THE TITAN YEARS
RICO DREDD

ABADDON
BOOKS

W W W . A B A D D O N B O O K S . C O M

An Abaddon Books™ Publication
www.abaddonbooks.com
abaddon@rebellion.co.uk

Omnibus published in 2019 by Abaddon Books™,
Rebellion Intellectual Property Limited,
Riverside House, Osney Mead, Oxford, OX2 0ES, UK.

10 9 8 7 6 5 4 3 2 1

Creative Director and CEO: Jason Kingsley
Chief Technical Officer: Chris Kingsley
Head of Books and Comics Publishing: Ben Smith
Editors: David Thomas Moore, Michael Rowley & Kate Coe
Marketing and PR: Remy Njambi
Design: Sam Gretton, Oz Osborne & Gemma Sheldrake
Cover: Neil Roberts

Rico Dredd created by
Pat Mills and Mick McMahon.

ISBN: 978-1-78108-648-3

Printed in Denmark.

THE TITAN YEARS

RICO DREDD

THE THIRD LAW • THE PROCESS OF ELIMINATION
FOR I HAVE SINNED

MICHAEL CARROLL

For Carlos

PART ONE

THE THIRD LAW

IT WAS AN accident, of course.

Yes, I was extorting that citizen. And, yes, that was a crime. I admit that. I've never denied it. I knew what I was doing, and I knew it was technically wrong. Especially for a Judge.

But what so many people have failed to understand is that there are *degrees* of wrongness. Killing a man without due cause is clearly wrong. Accidentally killing a man when you only intend to wound him is marginally wrong, but mostly just unfortunate.

My brother Joe didn't see it that way. To him, the world is divided into two groups: lawbreakers, and Joe Dredd.

I tried to explain, of course, but Joe wouldn't listen. All he saw was me drawing my Lawgiver on Virgil Livingstone. Without context, it looked like I was gunning down an unarmed citizen. But Livingstone wasn't a citizen, not really. He'd given up that right the moment he chose to be a lawbreaker.

And breaking the Law *is* a choice, no matter what any smug liberal do-gooders might tell you about "poor upbringing" and "broken homes." That stomm doesn't sit well with me. Never has.

Some perps will argue, "Hey, I didn't *know* that was against the Law!" but that's not a valid excuse. Just as it's our duty as Judges to make and enforce the Law, it's the citizens' duty to learn and understand it. The basic rule of life in Mega-City One is this: if you wouldn't do it when a Judge was watching you, then *don't do it*. That shouldn't be a difficult concept to grasp, but apparently it is.

A few days after we graduated, Judge Wagner was approached by a perp who wanted him to arrest her friend because he'd sold her a dud batch of crawbies. Wagner asked her, "You understand that crawbies are illegal, citizen?" and the woman said, "Yeah, real ones are, but these ones are *fake*. So are you going to arrest him or what?"

I've seen it myself, too. During my final assessment as a rookie, Judge Kenner and I were on foot-patrol when an ordinary car pulled into a taxi-only bay right beside us. The driver jumped out, saw us, realised what he'd done, looked back at his car for a moment, then turned to us and said, "It's all right—I *am* a taxi-driver. I'm undercover."

So sometimes the people need a reminder of who's in charge. They need to be shown that the Judges are there to protect them from themselves, as well as from each other. In the average week in Mega-City One, four citizens die as a result of possessing a strong sense of curiosity, a fork and a power outlet.

I believe that, in general, people are reasonably smart. But by Grud the dumb ones are *so* dumb they drag the whole damn human race down. This is why you'll always find finger-marks on a wall next to the *Wet Paint* sign. It's why the hinges on car doors are at the front: so that if the idiot driver chooses to open the door while hurtling along the freeway, the wind won't rip the door off and take her arm with it. It's why the food safety laws insist that banana skins and coconut shells must be printed with a warning notice that reads *Don't Eat This Part*.

My first week on the job I stopped a citizen from attempting to pry open the elevator doors on the fiftieth floor of the No-tell Motel. Poor drokker didn't understand the concept of elevator shafts: he thought that there was an endless stream of elevator cars, one after the other, like train carriages, and all he had to do was open the doors and step in.

That's why the citizens need Judges.

I graduated the Academy of Law with the highest cumulative score ever recorded. Joe was a little behind me. Not much, but it was clear which of us was the better Judge. In fact, that had been obvious pretty much from the start.

October 2073, six years away from graduation, Judge-Tutor Semple called our class to assembly. Semple was a stern man. Never smiled, never gave praise, but by Grud we sure knew it when he was disappointed. There were thirty-one of us, then, down from forty the previous year. Semple lined us up and strode back and forth along the line, scowling down at us in silence.

That's all he did. Striding back and forth, glaring with his good eye, saying nothing. And then, maybe ten minutes in, Cadet Milo Lange sagged, turned around, and walked away.

Semple seemed pleased with that. He said, "Hope the rest of you learned something here. Dismissed."

Cadet Gibson wouldn't let it go. He said, "Sir? What did Lange do?"

"Hell if *I* know," Semple said. "Did *something*. Guilty conscience. He'll be gone by morning."

Later, back in the mess hall, Gibson said, "That wasn't right. Lange's a good cadet. He's never done anything wrong."

Joe said, "He must have; he cracked. Semple didn't accuse anyone of anything, didn't give Lange the evil eye any more than he did the rest of us. It was a fishing expedition, that's all. He played the odds, figured that there was at least *one* of us has done something we shouldn't have."

"It's sick," I said, and Gibson and Hunt agreed with me.

Joe sat back in his chair and scratched at the fuzz on his chin. "No, it was a good move. Weed out the weak. I reckon we can expect a lot more stuff like that in the next few years. We're down to thirty now, started with over a hundred. By the time we hit the streets in '79 there'll be maybe ten of us left."

Before I go on, I should make something clear that many people don't seem to realise. The Academy of Law graduates a lot more Judges than that every year, of course. I mean, ten extra Judges hitting the streets each year isn't going to make a lick of difference in a city of eight hundred million citizens, is it? There are multiple classes taking place all the time: our class was one of forty-six. As the numbers whittled down they'd sometimes merge two classes, but mostly the tutors tended to keep the classes separate. The *actual* number of graduating Judges in 2079 was around five hundred, I think.

Anyway: Gibson said, "You and Rico'll be safe, whatever

happens. The two of you could piss on the Chief Judge's boots and he'd give you a free pass." Then he grinned. "Maybe that's what they want, huh? Hound the rest of us out so that the only Judges on the streets will be Fargo's sprogs. An army of interchangeable clone Judges stomping around without minds of their own."

And then he added, "No offence."

I didn't care—Gibson was always saying things like that, trying to get a rise out of Joe. My brother didn't respond, but I could tell he wanted to. Even then, Joe was a Lawbook on legs. He knew the regs inside and out, and never once broke a rule. I knew the regs as well as he did, of course, but I understood the difference between blindly following the rules and understanding their intent.

Judges don't just dispense the Law, we *make* the Law. That's why we have to be the best of the best. That's why, I guess, Semple and the other tutors were right to have been so hard on us.

Long before I graduated, I came to understand the need for Judges to be flexible. If we see two creeps beating the stomm out of each other on the street, protocol says we arrest both and sort it out later. So that's the arresting Judge, a crew on a pick-up wagon—three Judges at least—to take them to the closest Sector House, another couple of Judges there to process the arrest. And then we find out that the creeps are brothers or something like that, and neither will press charges. Best we can do is fine them for disturbing the peace. Fifty creds each, if it's their first offence. That's anywhere upwards of six Judges involved, all for a measly hundred credits.

But say the Judge on the scene breaks up the fight and instead of arresting them on the spot he demands to know why they're fighting. He figures out it's just a scuffle, no harm done. He gives them a warning—not anything official, just a scare—and sends them on their way. Now instead of five or more other Judges having their time wasted, we've got two scared citizens who'll be keeping their heads down for a long time afterwards.

That's why my arrest numbers weren't as high as Joe's. That's why the citizens on my regular patrol routes grew to respect me, not fear me. I'd pass them on foot or on the bike and they'd nod a greeting. A couple of months on the job and I had most of the local juve gangs in line. Half of Joe's were in the cubes.

Sure, the juves would get a bit wild from time to time—they were kids, it's to be expected—but I'd wade in with the daystick and crack a few skulls. Let them know who's boss.

I guess that's where the split between me and Joe really started.

At the investigation, it was suggested an incident in the Cursed Earth when I was a cadet exposed me to radiation that, somehow, affected me. I'd broken my arm and fractured my skull. This was thrown into the mix as a possible explanation for why I "turned bad."

But I didn't turn bad. Not then, not ever. "Bad" and "good" are not absolutes. They're points of view.

Even if I hadn't fully recovered, that theory doesn't make a lick of sense, no matter how thin you slice it. Joe was with me the whole time, only a few metres away. He was exposed to the same levels of radiation that I was. Anything that affected me would have had the same effect on him. After all, we're physically identical.

There were other theories raised at the investigation... My

DNA was tainted. I'd been exposed to the wrong sort of propaganda. My constant top-of-the-class scores had gone to my head, made me believe that I could do no wrong, and—therefore—I'd developed the notion that anything I did was right.

But the truth is a lot simpler that any of that. Joe concerned himself with maintaining the status quo, a case of "If it ain't broke, don't fix it." But I could see that it *was* broken. I saw the flaws in the Justice system, and I was smart enough to know how to make everything better.

MEGA-CITY ONE
2079 A.D.

One

THERE WAS THIS juve, Evan Quasarano. Seventeen years old, built like a tank and almost as smart. Quasarano was a rising star in a gang called the Beadles. They didn't get up to anything too serious; at worst, they did a little flash-mobbing every couple of months, swarm through a store and pick the shelves clean.

Some Judges follow the regs and will do whatever it takes to break up the gangs, but right from the start I knew that was the wrong call. Leave the gangs intact and let them police each other, but keep an eye on them—that's the best approach. If they do become a problem, it's a lot easier to corral a thirty-member gang than thirty individuals each with their own agendas, bolt-holes and alibis.

Quasarano was inducted into the Beadles when he was fourteen. At that age, he was already close to two metres tall, though he was skinny then. A couple of the older kids started giving him a hard time—part of his initiation, I guess. Quasarano took a few punches, hit the ground, then got back up and really laid into the drokkers, just using his bare fists. One of them ended up in the infirmary with cracked ribs and a dislocated shoulder.

They admired that, and soon Quasarano became their foremost enforcer. He kept the younger kids in line, and he was the one they sent out to "negotiate" with the other gangs in territorial disputes.

Like most of the juve gangs, once the kids reached eighteen they were nudged out, whether they wanted to leave or not. Around the time I came on the scene, Quasarano was fifth in line, and the four guys ahead of him were long past their eighteenth birthdays, but they didn't want to go. I can understand that, from their point of view: they'd spent years building up their little power-base and there was no way they'd be happy to just hand it down to someone else.

Quasarano didn't do anything, but he made it clear to the others that they weren't welcome any more. He began to ignoring the older kids' instructions, started telling the younger kids how things would be run. The older guys didn't like that, so one night they ambushed him coming out of a shuggy hall. Four against one.

I got the call and arrived to see Quasarano pushing himself off the ground, covered in blood. The other four looked like they'd tried to take down a tank by running at it with their faces.

"We were jumped," Quasarano said. "This buncha guys... They came outta nowhere and..." He stopped when he realised it was me. "Aw, man. Rico, look... I was defending myself."

I climbed down off my Lawmaster and strode over to him, hauled him to his feet. "I warned you about fighting on my patch, Quasarano."

"Rico, come *on*, man." He painted a bloody streak across the back of his hand with his mouth. "You know me. You know these guys. And you know the situation. They're too old for the club."

I planted my hand on Quasarano's jaw. "Hold still and shut up." I turned his head left and right. "Doesn't look like your nose is broken."

I stepped back and looked around at the other gang members. Three of them were unconscious; the fourth, a nasty little scuzzball called Paxton, was faking it. Compared to the others, there was barely a scratch on him. I'd seen that before, with street-fights; someone quickly realises that he's out of his depth, so he hugs the dirt in the hope he'll be able to slither away when it's all over.

Quasarano said, "Rico, I—"

"You weren't here. Go home. Now."

He hesitated for a second, then took off.

I pulled out my radio. "Control, this is Dredd. Four to pick up, my location. Brawling, four years in the cubes."

From the ground, Paxton said, "Four *years*? No way!" He rolled onto his side, pushed himself up.

I put away the radio. "Then it's a good thing for you that I didn't *actually* call it in. This is how it's going to be around here, boy. You and your friends stay away from Quasarano and the rest of the gang. Understood? Your time is over. You're done."

Paxton slunk over toward me. "Look, Judge... That guy

doesn't know stomm from stew. There's no written rule about how old someone hasta be to be in the club. And it *is* a club, not a gang. We're not—"

He shut up, then, because a fist in the face will do that.

I reached down, grabbed his arm and hauled him to his feet again. "I asked you if you understood, Paxton. All I want is a *yes* or a *no*."

He squinted at me through bloodshot eyes. "I'm just sayin'..."

It took two more punches and a solid kick to the ribs before Paxton came around to my way of thinking.

The next day, I saw Paxton and his friends on the street. Not one of them gave me any sass. They kept their heads down as they passed me by. That's part of what it means to be a Judge. We don't just rule the people, we *guide* them. It's better to steer the citizens away from trouble instead of just waiting for them to break the Law and then punishing them.

Joe could never see that. A week after the incident with Quasarano and Paxton, Joe and I had some downtime, a half-hour between shifts where we both happened to be in the same Sector House at the same time. We were only four months out of the Academy, and already we had better arrest records than Judges twice our age.

I spotted Joe in the mess hall. He was always easy to recognise, even from behind, because he was the only one sitting alone. The only one paging through the Lawbooks as he ate.

Joe turned around to face me before I was even halfway across the room. To anyone else, that might suggest some sort of mysterious link between twins or something, but I knew Joe better than that. If he *had* to sit with his back to the door, he'd arrange it so that he could see a reflection in the window, or in the side of a napkin dispenser. I'm not saying he was paranoid, just cautious. There weren't many people who could sneak up on Joseph Dredd.

Joe nodded to me, then to the chair opposite. I put my tray down, and for a moment I watched him eat. Even when we were kids, he was an efficient eater. Food was fuel to him, that's all. I don't ever recall him having a favourite flavour, or doing something like eating the pseudopeas first to get them out of the way. He just ate. Methodically, without any interest other than topping up the body's fuel and nutrients. He shovelled it in, chewed, swallowed, and stopped when the plate was empty, or when he was full. Those two things usually coincided, because Joe never put more food on his plate than he thought he'd be able to eat.

"Hey, Little Joe... Anything interesting today?"

"The usual. You?"

"Not much. Took down those three perps who've been tapping on the Galleria escalators. You'd have liked that—one of them had a zip-gun. Actually pulled it on me and took a hostage."

"Headshot?"

"No, there was no clean angle. Shot him in the knee instead."

Joe nodded, and speared another bright-orange mockarrot with his fork. "Intentional?"

It annoyed me that he felt he had to ask that. "Well, yeah. I'm surprised the whole *city* didn't hear the drokker's screams."

My brother's only response was to nod again, his attention now back on the Lawbook in front of him.

"Joe, you *know* all this stuff. Why do you keep reading it?"

"The Law isn't fixed, Rico. We have to keep on top of it."

He looked up, hitting me with that flinty gaze of his. "If we don't, then we might arrest someone for something that's no longer a crime, or let something go that now *is* a crime. You know that."

I started on my food. It was pasta in the shape of little Lawgivers; whoever had programmed chefbot that day had a strange sense of humour. "Yeah, yeah... It wouldn't do you any harm to relax now and then. Might even do you some good. Might make you a better Judge to be human. Look, we've got a lot of leave worked up already. Why don't we take a day off? We could get out of the city, go someplace where the predominant colour is green, not grey."

Judge Gibson dropped into the seat next to me. "I was thinking the same thing. Me and the guys have been talking about getting together sometime soon. You two in?"

"Yep," I said.

Joe asked, "Why?"

"Chew the fat," Gibson said. "Talk over old times."

"Old times? Gibson, we haven't been *alive* long enough to have old times. You guys are only twenty. And Rico and I are thirteen."

Gibson said, "Chronologically, yeah, but the geneticists sped up your aging, right? You've caught up with the rest of us." He sighed and shook his head. "And *you've* kept aging, Joe. You are *such* an old man. I remember the first time I met you guys. I was seven. We came into class one day and there you were, identical, sitting there looking like four- or five-year-olds." He laughed. "Me and Hunt, we used to give you such a hard time. Remember that?"

I said, "I remember that time when you spit in Little Joe's

breakfast and he beat the snot out of you."

Gibson laughed harder. "I went running to Judge Duane, crying my eyes out. Man, that was funny."

Joe wasn't amused. "You were a bully. Nothing funny about that."

"Has he *ever* laughed?" Gibson asked me.

That got me thinking. Gibson and I wracked our brains. We did manage to recall a couple of occasions when Joe had smiled, but actually laughed? We couldn't think of a time when that had ever happened.

Half-way through the discussion, Joe got up and left. Anyone else, you might think he was pissed that we were talking about him right in front of his face. But Joe didn't get offended by things like this. He'd finished his meal, so it was time to go back on patrol.

But let's get back to Evan Quasarano. His gang kept their heads down, pretty much, for a couple of weeks, then someone robbed a local synthahol dispensary and all fingers were pointing at the Beadles.

I got the call on a Sunday evening, eighteen hundred hours, so first stop was Quasarano's apartment. It was a ground-floor place, Brendan Behan Block. The whole floor stank of sweat and grease and boiled vegetables. Ragged lumps of filth burst out of piles of damp garbage and squealed as they scattered ahead of me. They could have been oversized rats or undersized children—it was hard to tell.

The door to Quasarano's apartment opened before I could knock. He stepped out and pulled it closed behind him. "What do you want, Rico?"

"Is that any way to greet the man who's keeping you out of

the cubes?" I nodded toward the door. "Anything you don't want me to see in there?"

His eyes narrowed. "You think me and the boys are responsible for turning over the boozery on Seventh, don't you? Wasn't us."

I stepped around him. "I'm gonna need to check inside, Quasarano."

"Rico... c'mon, man! I'm asking you as a friend. Don't do that."

It was hard not to smile at that. "A friend?" I placed my palm on the door. "Friendship goes both ways, kid. What have *you* ever done for *me*?"

"My mom's in there," he said quietly. "She doesn't know anything about... about anything. She thinks we're all angels."

I looked at him for a second, then pushed open the door. "I can be discreet, when I have to be."

Elizabeth Louise Quasarano was one of those women who are so deep into their fifties they look like they've got lost in there and they're never going to find their way out. She was stooped, frail, tiny—not even up to her son's shoulder. When she saw me, she almost dropped the casserole dish she was carrying toward the kitchen table. "Oh, sweet foetal Jovus! What's he done now?"

"Ma, it's okay," Quasarano said. "I'm not in trouble."

Mrs Quasarano regained her composure very quickly. "Right. Well, sit down. Both of you. There's enough to go around."

Staring at me from around the table were an old man who looked like he'd fought in the war and would bring it up in every conversation, Quasarano's two younger brothers, and his sister. The boys were twelve and eight, skinny but too tall for their clothes. The girl was nineteen, pretty but hollow-eyed, and seemed completely unsurprised to see me.

"I just need to ask Evan some questions, Mrs Quasarano. This won't take long."

She nodded. "Sit. And eat. Look at you—there's hardly a *pick* of meat on you."

Quasarano dragged over a chair, his brothers bunched up, and somehow I found myself taking off my helmet and gloves and sitting down, while Mrs Quasarano ladled the casserole into a small dish in front of me. "Uh, we're not really supposed to..."

"It's just a little goulash," she said. "Never hurt anyone. Better than that artificial rubbish you Judges eat. I don't know how you keep going. Thomas, be a good lad and pass the Judge some bread. No, don't use your hand! Pass him the *plate*. Grud above! Have I taught you nothing? I'm so sorry, Judge. I didn't raise my boys to be rude to guests."

She talked incessantly while we ate, telling me about the kids, her neighbours, her own childhood. No one else said a word; she never stopped long enough. At one point, I reached out to take the last bread roll and she slapped my hand. "In this home we *ask* before we take the last one. Where was I? Oh, right. So. My mother, Grud rest her, she was in the fashion industry. Well, that's what she *told* everyone, but between you and me, the truth is she worked in a clothing factory where she operated the machine that put buttons onto shirts. But she was a proud woman, very strict. Made sure we were brought up right..."

Eventually, the old man—Quasarano's paternal grandfather—pushed back his chair. "I'm done. Let the man ask Evan his questions, Liz. I'm sure he's got a whole backlog of innocent suspects to beat up."

Before the old man left the room, he pulled a litre bottle of Jepsom's Drunkifier from a cupboard. I didn't know much about booze, but I had a good idea of how much that bottle cost, and it was about as much as this whole family received from welfare in a month.

Quasarano paled at that, and looked away when I turned to him. "Your grandfather's right, Evan," I said. "You and I need to talk." I stood up and nodded to his mother. "Thank you for the meal, Mrs Quasarano. It was... tasty."

She beamed at that, and I moved toward the door before she could start talking again. "Evan?"

The kid followed me out into the apartment's narrow hallway, and closed the door behind him. He still wouldn't meet my gaze. "Rico, I'll get the boys to bring the booze and the money back to the store. Some of it's gone already, but..."

"Not them. Just you. And you weren't involved in the robbery. You found the stuff under the overpass. Got that? You don't know how it got there. You didn't keep it because you were scared that the Judges would blame you for taking it. If they offer you a reward—they probably won't—then you accept it. Don't pretend to be noble and decline it, all right? If you do, they'll become suspicious. In fact, if they *don't* offer you a reward, ask for one. Get annoyed if they say no."

He nodded. "Got it. Thanks, Rico."

I left him there in the hallway, and as I trudged my way through the garbage all I could think about was the meagre meal that his mother was happy to share with a stranger, and how Quasarano's brothers' and sister's clothes didn't fit.

I couldn't do much to help them, but I could do *something*. I pulled out my radio. "Control—Dredd."

"Go ahead, Dredd."

"Checked out the rumours of the Beadle gang's involvement in the synthahol robbery. Dead end. Looks like a rival gang's trying to shift the blame."

"Acknowledged, Dredd. We've got a 15-02 on the Westbound Narroway."

"On my way. And recommend you contact the owner of Brendan Behan Block. Damn place is knee-deep in garbage. That's a violation of city ordnance 4221. Tell him he's got twenty-four hours to get the block up to minimum standards, or he's looking at five in the cubes for neglect leading to possible endangerment."

That's how it began.

At my hearing, the investigators pinpointed that moment as "pivotal in Dredd's corruption." Their definition of "corrupt" didn't match mine, of course. Still doesn't.

Judge Rico Dredd became personally involved in the welfare of Evan Quasarano. Under the belief that he could steer the boy away from a life of crime, Dredd knowingly and deliberately covered up Quasarano's participation in a number of minor offences, one of which brought Dredd into contact with Quasarano's family.

Dredd was particularly impressed with Elizabeth Louise Quasarano, the boy's mother, and the manner in which she presided over her family and struggled to provide them with basic needs. Med-Judge Littman's psychological evaluation of Dredd suggests that Mrs Quasarano became a surrogate parent-figure, filling a void in the standard social structure that, as a clone raised in the Academy of Law, Dredd had never experienced.

Dredd personally intervened when Hector Quasarano, the boy's maternal grandfather, was arrested following a fracas involving three other war veterans. Dredd arranged for the charges against Hector Quasarano to be quashed, despite unequivocal evidence of Quasarano's willing participation in the event.

Though the defendant refuses to comment on this matter, we believe that it was around this time Dredd entered into a brief physical relationship with Stacie Quasarano, Evan's nineteen-year-old sister.

Stacie was quiet, thoughtful. The sort of girl that most guys wouldn't notice. And in truth I barely noticed her myself, the first few times I had dinner with the family. But one night, after the meal—I'd brought along a dozen re-Veal cutlets that I'd confiscated from a street-corner blackmarketeer—Stacie and I found ourselves sitting side-by-side on the sofa. Evan was out, the younger boys were in bed, and her mother and grandfather were taking the remaining cutlets to a neighbour.

It was a cold night, but I could feel the heat of Stacie's body even through my uniform. She wasn't saying much, just listening as I told her about my day.

I hadn't intended for it to happen. I hadn't intended for *any* of it to happen, of course. I used to call in to the Quasaranos' apartment maybe a couple of times a week. At first just to check on Evan, but soon it was because I liked it there. Most of the time the apartment was cold and damp, but the atmosphere was always warm and welcoming. The grandfather would tell stories about the war, and what America had been like back when it still *was* America. The kids would badger me with questions about being a Judge. Evan, too; I think he liked the idea, even though they were all far too old to sign up. Mrs Quasarano would tell me I was looking tired, or hungry. She'd fuss about me, making sure I was comfortable, giving me hot drinks. When I was leaving, she'd tell me to drive safely and not get into trouble. And one time, when I'd had a particularly tough day—a stolen truck had jack-knifed during a high-speed chase and killed Judge Ellard, who I'd known all my life—she could see that I was upset and she gave me a hug.

Stupid, I know. I was a Mega-City One Judge, trained in the best, toughest academy in the world. I shouldn't have cared. I didn't cry or anything like that, but this tiny woman wrapped her arms around me and told me that everything was going to be all right, and that meant more than any number of hours with a Department psychologist.

And so it happened. Stacie and I were the only ones awake in the apartment. I had a couple of hours free before my next shift. She was sitting next to me, her thigh pressed against mine as we watched some dumb game show on their crappy TV. We weren't even looking at each other, much. The sound was off and I was telling her how I'd chased down a perp.

Then Stacie's hand was on my leg. It seemed the most natural thing in the world to cover her hand with my own, to squeeze it a little and interlock our fingers.

She was the first girl I ever kissed. I didn't know what the hell I was doing, but I went with the flow.

Two

CELIBACY ISN'T EASY for most people. It's even tougher for Judges; there'll always be people out there who are drawn to power, and among them are those citizens willing to commit a crime just so that they'll be arrested.

In the Academy, we all had to pass a course called "Sexual Rebukes." It's not easy, and a good number of cadets utterly fail it. I like to imagine that they go on to have happier lives outside of the Department.

There are many reasons Judges can't have sex, and some of them are even credible. A Judge in a sexual relationship won't always have his or her mind on the job. That one makes sense, for most Judges. Despite the rumours, we're still human and detaching ourselves from our emotions isn't always easy. Then there's the danger of a Judge compromising a case by inadvertently revealing sensitive information to a lover, or of a perp hiring a hooker to seduce a Judge, filming the exciting parts, and embarking on a campaign of blackmail.

On top of all that, you really don't want a situation where some perp gets away with a crime because the Judge that might have stopped him is laid up in a med-centre with a dose of galloping crotch-rot.

They give other reasons, too, and some of them are less realistic. When we were hitting puberty, Judge-Tutor Semple told us, "Sex makes babies. The city's already over-populated and under-resourced. The Department doesn't want to have to fund a nursery for the illegitimate offspring of you little drokkers. So keep it in your pants."

And then there was this classic, which me and Joe got from Judge Morphy: "We belong to the Justice Department. They own us, and everything about us. That includes any DNA samples we might be inclined to deposit inside another human being. So you have sex with someone and the Department will be well within its rights to charge them with receiving stolen goods." I still don't know whether Morphy was joking about that, or if he believed it.

The first time I realised that I was under suspicion was when Judge Ernest Kenner took me aside one day and said, "Rico. Need to talk to you about Stacie Quasarano."

I put on my best poker-face and denied all knowledge of the girl, but Kenner wasn't an idiot. He *knew* me: he'd run my final assessment. "It *ends*, Rico. Understood? I should report you, but, damn it, you've got the makings of a good Judge. So you get it out of your system and you end that relationship. And do it *right*. Let the girl down easy. You don't want her going to the local Sector House looking for you."

"All right," I said. "I'll do it."

"If you can't keep your libido in check, pay a visit to the med-unit and get a suppressant. Doesn't always work one hundred per cent, but it helps keep you focussed. If that fails, there's always surgery."

I'd heard that some Judges underwent castration as an alternative to self-control or drugs, but the idea sickened me. "I can control myself."

"I hope so, Rico. My advice? Sign up for a two-man team. It's a lot easier to resist temptation when there's another Judge around."

I thanked him for the advice and told him that I preferred to work alone. He seemed satisfied with that.

I applied for transfer to another part of the sector, and while I waited for that to come through I kept clear of the Quasarano family. Stacie had been getting kind of clingy anyway, always wanting to see me. I knew that I was better off without her, especially if Kenner was watching me.

That bugged me, though. Kenner had no call to interfere with my life, especially since I wasn't doing anything wrong. It was against the rules, yes, but that doesn't make it *wrong*.

ON THE WEST side of the sector there was what the politicians like to refer to as a "house of ill-repute." Joe and I received a call one morning, about seven months into our first year: someone had beaten the stomm out of one of the girls. They didn't call it in themselves, mind. A passing motorist saw the perp on the street, giving the victim the full treatment with his fists and feet.

By the time we got there, the usual localised amnesia epidemic had taken hold. No one could remember exactly what the John had looked like.

The brothel was run by a middle-aged woman calling herself Madam Ozelle. Big hair, more make-up than clothes, permanently suspicious. But she treated the girls well, made sure they were safe. "I might recognise him if he comes around again," she told me.

We were in the lobby of the small block, and the victim— twenty-two years old, attractive in a cheap kind of way—was curled up in an armchair nursing her injuries. She was being taken care of by one of her colleagues, who was appropriately dressed, though the nurse's outfit was far too small and much too shiny to be practical.

Joe said to Madam Ozelle, "You can't remember what he looks like, but you might recognise him? I'm not buying that. Withholding evidence is a crime, citizen. Let's go through it again. *Do* you know the assailant?"

"No, I do not."

I noticed the hesitation in her voice—and I knew that Joe'd spotted it too. I asked her, "Why didn't you report the assault?"

"We don't want any trouble, Judge. Sometimes it's best to say nothing."

"Well, you've *got* trouble," Joe said. "Six months, failure to report. Call it in, Rico."

"Joe, that won't help anyone." I stepped closer to the woman. "You know the assailant. But you're afraid of him. You run this place?"

She nodded, clearly trying not to swallow audibly.

"But you're not the owner."

Joe said, "Registered owner is Forest Patterson Dechant, aged fifty-five. Resident of Umesh Benison Block. Three priors, all for assault." Joe had checked out the place on the ride over: he was good at remembering details like that.

"So he's the one," I said, still staring at Madam Ozelle. "All you have to do is press charges and Dechant's looking at a minimum of two years for assault."

The girl on the armchair said, softly, "And then he'll get *out*."

Joe asked her, "How many times has he hit you?"

Her voice even softer, she said, "This is the first time. But about every couple of weeks he goes after one of us."

"Habitual," I said. "Your testimony is enough to warrant detention on suspicion. Joe?"

Joe nodded. "You finish up here. I'll take him in."

When he left, Madam Ozelle turned to me. "We're still not going to press charges against him, Judge." She gave the young woman a nasty look, then added, "Bad as Dechant is, we *need* him. Our clients know what he's like. They treat us as well as they do only because they're scared of him."

"Your input is no longer a requirement, citizen." I nodded to the injured girl. "Her statement is enough. Joe will encourage a confession out of Dechant."

"It's not just that... The other houses around here, well, most of them have a Dechant of their own. It kind of goes with the territory. As soon as they learn that he isn't around, they'll come here, start trying to poach my girls. And not by offering them a bigger cut. More like, 'Come with us and you won't get maimed.'"

"Not really my problem, citizen. You need to hire better security."

That night, four thugs engaged by a rival brothel showed up, armed with obvious intentions and hidden guns. They barged through the place, kicking open doors and scaring the clientele.

Until they kicked open the *wrong* door. The door that had me waiting behind it.

The first guy was a bruiser. Fifty years old, ex-military. Knew how to fight and an expert at intimidation. I punched him in the throat, slammed my boot into his left knee as he staggered back, finished him with an elbow to the solar plexus.

The other three were no fools: they were already running before the bruiser spewed his guts onto the room's cheap carpet. They were maybe ten metres from the stairs leading down to the building's main entrance. They didn't make it.

They didn't know I was a Judge. I was off-duty, wearing civilian clothes. All they knew was that they'd got their butts handed to them by someone a lot younger, smarter, stronger and faster. They wouldn't be coming back.

First thing I did, after I hauled the thugs out of Madam Ozelle's place and watched them crawl, limp and bleed their way back to their crappy pick-up truck, was pay a visit to the brothel that had hired them.

I made it plain to the man in charge that his actions would not be tolerated in future. Four broken fingers and several shattered windows later, he was very much in agreement with me. And then, when he realised I was a Judge, he offered to make "financial reparations": a thousand credits not to arrest him.

I brought the money back to Madam Ozelle. She said, "But you should keep it. You earned it."

"Judges don't need money," I told her. "Use it to pay for the repairs, and to clean up."

The woman regarded me for a few seconds. "But... you won't *always* be a Judge. You'll need money when you retire, won't you?"

That caught me off-guard. I had never considered that one day I might no longer be a Judge. I realised that it was actually possible that at some point in my future—assuming that I wasn't killed on duty—I might decide to just quit.

In all my years in the Academy of Law, I don't think that I had even once asked myself, "What would I like to be, if not a Judge?" Judging was all I had been trained for, all I knew. I was Judge Rico Dredd, the best of a new breed of Judges. Mega-City One's finest. And I enjoyed being a Judge. Hell, I *loved* it. It was intense and relentless and unbelievably dangerous.

But was it *forever*?

Judges who quit are usually forced out by injury, or, in a small number of cases, old age. Either way, they just can't cut it any more. They're given a choice: teach at the Academy, work behind the scenes at Control, or take the Long Walk. That last one's a death sentence: they're supplied with guns, ammo and rations, and sent out to dispense justice in the Cursed Earth, or the undercity, or the Black Atlantic.

I'd always been aware of those options, but, now that I thought about it, I realised that I didn't like any of them. I couldn't see myself half-blind or maimed, limping through the corridors of the Academy and yelling at the cadets, or sitting behind a wall of monitors operating the spycams and guiding younger Judges through arrests.

Nor did I want to end up as some emaciated, self-righteous nomad choking on irradiated dust, trying to bring Big City

Law to a decaying town where the wiser inhabitants have long since bought themselves a copper-cased ticket to oblivion.

Still, I didn't keep the money. I'd nowhere to put it, for a start. Judges don't have bank accounts.

Madam Ozelle said, "Well, you need *some* sort of reward. That's only fair." She turned to one of the girls. "Amber?"

Three

It was what the psychologists called my "inevitable slide into corruption." A couple of nights a week I'd check on Madam Ozelle's place, just to make sure everything was in line. Yes, I usually spent an hour or so with Amber or one of the other girls while I was there, but that was just a bonus. The real reason I was there was to keep the peace.

And keeping the peace sometimes meant dispensing the violence. The owner of another local establishment took exception to the situation—she didn't like the idea of a brothel where the employees got to keep most of their own money—so I had to sort her out, too.

Ambrosia Cropper. Mid-sixties, face like something that would turn even a marine biologist's stomach. She came crashing in to Madam Ozelle's place with three sons and four grandsons, all armed with rockball bats, steel knuckles and a pair of ancient sawn-off shotguns. One of her sons said, "We're takin' over!" and that was the last thing anyone ever heard him say, apart from the screams, and they didn't last long. That's what you get when you're stupid enough to pull a gun on a Judge. I left the rest of them alive, but nursing a good collection of fractures, breaks and dislocations. Cropper and I came to an understanding: she'd treat her own girls—and boys—better, and she'd donate a quarter of her take to Madam Ozelle. In return, I wouldn't arrest her and dismantle her entire operation.

I arranged for Madam Ozelle to hire three new security guys. They weren't the smartest, but they were smart enough to know that they should keep their heads down, and never mention my involvement to any other Judges. I made it clear to them what would happen otherwise.

Two were ex-military, both dishonourably discharged for "unruly conduct unbecoming a member of the armed forces." In other words, they had a tendency to settle disputes with their fists. That was why I chose them. In a place like that, you want the bouncers to quickly gain a no-nonsense reputation.

The third guy we hired was Evan Quasarano. He was still only seventeen, but even at that age he was bigger than me. He was a good brawler, and scared enough of me to follow orders. And he knew the streets and the sort of vermin who slithered through them.

It was not a nice part of the sector. On patrol, we'd encounter more—considerably more—dust-heads and drunks than sober citizens. Some of the older Judges ran a weekly book on who'd find the most bodies. Apparently, the Resyk truckers used to fight over the routes through the area, because their bonuses depended on the number of stiffs they brought in.

The district was home to low-rent data hackers and unlicensed medicians, document forgers and counterfeiters, bootleggers and head-wreckers. There were gambling dens, black markets and mobster hideouts.

My job as a Judge was to clean it up, but of course that was impossible if I only played within the rules. For years, Judges had patrolled the sector without making a dent in the crime levels, because in a place like that, if citizens see a Judge coming, they suddenly lose their memories and their ability to speak and even the most highly-feared local ganglords become beatified.

So my approach was to take the fight to *their* level. Be seen as one of them. Pretty soon, everyone who believed they were important got to know my name. Judge Rico Dredd can be bought, that's what they learned. I'd bust a backroom bookie, scare the crap out of his punters, and he'd beg me to let it slide. A stuffed envelope would somehow find its way into my hands, and I'd let him off with a warning.

Because what's the point in imprisoning a guy for something that—let's be honest here—is mostly a victimless crime? I send him to the cubes, that costs the city at least sixty thousand credits a year. But if I leave him with a warning, make it clear to him that his actions will only be tolerated to a point, then he's out there still running his little games and keeping his punters too busy to get into any real trouble. If someone's spending his day playing nine-card wallaby or making half-cred bets on snail-races, then he's not murdering his wife or heading to the bank to make a shotgun withdrawal.

Same with the gangs and the mobsters. I got to know them, explained to them that if they kept their heads down, they got to keep those heads. The mobs controlled the district's protection rackets. I didn't like that, but I tolerated it. It's hard enough for the average citizen to afford insurance; the big, reputable companies won't insure anyone who doesn't have much in the way of assets. But the mobs didn't care about background credit checks and payment histories. Say there's some corner-store owner who's plagued with kleptos, vandals and gangs of flash-mobbing juves; well, there's no way he can afford real insurance. But he pays the mob a couple of hundred each month, and they take care of him. They make sure that the local thugs and spug-heads understand that the store is off-limits. The owner mightn't like paying protection money—and sure as stomm stinks, he doesn't want to ever miss a payment—but he's in a better position than he would be otherwise. He doesn't have to replace stolen or damaged stock, and no-one's going to ram-raid his store if the consequences involve lead pipes and kneecaps.

The mobs ran the loan-sharks, too, and it was pretty much the same deal. Sure, their interest rates were exorbitant, but it was the only way the average citizen could get hold of some quick cash.

What I'm getting at is that most mob-run districts actually have less crime, and are a lot safer, than they would be if the Judges ever managed to get rid of the mobs. The mobs bring order. It might not be the kind of order we'd like, but it's better than chaos.

So the mob-bosses got to know me, and I made sure they didn't step out of line. I didn't tell them outright what I was doing, because that wouldn't work. You can't go up to a guy like Sparks Petrosky and start laying down rules: you'd end up occupying several widely-spaced buckets. So you get him thinking that you're working for him.

I'd meet Petrosky about every ten days. Sometimes he'd point the finger at someone causing trouble in the district, and I'd arrest the creep—had to keep my numbers up; I didn't want Justice Central figuring out what I was doing—and that would make things better for everyone. Now and then, I'd have to confront Petrosky about his own guys being too heavy-handed, like if maybe they came down too hard on a guy who owed them money and he wound up dead.

I'd tell him, "Justice has to be *seen* to be done, Sparks. So you hand over one of your boys—someone low on the totem pole, if you want, I don't care who—and I'll put him away for a five-stretch for involuntary manslaughter." Petrosky would quibble, but eventually I'd get my way.

I guess, from an outsider's point of view, what I was doing probably *did* look like corruption. But the Council of Five and the Chief Judge weren't out there on the streets with the rest of us, wading through the filth. They sat in their polished throne-rooms with their unblemished uniforms and made decisions about the lives of ordinary citizens they'd never met.

Well, I'd met those citizens. I lived among them. I protected them—from outsiders *and* from themselves—and I understood what it meant to be a Judge. Every decision we made affected people's lives. We gun down an opportunistic burglar, that's one creep off the streets. But what about his family? Suppose he was stealing because it was the only way he could make enough money to keep them fed and housed? The official system treated the symptoms, not the disease.

My way was better. I've always believed that, always will. I consorted with criminals because they're people too. It's just human nature to covet what we don't have. The solution is not tighter laws, but a clearer demonstration of consequences. Education, not incarceration.

I was *among* the people I'd been trained to Judge, not above them. Working with them, not against them. The other Judges were lion-tamers where I was a shepherd, if you see what I mean. And if I made some money on the side, so what? It didn't distract me from my job. If anything, the money was an incentive to keep going. Each credit was a token that proved I was going in the right direction.

I HAD MY guys on the streets keeping an eye on things. They told me what was going down with the gangs and the solo low-lifes. That's how I got word that Judge Kenner had been snooping again.

Kenner was coming into the sector when I wasn't around, talking to people. Asking them about me. But he hadn't approached me directly, and that's what worried me.

So I had Petrosky's hackers check him out, see exactly what he was up to. Turned out I was right to worry: Kenner was building a case against me, trying to find solid proof that I'd gone off-book. I had the hackers check out Kenner's arrest record, too... His numbers were down; he'd spent so much time investigating me, he was neglecting his beat.

That wasn't good. Even if Kenner himself couldn't find any evidence—and I'd covered myself pretty well—then it was only a matter of time before someone else in the Department wondered what he was up to. If they investigated *him*, that would lead them to me.

I couldn't let that happen. Ernest Kenner was a good Judge, but he was old-school. He was rigid in his understanding and application of the Law. One of us had to go, and I didn't plan on it being me.

Besides, he'd already been a Judge for a long time. He was hitting forty; his best years were probably behind him. A Judge gets old, he gets slow. Starts making bad decisions. Like investigating a younger Judge when he should be spending his time dealing with real perps.

I took a pragmatic approach and weighed up the options. I could stop what I was doing and toe the line—though that wouldn't be easy, what with everything I'd already set in motion—or I could retire Kenner. In the long run, he'd be just another Judge. He'd make a tiny difference to the city as a whole. But me, I was poised to make a *huge* difference.

It wasn't an easy decision, but it had to be done. I contacted Kenner—off the record, of course—and let him think I was Joe. Told him, "It's about Rico."

"What about Rico?" he asked.

"I'm not sure, sir. He... He seems just different, these days. And I've been hearing things... Rumours about excessive violence. Complaints about his off-duty behaviour."

The old fool agreed to meet me to talk and see what we could do about the situation before the Department had to be brought in.

I had to do it. It was him or me.

We met at the old turnpike at the edge of the atomic wastelands. The radiation from the rad-pits interfered with the public surveillance cameras, and made radio transmissions difficult to track.

Kenner showed up on time. Strode toward me with his hand extended. "Joe."

"Wrong."

I didn't shoot him. Bullets can sometimes be traced, and even when they *can't*, the fact that he'd been shot would immediately steer the investigation in a direction I didn't want it to go.

So I put him into a rad-pit.

Kenner didn't die quickly, or quietly, and I regret that. I didn't want him to suffer. Despite everything that's been said about me, I'm not a cruel man.

My spies told me that he was reported missing a day later. The Public Surveillance Unit tracked his movements through the city right up to the edge of the wastelands, and a week of pit-dredging turned up what remained of his body.

Petrosky's hackers wiped Kenner's file on me. He'd never logged his suspicions, never spoken to anyone. There was nothing to tie his death to me.

I was free and clear.

Four

I GOT MY own apartment. Not unusual for a Judge. It got me closer to the action, set me deeper among the people.

The investigation into my actions said I was "building a criminal empire," but that's plainly stomm. It wasn't an empire. It was me on my own, bringing order to the chaos. Sometimes things turned sour, that's bound to happen. Some people died, like Judge Kenner, but no one can deny that—thanks to me— more people *lived*.

Serious crimes were down in my district, *way* down, and that was because the citizens trusted me. Or they knew me, which amounted to the same thing. One time, a dealer moved in with a batch of high-grade endorphium. He approached Petrosky, tried to come to an arrangement where he'd sell the stuff and give Petrosky a good-sized cut.

Petrosky came to me, I arrested the perp, and the endorphium was seized and destroyed. Well, most of it. It's actually a very useful drug; pumps up the user's energy levels, keeps him sharp, keeps him going long after anyone else would have quit. I kept a small supply on me, just in case I was ever in a bind and really needed a boost. But the point is, Sparks Petrosky turned in that dealer and cut himself out of a huge chunk of money, all because he understood that was how the game was now played.

I knew what I was doing, and I was doing it well. A newly-paroled perp moved into the district, or a new gang, and I'd pay them a visit. It's a process, really. Almost an algorithm. You arrive unannounced, kick in the door, take down whatever muscle they have, and make it clear that if they want to operate in the area then there's a tax. And they play their part, too: they react with indignation and threats, you bust a few more heads—or even, if you really have to hammer home the point, you find the guy's second-in-command and you put a slug inside his skull. That one usually makes them realise that you're not messing around.

It's not like it's *murder* to kill a henchman, though my prosecution made it clear that they didn't agree with that. They were wrong, and they'd have known that if they'd been riding Lawmasters instead of desks. Like I said, it's an algorithm, an equation. A dead second-in-command perp is a lot better than a dead innocent citizen. And of course they'd never stop at just *one* dead citizen, so whichever way you look at it, my method saved lives.

So, yeah, my body-count was up, reported crime was down, and I figured that would be enough to keep the Department's nose out of my business. But I was wrong. It all came crashing down.

Thanks to my brother.

* * *

HE'D BEEN SUSPICIOUS of me for a long time, but hadn't said anything, so I didn't know. Joe was like that; the ultimate poker-face. You almost never knew what he was thinking.

He showed up at my place one day. This was my second apartment, a nice place. I was on the roof, enjoying the sun.

Joe strode across the rooftop straight for me, like he was approaching a perp, and I knew what was coming. I also knew that I could cope with it. I'd always been smarter than him. Maybe not academically, but I had the street-smarts that he lacked.

"You're out of uniform," he said.

"Day off. We *are* entitled to time off. You'd know that if you ever *took* it. What do you want?"

"Been checking your stats. Body-count's giving me cause for suspicion, and you've got an above-average number of complaints."

That bugged me. A lot. He had no right to pry into the way I ran things. And I knew that he didn't come up with it on his own. Kenner was still pretty fresh in my mind, and I didn't want things to have to go that way again. "So the bigwigs sent Little Joe to give Big Rico a *lecture*, huh?"

He stopped in front of me, scowled down. "You're drunk, Rico."

I'd had a couple of drinks. Not more than two. I was in no way drunk. And certainly sober enough to hold my own in a battle of wits with him.

Amber came out onto the patio. "Everythin' all right, honey?"

"Just my other half come to give me some earache," I told

her. "Better leave us be, honey. Little Joe can be real *mean* when he takes a mind."

Joe looked around. At the pool, the expensive planters, the fifteen-hundred-cred Taneasy lounger I was lying on. "Where did you get the money for all this?"

I said, "Wouldn't you like to know?" I hadn't meant to say that. I'd always planned that if anyone asked I'd say that the apartment belonged to some rich guy who was spending a year in Texas City, and he'd asked me to live there so that it wouldn't get burgled. But Joe was pissing me off. Or maybe I was drunker than I'd thought.

"It's got to *stop*, Rico! You can't keep breaking the rules!"

I put down my drink. "I do what I want. I'm a Judge—I *make* the rules." Yeah, I guess I *was* heading toward wasted by that stage. Part of me was thinking, *Shut the drokk up, Rico!* but Joe's holier-than-everyone attitude had long since lost its charm. He was turning into a self-assured scuzzball who'd forgotten which of us had received the higher marks in the Academy. Or maybe he *hadn't* forgotten; maybe it had stuck in his craw, and it was all he could think about. I said to him, "I say the word..." I snapped my fingers. "Boom. You're *gone*. So don't tell big brother what to do, Joey."

I'd meant that as a joke. I mean, he was my brother, he knew I'd never actually threaten him. Or he *should* have known. If he'd had a personality, he'd have been able to tell that I wasn't really serious.

Joe reached out and grabbed the collar of my shirt, hauled me up so we were face to face. "Get this through your head. You're *not* my big brother. You never were. You're *me* and there's something wrong with you! *Do* something—or I will."

He shoved me back into the Taneasy and stormed away.

Joe had kept his helmet on, but I didn't need to see his eyes to know what he was thinking.

He was scared. He saw that I'd strayed from the rigid path set out by the Academy, and he knew that he wouldn't be able to keep up. He wasn't prepared for the way the department would have to change if it was to keep control of the city.

A government can exist only as long as the people allow it. You might say, "Yeah? What about a dictatorship?" Well, the same rule applies. Dictators can only push so far before they're overthrown.

And that's what Mega-City One became when the Judges took over. There's no democracy, but then most democracies are that in name only: the citizens are allowed to choose their figurehead, but the people with the power remain the same. The elections make a difference to the citizens' lives in the same way that changing a hood ornament makes a difference to a car's destination.

Mega-City One's Justice Department was established by my clone-father, Eustace Fargo, as a way to return order to the chaos after a succession of devastating wars. It worked, too, for a while. But sooner or later every empire falls. The smart people either try to steer that fall, or they get the hell out of the way.

Joe was part of the establishment and it bothered him that I was able to stand outside of it, to see the cracks as they appeared. He would take me down, if the opportunity showed itself. And he knew that he could do it a lot easier and faster if he were prepared to break the rules, but if he did that, then he wouldn't be Judge Joe Dredd. Then he'd be just like everyone else.

* * *

JOE'S SUSPICIONS WERE confirmed when a routine speeder chase took him into my patch. The driver was just a kid. Fifteen years old. Young enough to still believe that he was indestructible and smarter than everyone else, and tall enough to be able to see over the steering-wheel.

The kid blazed through a red light coming off the elevated highway, and next thing a Lawmaster was roaring up behind, lights flashing. If he'd been smart, he'd have pulled over, grovelled an apology and silently prayed for a lenient term. But he was an idiot—he tried to outrun Joe Dredd.

The stolen car—a '78 Fellini convertible, with deep red body-work and fitted with a state-of-the-art hover-plate that allowed it to reach several hundred KPH—ended up embedded in a wall. The kid died, of course, his skull coming to a stop a lot later than the rest of his body, but that was no loss. Just natural selection in action.

But as Joe was waiting for a clean-up crew and trying to keep the Lookie-Lous away, he was approached by one of my guys, Evan Quasarano. Understand that I don't know for sure this is *exactly* how it went down—I had to piece it together from a couple of reports and a few things I heard—but the outcome was the same.

"Hey, JD," Quasarano said. He'd taken to calling me that, instead of using my first name; you don't let people know you're friends with a Judge.

Joe nodded to him. "What can I do for you, citizen?"

Quasarano peered past him at the wreckage. "What happened here?"

"None of your concern. Move along before I cite you for obstruction."

Quasarano laughed at that. "Yeah, right. Listen, old man Petrosky sent one of his guys over last night. They want to talk to you about some trouble they're having with Vijay McMorran and his crew. Figure it's the usual, you know? Pushing past the edges of their territory."

Now, my brother might be a cold-hearted, humourless, unimaginative, by-the-book stickler for rules, but he's not an idiot. Far from it. It was clear to him that Quasarano thought they knew each other, and that could only mean he thought Joe was me. And why wouldn't he? We looked the same, sounded the same, wore the same badge. So Joe played along to find out more. "Got it," he said. "So how did things go last night, anyway?"

"Pretty quiet. No trouble. Well, there was one guy who claimed he wasn't satisfied and he wanted his money back, but we took care of it."

"Glad to hear it. What did you do with him?"

"The usual."

"You get his ID? I might want to pay him a visit myself."

Quasarano nodded. "Sure, yeah. Name's Donald Fletta. Old guy. Maybe forty or fifty, or sixty. Lives over in the Crimson Furrows. You know it?"

"Yeah, I know it," Joe said. "Fletta still in one piece?"

"A few bruises and cuts, that's all. Like you always say, right? You can only take money off a dead man once."

"That's true," Joe told him. He gestured back toward the crowd. "Better get clear. Med-wagon's coming in. What you said about Petrosky...? He mention a time when we're supposed to meet?"

"No. Guess he wants you to call him to arrange it."

"Good work. Thanks, kid."

And Evan Quasarano smiled and nodded and felt pleased with himself, and wandered back into the crowd without the slightest inkling of what he had just set in motion.

Five

I SHOULD GO back a bit, I think; I'm getting ahead of myself. You see, the whole deal with guys like Sparks Petrosky was that they thought I was working for them, when really they were working for me. I got them to temper their actions— no more murdering innocents if it could be avoided, for example—and they got a certain amount of freedom. Together, we established an uneasy sort of peace. I let them run their protection, prostitution, drug-dealing and loan-sharking with the understanding that they didn't do anything too flashy that might draw the wrong sort of attention. You could say that I was acting as an unofficial intermediary between the criminal classes and the judiciary.

They gave me a cut, sure, because if I hadn't taken it they would have been suspicious. And I'm not going to lie, the money was nice. In the Academy, we were raised without luxuries of any kind. There were no soft pillows or foaming baths, no rich foods or pet dogs or birthday presents. No hugs from Mom, no stories at bedtime, no games or toys and not many jokes. We didn't get to have a real childhood. We didn't get to have an adolescence, either. No girlfriends or boyfriends, no staying out late and sneaking home just before dawn, no concerts or movie theatres or parties or any of that.

No *fun*. Judges are expected to sit in judgement on the ordinary people without really knowing what it's like to *be* a person.

So I'd decked out my apartment with the latest in cool gadgets and stocked the refrigerator with treats. I rented movies and bought music and dated girls and sometimes got drunk or high and enjoyed myself.

But my new life didn't come free. The price was that I had to do some things that were technically illegal. I had to be seen to be just as bad as Sparks Petrosky and the others believed me to be.

And that meant, sometimes, doing little bad things in order to prevent larger bad things from happening. It's a matter of scale, and that's what Joe could never understand.

Virgil Livingstone was a small-time dealer who worked on the fringes of the district. He had a four-hours-a-week job delivering office supplies, and the uniform gave him access to a lot of places where he'd otherwise stand out.

He sometimes sold weapons or banned publications, but he mostly dealt low-impact drugs like cane sugar, caffeine, snizz or crawbies. And every now and then he'd come into contact with someone who could get hold of endorphium or even powdered jetsam. He sold to the city's fairly-rich and mildly-famous;

mostly k-list celebrities and the kids of declining corporate empires.

And Livingstone and I had an arrangement. He told me who he was selling to, and I didn't arrest him. See, if I *had* arrested him, then his clients would have just bought their stuff from someone else. But with him free to deal, I was able to build a very nice dossier on the corrupt elements in the mid-to-high levels of Mega-City One society.

He didn't know what I was really doing, of course. He saw me as an enforcer who collected the tribute for Petrosky, so it was vital that I played that role with conviction. That meant that sometimes I had to hurt him.

For weeks, he'd been putting me off; "I've *got* the money, but I just don't have it *on* me." I let that slide. I knew from my other contacts that he was actually telling the truth. A large shipment of quality European chocolate was coming in across the Black Atlantic, and I wanted to wait until it was in before I made my move. I could arrest the buyers as well as the dealers and *really* make an impact.

And then the rumours started to spread that the shipment already *had* come in, that Virgil Livingstone was now starting to think that he was big enough to sell it without Sparks getting his cut.

So I had to teach him a lesson, plain and simple. It had to be a lesson he'd never forget.

Virgil Livingstone's office door opened and he grinned nervously at me. "Hey, Rico. Good timing. I was just going to see you, man. I got—"

"I hear you've been holding out on me, Virgil."

"What? No! No way! See, what happened was there were these guys who—"

He stopped then, staring down the barrel of my Lawgiver.

"You're three weeks late with the payment, Virgil. Hand it over. You've got four seconds."

"Okay, okay... I've got it here." Slowly, carefully, he moved his hand inside his jacket. "That's what I was trying to *tell* you." He pulled out a thick, plastic-wrapped bundle of cash. "Eighteen grand, Rico. I know that's less than I owe, but that's because I did a deal that got..." He stopped talking, just stared at me as he held out the bundle of cash. "Rico... Please..."

"Eighteen's not enough. You're disrespecting the situation, Livingstone. You're disrespecting *me*. What was your mark-up on the deal? Fifty per cent? Sixty? I want all of it."

He slowly shook his head. "No. Look, I did make a profit. Nothing like fifty per cent, though. That's what I'm trying to say, if you just let me *finish*. I sold the chocolate at a knock-down price because there's another shipment coming in, a much larger one. Two months, and we'll have the clients crying for more. I'm thinking we can quadruple the price, and they'll pay it. You see what I'm saying? Rico, this is the deal of a *lifetime!* This eighteen grand"—again, he waved the cash in front of my face—"is all I made on the first deal. That's all I've got."

I took the cash and weighed up my options. It sounded like a good deal, and Livingstone was too scared of me to lie. But I couldn't just leave it there. Something like this new deal should have been run past Sparks and me first.

But because he didn't do that, because he was trying to bump up his own status, Livingstone had to be taught a lesson. I grabbed him by the collar, forced him down to his knees.

One good scare is usually all it takes. I held my Lawgiver right in front of his face, side-on, so he could see the ammo-selector. "You see *this*, you sweat-soaked bag of stomm? Incendiary. You know what that round can do to a human head at point-blank?"

"Jovus! Rico, *please...*"

I flipped the gun's selector. "Or maybe you'd prefer a Ricochet, huh? Bounces around in your skull. You'll be dead in seconds, but they'll be the longest seconds you can imagine."

I'd used this trick before. It scares the hell out of the perps, makes sure they stay in-line. You let them *think* they're getting a Standard Execution shot when really you flip it back to Ricochet. Afterwards, they're so grateful to be alive that it'd take something really drastic to shatter their new-found loyalty.

"You don't like that, Livingstone? That's not how you want to go? Okay. Fast and simple." I flipped the selector. "See that? Standard Execution. That more your style?"

"Rico, show some mercy! Please!"

"This *is* drokkin' mercy, punk!" I yelled at him "This is me being lenient, doing it painlessly. More than you deserve. You knew the rules, but you tried to go it alone. Now you pay."

Livingstone was crying now. "I'll give you everything I get on the new deal! *Everything!* My entire profit!"

Gotcha, I thought. *You're mine now, creep. Forever.* After this, I'd be able to tell him to jump from the top of Power Tower, and he'd do it.

And then *he* was there, coming out of the shadows. Joseph Dredd. My brother.

"Step away from him, Rico. Now."

*   *   *

So Joe HAD been following me. Maybe he'd picked up a trick or two on the streets, because I'd had no idea.

A thousand thoughts ran through my head. I was fast, definitely faster than Joe, and my gun was already drawn. He wouldn't be expecting it. I figured I had a good chance of taking him out.

But if I did, then what? I didn't know who he'd told, or if another Judge had ordered him to watch me. If a Judge goes missing, the Department turns the city upside-down looking for him. Like they did with Kenner. They'd investigate me, if I wasn't already on their watch-lists, and they'd find out everything. There was no way I could convince them that I was doing the right thing.

Joe stepped closer, his hands empty. I still had time.

And there was still a way out of this.

I said to him, "I was wondering when you'd show up, Little Joe."

Livingstone muttered something under his breath about "two of them!" but although I was looking at him, my attention was on Joe.

"You're not going to let this rest, are you, little brother? Okay. Two ways it can go. Either we work together—or one of us doesn't leave here alive."

He said nothing, as I'd expected.

"Which is it to be, Joe? Stick with me, I'll show you how to become a very rich man."

Joe said, "I've seen all I want to see, Rico."

He needs a demonstration, I remember thinking. *Have to show him what this is really all about.* Aloud, I said, "No, Joe. I don't think you have. You haven't seen what happens to scum who don't do what I say!" I pointed my gun at Livingstone's chest, aimed down at his sternum. I'm a good shot; I knew exactly what damage a Ricochet bullet would do at that range, at that angle. Crack the bone, lodge in the body. He'd be out of commission for a few days. A good demonstration to Livingstone *and* to Joe.

Livingstone started to back away. "Please, Rico. I can't pay you any more!"

I smirked. "You'll pay with your life, then!" I squeezed the trigger.

I knew the instant that the gun fired that something was wrong. You develop an instinct for that in the Academy. Different rounds have different kickbacks. This one...

This one was *not* a Ricochet bullet. It was Standard Execution.

Joe's fault, damn him. Totally his fault. He'd distracted me before I could reselect Ricochet.

Livingstone collapsed face-down to the floor, a growing pool of blood spreading out from under him.

Out of habit, I dropped down into a crouch next to him, checked his pulse, even though I knew there was no point: the exit wound in his back was large enough to put my fist in.

I looked up at Joe. He was staring at me like he couldn't believe what he'd just seen.

I could barely believe it myself. I'd killed before, plenty of times, but that was always intentional. It wasn't like this. But there are no take-backs with a Lawgiver. There's no "Undo" button on a gun.

If I'd been anyone else, Joe would already have shot me. No, scratch that—he'd have shot me *before* I pulled the trigger on Livingstone.

"This... this doesn't have to be a problem, Joe!"

He said nothing, just slowly crouched and pulled out his Lawgiver from his boot-holster.

"We can make it look like an accident!"

Joe straightened up, still staring at me. "No way, Rico. I'm taking you in."

I wanted to make him understand. Had to make him see that my way was right. Why *couldn't* he see that? We were the same person!

He swapped his gun to his left hand. He's pretty much ambidextrous—as am I—but the left hand was important. He wasn't quite ready to gun me down.

Or maybe, I thought, *he knows he* can't *do it.*

"*You* take *me?*" I said. "Don't make me laugh! I was *always* better!" I wanted Joe to see reason here. Livingstone was scum. He'd have died on the streets long ago if it hadn't been for me. His death today was an accident. And it was more than he deserved.

But my brother—that humourless, stick-in-the-mud, festering *scab*—just stared me down.

All right, then, I thought. *He's not going to budge. He's going to make me do it. He's going to make me draw on him. If that's what it takes to get out of this, then fine. I could kill him and then switch the scene around a little, make it look like it was* me *who'd stumbled across* him *attempting to extort money from Livingstone.* But no, if I was already under investigation, they'd know not to trust me.

But if they caught me... I knew what happened to corrupt Judges. *Better to die here and now than to end up like that.*

And then a simpler thought occurred: *I could just kill Joe and pretend that he's me and I'm him.* They'd never be able to tell. Physically we're identical, right down to our DNA. I'd just have to get used to people calling me Joe instead of Rico. And if there were any discrepancies, like if I didn't know something that Joe was expected to know, then I'd be able to cover that by pretending I was in shock at having had to kill my own brother.

"Too bad, Little Joe," I said to him. "But *one* of us has to go."

"You're not going to shoot me," he said.

That's where I made a mistake, and who can blame me? He was my brother. I thought he meant that I wasn't willing to shoot him—which would have been dead wrong on his part—but he actually meant I wasn't going to be *able* to shoot him. Turned out he was right about that.

He stood staring at me, Lawgiver by his side, not moving.

"Damn you, Joe, fire!"

Nothing. Not even a flicker of a reaction.

I raised my gun. "Why don't you *fire*—?"

He rushed at me, moving faster than I was expecting. I pulled the trigger three times before a blinding pain in my jaw sent me flying backwards.

For a long time, I didn't know how he did it. How could he have moved so fast? How could I have *missed*—I was always the better shot, always faster on the draw. In the Academy, he never once beat me.

But he took me down without firing a shot, got barely a scratch in return.

Eventually, I figured out how he managed it, but of course by then it was far too late. It wasn't that Joe was better than me. I was always the best, and I still am. It was *because* I'm the best.

It was subconscious. I *let* him do it because I couldn't kill my own brother. He was part of me.

That's the only explanation that makes sense. See, Joe was well within the Law to kill me, but he didn't. He used his fists instead of his trigger-finger, because it was the same for him. He couldn't kill a part of himself.

Six

THERE WAS NO trial, of course, but there was an official investigation, and that was almost the same thing.

They kept me cuffed, gagged and under mild sedation while witnesses were brought in, scanned, questioned, cross-questioned, and dismissed. Few of the witnesses would look me in the eye, or even glance in my direction.

I'd tried to explain what I'd been doing. I showed them the dossier I'd compiled on Sparks Petrosky and the other mob leaders. I gave them the names of the losers, users and abusers I'd encountered. And I did a damn good job. Anywhere else, they'd have understood. They'd probably have pinned a Grud-damned *medal* on me.

But none of it made any difference. I'm sure they went out and made all the appropriate arrests afterwards, but the investigation was really about one thing: punishing me because I'd tried to make a difference. Because I'd rocked the system. Because I'd shown them a better way, and made them look bad in the process.

The Justice Department exists because they have the only voice in the city. They're untouchable, unimpeachable. They wield absolute power over the citizens. And they hung me out to dry because I showed them how tenuous their position really is. I was an embarrassment to them because I was *right*.

On the evening of the third day, at the hearing's closing session, I said nothing; there was nothing left to say. I could have protested my innocence one more time, but that would have been pointless. They wanted me gone, and there was nothing I could do about that.

And then I was instructed to stand.

Chief Judge Clarence Goodman looked down at me and hesitated for a moment. "Rico Dredd, on the charge of the premeditated murder of citizen Virgil Alain Livingstone, this board has taken your testimony, witness statements and the physical evidence into consideration. We have concluded that citizen Livingstone's death was unintentional, and on said charge this board finds you innocent."

A murmur broke out among the gathered Judges, and for a moment I almost believed that I'd be exonerated. But I knew better. I knew how the Justice Department worked.

Goodman waited for the noise to subside. "But Livingstone's death was not unavoidable. Rico Dredd, you abused your position as a Judge for personal gain, and in doing so you put the life of citizen Livingstone—and countless others—at risk. A Judge's first duty is to serve the citizens, and in that duty you have failed."

I looked around. Joe was there, standing at the back with

his arms folded, looking only at Goodman. Next to him was Gibson, but at least *he'd* had the decency to remove his helmet and appear concerned for his old friend.

"Rico Dredd, this board finds you guilty of conduct unbecoming of a Mega-City One Judge. Specifically, multiple counts of extortion and theft, and deliberate actions that led to the manslaughter of citizen Virgil Livingstone." Goodman looked around the room. "If any Judge present has anything to say before I pass sentence, speak now."

I glanced toward Gibson again, but he just looked away. *Can't blame him,* I remember thinking. *He's not exactly squeaky-clean himself. But Joe...* That hurt. Joe could have said something. Sure, it mightn't have made the slightest difference, but he could have *tried*. He could have stood up for his brother. Even if he was never going to help me dispose of Livingstone's body and let me go—and I'd been mistaken in thinking he might be flexible enough to see things my way—he could at least have appealed for leniency.

Hell, it wouldn't have surprised me if he'd actually done the opposite and told the Chief Judge to throw the book at me.

With me out of the way, Joe was all set to become top dog in Mega-City One.

And so there was only silence, and my last hope flickered out.

Few of my tutors or mentors were present, and for that I was glad. Judge Morphy, who'd always had the air of a kindly old uncle when he spoke to me and Joe, would have given me *that* look, the look that said, "Rico, you let me down." The same look I'd seen on Kenner's face that time he confronted me about Stacie Quasarano.

Goodman cleared his throat. "Very well. Rico Dredd, you

are dishonourably discharged from the Justice Department, and sentenced to a period of no less than twenty years penal servitude."

And that was it. More than a decade as a cadet, a year on the streets, and it was over.

Goodman left the podium and the public gallery was cleared, then six senior Judges marched me toward the side-entrance and into the long corridor that led to the Judge Cubes, where Goodman was already waiting.

To the senior Judges, Goodman said, "Give me a minute with him. Alone."

The Judges hesitated for a moment, then moved away.

Goodman glared at me. "What the hell is *wrong* with you, boy? Top of your class year after year in the academy. Even before you graduated, I had the heads of every department begging me to give you to them." He thumped his fist against his ornate golden chestplate. "You could have been wearing *this* one day. You threw all that away, and for what? For a few handfuls of credits? Grud-damn it, Rico... You know the Law better than anyone!"

For the first time since the investigation began, I spoke. "*Almost* anyone."

"What? What's that supposed to mean? You're talking about Joe? Don't go thinking *he* gets off scot-free. If he'd turned you in earlier, Livingstone would still be alive."

"So now what?" I said. "I spend the next twenty breaking rocks in the Cursed Earth? I can take that. I'll still be younger than you are now when I get out."

"Cursed Earth *nothing*," Goodman snarled at me. "You're going to Titan."

TITAN
2080 A.D.

Seven

WHEN YOU'VE LIVED all your life on Earth suddenly finding yourself on one of Saturn's moons is unbelievably unsettling. The atmosphere on Titan is toxic to humans: mostly nitrogen, with a tiny percentage of methane and hydrogen. And the moon's gravity is only about a seventh of that on Earth, which takes a lot of getting used to.

Most of the time you can't even make out the sun, the atmosphere is so hazy. On the rare occasions when the air is clear and the sky is cloudless, it's just a weak dot in the sky, not much brighter than Venus appears from Earth. And it barely seems to move because—like Earth's moon—Titan's day is the same length as its orbit, which means that one side is always facing Saturn. That's one sunset every sixteen Earth days, just about.

But then there's also a planet-set, when Saturn eclipses the sun. The first time you see that, it's spectacular. It takes hours, of course, with the sunlight rippling through the rings. It's honestly one of the most breathtaking things I have ever seen.

The feeling doesn't last, though. Not when you're working back-breaking twelve-hour shifts out in the low gravity, chained to your fellow inmates, sweating inside your environment suit as you swing a pick-axe over and over at the unyielding ground. Knowing that in all likelihood you're going to die in that Grud-forsaken place, and that meant some other poor drokker would have to spend a day digging your grave.

On my second day on Titan, one of the inmates—a hulking ex-military guy called Cronyn—hit a particularly tough rock and the head came off his pick-axe. It bounced and struck another prisoner right in the environment suit's visor, cracking it.

He was dead in seconds.

The guards' only response was to order Cronyn to pick up the dead man's pick-axe and keep digging.

We worked alongside the corpse for another three hours, until shift's end. Then we carried him between us—still chained—back to the prison.

I WAS SENTENCED in the dying days of December 2080, when Saturn was on the opposite side of the sun to Earth, a distance of one-point-seven billion kilometres. So it wasn't cost-effective to send me to Titan then. I was held in an iso-cube until the following July, when Earth's orbit took it closer to Saturn, only one-point-two billion kilometres.

Even so, the trip took almost two months. Eighty-four prisoners and eight warders trapped in a craft not much bigger than a standard passenger airliner.

To avoid any trouble, we were kept under constant mild sedation. Aware of what was going on around us, and of time passing, but unable to muster the energy to even complain about it. We had been strapped into our seats and hooked up to intravenous lines to keep us alive.

For the most part, the warders stayed in cryogenic suspension. They woke in shifts, two weeks on, three weeks asleep, but there wasn't anything for them to do while they were awake except read or watch movies. That simple privilege was denied to the prisoners. The best we got was every two days being released from our seats—one at a time—and allowed to walk the length of the shuttle a couple of times.

The shuttle touched down on Titan in the late summer of 2081, and the final three days before landing were excruciating. The shuttle had been under constant acceleration since leaving Earth's orbit, and that acceleration provided gravity. But then it had to flip over and use its thrusters to decelerate in order to avoid overshooting its target. For those seventy-two hours, we were subject to five times normal gravity. We could do nothing but sit there and ride out the pain.

One of the prisoners didn't survive that part of the trip. When finally we touched down, the prison's doctor examined him and declared that his heart had failed, probably within the first few minutes.

The rest of us were fitted with electrocuffs, linked together with chains, and led shuffling from the shuttle through a succession of bare, damp, brightly-lit corridors and stairwells into a large glass-domed room, where ten heavily-armed guards were waiting.

One of them stepped forward as we filed into the room, a big man, maybe forty years old. "I am sub-warden Martin Copus. It's my job to keep this operation running smoothly. I take that responsibility very seriously, so you do what you are told and there's a chance that you'll live long enough to see the end of your terms." To the guards, he said, "Line them up. Strip them and scan them. Check their fingerprints, retinas, voice-patterns and DNA against the manifest."

This process took the best part of an hour, but we could deal with that. After the constant five-gees of deceleration, Titan's low gravity was like a long, cool drink on a sweltering summer's day.

Eight of the new arrivals had been smuggling contraband: cash, drugs and electronics that they'd somehow managed to hide from the searches back on Earth. It was confiscated, but none of them were punished.

And then came the needles.

First, they took something away: a litre of blood from every prisoner. "Blood's in short supply around here," Copus told us. "Get into an accident, and you'll be damn grateful we did this." This was followed by a powerful, general-purpose antibiotic, and a number of vaccinations and deep-tissue injections that left us clutching sore, swollen arms and cursing the medics. The last injections before we were issued with the one-size-doesn't-fit-all uniforms was the most painful; a GPS tracker implanted deep into the pelvic girdle. Some of the prisoners had to be held down for that one.

It was only when it was all done that Copus informed us that one of the injections had been a contraceptive. "Lasts about eight months. We don't have a childcare facility here, and we don't intend to start one."

The prisoners' names were read out in alphabetical order, so it wasn't long before they reached me. "Rico Eustace Dredd, former Judge. Mega-City One. Twenty years."

"Take him to the side," Copus said. Two guards grabbed hold of me and dragged me out of the line.

When the roll-call was done, I was one of eleven prisoners who'd been singled out, all Judges.

Copus ordered that the other prisoners be taken to their cells, then he addressed us. "There are rules. Most of them you're gonna find out as and when you need to know. But the chief rule is this: *break* the rules and you will be punished."

He walked right up to me. "You. Name?"

"Rico Dredd." Some of the others had their heads down, but not me. I looked him in the eye. It was the first time anyone had spoken directly to me since we'd left Earth.

"What did they get you on, Rico?"

"They called it corruption."

"It's got to be more than that."

One of the other guards said, "Sir, he killed a civilian. Cleared of murder, but guilty of manslaughter, accepting bribes, subverting the Law for personal gain, possession of illicit substances, abuse of his position—"

"That'll do, Siebert." Copus took a step closer to me, and said, "You look familiar... You're one of Fargo's clones, right? I heard about you. He was a good man. A *great* man. Hard to imagine that his progeny could have sunk so low."

He stepped back and looked around at the rest of the prisoners. "The minimum sentence on Titan is twenty years. You know why that is? Because that's how long you have to work here to justify the cost of the trip. This is a mining colony, just like the old one on Enceladus before that moon became too unstable to mine the iridium. The work here is hard, and dangerous, and for that they want people like you. Tough guys." He said that last part with a snort. "All of you have been deemed too dangerous to imprison on Earth or even the Lunar colonies. Titan is about as far away as you can be sent while still being cost-effective."

Copus began to pace back and forth, staring at each of us as he passed, and I figured he was memorising our faces. "And you used to be *Judges*. Five from Mega-City One. Three from Texas City. One each from Mega-City Two, Brit-Cit and East-Meg One. You were raised in the toughest academies on Earth, so that means you think you understand how hard life can be. Well, you're going to learn exactly how wrong that is. I guarantee that by the end of your first week, you'll be wishing you'd been executed instead."

He turned to me again. "You. Rico... They must really be scared of you, huh? Fargo's little boy turned bad. I can see that. And you've got that 'I can take it' look in your eyes." He smiled at that. "You'll learn, boy."

I said, "Don't call me 'boy.'"

I steeled myself for a beating, but it didn't happen. Instead, Copus's smile grew even wider. "I'll call you whatever the hell I like. You're not in charge any more. All of you are gonna have to understand that. You've got no power here. None. You have fewer rights on Titan than even the lowest citizens in your cities."

Copus turned to the prisoner next to me. "You. The sov. Sentence?"

The other guard, Siebert, said, "She doesn't speak English, sir. Zera Kurya. Thirty years for killing four other Judges. The exact circumstances aren't clear, but apparently she's never denied the charges."

Copus moved on down the line, checking us out one by one, and then returned to the centre of the room. "All right. Your first shift starts in a little under four hours. Shifts are twelve hours on, eight hours off. You get one day of rest for every eighteen days worked, and that's the only vacation you'll have. You get sick enough that you can't work, those days don't count toward your time here. So if your sentence is twenty years, then by Grud you'll *work* those twenty years. And speaking of that... Today is Day One. The time you spent waiting for the shuttle to leave Earth, and the sixty-two days you've just spent in space, do *not* count toward your sentence."

He gave us a few seconds to let that sink in, then said, "Insubordination will result in days added to your sentence. Harm a fellow prisoner to a degree that he or she can't work, days added. Each escape attempt will result in *months* added. Not that there's any *point* in trying to escape: we're alone on Titan and there's no way off this rock without a ship, and even if you somehow managed to steal one, there's nowhere to go. Head for Earth and you'd be shot down before you reached the asteroid belt. So you're here, and you work. Simple as that."

I asked, "The rest of the prisoners get the same lecture?" Then, quickly, I added, "I'm not being insubordinate, boss. I'm just curious."

Copus walked slowly toward me. "The other new inmates, Rico, are civilians. I know that Mega-City One rarely sends civilians here, but the other cities do. The civilians get a different lecture. But you lot are special. You were Judges. You all think you'll be able to ride this out, to coast your way through. Trust me, it won't be like that. I hate bent Judges, Rico, so I'm gonna bend you 'til you *break*."

I smiled. "That sounds like a challenge." Again, I braced myself for a beating, but again it didn't come.

Copus turned to Siebert. "Chain them, take them to their cells. And prep them for the first shift."

The guards chained our cuffs together, and as we were being filed out of the room, Copus called out, "Rico? That smart-mouth attitude? You'll want to drop that. It'll do you no favours here. The only way off this rock for you people is to keep your heads down, work hard and pray to whatever god you believe in that you can make it through. *I'm* the law here. Remember that. You push me too hard, and you'll get the treatment."

He didn't say what "the treatment" was, and we didn't ask, but he clearly meant it to sound unsettling.

We found out a few hours later. Some of the other prisoners—hardened men and women who could crack open a human skull and eat its contents with a spoon and not think twice about it—broke down when they realised what it meant.

Eight

"INSIDE," SIEBERT SAID, gesturing to what was to be my home for the next two decades. It was barred on three sides—there were occupied cells on either side of mine—with a solid stone wall at the back.

I was last in our group to be assigned a cell, so I knew what to expect: "Walk to the wall. Stand facing it with your feet apart. Rest your forehead on the wall."

I did as instructed, and Siebert unlocked my cuffs. "Next meal's in two hours, inmate. Twenty minutes allocated. Then you'll be fitted for your environment suit." He'd said the same thing to every prisoner, in the same bored tone.

Siebert was tall and wiry, a mean-looking drokker who was smart enough to never find himself alone with a prisoner. This wasn't like a prison movie, where there's always one guard who's unbelievably sadistic, who punishes the inmates to the point where they snap. Siebert was tough, unpleasant, but he had a full understanding of who he was dealing with.

The meal was simple; a scratched plastic bowl containing some kind of bland oatmeal-like paste, a cup of warm water that had a mild metallic tang, and a handful of raw carrots that were so pale they could have been parsnips.

Some of the other new prisoners weren't able to keep it down, they had been so long without solid food. Me, I got cramps and a bad case of the sweats after only a few mouthfuls. Another prisoner, a lank-haired, hawk-faced man in his thirties, was hovering around our table, constantly asking, "You gonna finish that, fish? You eatin' that? Lemme lick the bowl, huh?"

He tried it on me. "Hey, fishy-fish. You gimme the rest of your dinner an' I'll make it worth your while."

"Take a hike, creep," I told him.

"*Not* a creep," he said. "*Not* a creep, new fish." He stared at me with wide, twitching eyes that didn't seem to be able to blink in unison. "You're goin' out today, first time steppin' out into the Bronze, right?" Then he paused. "Damn, I probably sound like a crazy person. The Bronze is what we call the outside, because it's all brown and stuff. Guy who came here from Enceladus fancied himself as a poet, he called it that. My name's Pea. Yours?"

"Rico." I decided to give the scuzzball a break. I'd learned on the streets of Mega-City One that crazy people could be very useful. Everyone underestimates them, and their behaviour can cover up a lot of actions that might otherwise draw suspicion. In a place like this, it might help to know someone who could get around without being noticed.

"You here for the twenty, Rico-fish, or did you earn more

than that?" Pea asked.

"Twenty," I told him. I figured that was his way of judging how dangerous someone was. "What about you?"

"Thirty-five. I'll be seventy when my time is up, if I make it." He grinned, showing off his meagre collection of brown teeth. "You were a Judge, weren't you? Word gets around. Me, I got rail-roaded. I'm innocent."

"Sure you are."

"No, seriously. Totally innocent. I was a quality controller at Resyk in Meg Two. There was an accident, people died, I got the blame."

"I remember that," I said. "It made the news in Mega-City One. You were supposed to be monitoring the fluid filters but instead you were pilfering the corpses for gold fillings and pace-makers to sell on the black market. A valve failed and thousands of litres of body fluids bypassed the filters and ended up in your sector's drinking water. Seventy thousand citizens poisoned by the faecal matter of four hundred corpses. Twelve deaths."

Pea nodded. "That's the story they reported. The truth is, I was off-shift when it happened but the Resyk controller had been angling to replace me with a droid, and this was the perfect chance to get rid of me." He reached out his hand. "Elemeno Jameson Pea."

I shook his hand, but I still didn't believe his declaration of innocence. "Elemeno Pea. Parents had a sense of humour?"

"Yeah. Still, coulda been worse. My old man wanted to call me Asparagus." He shrugged. "You want my advice, Rico? You hafta be like a raft on the ocean, got that? Don't make waves...." Pea put out his hand, palm-down, then slowly and smoothly moved it away. "Just go with the flow. You might make it. You might. You don't wanna end up a mod, like *this* poor drokker." He pointed toward the door, where a figure was entering.

The man was tall, with a strong build. He was shirtless, and it looked like his skin was covered in grey dust. Later, I found out that *was* his skin.

Outside, in Titan's dense atmosphere, a human cannot survive without an environment suit. It's cold—eighty below, on a good day—and the air is toxic. But there were certain parts of the mines where an environment suit isn't practical. Many of the tunnels have narrow passages where a suit will snag, and on the open plains during a dust-storm a suit'll be shredded to rags in minutes.

So some prisoners are modified. Their skin is injected with an almost indestructible polymer. Their eyes are coated with a thinner, transparent layer of the same thing. Their lungs are replaced with a biomechanical breathing apparatus that converts the methane to oxygen. Their noses are removed, replaced with dust-filters, and their mouths sealed. For as long as the prisoner is on Titan, he or she won't be able eat or drink or even breathe normally.

This is "the treatment." Those who've been subject to it are called "mods" by the other prisoners.

My new friend Elemeno Pea said, "They say it hurts like Hades on a hotplate getting it done, hurts ten times more getting it reversed. But it allows you to work in the Bronze without a suit, and Copus likes that. Makes him less inclined to add days. Plus these mods don't do twelve hours on and eight hours off like us. They do ten-on and ten-off. Has to be that way, because they hafta purge their nose-filters every ten hours. That's something you don't wanna see if you've just eaten." He slapped me on the shoulder. "What do you say, Rico-fish? Sound tempting?"

"Not especially."

"Doesn't matter none if it *is* tempting, anyway, because it's not up to us to decide if we want it done. That's up to the sub-warden. You get on his wrong side, an' he will literally tear your lungs out. And I literally *do* mean literally."

THE REASON THE prison existed really was simple economics: the surface of Titan was rich in iridium deposits. Donny Guildford, a prisoner from Brit-Cit in the cell to the left of mine, told me about it.

"Iridium is the most corrosion-resistant element known. Very useful stuff, when alloyed with platinum or osmium or titanium. It's really hard to find on Earth, but it's common in meteorites and here in the outer system."

Donny Guildford had been a civilian, a research scientist who'd taken to settling inter-departmental disputes with tiny amounts of thallium. He was quite an expert with poisons and, according to his prosecutors, had more than ten kills under his belt.

Guildford was also a mod. He'd been caught attempting to strangle another inmate to death—self-defence, he claimed—and sub-warden Copus had ordered that he be given the treatment.

"The operation takes five days, Rico," Guildford told me late one night. "Heard they've got new drugs now that can make you forget the pain, but not when they did it to me. Five days of the purest hell you can imagine."

Guildford was sitting on the floor, resting against the bars that separated his cell from mine.

"They strap you down first. Arms, legs, head. Make sure you can't move. The eyes are the worst. Some guys say that the lungs hurt more, but not me. They hit you with a paralysing agent so you can't squirm away, then they use a suction device to pop out your eyes. Spray them with the polymer. And even if they do now have something to make you forget the operation, it still hurts like drokk for months afterwards. Every breath, every blink… You won't *believe* the pain, man. Just pray that they don't do it to you."

He twisted around and looked at me. It was hard to look back, but I wasn't going to let myself flinch. He tapped the voicebox fitted to his throat. "Wasn't for this, I wouldn't even be able to speak."

"Your mouth's been sealed—how do you eat?" I asked.

Guildford took hold of the voicebox and pulled. It came away from his neck with a wet sound. He handed it to me, but I didn't want to touch it. It was covered in saliva and mucus. Guildford reconnected the voicebox and said, "They give us a paste, like baby-food. Have to push it in with my fingers. It's drokkin' *disgusting*, man." He shrugged. "But I suppose it does have its advantages. Out in the Bronze, before they did this to me, I was constantly watching the oxygen pressure on my suit. Don't need to worry about that now."

EVERY PRISON HAS its own hierarchy among the inmates. It didn't matter how tough you'd been on the outside, when you arrived in the prison you were a new fish, on the bottom rung of the ladder, and the older fish did anything and everything to make sure you stayed there.

I quickly learned that many of the established prisoners particularly despised former Judges. Donny Guildford had warned me to watch my back, but I hadn't paid him any attention. I was a Judge. I'd excelled in the toughest environment on Earth. I could take anything they decided to throw at me.

My first encounter with Register Forbes came a week after I arrived. Forbes was fifty years old, slightly balding, a once-solid build now heavy with age and lethargy. He had a lot of connections and he knew how to acquire things for other inmates. That made him powerful, and powerful men get to thinking they're untouchable and immortal.

I didn't know who Forbes was when he shoulder-bumped me as I passed him in the corridor, but I knew enough to tell that it was a test.

I called him on it. "Watch where you're going, stomm-sucker."

And instantly I was surrounded by five very large, dangerous-looking inmates, all scars, tattoos and knuckles.

One of them pushed his head so close to mine that when he spoke, tiny specks of spittle landed on my face. "*You* watch who you're talking to, fish! Mister Forbes doesn't get out of your way. *You* get out of *his*."

I said, "If Mister Forbes has a problem with me, Mister Forbes can grow a pair and tell me himself."

The bruiser telegraphed the punch. I dodged it easily, but didn't strike back: I was testing them, too. I'd figured it wouldn't be long before something like this happened.

The bruiser took another swing—I swear his fist was almost

as big as my head—and again I dodged it. And then two of his friends grabbed hold of my arms.

They knew I was a Judge. How could they have *not* known? Sub-warden Copus had effectively tagged all the Judges the day we arrived by separating us from the other prisoners. So if Forbes knew I was a Judge, he must have known what was coming next.

It was over in seconds. I kicked the bruiser in the groin, he doubled over and—using his friends' grips on my arms as leverage—I jerked both my feet up and slammed them hard into his head. Hard enough to send him sprawling and force the others to loosen their hold. I fell back between them, rolled onto my feet and crouched.

The two who'd grabbed me started to move toward me again, but Forbes called them off. "Let him be."

He came closer, looked down at me. "You're fast. I've heard about you, Rico Dredd. They say you were one of the best, until you turned bad."

"They're wrong on both counts," I said. "I never turned bad. I just had my own way of doing things that didn't sit well with the rest of the Justice Department. And I was not *one* of the best." I straightened up. "I was *the* best."

"They caught you. Can't have been *that* good."

"There were extenuating circumstances. What do you want, Forbes?"

For a moment he peered at me as though he was asking himself that same question, then he said, "I'm always on the lookout for people who might be useful to me, and I've a feeling you could be very useful indeed." He extended his hand. "I think you and I will be strong allies."

I ignored the hand. "That's not your decision. What are you in for?"

"Murder. Multiple counts."

I didn't ask him if he was guilty. I could see it in his face. "I don't ally myself with scum."

Still with the same calm, detached manner, Forbes said, "Then you're going to be lonely in this place. Listen to me, Rico. I can smooth the path for you. Make things easier."

"Things are not supposed to be easy, creep," I said. "This is a prison, not a day-centre. The Law put us here to punish us. We do our time, and we do *not* coast on the backs of others."

Again, he regarded me silently for a few seconds. "You're not a Judge any more. You're one of us. Here, you play by our rules. Or you don't get to play at all. See, there are *degrees* of punishment. Some prisoners—the weak—have no choice but to lie down and let the strong walk all over them. But some of us, by our very nature, will always rise to the top of any given situation. You strike me as a survivor, Rico. You should—"

By then, I had turned around and was walking away.

Forbes called after me. "You're making a mistake. This offer only comes once. If you're not with me, then you don't get my protection. You know what that means in this place? It means you're a *dead man walking* unless you get back here and *pay attention when I'm talking to you!*" He had to shout that last part.

In the cells that night, Guildford told me that I had written my own obituary. "He's gonna come for you. Well, not him, but one of his guys."

"Let them come," I said. "I can take them."

"No, Rico, you don't get it. Forbes knows this place inside-out and upside-down. He knows all the guards, and he's friends with most of them. That's how he gets stuff in. It's why he's *protected*. He used to *be* a guard, back in the old prison on Enceladus. That's where he got his nickname; he pretty much ran the prison, got all the day-to-day stuff done. The warden would say, 'I need ten prisoners to swamp out the lower cells' and Register would schedule it and pick the prisoners *and* the guards. He gave all the easy duties to his friends, dumped the crap on anyone who complained or criticised him."

"He was the power behind the throne?"

"And then some. When they were preparing to evacuate Enceladus he was in charge of the flight manifests and the supplies and everything. A couple of the other guards caught him short-loading the iridium shipments back to Earth, and they threatened to squeal on him if he didn't cut them in. He made like he was going to do it, but on the next shift he sent them out into the Bronze with sabotaged oxygen tanks. They were rigged to read like they were full, but they only had a couple of minutes of air."

I nodded slowly. "He was caught, arrested, and ended up back here."

"No. They didn't even send him home first. The warden's a Judge; he sentenced Register on the spot. One day Register's got a cushy room in the guards' quarters, next day he's in a cell. But the thing is, he didn't rat out anyone else he was working with. So the next day after *that*, Register is moved to a *better* cell, and his pals let the other prisoners know that he's protected. Anything happens to him, they'll get the treatment."

I said, "I thought that Copus was the one who decided who got the treatment?"

"Officially Copus and the warden both have to agree to it, but the warden doesn't care and Copus listens to Siebert. And Siebert is one of Register's friends."

With this new knowledge, the next day I made peace, of a sort, with Register Forbes. I found one of his thugs—the bruiser, now sporting an ancient, grubby neck-brace—and told him I wanted to meet.

I was brought to Register's cell. Compared with the rest of us, he lived in a palace. It was twice the size of the other cells, and featured four stone walls—not a bar in sight. There was a toilet with an actual seat, and more than one blanket on the bed. Not that he'd need them; his stone-walled cell was considerably less draughty than any other place I'd seen in the prison.

Register was lying on the bed, and when he saw me enter he tossed his book aside and stood up. "So you changed your mind, Rico? Someone's been talking to you, is my guess. Someone who knows the score."

"You have friends back on Earth," I said.

"This much is true."

"So do I. And *my* friends are Judges. You think you can make things tough for me here? That's a hangnail compared to what my friends can do to yours. To your family."

"Huh," he said. "That a *threat*?"

"Yes. And if you want clarification, try this: you hurt me, and every one of your friends back home will lose their eyes."

I stepped closer to him, and his bodyguards rushed at me from the doorway. I elbowed one in the face, hard. I grabbed the wrist of another with both hands, then jerked him toward me and kicked him deep in the armpit. I let his dislocated arm drop as he screamed, then rounded on the third guard—a woman I hadn't seen before. She was a lot shorter than me, but that didn't stop me launching a right jab at her throat.

She expertly blocked it, then swung at me. I dropped into a crouch and kicked out at her knees. She side-stepped the kick, but her movement took her away from me long enough for me to get back on my feet.

There was a flurry of vicious punches, jabs and kicks on both sides, all of which were dodged or blocked.

It only came to an end when two of Register's other guards jumped me from behind. They dragged me away from the woman and held me tight while Register checked her over.

"You're not hurt?" he asked. He sounded genuinely concerned.

She shook her head as she continued to glare at me. "Nothing that won't heal. Drokker's stronger than me. Faster too. He's a keeper."

Register glanced at me. "I don't know... He's dangerous. And he can't be trusted."

"We'll need him." She pulled herself away from Register, and approached me. "Where'd you serve?"

"Mega-City One. You?"

"Same. Four years in Meg-South." The woman was in her mid-twenties, and very definitely had the look of a former Judge; determined, confident, capable. She wasn't what you'd call attractive—certainly not my type—but there was something about her that piqued my interest.

"What did they get you on?" I asked.

"Riot control. I opened fire on the crowd. Turned out there was a couple of undercover Judges among them. One of them survived, testified against me." Without blinking or looking away, she continued, "Seems the Department has a problem with Judges walking up to fourteen wounded, unconscious rioters and putting bullets in their brains. What about you?"

"Corruption, they called it. And there was a death. Accidental, but... a fellow Judge didn't see it that way."

She tilted her head a little to the side as she gazed at me. "Has to be more to it than that."

"There is." I offered her my hand. "Rico Dredd."

She shook it. "Adelaide Montenegro." Her hand was warm, and she held onto mine for a second longer than necessary.

To the side, Register Forbes said, "If you two are done sizing each other up? Rico, we were in the middle of threatening each other. Where do we stand on that?"

I said to him, "Forbes, I don't want to be part of your crew. You stay the drokk away from me, I leave you and your friends with all limbs and digits intact. How does that sound?" I turned and walked toward the door.

"You'll be back, Rico!" he called after me. "Sooner or later, you'll *need* me for something. You'll come back. And when you do, if you don't want to end up like your friend Donny Guildford, you'll come back on your *knees*!"

Nine

I WAS ALMOST eight months into my sentence on Titan when I first realised that escape might be possible.

The other prisoners talked about escape all the time, of course, but most of them didn't have the understanding to grasp just how unlikely it was. They'd talk about using the mining tools as weapons to hold the guards hostage, or hiding out in one of the exhausted mine-shafts.

Elemeno Pea was particularly excitable when it came to escape plans, and he had a hundred of them, not one of which was remotely practical. "We hide all the iridium we find," was one such plan. "We dump it deep inside one of the exhausted mine shafts. Then when the bosses see that there's no more iridium, they'll have to abandon the prison 'cause it'll not be, whaddayacall, cost-effective any more. That means sending us back to Earth. From there, we can get away easy."

Another of his great plans was that we'd kill a random prisoner every day, but make it look like suicide: "They won't keep us here if they think we're all gonna top ourselves!"

And then there was Pea's masterpiece of lateral stupidity, which he explained to me and Guildford one day as we were picking fruit in the prison's huge hydroponic gardens: "Gravity's so low on Titan, escape velocity is *way* down. So, see, what we need is to build a giant sling-shot. One of those tree-bucket things."

"A trebuchet?" I asked.

"Yeah, if you want to get all fancy about it. So we build one of them and fling ourselves out of the atmosphere."

Guildford said, "Where we'll die in space."

"Yes. No! See, we make the tray-bushy thing big enough that it can fling a cargo container. We'll be inside it, with supplies and so on. And we'll seal it up first, make sure it's airtight."

"And *then* what, Pea?" I asked. The man was peering over the edge of insanity at the best of times, but he was just about the only entertainment we had. "We'd need some form of propulsion or we'd just get pulled back to Titan. Or get caught in Saturn's gravity well."

"Hey, I thought of that too. We take along a whole bunch of other prisoners, then, when we're in space, we throw them out one at a time. It's Newton's Third Law of Motion, right? Every action has an equal and opposite *re*action. We throw out a guy, and he goes one way while we go the opposite way."

"And after the first guy we throw out, why would the others allow us to throw *them* out?" I asked.

"Well, they'll be dead. We'll kill them first. Dead bodies are lighter than live ones, which'll make it easier for the traybushay to get the cargo container into space."

Guildford said, "Dead bodies *aren't* lighter, Pea. Someone who worked in Resyk ought to know that. They..." He stopped himself. "Why am I even *arguing* this with you? We can't build a trebuchet because it would take years and the guards would *see* it!"

"Not to mention that it wouldn't work," I said. "Besides, it's asking a lot that we put our faith in someone who pronounces the word 'escape' with an X."

A guard yelled over at us: "Shut up and get back to work!"

We'd been on garden duty for a week already, working in the vast dome, picking the fruits and vegetables that grew to enormous size in the low gravity. Some prisoners believed that it was preferable to working in the mine-shafts, but not me. It was tough, endless, back-breaking work, and we sweltered under the powerful lamps and choked on the rich, cloying scents of the flowering trees. So much greenness made me uncomfortable: I was raised in a concrete-and-steel city where ninety per cent of the population had never seen a real tree.

There were fewer guards than in the rest of the compound since we didn't have power-tools, but they kept a close watch on us nonetheless, in case we ate as we picked.

When the shift was done, we were frisked, then chained once more and led back to our cells.

As we reached the exit and the guards fumbled with the ancient locks on the huge gates, I looked back over the gardens. It was an impressive sight: a dozen square kilometres of fields of wheat and corn, orchards and vegetable patches and herb gardens. The plants provided the prison with oxygen as well as food. Without them, the prison would not be viable.

And an important thought began to form...

I did some quick mental calculations, but the answer didn't seem right, so I started over. Again, the same answer.

By the time I reached my cell, I realised that I had stumbled upon something that I was sure none of the other prisoners had discovered.

There *was* a way off Titan. It wouldn't be easy, but it could be done.

I WAS OUT in the Bronze when the storm hit us. We were a chain-gang of twenty inmates and five guards working on a newly-discovered deposit about three hundred kilometres east of the prison.

We'd been there for three days already, spending our off-time in the huge, low-slung, wide-wheeled transport vehicle that the guards jokingly referred to as the School Bus, and were scheduled to stay out there for another week.

The new iridium deposit was the debris from a large meteorite strike a few thousand years ago. Our job was to scan the surface for fragments—in Titan's low gravity, even a low-velocity impact could spread the fragments up to a kilometre away—then dig them out of the surrounding dirt. Any fragments too large to lift were flagged for later retrieval by a powered digger. We loaded the smaller fragments into two-wheeled barrows, pushed them over the rough ground to the massive trailer attached to the back of the bus. It was exhausting and mind-numbingly tedious, but then I'd yet to discover a job in the prison that was anything but.

Siebert was overseeing the dig, which meant that he'd had his pick of the prisoners. Since it meant time away from the prison compound, there'd been a lot of volunteers. Siebert picked Register Forbes and his crew, and Register had told him to pick me, Guildford and Pea.

In the months since our encounter, Register had made it clear that he wanted me working for him. He could have strong-armed me, or threatened my friends, but he was smarter than that. About once a week he or Montenegro would call on me and ask, "Changed your mind yet?" My answer was always in the negative, but that didn't stop them.

So twenty inmates and five guards piled into the back of the School Bus and set off on the last journey that most of us would ever make. But of course we didn't know that.

The storm hit hard, and fast. The sensors on the bus were barely adequate; we had less than a minute's warning.

Siebert's voice came blaring over our helmet-radios: "Get back to the bus! Now! Storm coming—a bad one!"

On Titan, the weather comes at you like an invisible psychopath wielding an irresistible grudge and a stealth chainsaw. One minute it's all calm and clear skies—well, as clear as they ever get, which isn't saying much—and the next, there's two-hundred-KPH winds and hailstones the size of your fist. I've heard that it wasn't always so extreme, but a few years back some of the bigger cities collaborated in an attempt to terraform Titan, to turn it into another Earth. They installed atmosphere processors and weather-controlling satellites, and attempted to cap a couple of active volcanoes. They didn't want the same thing happening on Titan that had destroyed the mine on Enceladus.

It failed quite spectacularly when one of the volcanoes

erupted prematurely and incinerated eighty-one engineers and a billion credits' worth of equipment. The project was abandoned, leaving only the engineers' mining base and a handful of outstations. But the volcanic eruption had released millions of tonnes of iridium ore... No one wanted to leave that behind, but no one was dumb enough to volunteer to stay and mine it. The best compromise was to give the hard work to those members of society whose lives weren't worth much.

The prisoners were always chained around the waist. The chains were hardened steel, tough enough that it would take several hours to cut through with the tools we were given. I was chained to Guildford, Pea and a guy I didn't know. We'd been maybe two hundred metres from the bus, returning with barrow-loads of iridium ore, when we got the call. We made it back seconds before the first hailstones slammed into the side of the bus.

The bus's windows were made of thick plastiglass. Tough enough to withstand the storm, clear enough that we could see the others caught outside, abandoning their barrows and pick-axes and running hell-for-leather for safety.

Guildford was next to me at the window, looking out. A hailstone exploded against the glass right in front of us. "Jovus... This is gonna be a bad one!"

To the east, the sky was darkening.

Ten

OUTSIDE, A HAILSTONE struck one of Forbes's men in the back of the head. He went down at once, and never moved again. Or not voluntarily: his colleagues were still chained to him.

As they tried to drag the corpse over the hail-scattered ground, one of them was hit in the elbow. Though it should have been impossible over the roar of the storm, I swear I heard the crack.

"Get out there!" I shouted to Siebert. "Unlock them!"

He shook his head. "There's no point. It'd take too long for me to put on my suit."

"Then give *me* the key. I'll do it!"

He looked at me like I was crazy. "No drokkin' way are you getting my key!"

Another flurry of hailstones ripped into the side of the bus, hard enough to rock it, and outside I saw the dead man's colleagues drop. The last one alive was smart: with considerable effort he pulled his friends' corpses over himself.

All we could do was wait. All five guards—unencumbered by chains—were back in the bus, but of the twenty prisoners, only eight of us had made it.

Someone said, "Food and water'll last longer this way, I guess."

I turned from the window to see who'd spoken, and saw Register Forbes slam his fist into the side of another prisoner's head. "Those are my people out there!"

Again, I said to Siebert, "Give me the key."

He backed away from me. "No. It's policy. No matter what happens, I can't give a key to a prisoner."

"I'm not going to *report* you, damn it! That guy's still *alive* out there—better to go back with nine prisoners than eight! Just give me the drokkin' *key!*"

Forbes said, "Do it, Siebert. Where's he going to run to?"

Siebert wouldn't look me in the eye as he unclipped the electronic key from his belt.

Guildford said to me, "Let me do it. I don't need a suit."

"I'm faster than you, and smaller," I said. "Less of a target. Siebert?"

Siebert placed his thumb on the key's scanpad. "You've got a hundred seconds before—"

"I know," I told him as I grabbed the key from his hand and ran for the airlock. After one hundred seconds the key would become inert again. It was a security measure, in case a prisoner ever managed to snatch a key from a guard. "Keep the airlock open!"

Outside, the wind threatened to lift me off my feet as I half-ran, half-crawled toward the downed prisoner. I tried shouting, letting the fallen man know that help was coming, but my voice was swamped in the roar of the storm.

The ground was treacherous, slick with fragmented hailstones as a fresh flurry pounded down around me, ripping chunks out of the dirt.

As I reached the bodies, a hailstone the size of a football missed my head by centimetres. Later, Pea told me that they had watched it strike the ground behind me and bounce clear over the bus.

I saw a gloved hand protruding from beneath the bodies, and grabbed it. It grabbed back—he was still alive.

I took hold of the topmost body—it was a prisoner I'd seen working in the gardens—and dragged it clear, then lost a few seconds trying to get the key to work.

It was only when I was hauling the man free that I realised it wasn't a man at all, but Adelaide Montenegro, my fellow former Judge.

She nodded at me as I helped her to her feet, then she began to scramble over the growing piles of hailstones toward the bus.

I followed her, aware that at any moment we could be struck from behind.

By the time we reached the bus, the hail was already up to the airlock's outer door. Forbes was inside, kicking out the hail almost as fast as it was piling up.

Montenegro lunged for the airlock, and Forbes grabbed her hand, helped her the rest of the way. Then he reached out for me.

I almost hesitated. I didn't want someone like Forbes to have any reason to think I owed him, even in a situation like this.

But then, I *had* just saved his colleague's life.

I grabbed his arm and allowed him to help me into the airlock.

He slammed the outer doors closed, and the roar from outside subsided a little.

As we left the airlock, Siebert was waiting for us. "I've heard of storms like this lasting hours. Then we're looking at digging the damn bus out."

Forbes said, "Well, now, thanks to Rico, we have one more person to dig."

"Right," Siebert said. He held out his hand, palm up. "Key?"

I pointed outside. "I had more important things on my mind than your stupid key. You want it, go out and fetch it for yourself."

Naturally, Siebert ordered the other guards to search me, but it wasn't hard to hide the key in the folds of my environment suit when I removed it.

The storm lasted for nine hours, a relentless, deafening assault that shook the bus with every impact and more than once threatened to shatter a window.

I eventually fell into an uneasy sleep and woke to a darkened bus, thinking that night had come; but no, this was Titan. Night was another six days away. We were just buried under countless tonnes of hail.

Siebert and another of the guards—a thin, stoic man called Vickers—were awake, sitting in the cab. When Siebert saw me move, he beckoned me closer.

In a low voice, he said, "Rico... The engine's dead. Don't know whether it's just a loose connection or something more serious, but"—he tapped the dashboard readouts—"there's nothing happening here. Radio's shot, too. Copus knows where we are, but we don't know how badly *they* were hit by the storm. It could be some time before we're rescued."

"So we rescue ourselves," I said. "Dig our way out."

"And go where?" Vickers asked. "We're hundreds of kilometres from the prison and we're the only people on the whole damn planet."

Siebert said, "It's a moon, not a planet."

"Like *that* makes a drokkin' difference."

"We're not alone," I said. "But right now, getting out of here is our first priority. Even if Copus sends people after us, we don't know how deep we're buried. From the air, they might not spot us. We might never be found." I tilted my head back, looked up at the roof. "How thick is the armour plating on this thing?"

"Three centimetres, maybe four," Siebert said. "We don't have anything that can cut through it. And we can't go out through the airlock. There's a wall of ice out there, and all the digging tools are outside. I say we sit tight."

Vickers nodded. "Food'll last us a couple of weeks. Three if we're careful. Same with the air, plus there's oxygen in the suits. And if we want water, we have all the ice we'll ever need outside."

"The ice isn't *water*, it's frozen methane," said Guildford, coming up behind me. "Though it might come in useful if there's no sign of rescue and we're slowly starving to death. We could thaw some out and gas ourselves instead."

"Methane gas is flammable in oxygen," I said, thinking aloud.

Siebert said, "You think we could burn our way out?"

I started to say that it might work, but Guildford interrupted me. "Unlikely. If the mix of oxygen to methane is too thick or too thin, it won't burn. A bigger problem is that if the ice *is* methane, it won't be around long. It's got a much lower melting-point than frozen water. That's not as good as it sounds: if it melts too quickly there's a possibility we could drown. I doubt this bus was built to float."

THE BUS'S BACK-UP power failed on the evening of the second day. That is, the second Earth day.

Most of us were awake when the interior lights dimmed and faded. The darkness wasn't complete—it was still daytime on Titan, and enough light filtered through the hail outside that we could still just about see.

"Damn, it's *quiet* out there," Vickers said.

He was right. There was the constant dripping of melting methane-ice, but that only served to heighten the silence. There was no wind, no engine-hum of an approaching rescue craft... And something else was missing. It took me a moment to realise what it was. "It's quiet in here, too. The air-recycler must be on the same circuits as the lights."

Pea jumped to his feet. "Drokk! How long is the air in here going to last?"

"Don't worry about that," Donny Guildford said. "You'll freeze to death before you suffocate."

Siebert said, "Everyone, suit-up. And if any of you have any ideas how we can get out of here, now's the time to let the rest of us know."

Guildford said, "Bet you all wish you'd had the treatment now, right?"

"Yeah, that doesn't help," I told him, pulling on my environment suit. "The first thing we need to establish is how deep we're buried. I say we have no option but to start digging. We open the outer airlock door and see what happens. If the hail spills in, then it's not all frozen into one mass. That means we'll have a chance of getting out."

Siebert nodded. "All right. But we're only sending out *one* person. And that's Montenegro."

The former Judge looked up at him. "Me? No way."

"You're the smallest. That means you won't have to dig so much."

Guildford said, "It's not about size, Siebert. It's about *strength*. And one isn't enough. Me and Rico will do it."

There were no objections, not even when I took the oxygen tank from one of the spare suits.

Without power, we had to open the airlock doors manually, which took some effort. The guards closed and sealed the inner airlock door behind us, then Guildford and I stood facing the outer door.

"Ready for this?" he asked.

"Don't have a lot of other options."

We grabbed hold of the lever next to the door, and pulled. I had to brace my feet against the wall, but we managed it. The methane ice on the outer door cracked as the door swung in, revealing a densely-packed wall of apple-sized hailstones. They didn't fall.

"That's not good," Guildford said. He reached out and poked at the wall with his fingertips, hesitated a second, then pressed harder. "Seems solid... although it's melting."

Together, we tried pushing at the wall, then kicking at it. Too solid to move, and too slick to hold onto.

Guildford said, "Rico, we could be looking at two or three metres. Maybe more. Nothing short of a concussion grenade is going to get us through this. We're going to have to wait until it melts further."

"That might not be as long as you think," I said. "Look down."

He looked. At our feet was a pool of liquid methane about a centimetre deep, and growing. "Damn. That a good sign or a bad one?"

"Wish I knew. Could be that it's melting from the ground up rather than from the top. If that's the case, then—" We felt the bus shift, very slightly, to the left.

Guildford said, "Okay... That's definitely *not* a good sign."

The bus lurched again, more noticeably.

"I know we're not parked on a *hill*," he said. "So what in Grud's name is happening out there?"

We never found out exactly what happened. The best guess is that the bus was frozen into the ice, and the ice was melting under it.

The bus rocked and swayed for another four hours. At times, we had no doubt that we were moving, that the whole ice floe was sliding, dragging the bus with it.

Many of the more serious lurches—the ones that had us clutching at walls and seat-backs for support—were accompanied by deafening cracks from outside.

The walls trembled as the bus's wheels were dragged over the ground, and there was nothing we could do but wait it out.

The air inside the bus grew stale, our breath misting as the temperature dropped. Frost formed on the inside of the windows, and we were forced to seal our helmets and pray that the oxygen lasted long enough for us to be rescued.

Except for Guildford, of course.

I saw Vickers and Siebert at the bus's controls. They had the dashboard panels removed, and had been poring over the wiring for hours, to no great effect.

I sat with Pea and Montenegro and Forbes and Guildford, and countless ideas were raised, discussed and dismissed. Except for Pea's ideas, which were dismissed without discussion to save time.

And gradually I became aware that Vickers kept looking in our direction, and of the air of conspiracy about him and Siebert. You quickly develop a feel for that sort of thing when you're a Judge.

Montenegro seemed to be aware of it too; she moved closer to me and said, "Something's wrong."

"I know," I told her, keeping my voice low. "We should have been found by now, no matter how far the ice has carried us. I think we need some answers." I stood up, stepped over sleeping bodies on my way to the cab.

"That's close enough, Rico," Siebert said, his hand drifting toward his gun. "What do you want?"

"Why haven't they come for us?"

Vickers said, "We talked about that. The bus's controls are shot; they can't lock—"

"Drokk the controls," I said. "Every prisoner on this bus has a GPS tracking implant. You know that."

The two men briefly exchanged a glance, and my suspicions were confirmed. There was no GPS implant. It was just another ruse to keep the prisoners in line.

And I was sure that even if we *were* rescued, sub-warden Copus would have us killed before we could let the other prisoners know that the GPS wasn't real. I gave them a way out. "It doesn't work this far from the prison, does it?"

"Radius of about ninety kilometres," Vickers said. Lying.

Siebert added, "And if you even *think* of mentioning that to the others, I'll happily put a bullet in your brain."

"What would be the point of telling them?" I asked. "If someone escapes from the prison there's nowhere to *go*. Look, we want to get out of this situation as much as you do. We don't know where we are, we can't even take a guess at how far we've been carried. The weather on this moon is so drokked up we could be a thousand kilometres away from where we started."

Vickers said, "You think we don't *know* that? Until the ice melts, we can't use the doors or windows. We don't have anything strong enough to cut through the roof; and for all we know, there's still a couple of metres of ice up there."

"So we go *down*," I said. "We go through the floor."

Eleven

WITHOUT PROPER TOOLS—the bus's toolbox was fixed to the outside—it took us almost two hours to undo the heavy bolts securing the access panel in the floor.

Once the bolts were removed, Guildford hacked through the thick silicon sealant around the panel with a screwdriver. "Okay. Everyone ready? Make sure your helmets are sealed, because once the air in here hits the methane, the moisture in the air will freeze and the methane will start to evaporate. You won't be able to breathe."

We gave him the all-clear, and he prised up the panel. The air clouded; the frost patterns on the windows briefly cleared before reforming into thick crystals.

Guildford pointed the one remaining flashlight down into the darkness. "Rico was right. It's liquid. Can't see much through it, but I think it's pretty deep."

"Can you swim through it?" asked Forbes.

"Not without a suit. I don't feel the cold and my skin is probably tough enough to survive it, but"— he tapped the voicebox at his throat—"This isn't waterproof. I'd drown."

"Then take one of the spare suits." I dropped down flat next to the hatch, and reached my gloved hand down into the thick liquid. "Triple insulated gloves and I can still feel it."

"You could put the other spare suit on over yours," suggested Pea. "That might help."

Montenegro shook her head. "He wouldn't be able to seal the second one. The methane would seep in, get trapped between the suits. That'd be worse."

Forbes handed me a roll of suit-repair tape. "This could work. I know it's only designed for small rips, but it'll help keep out the methane."

"No," I said. "It's hard enough to move in these suits as it is. I definitely wouldn't be able to swim wearing another one on top of it." There was a strong chance that I wouldn't make it more than a couple of metres, anyway, but there was no choice. It was either this or stay on the bus and suffocate.

I stood up again, watching as Forbes and Vickers helped Guildford into his suit.

Siebert passed me the large screwdriver, the only useful tool inside the bus. "You get us out of this and I'll talk to Copus. Get him to put in a word with the warden. I'll see what we can do to reduce your sentences."

"Sure," I said, but I didn't believe him. In the history of the prison, no one had ever had a sentence reduced. "Close it up after me. But if you hear me knocking, open it up *immediately*."

Siebert nodded. "Will do."

It was hard to be sure, through the helmet's visor and with his mutilated face, but it seemed to me that Guildford was grinning as he patted me on the shoulder. "I'll lead. I get into trouble, you head back, got that?"

Before I could answer, he was crouching down over the mist-obscured hatch and lowering himself into the liquid methane.

"Rico..." Pea said, "swim *fast*."

"Good thinking," I told him.

Register Forbes patted me on the shoulder. "Good luck, Rico. Whatever happens out there, you've earned my respect."

Yeah, that'll *do me a lot of good,* I said to myself as I followed Guildford down through the hatch. The instant my feet hit the liquid, they started to burn with the cold. I kept going; better to die quickly.

The methane was so cloudy with sand, dirt and swirls of oil and grease from the underside of the bus that I could barely see Guildford ahead of me.

We'd already agreed on the direction, the same way the bus was facing. The meagre sunlight seemed to be strongest that way, so we figured that the ice might have melted more on that side.

A hand swung down in front of my face, and I'm not ashamed to admit that I screamed.

The arm hung limply, drifting with the invisible currents, and it took me a moment to realise what it was. Another prisoner, suit mangled, faceplate crushed. Whoever he was, he had taken refuge under the bus when the storm hit, become entangled in the suspension mechanism.

How long? I wondered. *How long was he out there, only a metre away from the rest of us, and we didn't even know? He could have been screaming for help for* hours, *and we didn't hear him over the storm.*

Guildford hesitated too, but moved on, now upside-down as he kicked with his feet and used his hands to pull himself along the underside of the bus.

I followed, arms and legs already numb. The inside of my environment suit's visor had completely misted over, and I could only see Guildford as a thrashing shadow.

It seemed to take forever, though it was probably only seconds. Eventually the light ahead brightened as I reached the front of the bus and came out under the ice.

Guildford stopped in front of me and pointed up.

I looked. Maybe two metres overhead was a bright patch. Not an actual break in the ice, but a thin patch. Possibly thin enough to smash through.

Guildford kicked upward, braced his fists ahead of him and hit the underside of the ice. It didn't look as though he'd had an effect at all, but he wasn't giving up. He swam back down, pointed at me, locked his hands together in front of him, and again looked up.

I nodded and linked my hands, fingers locked, as though I was boosting him over a wall. He put one of his feet into my hands, and I hoisted him up while he kicked off.

Travelling a little faster this time, he again struck the ice with his fists.

Then we did it again. And again.

After the fifth attempt, Guildford shook his head and pointed off, suggesting that it might be better to try elsewhere.

But I wasn't ready to quit just yet, certainly wasn't willing to go searching for another thin patch, or for the edge of the ice.

By now I could barely move, let alone boost him. The cold had seeped through into my bones, and every breath was like fire.

I held up my index finger—one more try—and this time I got him to boost me.

I saw the uneven, glassy ice approach, and at the last second I stabbed upward with the point of the screwdriver.

The impact rippled through my bones, threatened to tear my muscles free... But there was a crack in the ice. Without dropping back, I stabbed again, in the same spot, and the shock knocked the screwdriver from my grip. I grabbed for it, and missed.

I watched it drift down and I remember thinking, *This is* not *how I'm going to die! Not after everything!*

I was going to live out my twenty years on this glacial moon. I'd serve my time and go back to Earth, back to Mega-City One, and find my brother. Make him pay.

Because *he* did this to me. He had refused to see things from my point of view, to even consider the possibility that I'd been right. But that's how he's always been. Sure, he'll listen to advice and he'll pay attention to new ideas, but in the end Joe Dredd does whatever Joe Dredd wants.

And one day, I'd go back. I'd see him. Look the drokker in the eye and show him what he'd done.

Twenty years in this hell-hole for what? For having different ideas. For having the intelligence and the empathy to understand that the Law isn't everything. That without mercy, it's *nothing*.

Maybe it was because I was exhausted, and desperate. Maybe it was because I didn't like being trapped. Whatever it was, it fed my anger and my anger gave me strength.

I slammed my fist upwards, and it punched clear through the ice.

* * *

I KNEW THAT, inside my gloves, my knuckles were cracked, the skin raw and seeping, and I was grateful that I could feel nothing but the cold.

For a long time I didn't have the strength to pull myself up, so I clung to the edge of the fracture, trying to summon that anger again.

But it eluded me. All I could do was hold on, the faceplate of my environment suit barely above the misty surface of the liquid.

Through the soul-chilling numbness I felt Guildford's strong arms wrap themselves around my legs, and for a moment I imagined he was trying to pull me down, to drag me into the suffocating, freezing death.

Then he was lifting me from below, pushing me until I could get my elbows over the edge.

I hauled myself up, Guildford still pushing me, and collapsed onto the ice, face-down.

I allowed myself a couple of seconds to rest, then twisted around, reached into the hole, grabbed hold of Guildford's flailing hand, and pulled. It took the last of my strength to get him out, and I wouldn't have been able to do it had he not used the screwdriver—he'd seen it fall from my hand and caught it—as a piton.

It was only when he was out of the liquid and onto the ice that I understood how close we had come to failure. Twenty metres in front of us was the bus, trapped inside a hill of compacted hail. Guildford and I were in a shallow, inexplicable depression. Otherwise, the ice stretched for hundreds of metres in every direction.

The floe was drifting across a vast plain. There were mountains in the distance, but nothing recognisable. The only clue I had as to how far we'd come was the position of Saturn in the sky.

From where we were when the storm hit, Saturn should have been a few degrees above the horizon; here it was well up in the sky.

Guildford joined me, his helmet now removed, and we stood together looking at the planet. "What do you think, Rico? A couple of hundred kilometres?"

"At least," I said. "Probably a lot more."

"Then all that was for nothing. They're never going to find us before the oxygen in the suits runs out."

"*You'll* have to tell them what happened, then."

He barked a harsh, mechanical laugh, then slapped me on the shoulder. "We should get the others free. And then maybe there's a way we can break the bus loose. Probably won't work, but it'll keep us all occupied while death sneaks up on us."

We returned to the bus and circumnavigated it, looking for the easiest access point. As we walked, I told Guildford about the GPS fraud. He didn't seem surprised. He said, "They think we don't know, so we let them believe that. If they figure we know it's a con, they'll do it for real."

"How do *you* know?"

"I was a scientist, remember? And it doesn't take a genius— which I *am*, for whatever that's worth on this Grud-forsaken rock—to figure it out. You know how everyone keeps telling us that escape is impossible? Well, about four years ago three prisoners *did* escape. They weren't able to get off-planet, but they did manage to get out of the prison. Copus made a big show of bringing back the remains of their bodies, but it wasn't them. They'd dug up a few graves instead. For all we know the real escapees could still be out here somewhere." Guildford began to climb up onto the ice-sheathed front of the bus. "So they're free, but dead, of course, because there's nowhere on this rock to actually escape *to*."

I said, "Yeah, everyone keeps telling us *that*, too. But they're wrong."

Guildford looked back at me. "Meaning?"

"Meaning I'm pretty sure we're not alone on Titan."

Twelve

THE COMPACTED HAIL on top of the bus was a metre thick, and without proper tools the only way we could get through it was by hacking at it with the screwdriver and pulling at the chunks of ice with our hands. The constant freezing and thawing of the methane ice had solidified it into a single mass peppered with tiny pockets of air.

As we worked, we talked. "You look at the size of the prison's gardens," I told him, "then think of the portion sizes of our meals, and the number of prisoners. The gardens produce a lot more food than we consume. About three times as much."

"I guess the rest is used to create biofuel or ethanol to power the vehicles," said Guildford. He stamped the heel of his boot down onto the ice. "Like the bus. It's certainly not nuclear."

"That doesn't account for all of it," I said as I stabbed at what looked like a weak seam. "And every six days one particular truck heads out to pick up loose ore fragments. Or so they say. But from where? I've never been on that duty, nor has anyone I've asked. You've seen it—it's red and has a massive dent in the side of the cab. I've been keeping track... Sometimes it goes west, sometimes east, but that's a diversion. It always heads south." I dropped back, exhausted.

Guildford pulled the screwdriver from my hand, and took over. "How did you work *that* out?"

"Because *we're* sent out every direction but due south, and I've never seen the red truck out here, although I've seen every other one many times." I pushed myself to my feet, and turned in a slow circle. "And the red truck never comes back with a full load. In fact, it always comes back with pretty much the same amount of ore. Ore that *I've* never been assigned to unload. Have you?"

"Can't say that I have, no. So what are you saying? That there's another base somewhere on Titan and the prison is supplying it with food?"

"Yeah, I think so. It just carries the same ore out and back every time. And because they're keeping it a secret, I figure it's either a research station working on something big, or it's a military base."

Guildford stopped working, and turned to face me. "Military. Out *here*?"

"We know we're not alone in the galaxy. Have you ever heard of a society that *wasn't* paranoid about invaders? I'd put money on it, if I had any. There's a military base here. Probably one on every major moon in the system. And military bases have ships. And guns."

After some consideration, Guildford said, "If we knew exactly *where*..." Then he shook his head. "It'd be a lot better defended than the prison." He stepped back and handed me the screwdriver.

"I know," I said, as I crouched down and resumed working. We were above the roof of the bus, slowly working our way down through the ice toward the door. The plan was to clear away enough ice that Montenegro could get out, then she could take over for a while.

And we couldn't stop. Being a mod, Guildford had turned off his oxygen, but mine was already running low. When it was gone, I'd swap tanks with him, but even so, time was against us. The sooner we got Montenegro out, the sooner she could free the others.

We worked in silence for a while. Holding the screwdriver in both hands, I stabbed at the ice, over and over, while Guildford stood next to me, watching, ready to take over when the cold and constant jarring in my arms became too much.

"Suppose we *did* get to the military base," Guildford said, "And we managed to get a ship that we could somehow actually fly. What then? Where would we go? You've said it yourself many times—if we go back to Earth, we'll be shot down."

I told him, "We don't go to Earth. We go... elsewhere. There are races out there who'd pay a lot for our knowledge of Earth."

Before Guildford could reply, a head-sized portion of the ice collapsed under my hands.

We stared down into the small hole, and heard Siebert's voice call out, "We're through!"

* * *

IT TOOK ANOTHER half-hour to free enough ice for Montenegro to squirm out.

Vickers came next. He threw a large cloth-wrapped bundle ahead of him, then reached for me and Guildford through the opening. "Don't try anything," he warned us. "Siebert's still armed. You don't want to lose your friends to a gun after all you've been through, right?"

We hauled him free, and he ordered us to back away. "Toward the front of the bus. Move." Still watching us, he called over his shoulder, "Mister Siebert? It's clear."

Vickers crouched down next to the opening and Siebert passed him up the gun.

Vickers held the gun on us as he tapped the bundle with his foot. "Spare oxygen tanks, the rest of the food and water. You'll be carrying it."

"Where are we going?" Guildford asked. "We don't know where we are, and—"

"No questions," Vickers said.

It was a few minutes before Register Forbes emerged, clambering awkwardly out of the hole, almost slipping back a couple of times. He hoisted his stomach over the edge, then turned to help Siebert out.

Siebert was also carrying a large bundle, and I could see now that they'd been fashioned from the thick rubberised cloth that covered the seats inside the bus.

Vickers helped the other guards out, Guildford, Montenegro and I watching, as Siebert and Forbes peered around at our surroundings. "I don't know this place," Forbes said. "We could be anywhere. What do we do?"

Siebert examined his gun. "We have one high-ex shell. We

can use that as a flare if we see anything. Right now, we head west." Then he looked directly at me. "You were right about the military base."

"You heard that," I said.

"We heard *everything*," Siebert said. He kicked at the bundle at his feet, and it slid over the ice toward me. "Pick it up. You three walk ahead of us, not more than ten metres, not closer than five. We stop only when *I* say we stop. Understood?"

"What about the others?" asked Montenegro. "We can't just leave them here!"

Even before I picked up the bundle, I knew what had happened. It was heavier than it should have been, and that was because it contained more oxygen tanks. Not just the tanks from the spare suits. "There *are* no others," I told her. "They're dead."

Thirteen

NAVIGATING ON TITAN isn't as tough as it would be on Earth, where the sun is only a useful pointer if you know the time of day. Titan's day is the same length as its orbit, so Saturn never moves in the sky. If we'd been on the other side of Titan, it's almost certain that none of us would have made it.

The ice-floe continued to melt as we walked, in pockets that evaporated into thick, tall columns of mist that twisted and writhed like giant agonised snakes. In some places, the mist remained at ground level, hiding the deep, jagged-edged pits from which it had evaporated.

Forbes and the guards walked behind us, mostly in silence but occasionally talking or even joking.

I couldn't take my mind off the prisoners inside the bus. I didn't know most of them—Pea was the only one I'd have considered a friend—but that wasn't the point.

Siebert had ordered them killed just to give himself a better chance of survival. And I had no doubt that if they hadn't needed me, Montenegro and Guildford to carry their supplies, we too would have been left behind.

After a few hours, the wind picked up a little, coming at us from behind, blowing away the mist and allowing us sporadic glimpses of the pockmarked landscape ahead. The wind was loud enough that the guards could no longer hear us talk.

"They won't admit what they've done," I told Guildford and Montenegro. "They'll kill us before we reach the military base."

Montenegro said, "So we have to remain useful to them as long as possible. And that means not using up the supplies too quickly."

A few minutes later we lost one of the guards. Frazier, a quiet man who'd always looked to me like he was continually running a mental countdown of the days he had left until retirement, walked across a patch of ordinary-looking ice and it cracked under his feet.

The rest of us barely had time to register the sound of the crack before he was gone: fallen through, dragged under by the liquid methane's strong current, and swept away. It took a second, maybe less.

Frazier had been carrying one of the makeshift sacks of supplies.

We carried on—there was nothing else we *could* do—with increased caution, and growing concern from Guildford. He sidled closer to me. "Most of my food-paste was in Frazier's pack."

"The rest of us will share," I told him.

He tapped his grey, surgically-sealed mouth. "I can only eat the paste, remember?"

There was a solution to that, of course, as we discovered on our next food-break. The environment suits featured a small airlock on the underside of the helmet, so that non-mod prisoners working outside could eat by breaking up the food and inserting it one mouthful at a time. The food was compacted lumps of dried fruit and vegetables. We'd break off a chunk, put it into the food-airlock where it'd be warmed up.

That wouldn't work for Guildford—he couldn't chew. So I had to do the work for him, and that wasn't pleasant for any of us. I took his meagre portion of food and chewed it up, spat it back out into his hand so he could quickly force it into the voicebox-hole in his throat before it froze.

Vickers and one of the other guards—I never learned his name—thought this was tremendously amusing.

We reached the edge of the ice-floe shortly after that, and by luck it had butted up against a gentle hillside. If we'd had to wade through the lake of liquid methane I doubt any of us would have survived.

We trudged on through the Bronze, sleeping a few hours at a time whenever Siebert grew too tired to carry on. We left in our wake a widely-spaced trail of discarded oxygen tanks and food packaging, until Montenegro, Guildford and I could no longer fake how light the makeshift bags had grown.

Siebert ordered a stop. "Food and water are getting low, and night's coming in. We don't need all three of you to carry the gear. You can decide amongst yourselves which of you won't be coming any further."

Montenegro said, "Siebert, if you show up at the military

base with Forbes as the only surviving prisoner, they'll figure out what happened. No matter what we've done, you have a duty of care to your prisoners, and—"

Siebert shot her in the face.

I HAD ALREADY decided to kill Siebert, so the suddenness and brutality of his action made little difference to how I felt. But it did crystallise the timetable. Siebert and the others, Forbes included, had to die before they killed me. Or Guildford; I'd never make it to the military base alone.

But I needed Siebert alive to *find* the place. That was the only reason I hadn't already smashed open his helmet and watched him suffocate.

"Rico, get her tank and supplies," Siebert ordered. "Then we pick up the pace. It won't be much longer now. We get within a hundred kilometres of the base, they'll detect us and send someone out to investigate."

Guildford and I took a last look at Montenegro as we removed the oxygen tank from her suit. While we crouched over her he quietly asked me, "You still got Siebert's key?"

"Yeah. Can't see what good it'll do us, though. We're not chained."

"It's got a power-source. First chance you get, give it to me."

We marched on, always heading west. Though Guildford was bigger and stronger than me, and had been adapted for the climate, he wasn't holding up too well. Maybe it was because I'd been trained as a Judge. Or maybe it was because, despite everything, Donny Guildford of Brit-Cit wasn't used to seeing someone he knew gunned down in cold blood.

He spoke about that as we walked. He'd rarely mentioned anything about his past before, and I knew then that he was certain that he was going to die. This was his confession. Perhaps telling it to a Judge made things easier, I don't know. But I listened, because he was my friend.

"I did it," he told me. "There. Never admitted it before, not even when the prosecution showed absolute proof. I did it. I killed them. Deliberately, too. I intended to kill them, and I succeeded."

"So who were they?" I asked.

"Colleagues. One in particular. We were working on a way to create liquid glass." He turned to me and smiled, as best as his sewn-up mouth allowed. "Pointless, I know. There's not a lot of practical applications, but we weren't exactly in a cutting-edge industry. Everyone thinks that research scientists spend their days trying to come up with a smarter rat-trap or a cure for something horrible, but most of us are in the private sector working on stuff intended to save a private company tiny sums of money. Liquid glass was probably going to be a novelty item. It'd be liquid at room temperature." Guildford shrugged. "Like I said, pointless."

Behind us, Vickers called out, "Shut up!"

I shouted back, "Why?"

He didn't have a real answer for that. "Because I said so!"

Guildford resumed talking anyway. "So, there was this guy in the company, one of those people who just really wind you up the wrong way. They never actually do anything bad, nothing you can point your finger at and say, '*That's* why he's a complete spugwit!' but still, you can't get along with them. You know the type?"

I said that I did. I was, of course, thinking of Little Joe.

"Herman, his name was. He joined the company after I did, and everyone liked him immediately. *I* did too, for a while. But Herman just kept pushing my buttons, over and over. Wouldn't stop no matter what I said or did. It was stupid stuff, mostly. Like, we'd go together to the canteen for lunch, and he always—*always*—ended up ahead of me in the line. Somehow, we'd be walking along the corridor and no matter what I did, it was always me holding the door open for him, so that he'd go through first and go straight to the end of the line." Guildford shrugged. "Like I said, stupid stuff. But imagine that happening every single day for eight drokkin' *years*."

I was about to make a comment, but he wasn't done yet.

"Herman always found a way to get under my skin. Subtle things, but the sort that build up. Leaving stuff on my desk. Taking my pen and chewing the end of it. And he'd go out with the others after work and not invite me, but the next day he'd tell me what a great night it was, and that I should have been there."

There was more like this, a *lot* more, and it was all I could do to rein in my Judge training and resist punching his arm and telling him to grow a pair. What it all boiled down to was that this guy Herman had supplanted him in the company's social hierarchy, and so Guildford poisoned him with thallium. "It was simple, in the end," Guildford said. "I dipped my pen in thallium dust and left it on my desk. I mean, I'd told Herman a hundred times not to chew my pens, but, true to form, he did it anyway."

"How did you get caught?" I asked.

"Well, Herman was only the first. I had problems with

another colleague, in a different department. We'd talk about work and he'd take my ideas and present them to his boss like he'd thought of them. So he had to go. So did his boss; that drokker *knew* they were my ideas and he didn't care. And there was a neighbour, too. And a few others."

"How many in total? Someone told me it was at least ten, is that right?"

"Seventeen. They caught me because some hot-shot young Judge took over the investigation and just wouldn't let it go."

After a long pause, I said, "*I'd* have executed you on the spot."

"I know. But that was Brit-Cit, not Mega-City One. You have your Laws, we have ours."

I glanced back at our captors. "And here, they have their *own* laws. It all seems so... arbitrary."

An hour later, Siebert called for another rest-break. Guildford and I strolled back to the others, but kept our distance.

Vickers dropped to the ground and said, "We must have walked a thousand kilometres by now."

"A couple of hundred, at most," I told him. To Siebert, who was gulping water from his bottle, I said, "Slow down. We don't know how long we'll be out here."

Siebert glared at me. "You don't tell me what to do, Rico. *Never* tell me what to do." He looked around to make sure the others were listening, then said, "Rico Dredd was a Judge, can you believe that? A *Judge*. Supposed to be the best of the best. Turned out he was nothing but a thug. A perp. Best-trained perp in the world, maybe, but still a bottom-feeder. Still nothing more than a piece of murdering scum." Siebert lowered himself down to the ground next to Vickers. "You think your old man would be proud of you, Rico? I doubt it. He'd have put you away himself. Like your brother did."

Standing close to them, Register Forbes said, quietly, "Siebert, it's time."

"Yeah, I know." Siebert looked from me to Guildford and back. "One of you has come to the end of his journey. And it's *you*, Rico. We still need one of you to carry the stuff, and Guildford doesn't need an oxygen tank." He smiled. "Told you I'd reduce your sentence if you got us out of the bus, didn't I?"

"I understand," I said. "Believe me, if I was in your position I'd do the same. Give me a few minutes to make my peace with Grud?"

"Never took you for a believer, Rico. But go ahead. Say whatever prayers you think might help you. But try not to breathe too much—no sense in wasting that precious oxygen."

"Of course." I dropped to my knees, facing away from them. I took a few deep breaths, then disconnected the tank from my suit. Hidden in the palm of my other hand I had Siebert's electronic key.

Guildford had explained how it worked. It was about the size of a thumb, and the only reason it needed to be that big was because it contained a thumb-scanner. When Siebert wanted to unlock a chain, he put his thumb on the scanner, the key's internal circuits recognised it, and for the next one hundred seconds it would disable the appropriate lock. But I didn't care about the scanner, or the circuitry. I was interested in the tiny lithium battery inside the lock.

It had been tricky work, with the insulated gloves, but I'd managed to disconnect the battery from the rest of the key, exposing the hair-thin wires.

Guildford said, "I don't want to see this. Been nice knowing you, Rico." He walked away.

There was no time to experiment, to check that what I was planning was even possible. When you're a Judge, you're trained to work with whatever you have to hand.

I had a half-full oxygen tank, a methane-rich atmosphere and a device capable of making a spark.

Behind me, Siebert got to his feet and said, "You've had long enough. You'll be seeing Grud in person in a few seconds anyway."

"Okay," I said. I stood up, and turned to face him. I had the oxygen tank, with the key taped to it, in my left hand.

All four remaining guards, and Forbes, were clustered nicely. The explosion, if it worked, would certainly take them all out. But it would take me out too. Guildford and I had talked about that, and agreed that it was worth it if only one of us was going to make it.

I honestly believed that was *it* for me, that I was going to die right there and then. It might have looked like a noble sacrifice to save my friend, but the truth is that I just wanted those drokkers to suffer.

Forbes said to me, "Rico, no hard feelings. You understand that this is how it's got to be?"

"You'll be next, Forbes. They need Guildford alive more than they need you."

"I doubt it," he said, smiling. "If I die under suspicious circumstances, certain information about certain guards will become public. Right, Siebert?"

"That's right," the guard said, nodding.

I said to Forbes, "I know this is coming a bit late, but you wanted me to shake your hand, first time we met. I refused." I extended my right hand to him. "Well done. I'm man enough to admit that you beat me. But don't die *here*, Forbes, got that? Don't let them win. At least *one* of us has to get out of this alive."

Forbes shook my hand, a smug little grin on his face. "Sure, Rico."

I stepped closer to him, turning the handshake half-way into a friendly embrace. With my left hand around his back.

Vickers said, "Wait, what's that he's got—?"

He never finished that sentence, because I pressed my thumb into the inside of the key. The battery's exposed wires sparked, and ignited the pure oxygen invisibly spraying from the tank's half-open valve.

I let the tank go and whipped my hand back just as the tank exploded. Forbes slammed against me, shielding me from the blast as shards of the tank tore through the guards.

One shard, quite a large one, passed straight through Vickers's chest. He was the first of them to die. The others merely had their suits ripped open. There was plenty of repair tape, of course, but that was with the bundles of supplies that Guildford and I had been carrying.

The guards desperately tried to cover the rips in their environment suits. Siebert ran for the supplies, and Guildford tackled him from behind, brought him crashing face-first onto the frozen ground.

My own suit had been torn, too. Not as much as Forbes's had, but enough that I was losing air, and fast.

I rolled Forbes's mangled body off me, then scrambled to my feet.

I ran past Guildford, who was sitting on top of Siebert's prone body and methodically slamming the screaming man's face into a sharp-pointed rock, and skidded to a stop next to the supplies.

Obviously I survived. I'm still around to tell the tale.

Siebert didn't. Guildford cracked the face-plate on his suit, and—ignoring my suggestion that we sit and watch him die—continued to slam his face against the rock. Over and over, until I swear I could see the rock making dents in the back of Siebert's helmet.

GUILDFORD DIED SIX days later.

We'd carried on walking, always going west, because the only other option was to lay down and die.

We dragged the supplies behind us, and as the days progressed that became both easier and harder. Easier because there was less and less to drag, harder because we'd run out of food and fresh water.

The environment suits are capable of recycling the body's waste water—sweat and urine—but that only works for so long before the filters become clogged.

Night had fallen on Titan, but there was enough light from Saturn that we could mostly see where we were going. Mostly, but not perfectly. Guildford stepped on a loose rock, tripped, and his left ankle snapped.

He couldn't walk, and I didn't have the strength to carry him.

I had Siebert's gun—there was no way I was going to leave *that* behind—and Guildford begged me to put him out of his misery.

"Do it, Rico! Make it fast. I've always known I wasn't getting off this rock. Better to end it now, because even if we get back, I don't think I can last another week in the prison." He looked up at me, through plastic-coated eyes that, if they'd been capable, would have filled with tears. "I *deserve* to die, Rico. I murdered all those people because I cared more about my feelings than I did about their lives. So do it. Shoot me."

I looked down at him, and did my best to give him a brave smile. "Good-bye, Donny."

The echo of the shot seemed to last a lot longer than it should have. Maybe that was the strange atmosphere on Titan, or maybe it was just my imagination.

Fourteen

I DON'T KNOW who found me. I asked, but they wouldn't tell me. The last thing I remember, when I couldn't go on any further, was using the high-explosive shell in Siebert's gun to blast a large chunk out of the side of a hill, in the hope that someone would see the explosion and come looking.

I guess it worked. Hell, for all I know, the military base could have been on the other side of that hill.

I woke up in the prison infirmary, surrounded by too-familiar sounds and smells. And I was glad to be back; the only alternative was a slow, suffocating death. I'd no idea how long I'd been unconscious, or how I got there. All I knew was that I was alive and, for the first time in an eternity, I wasn't hungry or thirsty.

I couldn't see too well—everything seemed out-of-focus—and I couldn't move, could barely even turn my head, and it took me a few moments to understand that I'd been strapped to the bed.

On my left side a hazy face came into view, close enough for me to recognise it as sub-warden Copus. I was genuinely pleased to see the man.

"Don't try to talk, Rico. You probably can't, anyway. You've been through quite an ordeal. Twenty-five went out, only one came back." Copus moved closer in an odd jarring motion, and I realised he was sitting on a chair and had shuffled forward. "We back-tracked your path... Found a few of the others. Took us some time to identify Siebert." He paused for a long time, then said, "There were a couple of hidden cameras on the bus. Siebert and his friends weren't aware of them. So we know a lot of what happened. The bus got trapped in that hailstorm, is that right?"

I nodded.

"You and Guildford managed to get out. You freed the others. Then Siebert decided you should all head for... a place he'd heard about. Correct?"

Again, I nodded.

"That place doesn't exist, Rico. You know that, don't you? It *can't* exist. Siebert was delusional, or maybe he was lying in order to keep morale up, to give you the motivation you all needed to survive. I *know* that's what it was, because there's nothing on this moon but us. Only us." Copus leaned back a little, and seemed to be lost in thought for a moment. "I was never able to prove that Siebert was dirty, but the hidden cameras caught him and Frazier strangling the other prisoners to increase their own chances of survival."

Then, more to himself than to me, he added, "We're gonna

have to make some changes around here. *Big* changes. It was a mistake to have Register Forbes serve his sentence in the same place he committed his crimes."

He looked at me again. "But *you*, Rico... Fact is you probably should have been left out there. Your return has been giving the other inmates the idea that it's possible to survive out on the surface. That's not what we want. Not what we want at all. So the warden and I made a decision. You understand that this was the only way, right?"

This time, I shook my head. I had no idea what he was talking about.

Copus's head moved out of view and I felt him working at the straps holding my left arm in place. "Raise your arm," he told me.

I did so, and though I couldn't see it too clearly, it seemed that it was thinner than before. That was reasonable, after what I'd gone through. But I didn't expect my skin to be grey.

When Copus said, "We had to make some modifications," I understood why my vision was blurred.

A WEEK LATER I was released from the infirmary and returned to the general population. No one would look me in the eye, and I don't blame them. I could barely look *myself* in the eye.

They turned me into a monster. Not because they had to, but because they *wanted* to. They were in charge, and they wanted the other prisoners to understand that.

Guildford had been right about the memory-altering drugs they'd administered before the operation: I have absolutely no recollection of it. And he was also right about the pain afterwards. Breathing and blinking were agony for the first few days. Took me a long time to get used to the new sensations.

But it's nice not to feel the cold any more.

Before I left the infirmary, Copus told me, "When your time here is done, we'll reverse the process. You'll be left with some scarring, but…" He shrugged. "Until then, you *play ball,* Rico. There is no military establishment on Titan."

I said, "I understand. I genuinely do. I was a Judge, remember? A damn good one. I understand the need for secrets. And who would I *tell,* Copus? All of my friends are dead." I looked at him steadily for a few seconds. "They all died in the storm. It was only by luck that I managed to survive."

What they did to me was horrific, but—from their point of view—it was necessary.

There's an upside, I can't deny that. Copus arranged with the warden that my sentence should be reduced. Officially, that was in light of what Guildford and I did to free the others. Unofficially, it was a bribe to encourage me to forget about the military base that they denied existed. Plus, let's be honest here, I'd been a model prisoner. Never started any trouble, never tried to escape. Being turned into a freak is fair price for getting out a year early.

And mods work ten-hour shifts instead of the usual twelve. I use those extra two hours to read, or work out, or play chess with anyone brave enough to take me on.

I have to keep myself sharp, you see, because I *will* get out. One day, I'll return to Mega-City One and then… And then Little Joe and I will settle things. We'll talk, he and I. And I know I'll be able to prove to him that I was right all along.

Justice must be tempered with mercy. It must be flexible, and that goes both ways. Sure, what Copus and the warden did to me is inhumane, but it was necessary for the greater good. They had no reason to trust me not to say anything, and they didn't want to just execute me, so they came up with a compromise. It's not a perfect solution for any of us, but it *works*.

It's just like it was back in the Meg. What happened with Virgil Livingstone, well, that was an accident. He shouldn't have died. No, scratch that. I shouldn't have killed him. But I was making a point about the Law, and it's a point in which I still believe: If the Law is too rigid, the citizens will eventually rise against it. But if it bends, even just a little, then the citizens will come to understand and respect that.

The Judges present themselves as untouchable, as incorruptible, and the people don't like that. They don't like being made to feel inferior. The way *I* ran things, that wasn't the case. Sure, it was clear to everyone that I was on the top of the heap, but they knew that they could come to me. They knew that I could change the things that needed to be changed. The other Judges said, "This is the Law, and it is immutable. Put up or shut up." Okay, so it's not actually immutable, since the Judges change the Law as they see fit, but that's part of the problem. They change it to suit themselves, not to suit the citizens.

Is it any wonder that they're despised?

In my year on the streets of Mega-City One, I worked hard to be seen as one of the people, and I know that they respected that. They respect a Judge who, if he catches them littering, will slap them across the back of the head and tell them not to do it again. They don't respect a Judge who'll imprison them for it.

So I'll get out of here when my time is done.

I'll go back to Earth. To Mega-City One.
And I'll find my brother.
And then we'll see who was right.
Then we'll see.

PART TWO

THE PROCESS
OF ELIMINATION

EVERY PRISONER HAS a mental clock that counts down, slowly eroding the days until release. They might not admit it, but they *watch* that clock. Constantly. There's always a part of their brain that's aware of how much time they have left to serve.

Except in cases of brain damage or illness or just plain stupidity, no prisoner in the history of the universe has ever been surprised to hear a guard say, "Today's the day. You're outta here. You've done your time."

Sometimes that countdown clock gets nudged back up a little. An extra year for an escape attempt, maybe. Or a couple of days for being involved in a fight. A month for hiding contraband. That kind of thing.

Once in a very long while, the countdown clock gets nudged in the *other* direction.

That happened to me.

It was quite a neat way of doing things, I suppose. Instead of telling the prisoners that you'll add time to their sentence if they don't cooperate—the prisoners might react negatively—you take time away and let them know that it just as easily could be returned. With interest. I saw the same thing when I was a Judge on the streets of Mega-City One: warning a citizen not to do something or she'll go to the cubes is far less effective than telling her that if she *does* do it, her benefits will be cut.

The word around the prison was that I had only barely survived my time out in the Bronze, that the search party had pulled me back from the edge of death. That's close to the truth, anyway. Close, but not all the way there. Someone else had found me.

I still didn't know who, or how. I remember the readouts on my last oxygen tank. The needle steadily dipping toward the red line. I remember thinking that suffocation was probably a better way to go than starvation. And then I fell—again—and that time I didn't even have the strength to rise up against Titan's weak gravity.

So I lay there, lacking the ability to roll onto my back and look up at the stars as I waited for death, until even keeping my eyes open became too much for me.

I was the only one who'd survived the storm, which presented the warden with something of a dilemma. I was a liability—I knew that the prison was *not* the only installation on Titan—but if they brought back nothing but bodies, the inmates might get it into their heads that we'd been found and executed. Letting me live hammered home the futility of an escape attempt. You get where I'm going with this? I *had* to survive, to prove that it wasn't *possible* to survive.

But they couldn't restore me to health and leave me intact. That wouldn't look good at all. It had to be clear that I'd suffered.

Sub-warden Copus said there was some debate as to whether I should lose an arm, or a leg. But I'm here to work, he said.

I don't feel cold any more. I can walk out into the Bronze without an environment suit. No oxygen tanks to carry, no constant fear that the suit will snag on a jagged edge, no more getting to the end of a shift feeling like I've been marinating in my own sweat and urine.

They laced my skin with a tough insulating polymer. Coated my eyes with transparent plastic. Cut out my lungs and fitted me with a biomechanical apparatus that allows me to breathe in Titan's toxic atmosphere. Replaced my vocal cords with an electronic voicebox. Augmented my blood with an artificial fluid, resistant to sub-zero temperatures.

They stripped away my humanity and turned me into a gruddamned monster. A grey, ugly-as-sin cyborg.

But they knocked a year off my sentence.

So, y'know, swings and roundabouts.

TITAN

2084 A.D.

Fifteen

IT'S SAID THAT even the toughest prisoner is no match for Titan. *Everyone* breaks, they say.

The cold, the storms, the darkness, the endless labour, the sporadic nocturnal screaming sessions, the ever-present danger from the guards and the other prisoners, the days that last three hundred and eighty-two hours, the constant risk of suffocation in Titan's toxic air, the food so utterly bland that sometimes you'd happily murder everyone on the whole drokkin' moon just for the chance to lick the pot a potato had been boiled in.

Most prisoners broke, eventually; a few didn't. I didn't. Never broke down, never once allowed myself to roll over and expose that emotional underbelly. Displaying a weakness like that in such a hostile environment is the equivalent of handing the other guy a gun and showing him where on your chest you wanted him to aim.

Cadmus Robert Holland—male, Caucasian, fifty-something—finally crumbled, more than a year into his sentence. We'd long since exhausted the pool on him and just taken it as solid that he wasn't going to crack.

We all knew *why* Holland was there, of course, known that from the start. He'd murdered his brother. Bludgeoned him to death with his fists in a frenzy of pure rage. For someone not trained in hand-to-hand combat, that's a pretty impressive feat. Sure, anyone can knock someone over so they hit their head and that kills them, but to actually cave in a human skull using only your knuckles? That takes a special kind of fury.

Otherwise, the only remarkable thing about Cadmus Holland was that he was one of the final batch of Mega-City One citizens sentenced to Titan. Other cities kept sending civilians for the next few years, but someone in the Big Meg had decided that the mining colony on Titan was too harsh a punishment for cits, and fit only for wayward Judges.

It was late November, 2084. A bunch of us had been assigned to cable-duty on J-shaft. Assignments were usually fixed, and most of the time I was outside the prison compound, but sometimes a dig would be picked clean and we'd have to wait until another one was found; or sometimes, the weather was just too bad. That was when they put us on J. It wasn't the worst duty—that would be waste management, and believe me, you do *not* want to know the details—but it was hard work, especially pulley duty.

The shaft was inside the prison compound, and was the primary reason the prison had been built just there. A rich, almost vertical seam of iridium ore that even after all these years still hadn't been exhausted. The yield was about a kilogramme of iridium for every two tonnes we dug out. That might not sound like much, but it gave the average astrogeologist palpitations.

The shaft was a narrow cone, fifty metres across at the surface and three hundred metres deep, with a few small side-tunnels that snaked away, following smaller deposits. It was covered by a sturdy, three-storey-high framework, housing thirty or so mechanical pulley blocks.

That day, former Sov Judge Zera Kurya and I joined eighteen other prisoners hauling on the pulley cables, two prisoners to a cable. We nodded the usual greetings to the teams on either side of us—Cadmus Holland and Artherus Schiller were on our right—and then untied our cables and started to pull.

Arm over arm, steadily hoisting up huge steel buckets of ore. When they reached the pulley block, we switched to a second cable that pulled the bucket forward until it was clear of the pit, then tipped it into the back of a waiting truck.

The trucks took the ore to the smelter, which refined the metal, depositing bars of iridium in neat stacks. Back on Earth, any one of those bars could set someone up for life. Here on Titan, they were just piled up, waiting for the next ship to collect them.

It took an average of four hundred arm-pulls to get a bucket up from the lowest level of the pit. I know: I'd counted. It was exhausting, tedious, back-breaking work and everyone hated it. Most jobs in the prison you'd find someone who didn't mind it, but not this.

New fish always think that they'll be okay with it, and for the first few hours it's not so bad. The buckets weigh about half a tonne fully laden; but with two people lifting, that's only two-hundred and fifty kilogrammes each. And the pulley block has a ten-to-one ratio—for every metre you pull, the bucket is raised ten centimetres—so you're really only lifting twenty-five kilograms. In Titan's low gravity, that's hardly any work at all.

Until you have to do it over and over, a twelve-hour shift, in your bulky, uncomfortable environment suit, on your feet the whole time. You get three twenty-minute breaks per shift, and no talking if certain guards are supervising.

I had it a little easier because mods only do ten-hour shifts when we're working outside: after that, we have to purge our sinus filters, and no one wants to see that.

Six hours into the shift our supervising guard, Delaney, called second break. Delaney was a barrel-chested man with rosy cheeks and white bushy eyebrows. Donny Guildford had once whispered to me that he looked like Santa Claus had gone into witness protection, and it'd stuck with me ever since. We liked him; he was one of those guards who wasn't paranoid enough to equate casual conversation with sedition.

As we all gratefully tied off our cables and sat down on the frozen ground, Cadmus Holland said, "I'm done."

Artherus Schiller asked, "You've done what?"

Inside his helmet, Holland slowly shook his head. "I can't go on. This drokkin' place... The air is poison, nothing grows in the frozen dirt, the storms wind can tear you apart. And for what? For *this*." He picked up a small chunk of rock and bounced it in the palm of his hand. "Iridium." He pointed straight up. "There are whole *asteroids* made of the stuff up there. Much closer to home than we are." To Kurya, he said, "I heard your people are talking about setting up a mass-driver in the asteroid belt. Shoot the damn things at Earth, let them burn up in the atmosphere, save the cost of smelting them to get the ore out. That's the way it should be done."

"Probably wasn't their idea," Schiller said. "The Sovs don't invent. They just take other people's ideas. You know? Communism. Even the ideas belong to the state. No offence, Kurya."

"Die in pain," she responded calmly.

I said, "Schiller, shut that down right now. And you can drop the 'I can't take it any more' attitude too, Holland. You can and you will. Your first week, you thought you weren't going to survive, am I right?"

He nodded. "Yeah, but—"

"You were wrong then. Never thought you'd make it through your first month either, or your first year. Same as the rest of us. But you were wrong then too. You *did* make it. Now you think you can't make it to the end of your sentence. What makes you right about that when you were wrong before?"

Schiller gave a half-laugh, half-snort. "Dredd's right. You'll get back to Earth. Start your life over."

Then Holland said, "Without my brother."

"Yeah, well, *you're* the one who caved in his skull. You crack an egg, you can't go complaining that the yolk is leaking out, right?"

Normally, Holland would have either completely ignored that, or responded with a brisk head-butt. This time, he just nodded.

Schiller flashed me a look that said, *That's interesting...* Then he asked, "Why'd you do it, Holland? You spent eighteen years taking care of your brother, and then one day you just snapped."

Holland sighed long and deep, and the strength and life just seemed to slip out of him like a punctured airbed.

I knew from previous conversations that Holland had grown up believing in Mega-City One, in the Justice Department. He'd lost friends and family in the war—on both sides—but had never lost his faith in humanity. In the end, no matter what the odds, the good in people will triumph.

That's what he believed. That was at the core of Cadmus Robert Holland's being: the notion that people are inherently good. There are some who stray from time to time, but there is always a nucleus of goodness deep inside even the most hardened, most bloodthirsty criminal.

I guess he was right about that. Back in the Meg I got to know a lot of people who have one foot firmly in the gutter. The department classifies them as criminals, but ignores the good that they do. A woman can spend her entire life and all her pay making clothes for the homeless, but she shoplifts one can of lettuce-freshener and she's labelled a thief.

I've already mentioned my friend Evan Quasarano. Grew up in the ghetto, joined a gang, became a small-time crook. Why'd he do that? Because he knew nothing else. His mother struggled to keep the family fed and clothed, his father was long gone and his grandfathers constantly bickered. They'd been on different sides during the war and every family get-together was destined to go down the 'What the *drokk* did you just say?' route. More than once I'd had to pry the two old guys apart, stop them from killing each other over the dinner table.

Evan was a thief, a thug, a lowlife numbers-runner and occasional bodyguard. All before his eighteenth birthday. Did that make him a bad person? No, just misguided. I'd spent a lot of time with him, listening to his barely-formed opinions and regurgitations of other people's ideas, and I could tell that Evan was just ignorant, and maybe a bit dumb. But I once saw him give half a bag of crawbies to a kid who'd had his own stash stolen before he could sell it, all because he knew that kid's mother would have beaten him if he'd come home empty-handed. You can't tell me *that's* something a bad person would do.

People are a little selfish, maybe, but when they take the time to step outside their own lives and see things from other perspectives, they generally do realise that we're all in this together. I'm not saying that it's altruism, doing good for no reward or recognition, but that's not the point. Every good thing we do helps make the world a better place—and who doesn't want to live in a better world?

That had always been Cadmus Holland's stance. Broderick— his younger brother—had apparently been a nice guy, doing pretty well at school, had some good friends. He'd been well- adjusted and well-liked by most people.

Holland said, "Something happened to him the day after a bunch of us went to the Festival of Wheels."

Schiller said, "I remember that. We couldn't go—Papa said it was too expensive to get to Mega-City One."

Holland nodded slowly for a moment, then calmly said, "You've been begging me forever to tell you, so shut the drokk up and listen."

Schiller grinned. He was never the sort to take offence easily.

"Broderick was thirteen years old," Holland said. "We'd had a good time at the festival but the next morning he didn't respond when I woke him up for school. I mean, he got up, but he didn't say anything. Went off to school still not talking to me. I figured he was angry with me for something, but you know kids—you can't read their minds. That night I got a call from his school. Broderick hadn't spoken to anyone all day, not even when his teachers asked him directly.

"So I went into his room and said, 'The hell's the matter with you?' Nothing. 'You're not talking to me?' Still nothing. I figured it would blow over in a few days, but I was wrong. I could see it in his eyes sometimes that he *wanted* to speak, but he just couldn't. I gave him a pencil and a pad, but he just threw them aside. Same with the datapad. After the second week I brought him to the doctor. Those first brain-scans alone cost me a month's salary, but they didn't show up anything wrong. No damage, no lesions, no parasites. Broderick had just lost the ability, or the will, to speak.

"We did have some medical insurance, but the drokkers refused to pay up without an official diagnosis, so I had to pay for everything. Sold the car. Sold the house to cover a four-week stint in the Tremaine Clinic, but still they couldn't find anything wrong. Had to move into a crappy one-bedroom stomm-hole on the west side after that. And then..." Holland looked up. "*That* day. Broderick was thirty. We'd been living with his condition for seventeen *years*. We were out, scouring the market down under the flyovers... I thought that maybe I could get him a job somewhere that it didn't matter that he couldn't speak. At that stage we were so broke I was dealing zizz to juves. So we saw this market stand where an old guy was selling dead-shirts. He—"

Kurya interrupted. "Dead-shirts?"

I answered for him. "Clothing taken from bodies at Resyk.

Used to be that the Resyk centres just incinerated the stiffs' shoes and clothing, but then they started using it as landfill. Some people steal the clothes from the landfills and sell them. It was actually quite the fashion for a while. I remember—" I caught the look in Holland's eye. "Sorry. Go on."

Holland said, "I asked the old guy if he needed help getting the stuff, and he said, 'Yeah, maybe. Not easy work, though. You strong?' I said, 'I am, but it's not me looking for the job. It's my brother Broderick here.'

"And then Broderick said, 'It's about drokkin' time!'"

Kurya said, "So he had *not* lost the ability to speak?"

"No. No, he hadn't. I asked him what the hell was going on, and he told me that seventeen years earlier, the night before that first morning, just before he went to bed... We'd been joking about someone we knew. He didn't even remember *who* it was, but that's not important. What *is* important is that we both said, 'Yeah, that guy's *insane!*' at the same time. And... and then *I* said, 'Jinx.'"

We all stared at Holland.

Schiller muttered, "Stomm..."

I said, "No way. No *way* he kept that up for seventeen years!"

Holland said, "He did. Stubborn little *drokker*. That was the rule, see. Two of you say the same thing at the same time, then if one of you says 'jinx' before either of you say anything else, then the other one can't speak until the first one says their name."

Schiller asked, "In all that time you never said his name? Not even when you were speaking to a doctor about him?"

"Sure I did, but apparently not when he was around to hear me use it. He said I'd just referred to him as 'my brother.'"

Holland stared down at his hands. "I'd put my entire life aside and spent every credit we had trying to find out what was wrong with him and he could have put a stop to it at any time with a note on a scrap of paper. So I hit him. And I couldn't stop. He was long dead by the time the Judges came, and even then they had to shoot me to get me away from him."

No one could think of anything to say after that.

Sixteen

KELLAN WIGHTMAN CAUGHT up with me after the shift, as I was making my way back towards my cell.

"What was *that* about?" he asked, gesturing back towards the way he'd come. "Takenaga got a message on her datapad and muttered, 'Aw crap.' And then she just walked away."

"Since I wasn't there, I obviously have no idea," I said.

If Kalai Takenaga had been supervising him, that probably meant that Wightman had been on machine maintenance again. He usually griped about that, but I knew he secretly enjoyed it. Tinkering with an engine was a great way to lose yourself for a few hours.

Wightman was like me, a mod. A bulky man, taller than me and impressively strong. He sported a thick beard—now flecked with grey—in a futile attempt to hide the cybernetic modifications to his face. Wightman was coming to the end of his fifteenth year, almost half his sentence behind him, which was something he managed to bring up at every opportunity. "Two weeks from Wednesday and I'm over the crest of the hill," he said. "Fifteen whole *years* in this crap-cluster, can you believe that, Rico?"

"I've got seventeen to go, so, yeah." But I couldn't resent Wightman's buoyancy. Fifteen years without a shiv in the back was something of an achievement.

"We are gonna get absolutely stomm-faced," he said. "The stuff's been fermenting nicely. It should be pretty powerful. Probably tastes like what it is—rotten vegetables—but I don't care."

"Not for me," I said. "But knock yourself out. Which you probably will."

Wightman lowered his voice a little as we passed two anxious-looking guards. "We're not Judges any more, Rico. You can let go of the good-little-angel act."

Wightman had been on the job in Mega-City Two for eight years before he was arrested for setting fires in city blocks and then fabricating evidence to frame the Californian Secessionists. "Just a moment of madness," he'd said, the first time he talked to me about it. "Damn Fornies were causing so much trouble, something had to be done. It's not like I *murdered* anyone."

His 'moment of madness' had led him to torch seven city blocks, with damage estimated at the best part of half a billion credits. It was a wonder they hadn't executed him, and an absolute miracle more people hadn't died.

The only reason he got caught was because he'd always taken great care to ensure that each block's alarm systems were fully functioning to make sure that everyone go out before the fire really took hold. But on that seventh block the alarms worked fine for the first minute, then abruptly shut off. By that stage it was too late to quench the fire. Wightman risked his own life getting everyone out. Four of them later died due to severe smoke inhalation.

I'm not saying that getting all those people out makes him a hero—I mean, he'd started the damn fires himself—but he wasn't technically a murderer.

Wightman had settled into prison life neatly. He quickly became the prison's chief booze-hound. He knew alcohol inside and out, and there was a running joke that the guy could ferment a sack. He had the advantage that most of the other prisoners were Judges with little experience of real alcohol, so even a thimbleful of the hard stuff was enough to get them swaying.

"You'll like the latest batch," he said. "Grapefruit wine. It's been ready for weeks, but this is a celebration, so I want it to be something special. Fermentation can only get you so far. Now I'm looking into distillation."

"There is no way you can build a still and not have the guards find it," I said.

"Don't need to. Distillation is just separating the alcohol from the water, right? Don't need to evaporate the stuff to do that. The freezing point of alcohol is negative one hundred fourteen degrees. So I'll drop the temperature to about negative eight"—Wightman's sewn-up lips formed into a rudimentary smile—"the water freezes, but the alcohol doesn't. Then I'll just take out the ice."

That sounded right, but I still didn't want to get involved.

It wasn't that I was afraid of reprisals: I just wasn't interested in getting drunk. It was important that I kept my head clear. Most of the time the prison was peaceful, but that was only because ninety per cent of the prisoners were biding their time before they made whatever moves they felt were vital to their own well-being.

Fights could, and did, break out seemingly spontaneously, but luckily few of them descended into full-scale riots: that was when this place got *really* dangerous.

The unspoken prison hierarchy would be upset for a day or two, then settle down again. The big storm disaster that led to me becoming a mod wiped out the prison's most sadistic guards and some of the worst of the prisoners, but the power vacuum was filled in a matter of weeks.

I could have seized power then, probably, but I chose not to, because while *technically* I was a criminal, I wasn't a crook. I was one of the good guys.

So my reputation kept the small-fry clear of me, but it attracted the bruisers. You don't want to be drunk when someone is charging at you with a shiv.

And there was one bruiser in particular who'd been gunning for me. Southern Brennan. He'd come in on the last ship, and the first thing he did was put out the word that he wanted my head on a pike.

Brennan was one of the biggest guys I'd ever seen that wasn't a mutant. His fist was the size of my head. He hadn't even made it all the way through the Academy of Law before he'd committed so many brutal crimes that he was shipped straight to Titan. I heard that he once threw a Lawmaster at another cadet. I dunno about that; a Lawmaster weighs the best part of a tonne.

Someone screwed up in the cadet screening process, that was certain. Or maybe something happened to him along the way, something that changed him. I guess that's more likely, because cadets go through stringent psych tests right from the start. Brennan's aberrations would have been caught a lot sooner if they'd been there all along.

Anyway. The reason I bring him up now is that as Wightman and I were walking, Brennan appeared at the far end of the corridor.

Wightman muttered a few select swear words and there was a definite hesitation in his step, but I kept going. I knew what I was doing. Keep a steady pace. Don't try to stare Brennan down, but don't ignore him either.

I'd done this before, a couple of years earlier, shortly after I became a mod. A similar situation: a guy who wanted my intestines between his teeth solely because everyone knew that mods were hard to kill. In that case, I was able to put him off for months by telling him, "Not now. This is not the time, and you know that." Kept that up for ages, until one day he was expecting me to do the same as I passed him on the way down into one of the northern mineshafts. Idiot. You never tell a man you want to kill him and then let your guard down. They found his body after a brief search at the end of the shift. All the signs indicated that he'd snagged his environment suit on something and for unknown reasons he'd ignored the suit's low-pressure warnings.

Now Southern Brennan was striding towards me, and I could tell that Wightman was ready to turn and run. But he held his ground. I was proud of him for that.

Brennan was flanked by Vivean Kassir and Lorne Sims, both

former Mega-City One Judges. They'd adopted him into their little clique, nurtured his psychopathic tendencies to use him as a weapon. It hadn't worked the way they'd planned: they'd made the mistake of assuming that Brennan's size and strength were balanced by a lack of brains.

Now Brennan stopped in front of me, and Sims and Kassir spread out a little, making it very clear that Wightman and I were not expected to simply step around them.

We were about four metres away when Brennan called out, "You *cosy* in there, Rico Dredd?"

I slowed to a stop, regarded him as casually as I would if anyone else had asked me the time. "Meaning?"

"You keep to yourself, feeling all safe and snug and protected. Tucked away in the warden's pocket. You think we don't know? Comes to a fight, Rico doesn't take sides because he's already on the side of the establishment."

I was watching Brennan as he spoke, and it was hard to focus on his words because the man was just so damn huge. He was a head taller than me, and I'm no shrimp. Zero body fat. He looked like he'd been sculpted by someone who'd accidentally bought enough muscle for four people and didn't want to waste anything.

"You're wrong about that," I said. "I *do* take a side. Mine."

"They say you went out into the Bronze with twenty-five others and you're the only one who made it back." He took a step closer, and peered down at me. "You kill them?"

"What do you want, Brennan?"

"Same thing *every* drokker in this place wants."

"Freedom."

He shook his head. "Freedom's just a point of view. What we

want is control over our own lives. I aim to regain mine. A lot of people are going to get in my way. I think you're going to be one of them, so I'm putting you on notice right now." He tilted his head closer to mine, and I could almost hear the muscles in his neck creaking against each other. "You're either on my side or in my way. There's no neutral ground. You make your choice, Dredd." He stepped back and glanced around. "And make it fast. All of this will come crashing down."

On Brennan's left, Lorne Sims said, "I wouldn't trust this drokker if he told me my own name."

Brennan calmly looked at me for a few more seconds, then said, "You think you're a tough guy, Rico. I can see that in you. You think you're top dog here, that nothing can touch you, because you and Copus made some kind of deal after you got back from the Bronze. You're going to tell me what that is."

A voice from the far end of the corridor yelled out, "The hell is this, blockin' the corridors? Keep *movin'*, you drokkers!"

Brennan quietly said, "De Luyando. He'll be the first to go."

I tried not to sneer as I said, "Right. When you seize control of a prison mining colony that'll fall apart without support from a homeworld a billion kilometres away."

De Luyando yelled, "I said *move*, you spugwits! You want me to come over there and *make* you move?"

Brennan turned around, muttering, "Pick a side, Dredd. I won't tell you again." He strode away, Sims and Kassir almost running to keep up.

Wightman—when he was sure that Brennan was out of earshot—asked me, "How the hell did that animal get so close to making Judge?"

There was no answering that. The same question had been

asked about me, and probably a good number of the other prisoners on Titan. How could an institution as strictly controlled and as heavily monitored as the Mega-City One Academy of Law produce Judges who are anything less than perfect? For fifteen years, every aspect of our lives is scheduled, studied and logged. There's almost nothing a cadet can do that falls outside the attention of the system.

When my class was seven years old—Joe and I were the *equivalent* of seven, roughly, but it's hard to be accurate because of the accelerated ageing process—Cadet Sabrina Han quietly told me that she hated Judge-Tutor Rowley. There was no one else around, and I never mentioned it to anyone, but the next morning Rowley strode up to Han and told her, "We're not here to be liked, Han. We're here to teach you. You don't like that, you can quit. Is *that* what you are, Han? A quitter?"

I don't know, maybe Han had told someone else, and they'd mentioned it to Rowley. Still, the incident stands out in my memory as the first time I realised that my life wasn't my own. The Justice Department owned everything about me, even down to the thoughts in my head. For a long time I was afraid to even think of anything negative about the tutors or the training, just in case. And this was *before* I understood about psychics.

Wightman kept his voice low as we passed the scowling De Luyando. "Rico, if you *had* to take down Brennan, how would you do it? I'm not saying it will come to that, but if it does."

"Blind him," I said. "Simplest, quickest way to take him off the board."

"Jovus, that's cold. You go for a guy's eyes and miss, he is *not* going to let that slide. There's no going back from that."

"You think I'm the sort of person who'd beat someone into submission so that later we can be pals?"

"No, but... I mean, you might need them later, right? Say you were going to try to take control of the prison. You can't kill *everyone* who stood against you, because that'd be all the wardens and guards, and they're the ones who know how to keep the lights on and the air working."

"Kellan, we're not talking about this," I told him. "Seriously. We are prisoners here for good reason. There's not one of us who doesn't deserve this."

He stopped walking and stared at me. I had to stop too: didn't want anyone else listening in on whatever he was about to say next. I knew what it was going to be, though.

"Even you?"

"I broke the law."

"But you said that the laws you broke were unfair. The *system* is unfair."

"Come on..." I nodded in the direction we'd been walking, and Wightman fell into step beside me. "Look, I still broke the law. Doesn't matter how wrong a law is. If you break it willingly, you have to be prepared to pay the price." I could see that he still wasn't getting it. "Wightman, from the minute I hit the streets I tried to subvert the Department of Justice's training. I thought I knew better, that their way was too restrictive, too inhuman."

"And now you don't? Three years here have changed your mind?"

"No. I was right then, and I'm still right. But if you take an action—regardless of the nature of that action, or the reason you've chosen to take it—and you're fully aware of its impact and possible consequences, then you can't complain if you end up *suffering* those consequences."

The corridor opened onto the transparent plasteen tunnel linking the prison's administrative quarters to the hydroponic domes. On a clear day you could see the sun sinking behind Saturn, its light rippling through the rings. A breathtaking sight. But this was not a clear day. Visibility was down to about five hundred metres, I guessed. Titan's atmosphere was brown, cold, dark. It was hard to shake the impression that there was oil in the water and grit in the clouds.

Wightman said, "I'm beginning to think maybe you *like* it here, Rico."

I snorted, as well as anyone with mechanical lungs can snort.

"Seriously. You weren't even on the streets for a *year* before they arrested you. I think that maybe you became institutionalised in the Academy of Law. There's no way to return to that once you graduate, so you put yourself in a position to get arrested and imprisoned. There's not much difference between the Academy and this place, if you look at it in a certain way."

I honestly hadn't considered that before. He was wrong, I was sure, but only an idiot dismisses an idea just because it makes them uncomfortable.

I told him, "If you look at *any* two things in the right light, you can find similarities. That's cherry-picking, Kellan. Shouting excitedly about the few similarities while brushing the many differences under the carpet is like trying to convince a fish that it can live in gasoline. Gasoline and water are both liquids, both have hydrogen as a key element, you can store them both in buckets."

"That doesn't mean I'm wrong."

"That's true," I said. "But I *don't* like it here, any more than you do." I held out my hands, palms-up. "Look what they've done to us."

Wightman glanced at his own hands, but didn't say anything. He'd never spoken of the reason behind his own transformation, but others had told me.

He'd been out on the surface, part of a chain gang slowly sweeping across what had once possibly been a lake-bed. A scan had detected iridium deposits on the surface and the initial on-the-ground survey had provided confirmation: at some point in the past thousand years a very large iridium-heavy asteroid had skimmed the atmosphere; chunks of it had broken off and deposited an estimated nine billion credits' worth of the precious metal across the surface. The easiest and cheapest way to find and retrieve the fragments was the chain gang: fifty prisoners chained together for four days, carefully sieving through the sand- and dust-covered lake-bed.

On the third day, Wightman had noticed that his environment suit was telling him its urine pack was full. He signalled to the nearest guard and said, "Need to purge here, chief."

"Not now," he was told. "Shift ends in four hours twenty. Hold it."

"I *have* been holding it, chief," Wightman had replied. "All morning. It'll auto-purge if I don't—"

"Just keep working, Wightman."

After another hour of ignoring his suit's signals that the artificial bladder was dangerously full, Wightman again asked for permission, and was again denied.

Ten minutes later, he decided drokk it, what were they going to do? Fire him? He turned around and released the bladder's valve. The stream of urine had been under more pressure than he'd realised, and in Titan's low gravity it arced out pretty far. The urine froze almost instantly, of course, but it still had momentum and mass.

It hit another guard square in the back of his helmet. I haven't read the report but it's easy to guess that the guard thought he was under attack.

He spun around and opened fire. His shot drilled a hole in Wightman's chest and emerged between his shoulder blades, then passed straight through his oxygen tank.

It had been a million-to-one chance that Wightman didn't die before they got him back to the prison. As it was, he suffered oxygen deprivation, hypothermia and severe blood loss. Turning him into a mod was the only way to save his life. No, let me be more accurate: it was the only way to save his life that would leave him still able to work.

I knew he didn't accept what they'd done to him, that the sense of betrayal and horror and loss had never left him.

As we walked through the transparent tunnel—only occasionally glancing up to see if there was a break in the clouds—he said, "I'm going to sue them, soon as I set foot on Earth. I heard that when the Titan shuttle comes in to San Fran, there are solicitors just waiting for the prisoners. They're all desperate to make media-deals and help the parolees sue anyone and everyone they can. And what with the hard-luck aspect you can double your income if you're a mod, is what I heard. 'They turned me into a monster' kind of thing."

"*Has* anyone ever successfully sued the Department of Justice?" I asked.

"Probably not. And I probably won't be successful either. But I'm going to do it anyway. Make a big noise about how they've treated me."

"Maybe it would work in Mega-City Two, but not where I come from. We got rid of most of the lawyers back when—"

Wightman slapped my upper arm and pointed ahead. "What's this?"

Three guards were striding quickly towards us from the hydroponic domes. "You tell me," I said. Wightman had much better eyesight than I did—the modification process isn't exactly precision engineering.

"Giambalvo, McConnach and Sloane. And they're looking at us."

We both stopped walking. That was just something every prisoner learned to do, one of those unwritten, unspoken rules. If a guard doesn't give you a direct order to approach, you stand still and let them come to you. I never thought about it much, but I guess that subconsciously you're expecting a fight, so letting the guard cover the distance, however short it might be, is a way of ensuring that they've expended more energy than you have before the potential trouble begins.

When they were close enough that they didn't have to shout, sub-warden Giambalvo said, "You two. Warden's office. Right now."

Wightman said, "What for? We haven't done—"

McConnach's daystick lanced out, striking Wightman square on the voicebox. He staggered back, then dropped to his knees, gagging and groaning. I've had that done to me more than once—by McConnach herself—and it hurts like you've been gargling chunks of broken glass.

"After fifteen years anyone would think that you'd learn, Wightman," McConnach said. "Your days of giving orders are long over."

Giambalvo looked at me. "We don't have time for drokking around," she said. "Pick up your friend and come with us."

Seventeen

IN THE THREE years since I'd arrived on Titan I'd only twice seen the warden in person. Governor Myles Dodge, seventy, completely bald—didn't even have eyebrows—with African and Caucasian heritage. He had the look of an old-time circus strongman whose body had finally succumbed to age: a broad frame supporting a body draped with far too much loose skin.

It was easy to get the impression that Dodge spent his days sitting in his office watching TV while he left the running of the prison to the sub-wardens and guards, and maybe that was the impression he *wanted* to give, for some reason. But the fact is he had his finger on the pulse, as I'd learned the first time I met him.

That had been shortly after my modification surgery. I was in the infirmary, with sub-warden Copus in the middle of explaining certain truths to me, when the door opened and Dodge entered.

He looked me up and down, and said to Copus, "Good job. What does he remember?"

"About the process? Nothing."

I said, "Who the hell are you?"

He ignored that, and asked Copus, "Who was on the airlock when he was brought in?"

"Giambalvo." Copus hesitated for a second. "So far she's said nothing, but I don't know her well enough to trust her."

"I do. She can keep her mouth shut." He turned to me. "Dredd, I'm Governor Dodge. You understand why we did this to you?"

"Sure, I understand." He looked as though he didn't believe me, so I repeated it more firmly. "I understand. The other inmates have to believe that Titan is so hostile that this was the only way to save my life." I shrugged. "I hate it, but I get it. If they believe there's even the slightest chance of surviving out there, they'll spend all their time plotting their escape. That's not going to get the ore out of the ground, and the ore is the only thing that makes this place viable."

Dodge watched me as I spoke, nodding slowly, then said, "Your voicebox gives you an advantage over non-modified prisoners, Dredd; it's harder to tell whether you think I'm a piece of toast. So we're going to have to judge you by your actions, not your words. Work hard and keep your head down, and you might find yourself in my favour. The journey from Earth to Titan is expensive, so anything less than a twenty-year sentence is just not cost-effective... But say an inmate was to help keep the peace. Fewer fights means fewer injuries. That means fewer days in the infirmary and lower running costs. Something like that might weigh heavily in your favour, Dredd. It's all economics. Do you understand what I'm saying?"

"I do. Aside from the reference to toast."

Copus said, "Don't butter him up."

"Right, got it."

Dodge continued, "Then there's the opposite approach. Push against the system, the system pushes back, and no one man—no matter *how* impressed he is with himself—can win against the system."

He tapped the centre of his chest with his index finger. "The system. In case there's any confusion."

The second time I met Governor Dodge was sixteen months later, when former EuroCit Judge Ren Tramatky lifted a guard's gun and managed to deactivate its handprint scanner. Exactly how he did that we still don't know, but the result was chaos: two guards dead and fourteen wounded, six prisoners wounded, and more than fifty almost suffocated when Tramatky realised there was no possible way to escape and blasted a hole in the mess-hall windows. I'd ordered Wightman and a couple of others to block the cracked windows with tables and plastic trays while I took down Tramatky with my bare fists. Afterwards, Dodge had called me to his office to—he said—commend me on my quick thinking. I figured he was checking up on me. Wanted to look me in the eye, see if he could work out what I was thinking. And maybe because the whole hands-off image he worked so hard to maintain kept him a further step removed from what was happening on the ground. He asked me to explain what had happened, how I thought Tramatky might have disabled the handprint scanner—I didn't have an answer for that one—and if there was anything else I wanted to report. I wasn't able to think of anything that might fit, so after a few awkward exchanges he concluded that we were done, and he dismissed me.

It wasn't until months later that I realised the real reason Myles Dodge had called me in. He liked me. Liked my company. Unlike most of the prisoners, I wasn't permanently arrogant or terrified. I wasn't raging against the system that put me there. I'd accepted that they'd made me into a mod without too much in the way of complaint.

And maybe there was a philosophical connection too: pretty early in his career, Dodge had been wounded during a riot at an aeroball stadium: spine broken in four places. He'd never quite recovered, and had spent the next decade driving a desk, despite his protestations that he was strong enough to return to the streets.

Then in 2076, Governor Nkambule decided to see what bullets tasted like, and her job was suddenly vacant... and tantalising for Dodge. Solid work, a twenty-year contract with the option to retire at the end of it, and a hefty pension.

Judges don't normally get paid, but the mining corporations on the outer planets' moons are multinational, so they don't answer to any one city. Plus it's hard to persuade *anyone* to go, so the corporations tell potential guards and wardens, "We'll put your salary aside for you, every month, in a high-interest account. When your term is done and you come back to Earth, you'll get it all in one lump sum. You'll never have to work another day in your life."

And for Dodge there was the added attraction of Titan's low gravity, about a seventh of that on Earth. Sure, inside the prison we had grav-plates on the floor to make it easier to get around, but they were rarely running at full-G. That had to be bliss for someone who's suffered decades of back pain.

So I got to thinking that maybe Dodge saw something of himself in me: we'd both wanted to be Judges, but the system wasn't flexible enough to accept that we were different to the standard model of a Judge.

I don't know, maybe I'm wrong about that. Certainly, Dodge didn't seem to have anything like that on his mind when Giambalvo and the others escorted me and Wightman into his office.

Sub-warden Copus was already there, standing beside Dodge's desk with his arms folded and his brow furrowed. And so was Zera Kurya.

Copus said, "This is everyone," but I couldn't tell from his tone whether that was a statement or a question.

Governor Dodge looked around, nodded, and said, "We have a situation, and you people are going to resolve it. Four days ago a freighter outbound towards Mimas suffered a catastrophic failure. Its crew managed to regain enough control to steer it towards Titan. One hour ago it breached our atmosphere. That slowed its descent a little, but not enough. It hit the ground *hard*... and our long-range scanners are picking up possible life signs." He looked directly at me. "You and Wightman are going out to find the crash site and retrieve any survivors and supplies. Kurya is here because back in East-Meg One she was a top-rated Med-Judge."

Wightman said, "Yeah... I don't *think* so. I've just come off a shift. There's no law that says we have to..." He noticed Dodge's scowl and slowed to a stop. "Damn it. All right."

I asked, "Where did the ship hit?"

"A few kilometres south of Brunel's Ridge."

I knew enough about Titan's geography to get an inkling of what we were facing. "That's got to be five hundred kilometres from here."

Giambalvo said, "Closer to *six* hundred."

Copus glanced at Dodge, who very slightly shook his head. Copus turned back to us. "Since our friends in Texas-City have yet to deliver on the shuttles they promised us eight drokkin' *years* ago, we've got to go overland. The rescue party is the seven of us here. Not counting the warden, of course."

Giambalvo said, "Sir, I can't. The low gravity outside... you know how much it affects me. I was invalided out of the Department because my sense of balance is shot to stomm. In the low gravity it gets even worse."

"The transport has grav-plates, Giambalvo. You'll be okay."

"I won't be able to function effectively. I recommend Takenaga take my place. She understands discretion. Plus she's logged more time on the surface than I have."

Copus exchanged another look with Dodge, but this time the warden nodded. "All right," Copus said. "Find her, brief her. Sloane, you're the driver—get down to the compound and requisition the best vehicle you can find. Nothing smaller than a four-tonne. The freighter's complement is seventeen. It's unlikely that they all survived, but we have to prepare for that."

Sloane said, "The *big* bus would do it..." He checked his watch. "It's due to head out on the next shift."

"Okay. Tell the quartermaster to talk to me if he gives you any trouble."

As Sloane and Giambalvo left, Copus turned to me, Wightman and Kurya. "You all know how dangerous it is out there. We're aware that with danger there comes opportunity. Any of you even *think* about turning on us, you'll find yourselves—"

Kurya cut him off. "We understand. We are still prisoners."

Wightman asked, "Just wondering, chief. Do we get anything for this? I mean, we're risking our lives."

Governor Dodge said, "We'll talk about that when you return. They..."

He looked away as his voice trailed off, and that was when I knew that they were lying. This was not a rescue mission.

This was something else.

Something a lot more dangerous.

Eighteen

"THE BIG BUS" was the name given to the prison's most powerful vehicle. It wasn't the largest—that was our General Dynamics H88 Crawler, which could haul a hundred tonnes of ore at a maximum speed of fifteen kilometres per hour—and it wasn't the fastest, which was a Mega-City One Justice Department Lawmaster that had been modified to run on sand. We only had one of those, and it wasn't going to be much use for this mission.

The Big Bus was a double-width version of our standard personnel carrier. Range of over three thousand kilometres and capable of carrying a hundred passengers in relative comfort, if all the seats were installed, one-sixty in misery if they weren't.

The reason it was double-width—actually wider than it was long—was that it had once been two standard vehicles, and some engineering genius had bolted them together. The original plan had been to join them end-to-end, but the surface of Titan is pitted with so many crevasses and craters that the long bus would have got stuck every time it crested a hill.

Wightman knew a lot more about engineering than I did, and he'd always wanted to travel on the Big Bus.

In the airlock, as we waited for Kurya to seal her environment suit, Wightman was growing more and more excited, like a kid on his Birthday Eve. "You know how intricate a differential gearbox is in a normal vehicle? This one has got to be ten times as complex!"

He took the lead as we left the prison's hangar and headed towards the bus. Not caring whether or not Kurya and I understood—or cared—he launched into his lecture: "Your standard wheeled car has wheels on both sides, right? This means that when it's turning, the wheels on the inside of the curve have a shorter distance to travel than those on the *outside* of the curve, which means they have to turn slower. Now, in most cases only the rear wheels have drive—the front ones aren't connected to the engine. So when it's turning, the front wheels can turn however much they need to, no problems there, but the rear wheels are connected to the engine via a common drive-shaft. So the whole mechanism needs to work in a way that the engine provides different rates of power to the inside and outside wheels. It gets even more complicated with a four-wheel-drive vehicle." We'd reached the bus; Wightman had already dropped to his knees and was peering underneath the chassis. "But in this case it's *way* more complicated because all the wheels are driven—"

"We get it," I told him.

Wightman twisted around and lowered himself onto his back, started shimmying underneath the bus. "Man, I'd love to see the schematics for this. Two separate engines, sixteen wheels, four drive-shafts! Just the braking system is giving me palpitations! I tell you I was planning to retrain as a Tek-Judge? I always got along better with machines than with people." He drew up his legs, dug his heels into the dirt, then pushed himself further under the bus. "Rico, go get me a flashlight. I want to see how they've linked up the two suspension systems."

Kurya nudged my arm, and I looked up to see Copus and Takenaga approaching, cautiously making their way across the packed-dirt ground.

I kicked the sole of Wightman's boot. "No time for that. Come on."

Copus seemed particularly unsteady, but I quickly realised why. As second-in-command to Dodge he delegated work to the other wardens. He rarely left the prison himself, and wasn't used to the low gravity.

"Move it," Copus barked at us. "Departing in ninety seconds."

I grabbed Wightman's ankle and dragged him back out.

We followed Kurya onto the bus, and the engines coughed into life as the airlock doors closed and sealed behind us.

Guard Ernie Sloane was at the controls, flipping switches and checking read-outs more efficiently than usual. Copus was standing with his back to the windshield, already removing his helmet. McConnach was near the back, kneeling on one seat while she rummaged through an emergency pack on the seat behind it, and in the alcove behind Sloane, Takenaga was checking the seals on the weapons rack.

Copus said, "Sit down, strap in, and hold on tight. We've got a lot of ground to cover and not a lot of time."

Takenaga asked, "So what *is* this? Giambalvo said something about a crashed freighter."

"Not yet." Copus glanced at Sloane. "Gun it."

I'd barely lowered myself into a seat before the bus surged forward.

In the seat in front of me, Wightman muttered, "Holy crap!" and turned around to stare at me with wide eyes. "Talk about *torque!* I had no idea this bugger could move this fast!"

Sloane called back, "We should hit a cruising speed of about one-thirty, but the topographical data beyond the four-hundred-K radius is pretty sketchy. Rough estimate for our ETA—and don't hold me to this—is approximately six hours."

Takenaga said, "ETA already has the word 'estimated' in there. You don't need to repeat it, much less add 'rough' and 'approximately.'"

Sloane laughed. "Hah, yeah. That does sound a bit vague, doesn't it? But we're going to be crossing *terra incognita* so there's no way of knowing what we're going to hit."

Softly, Takenaga said, "Can't be *terra* incognita. This isn't *Terra*."

Wightman winked at me and whispered, "Remember I told you she was pedantic?"

Copus called out, "All right, everyone listen up. McConnach? I'm talking to you too."

"Double-checking the supplies, boss," she called back. "We're supposed to do it *before* we leave, but—"

"Turn around and pay attention, McConnach. Now."

My guts started to churn. They'd already been troubling me, but now they were hitting the spin-cycle.

Copus said, "Mister Sloane, disengage the vehicle's radio, GPS tracking, and the transponder."

"Eh... No."

"Do it, Mister Sloane. That's an order."

"Sir, if I do that, then I'm driving blind. It's not like there are road signs on this planet."

Takenaga muttered "moon" under her breath.

Copus said, "I didn't say disable the GPS *entirely*, just the tracking. I don't want anyone to know exactly where we've been or be able to retrace our path. That's why we're maintaining radio silence until we're back at the mine."

Sloane hesitated, but flipped some switches next to the steering column. "Okay. It's done."

"Good." Copus looked around at the rest of us. "There is no freighter."

We watched in silence as he passed a handwritten note to Sloane. "Stay on your current vector until you reach these coordinates, then head due south. Top speed."

Sloane began, "But this isn't—"

"Shut up. Just drive. And listen." Copus looked at each of us in turn. "The freighter is a cover story in case any of you decided not to participate. The real story is that twelve hundred kilometres south of the prison there is a small but vital military complex." Using the backs of the seats to steady himself, he moved forward until he was standing only a metre away from Takenaga, staring at her. "It's jointly run by the three North American Mega-Cities, and its existence is in violation of fourteen separate international charters and directives on extra-terrestrial military establishments."

From the back of the bus McConnach asked, "*Aliens?*"

"No, I mean extra-terrestrial as in 'not situated on Earth.' After the war every nation agreed to certain limitations on firepower and presence outside the planet." Copus returned his attention to Takenaga. "Hondo City does not know of the existence of this base. Do you understand, Kalai?"

She nodded. "Of course."

Copus hesitated for a second, then said, "We need to be clear about this. I'm not asking if you understand that the base exists and that it is secret. I'm asking whether you understand that it must *remain* a secret."

Again, she nodded.

"I want a verbal response, Kalai. And an affirmation that you will not inform your superiors of its existence."

"I understand, sub-warden, and I promise that I will say nothing."

Next, Copus turned to Kurya. "And you?"

A lot of the time it was hard to tell with Kurya whether she was even listening, let alone paying attention, but she nodded and said, "I have twenty-seven years remaining on my sentence. I have no doubt that by the time I return home and face my former superiors, your military base will either have already served its purpose or been exposed by some other means."

Wightman and I exchanged a glance. That was by far the most we'd ever heard Kurya say in one go.

Copus was about to respond when Kurya continued: "That said, I could easily inform other prisoners of the base's existence, and it's conceivable that one of those prisoners would return to Earth and inform my superiors. If you truly wish your base to remain secret, you should instead work to establish a bond of mutual trust, dependency or fear between all seven of us currently in this vehicle."

Copus nodded and said, "Right..."

I figured it was time to speak up. "Kurya's right, boss. I've known about the base for a couple of years and said nothing to anyone, because you made it worth my while to keep my mouth shut." I tapped at my sealed lips to reinforce the irony.

Wightman glared at me. "How the hell did *you* find out about it? Wait, was this back when you were trapped out there and...?" He frowned. "I always kinda wondered how you made it back to the prison on your own. You said it was just sheer determination, but that doesn't fill oxygen tanks, does it? So what happened, they rescued you?"

"I didn't know for *sure* that there was a base, but I figured there had to be something. Our hydroponics produce more food than we need, so what happens to the excess?"

Kurya said, "How you deduced the existence of the base is irrelevant. I am naturally curious about its purpose..." She looked at Copus. "But more curious about this *mission*."

Nineteen

COPUS TOLD US that he didn't know much. He'd never visited the base, never had direct contact with any of its personnel, didn't know a lot about it other than that it existed.

About once every six days one of the prison trucks was loaded up with food and supplies from the hydroponic farms and dropped off at a pre-arranged location. I'd already worked that out, a long time ago, but never had the means or the chance to find out much more than that.

Copus said, "There's a shielded comm-link between the base and the prison. A *physical* line, not just a radio link. It has one purpose: to send a distress signal. The only people who know about it are Governor Dodge, Giambalvo and myself. The long-standing agreement is that in the event of an emergency— an uncontrollable riot, an invasion, a natural disaster that threatens the safety of the prison—we trigger the alarm and they come to our aid." He glanced at me. "Got to say, the closest we came to hitting it was when your party went missing."

Sloane snorted. "I'm guessing that you never expected the alarm to go both ways."

"Correct," Copus said. "Twenty-eight minutes ago we received a video signal through that channel from Captain Apolla Harrow." He triggered a holo-projection, and a frozen image of a wide-eyed, pale-skinned woman appeared in the air beside him. She was too close to the camera to see much behind her other than part of a wall and the edge of a doorway. "We're assuming that she was in command, but we've no way of knowing that for certain. Sound's missing for the first few seconds."

He played the message, and the holo rushed into life. Harrow spun around to check behind her, then turned back. She silently mouthed something, then briefly looked behind her again. She was clearly anticipating something bad.

McConnach said, "She's scared."

Before anyone else could respond, the sound kicked in. "—the drokk *out* before he kills us all! I repeat: This is Huygens Base. We have a *code red* situation and require *immediate* assistance! At least eight dead with—" Something flashed behind Harrow and an exit wound appeared in her chest. As she toppled forward, the projection froze again.

"That's all we've got," Copus said.

We sat in silence for a few moments, then Takenaga asked, "How do you know her name? We can't see her tunic label from this angle, and even if we could, it would only show her surname."

"Governor Dodge identified her," Copus said. He dropped

into the nearest seat and turned to rest his arm on the seat's back as he faced us. "She sent him a comm through standard channels a few years back. He said it stuck in his memory because he had no idea who she was or why she'd established contact, and then his reply got bounced."

I said, "So she was sowing seeds just in case she ever needed him. Smart." I gestured towards the spot in the air where the projection had been. "Can you show us again, boss? Run it at quarter speed, see if there's anything else we can get from it."

Over the next hour, we watched the footage four more times, then frame-by-frame, all the while picking out anything that might be relevant.

It was McConnach who spotted that the faded and heavily scraped-away writing on the wall-panels behind Harrow was originally the phrase *'Until Inner Door Is Sealed.'* "She's in an airlock, no doubt about it."

Wightman said that the panels themselves were not what you'd expect to see in an established base: "That's a ship. Military, is my guess. The holo is too low-res to be sure, but I think we're looking at foamed-steel panels. There used to be a manufacturing station in the asteroid belt that specialised in foamed-steel. It's very light, very strong, and can only be made in a zero-g environment. But it costs three times as much as standard steel or titanium plating, so it's really only the military that can afford it. You wouldn't use it to build a base."

Takenaga said, "She used the word 'he' but didn't give a name. That implies that it's someone she knows."

My own contribution to the discussion seemed pretty minor at first. "The camera didn't move. That means it's fixed, not hovering or being held. And she was shot from behind... Could be they knew what she was doing and wanted to stop the message from getting out. Or they were not thinking clearly for whatever reason."

But it was Zera Kurya who spotted something that the rest of us were kicking ourselves for missing. "Captain Harrow broke radio silence so obviously this is a drastic situation; but she did not mention the prison. Her demeanour indicates that she was not in the right mindset for subterfuge, making it unlikely that she was hiding the recipient of her message. We cannot conclude with any certainty that the prison was the intended recipient."

I said, "Okay... But the comm link between Huygens and the prison is isolated, so no one is going to pick up that message by accident. If Harrow was hoping to contact her superiors on Earth—or someone else; who knows?—they didn't get the message." I looked up at Copus. "What's the base's complement?"

He shrugged. "Unknown."

Wightman said, "Well, it's at least eight people fewer than it was yesterday."

Sloane called out, "Hold tight—we're on those coords. Making a sharp left now."

I'd half expected a brief countdown, but Sloane wasn't playing around: we were all immediately flung to the right, and for a few seconds my stomach threatened to heave as the bus's grav-plating struggled to keep up with the shifting g-force.

When our path had straightened out, Copus said, "Jovus, Ernie! Next time, give us a heads-up!"

Sloane sighed theatrically. "Gotcha, boss..." He lowered his voice a little, but not so I couldn't hear him. "Reckon you shouldn't engage Dredd and the others. They're prisoners, for Grud's sake. Murderers. We can't trust a word they say." He glanced over his shoulder at me. "Especially *that* drokker. If he told me my name was Ernie Sloane, I'd contact my mother to check, and even then I wouldn't believe her."

"These three were Judges," Copus said, "just like us."

"Yeah? Well, forgive my candour, boss, but they turned their backs on their Justice Departments. Sold them out."

Takenaga laughed. "So did *we*, Sloane. There's not one of us here because we love guarding prisoners. We're here because we love getting paid."

"Enough," Copus said. "Rico, you were making a point?"

"Just that if very few people in the prison know about the comm link, could be true at the base too. The grunts know that the prison exists, but not about the link. They might be expecting aid from another military outfit. That could take days."

They all took a moment for that to sink in, then Takenaga said, "There are military and research bases on Jupiter, the asteroid belt and Mars—and probably a few in between—but Huygens Base is covert; even in an emergency they won't risk compromising it. Earth is about eighty light-minutes from Saturn, on average. That's two hours forty minimum to send a radio message and receive a response... Upshot is, even if there *was* a team geared up and ready to go on the next closest base, the message would still have to be relayed from Earth, and the team would have to *get* here. Unless there's a military ship in orbit right *now*, my guess is the earliest Huygens can expect backup is two days." She looked around and saw the rest of us staring at her. "What? I'm a military buff."

Copus nodded slowly at that. "So there's a chance they have no idea that we're coming."

"That's what I'm thinking," I said. "And we don't know what's there waiting for us. So unless some new intel shows up before we get there, I think we need to approach with extreme caution. If some hostile force has taken the base and they have access to military weaponry—judging by the distance from the airlock door and the size of the exit-wound in Harrow's chest, that gun was at least a point-five-oh calibre—then we're potentially walking into a firestorm."

McConnach pulled herself out of her seat and moved to the seat across from me. "Dredd's right. We don't know the situation, the topography, or *anything* about the base itself. For all we know there could be a thousand trigger-happy grunts there who're going to open fire on any unknown vehicle that gets too close—including us. They could be already tracking us."

That was a sobering thought.

I remained silent for a while, letting the problem stew in the back of my brain as I half listened to the others making plans for what they hoped was the most likely situation.

Between them Takenaga and Wightman worked out that Huygens Base couldn't hold more than eighty personnel, based on the amount of food that we supplied. That gave them a starting point. Assuming twenty-four square metres per person, that made the base around two thousand square metres in area.

"Sounds about right for an office," said Copus. "But military bases have crew quarters and vehicle hangars and weapons storage. So I reckon we can double it. Four thousand square metres."

"That's floor space," McConnach said. "It won't be a

conveniently rectangular single-storey building, will it? It'll be multiple floors. Some of the base could be underground, for insulation, and easier to defend. Or to hide: for all we know, it's *completely* hidden."

"That's possible," Takenaga said. "You heard the stories about Planitia Four? No? Story goes that it was a secret underground base on Mars, built by the Americans a hundred years ago. Staffed by a team of ten people, all sworn to ultimate silence. Whatever they were doing there was so secret that when the Roussom Corporation set up its first Mars settlement and chose the exact same location as Planitia Four—their computers used the same algorithm to find the best spot for sunlight-capture, bedrock solidity, storm-shelter, and so on—the staff at Planitia had no choice but to self-destruct the base and take their own lives. The whole thing was passed off as an unexpected underground cave-in."

Sloane said, "Bull. If it was *that* secret, there wouldn't even be rumours about it."

"The point is, Huygens Base might not be visible from the surface. So how are we going to know when we've found it?"

I had to admit, Takenaga had a point there. And even if their rough calculations and estimates were accurate, and even if we *could* find the place, it was still a military base. Finding it is one problem; getting inside would be something else entirely.

It wouldn't be impossible—no building is completely impenetrable—but it was going to be tough. Especially since my old friend sub-warden Martin Copus seemed to have forgotten why some of us were on Titan in the first place.

I decided that it would be best to deal with the problem now rather than when we reached the base and it was too late.

"Boss?"

Copus was sitting slumped forward in his seat. "What now, Dredd?"

"Why are we here?"

He raised his head and looked at me. "Have you not been paying attention?"

"No, I mean, *we* as in myself, Kurya and Wightman."

"Because you and Wightman are mods and you can go out into the Bronze without a suit. And Kurya's here because she was a Med-Judge and I'm not about to put Doctor Mollo's life at risk if I don't have to; plus she was training to be part of an elite strike-force before she was arrested."

Kurya said, "That is true."

I nodded. "Good. Fine. Now... *how* are we supposed to help? Wightman and I scout ahead, find an entrance? Kurya backs us up, using her skills to breach the base. So we get inside undetected, somehow, and we find Captain Harrow if she's still alive and then... what? If we come under attack, I'm not sure that I'm comfortable facing a potential shoot-out where their side is armed with military weaponry and our side is fighting back with nothing more substantial than hopes and prayers."

Copus stared at me, and even over the constant rumble of the bus's engines I could hear him dry-swallow. Under his breath he muttered, "Stomm."

I was enjoying this too much, I admit. Slowly, but cheerfully, I asked, "Isn't it kind of against the rules—and common sense— to equip your prisoners with guns?"

Twenty

OF ALL THE moons in the solar system, only Titan has an atmosphere with a density comparable to that on Earth. In fact, the atmosphere is *denser* than Earth's. Which means, of course, that Titan is the only moon that has powerful winds. That's one of the reasons its surface looks more Earth-like than almost any other moon: the winds mean erosion. Drifting sands, storms, the constantly freezing and thawing methane lakes... they all contribute to grinding everything down, stripping the rough edges from craters and crevasses and boulders and rocks.

The moon's air is almost completely nitrogen, with the remainder being methane and hydrogen. None of which are conducive to human health... unless that human has been modified.

So under a brown, poisonous sky, Kellan Wightman and I trudged side by side over the dusty, rocky landscape. It was like walking across an eternal stony beach at sunset on an overcast winter's day.

Not that we felt the cold much. Our polymer-laced skin and artificial blood helped keep us moving in conditions that would kill an unmodified person in seconds. Our coated eyes blinked without tears, our sealed mouths and noses kept the frost from forming within our paper lungs.

My friend Donny Guildford, now long dead, once explained to me that a mod's artificial lungs don't actually *breathe* methane, as most of the mods believed. "The body needs oxygen and there's no oxygen *in* methane. It's CH_4: four hydrogen atoms and one carbon atom. What the apparatus *is* doing is extracting water-vapour from the atmosphere and using molybdenum-sulphide to strip its hydrogen atoms. What's left is oxygen. It's a miniaturised version of the prison's atmosphere processing system, except that the big machines burn the hydrogen as fuel instead of discarding it. Besides, if they could somehow have modified our lungs to breathe methane instead of oxygen, we'd suffocate when there's no methane around, right?"

While I did understand the science, I didn't like to think about it too much. Tucked away in some cryogenic freezer inside the prison were my original lungs and a couple of kilograms of other body parts they'd had to remove to modify me. *That's* a much more comforting thought: that when my sentence is done, those pieces will be returned to me and the process will be reversed. I quite like the idea that my lungs are still going to be twenty years old when the rest of me is hitting forty. Well, roughly. It's hard to be accurate about how old I really am, being a growth-accelerated clone.

Halfway up an unusually jagged hill—so steep in parts that

we had to use our hands to climb—Wightman said, "Rico, suppose the base is gone."

"How do you mean, gone?"

"I don't mean destroyed. Let's say that everyone's dead, but the building is intact."

I guessed where he was going with this, but decided to let him take me there anyway.

"That means lots of weapons lying around. Plenty of supplies too. Who says we have to go back? We could just seal it up and defend it from the inside. I'm sure Kurya would be more inclined to take our side. That's three against four. Good odds. We might even find a ship. A military base is bound to have some sort of shuttle. We can get off this damn rock."

And now the conversation was back on familiar territory. "And go where?"

"Back home. Where else?"

A head-sized boulder slipped under my foot, and I turned to watch it roll and bounce its way down the hill. "Back home, to the planet that's protected by so many early-warning systems that they'd see us coming before we even left Saturn's orbit."

"Okay then, we just stay in the base."

"How is that better than the prison? At least there we know we get to go home when our time is up."

Wightman said nothing for a few minutes, then muttered a few choice swear-words. "You're not wrong."

"I know. So you're here for arson, right?"

"Mostly because of the people who died in the fires."

"Are you guilty?"

He stopped climbing and looked at me as though I'd asked him if he could count to four. "Well, *yeah*. You know that."

"So you deserve to be here, same as me. In Mega-City One I killed a citizen I'd intended to wound. Not *entirely* my mistake, but I did it. Virgil Livingstone would probably be alive now if not for me. He was a perp, but he didn't deserve to die. I broke a lot of other laws too. All with full knowledge of what I was doing and full understanding of the impact of my actions. I'm here on Titan because this is the latest stop on the path that I chose for myself. It's not a stop that I'd *wanted* to take, but it's certainly one that I knew was possible."

Close to the top, Wightman hauled himself up onto a ridge, and sat watching me do the same. He was taller than me, so the climb was a little easier for him. "You're telling me that rehabilitation works?"

"I'm saying that I knew the risks, so I can't blame anyone but myself. Except the whole *system* is wrong. Treat the citizens as though they're all potential perps, you can't complain if they act like perps."

He rose up onto his knees, then his feet, and looked towards the hill's apex. "About a hundred metres and we should have a clear view of the base. If it's even there."

He started to move on, but I put my hand on his arm. "Hold it... A secret base will be surrounded by alarm triggers."

"I know. We should watch out for booby traps too."

I shook my head. "No, probably not. One sure way to let everyone know that they're close to your secret base is to have booby traps. You don't want to confirm your existence, you want to steer people away."

There were times when I wondered how Kellan Wightman had ever made it as a Judge in the first place. Things were said to be a little more lax in Mega-City Two, but that couldn't explain how Wightman was sometimes so stunningly oblivious. It was like he had blind spots on his brain for things like tactics and empathy.

It's not that he was stupid, as such. It was more that he lacked the imagination a good Judge requires to put himself into the perp's position. Maybe that's how he'd been caught so easily.

I told Wightman to stay put and moved on, staying on hands and knees even when I reached the apex and the hill flattened out. Snake-like, I squirmed through a series of small boulders and drifts of gravel until I was able to see the land beyond.

The base was there, but it had been very effectively disguised. From directly overhead it looked like a simple plateau, and even from this angle it wasn't noticeably artificial... except for the light shining out through a ragged blast-hole in one side. With that as a starting point, I found it relatively easy to trace the edges of the building, ignoring fake boulders and dust-drifts that the manufacturers had strategically placed to help break up the outline.

Even so, it was hard to guess the size of the place. It needed a door, or a truck, or even a human body lying on the ground to lend it scale.

Softly, Wightman's voice called, "Well?"

"It's there," I replied.

"Okay. So... what next?"

I didn't have an answer for that, so I fell back on my training and started to analyse the situation.

It had been over six hours since Governor Dodge received Captain Apolla Harrow's call for help. Aside from the blast-hole, the base showed no signs of being under attack. No sentries, no equipment, no vehicles—or even vehicle tracks—outside. The warping of the metal plates at the blast-hole told me it was an internal explosion. There was very little debris ejected from the blast-hole, either, as far as I could see, which meant that either someone picked it up, or there had been nothing in that particular room or corridor. Unless, of course, the explosion had taken place in the room in which Captain Harrow stored her collection of rocks and dust.

That was a joke.

I heard something moving behind me and looked back to see Wightman slowly approaching, squirming with his belly to the ground as I had.

I returned my attention to the base. The light still streaming out through the blast-hole suggested that the situation was not under control: the top priority in a covert location was discretion, and that light might as well be a kilometre-high sign with a flashing message reading, *Secret Base Here!*

Wightman settled into place next to me. "Huh. Not what I was expecting, but it makes sense. Wonder what they do here?"

"We're going to have to make a decision," I said. "If this was back home, and you were still a Judge, what would you do?"

He peered down at the base for a moment. "Find a second entrance. That section is no longer airtight; they'll have sealed it off."

"That's what I'm thinking." The lack of oxygen didn't make any difference to me and Wightman, but whoever was inside the base would have isolated the compromised tunnel, maybe even welded the inner doors shut. It's a lot easier to get through an airlock door than a welded door. But an airlock door would be harder to find.

"I'd shut off the light, too, if I was in charge," Wightman said.

"So either they want someone to see it, or whoever's running things now doesn't realise."

"Or they're *unable* to shut it off." He began to squirm backwards. "We should go back to Copus, fill him in."

I'd been mentally weighing up the possibilities since Copus had shown us the holo of Captain Harrow calling for help, and I'd come to a decision. "No, I want to get closer."

"Rico, if someone hostile has taken the base, they'll see you coming."

"That's what I'm counting on."

Twenty-One

I TOLD WIGHTMAN to go back to the bus. "Tell Copus to give me sixty minutes."

"Then what?"

"That's up to him. But I want sixty minutes to check it out for myself."

I waited for Wightman to slither back down the other side of the hill, then moved forward.

The hill was steeper on this side, but craggier, which made climbing down a little easier. I was, of course, in full view, and for the first few metres I kept expecting a searchlight, or a shouted warning, or gunfire.

I half ran, half slid down the last few metres of loose scree, then took the time to dust myself off as well as possible: it seemed to me that if anyone *was* watching, then my casual, no-hurry, no-big-deal approach might be intriguing enough to keep their fingers off their triggers.

As I neared the hole in the wall, I was finally able to get an idea of the scale of the building: the hole was as tall as me, and had been blasted in a corridor wall. A few scraps of scorched metal were half-buried in the dust around me, but far less than I'd have expected from a hole that size: the explosion had pierced the wall but not shredded it.

My foot kicked against a fist-sized chunk and I picked it up. It felt solid, but it was lighter than it looked, even taking Titan's low gravity into account. A *lot* lighter.

That was when I realised something that should have been obvious from the start. In the holo message Wightman had recognised the wall panels as foamed steel, which suggested that Harrow was on a ship. But she contacted the prison through the physical comm-link: there was no way to do that without actually being inside Huygens Base.

See, you don't fly a billion kilometres to Saturn's largest moon and then spend months building a top-secret hidden base. That would be incredibly wasteful. What you do instead is fly to the moon, land your ship and then your ship *becomes* the base. It's already airtight, it's got power, it's outfitted with crew quarters and everything else you need. Plus, in a real emergency, the whole damn thing can take off and go somewhere else.

I tossed the lump of foamed steel aside and kept walking towards the ragged opening. Now I could see the damage to the wall on the other side of the corridor, and to the floor and ceiling: the explosion had not been caused by a shaped charge.

I climbed the slight incline leading to the hole and this close it was even more obvious that this was no natural plateau.

The exterior hull of the ship had been copiously but inexpertly sprayed with a plastic paint that was a reasonable match for the surrounding dirt, and many of the "plateau's" larger boulders and outcrops were clearly fake. They were covered with seam-lines and fingerprints, and here and there the wire-mesh framework showed through.

Once, in Mega-City One, I investigated the death of an actor on a set modelled on twentieth-century Detroit, and that set was what the half-buried ship reminded me of. From a distance, it was the perfect illusion; but up close it was a mess.

As I stepped inside, normal gravity returned—or close to normal, anyway—and I sniffed the air. My cybernetic olfactory system wasn't particularly well-calibrated, but I could still detect scorched metal and plastic.

Inside, the corridor seemed empty. To the right, it stretched on for about ten metres before curving away, and to the left, a few steps away, was a sealed interior door.

I walked up to the door and knocked on it.

My logic, which seemed sound at the time, was this: if someone hostile had taken control of the base, then they'd probably assume that a prisoner would be on their side. But if Captain Harrow or one of her people had regained control, then they were the ones who'd called for help. So either way, whoever was in charge would be pleased to see me.

Or, at least, not overtly hostile.

Wightman's idea of finding a second way in, on the grounds that any internal doors close to the rupture would have been sealed, seemed less likely now that I knew that this was a starship. Every internal door on a ship—especially a military vessel—has to be completely airtight.

I knocked again, much harder, and shouted, "Open up!" in the best Judge voice I was still able to muster.

I mentally pictured a bunch of low-rank soldiers on the other side of the door wondering what to do next. If there was anyone there at all.

Could be they're all *dead*, I said to myself.

I hadn't really entertained that thought until now, and that bothered me. I had been on Titan three times as long as I'd been a Judge: maybe I was starting to lose my edge. Certainly, back in the Meg, this situation would never have lasted this long.

I was about to knock for the third time when a voice said, "Identify yourself!" It wasn't Captain Harrow, but whoever she was, she was standing on the other side of the door.

I called back, "Rico Dredd. Prisoner in the Titan mining colony."

There was an awkward silence, then the woman asked, "You armed?"

"No."

"Alone?"

"Right now, yes. But there are others waiting."

Another pause. "Former Judge?"

I nodded, then realised she couldn't see me. "That's right. From Mega-City One."

"Wait there. I need to seal off this corridor before I can open the door. Two minutes."

"Understood."

As I waited, I thought about what she'd said: "*I* need to seal off this corridor." A strong indicator that she was alone. Everyone else dead. Did that mean that she was the killer, or the survivor?

Some mechanism inside the walls clunked and rattled into life. I pictured gears grinding together and a vacuum pump drawing the air out of the corridor. After just about two minutes, as promised, the door in front of me split vertically down the centre and slid neatly and near-silently into the walls.

Inside, the short corridor seemed clean and safe. Another door at the far end, ten metres away, and two more set into the right wall, about four metres apart. No debris, bullet-holes, scorch marks or body parts. That was a good sign.

I stepped in, and the first door closed behind me.

There was more clunking and rattling as the air returned, then the woman's voice said, "I'm coming out now. I'm armed. I want to see you standing with your forehead pressed against the door you entered through, hands visible at all times. Try anything else and you're dead. Do you understand and acknowledge?"

"I do."

I turned around, pressed my forehead against the cold metal of the door, and stretched out my arms, fingers splayed.

Another door opened behind me, and quiet footsteps approached.

"Don't move. Don't even *twitch*."

Something warm and metallic was pressed into the small of my back, felt like the muzzle of a large-calibre rifle. A black-gloved hand quickly and expertly patted me down, then I heard her move away.

"All right. Turn around. Slowly."

I turned. Looking back at me along the barrel of a rifle was a woman in her mid-twenties.

She was a redhead; I liked that. Rich brown skin, strong

build, short—barely up to my shoulder—and she was looking me square in the eye without flinching. I liked that even more.

"First Lieutenant Salome Vine. You?"

"I told you already. Rico Dredd. Former Judge, currently a prisoner at the iridium mine."

"The hell are you doing here, Dredd?"

"We got a call from Captain Harrow. There's an emergency line between here and the mine."

"And they sent you, an unarmed prisoner, into an unknown but certainly hostile situation?"

I shrugged. "I'm more expendable than a guard, and I can operate outside without an environment suit."

Vine lowered her weapon, and I got my first clear look at her face.

I'd met my share of attractive women back in the Big Meg, as a cadet and then as a Judge. Particularly as a Judge: women just gravitated towards me. And it wasn't just my looks; they weren't *that* superficial. I was physically identical to my brother and women generally steered away from him. Well, there were a few exceptions, but then the human race is peppered with crazies.

Women liked confidence, that was what I learned pretty shortly after puberty. Not arrogance, that's a different thing entirely. Confidence is when you know you'll be able to take care of something. Arrogance is when you think you're the *only* one who can take care of it.

I'd been the best Cadet in the Academy of Law and I knew it, but that wasn't arrogance, because everyone else knew it too. And I didn't dangle it over people's heads. I'm not a jerk. You don't point out your successes and tell others, "You're never gonna get there." What you do instead is tell them, "Yeah, this is me up here on top. This is your goal. I *want* you to get good enough to knock me off." It's a simple equation: the harder you try, the better you'll get. Practice can only improve your game.

But you don't get to stay at the top of the heap without putting in the work, and I guess that's what brought me to Titan.

I had been the best Judge in Mega-City One, but Little Joe had been right behind me, and he'd never slacked off. Joe never took a day to just chill and watch the world go by. He devoted every spare moment to the Law. When he wasn't hitting perps, he was hitting the books.

Have to say, a couple more years and maybe he'd have caught up with me. I'm not saying I got lazy, but my self-selected lifestyle meant that I *had* to take downtime. I worked hard to shake up the system, to make it fair for *everyone*, not just the Judges, and that included the unpleasant task of letting the perps see me as one of them. I let them think I was on the take, because a corrupt Judge can get a lot closer to a mob's centre of power than a Judge like Joe, who was always as straight and to-the-point as an arrow.

So if First Lieutenant Salome Vine was masking revulsion at my appearance, then that was a little annoying. She was the first new woman I'd met since being turned into a mod. Not counting some prisoners who'd arrived since, but then none of them had been interesting enough to snag my attention.

Vine, though... she was stunning. One of those people you know you're going to remember for the rest of your life. Maybe it was her aloofness that I found enticing. After all, the best way to get someone to want something is to tell them they can't have it. That's what her demeanour was telling me.

She stepped back towards the door from which she'd emerged. "How many others are with you?"

"Six. Four guards, two prisoners. One of the other prisoners is like me. Modified."

She watched me for a second, and it was clear that she was weighing up her options. "Okay. To be frank, Dredd, I wasn't expecting anything. The next supply ship is four months away, and it's pretty clear that this station operates under the radar. We are off the books. Do you know what that means?"

"I do. You can't call for backup through the normal channels." I took a step closer. "So for now *I'm* your backup. What's the situation?"

"One hostile, one survivor."

I said, "Got it. I'm going to operate on the assumption that you're the survivor." That was meant to be a moment of levity, but Vine didn't crack a smile. "So what happened?"

"Follow me."

She lowered her gun completely, and as she led me through the ship she filled in some of the background about the operation. "The hostile is Corporal John Armando. Thirty years old. Exceptionally skilled at hand-to-hand combat, weapons, tactics, anything you can name. Right now, he's sealed in the lower levels—but he's smart. He'll find a way through."

"What's he got down there?"

"Enough air, water and food to last five years, minimum. More ammunition than he'll ever need. Armoury, machine room, electronics lab, hydroponics... And access to the reactor."

"You're saying that he could just destroy the base?"

"The reactor is powerful enough to knock the whole damn *moon* out of orbit. But that won't happen. There's a lot of failsafes, and Armando doesn't have the clearance to bypass them. Or the skills to hack the computers."

"You can't just seal him in and leave him there?"

She slowed to a stop, and turned to face me. This close, I could smell her skin even with my altered olfactory system.

She looked as though she was about to say something, but frowned instead as she peered at me. Then she said, "I *know* you. I mean, I've seen you before."

"Maybe you've met my brother back in the Meg. Last I heard he's still a Judge."

"Unlikely. It's been four years since I last set foot in Mega-City One. It's your eyes. Something about them."

I guessed where she recognised me from, of course, but I preferred people to work it out for themselves. Kept at least one part of their brain busy. It had come in useful a couple of times when I was a Judge.

See, everyone was used to seeing pics of Chief Judge Eustace Fargo as an older guy. They recognise something of him in me and Little Joe, but they're not always able to place it.

But I was wrong about Vine. She leaned even closer—I swear to Grud, for a second I thought she was going to kiss me—and said, "It's you. The dead man."

"The what?"

"You're the one who survived that storm a few years back. It was my team who found you out in the Bronze, on the edge of suffocation. You were so far gone we almost didn't bother trying to resuscitate you." She stepped back, slowly shaking her head. "After everything you went through out there... What the hell did you do to end up like *this*?"

"Long story."

She nodded and resumed walking.

But before she turned away, I saw another look in her eyes. I'd seen it before, a couple of times, when I was on the streets of the Meg. Sometimes a Judge just *knows* everything has turned a corner and there's no way back.

Vine had that look now.

Twenty-Two

THE CLOSER WE came to the engine room, the more damage I could see. First the stink of cordite and thermite in the air, then fresh bullet-scratches in the walls. Blood spray across a glass door. A discarded ammo magazine on the floor. A first-aid box smashed open, its pills and bandages scattered like confetti after a particularly brutal wedding.

Through a synthiglass panel in a closed door, a boot on the floor with a small trickle of blood streaming past. No way to tell whether the boot was occupied.

More blood-spatter, running thickly down the wall—pooling at the ground around little tooth-and-bone islands.

"How many down?" I asked Vine.

"Thirty-four."

I didn't respond to that. On the bus we'd calculated that we were sending the base enough food for eighty people, roughly.

What were they doing with the rest of it?

And then a picture of Kellan Wightman's stash of fermenting fruit and vegetables jumped into my mind. That made sense. These people were soldiers, not prisoners. They probably had their own still somewhere on the base, and I was sure it would be more elaborate and more efficient than Wightman's collection of hidden barrels.

"So what is it that you do here?"

"That's classified," Vine said. I got the feeling that it was such an automatic response that she didn't register either the question or the answer.

She glanced back at me. "I know everything's fubar now, but that doesn't change the meaning of the word 'covert.' A former Judge should understand that."

"I do. But—"

"If and when you need to know, I'll tell you." No nonsense, to-the-point. I was liking her more by the minute.

Ahead, the corridor split, with a staircase on the right. Vine didn't say anything, but she'd slowed a little, her movements becoming more cautious, more deliberate.

"We're close?" I asked, as softly as my voicebox would allow.

She nodded. "He's down there."

We stopped at the top of the staircase and she hunkered down, then motioned for me to do the same.

Below, I could see yet another sealed door—this one cutting off a smeared trail of blood. Something had been dragged through: going from the crimson fingerprints low on the door frame, a person. One who, at the time, was still alive.

Vine said, "I've sealed every door out of there but that one."

"Makes sense," I said. "Leave Armando an obvious way out.

If he's as smart as you say, he'll know it's a trap and won't take it. Which means that's our way *in*." I stood up again. "All right. Eight of us should be enough to take him down."

She sighed. "Typical Judge. Ego the size of Jupiter. Dredd, Armando killed thirty-four highly-trained marines in the space of eighteen minutes, most of them with his bare hands. The only reason I survived was because I was out on the surface at the time."

I ignored that. "Can you patch into the base's internal cameras? See where he is right now?"

Vine lifted up her left arm, showing me the small datapad attached to her wrist. It was displaying a map with a slowly-flashing dot in the centre. "That's him. About twelve metres along on the other side of that door." She raised her wrist to her mouth and softly said, "Computer. Best visual on Corporal John Armando."

The datapad's screen switched to a security camera feed.

Armando was barefoot, and naked from the waist up; he had a large, well-defined build. He was standing perfectly still with his arms by his sides and his eyes closed. His chest rose and fell regularly and deeply. What I at first took to be an aberration of the camera lens or the screen was clarified when it switched to a different angle. Armando's skin was as grey as mine.

"Something you're not telling me?" I asked.

"There's a *lot* I'm not telling you."

"Can you open the door remotely? See how he reacts?"

"We tried that shortly before you showed up. He just stands there. Look." She tapped at the datapad for a second, and the image pulled back. On the edge of the screen were two very clearly dead bodies: human heads are just not designed to be at that angle. "Master Sergeant Wegryn and Second Lieutenant Matheson. They'd been outside with me. We saw Armando like this, and Wegryn approached. The corporal was totally unresponsive. He looked catatonic. But when Wegryn came within two metres, Armando struck. Matheson opened fire but..." She shrugged. "I'm not saying that Armando *dodged* the rounds, but I know how good a shot Matheson was. She could hit a running target between the eyes from two hundred metres."

I pulled the datapad off her arm—she didn't protest—and poked at the screen until I found the map again. "Straight line of sight between him and the door." I began to walk down the steps. "Vine, how about you give me a gun, open the door and I shoot him?"

"We *can't* kill him. Matheson shouldn't have even tried."

"Do you mean we can't, or we aren't permitted to?"

"We're not permitted."

"Why not?"

"That's classified."

"Of course it is." I'd reached the door, so I turned back towards the lieutenant. "How close did you say the Master Sergeant got to him? Two metres?"

"Dredd, he'll kill you just as quickly as he killed everyone else."

I couldn't help smiling at that. She really didn't know who I was. "I'll take the chance. I'm clearly not a soldier, so he might not register me as hostile. Otherwise, what do we do? Wait for him to snap out of whatever trance he's in and decide to blow the reactor?"

"I told you, he can't do that," Vine said, following me down the stairs.

I handed the datapad back to her. "Keep the door open wide

enough for me to get back through if I have to. And have your gun ready."

"Dredd, your life is worth less than his."

I gave her another smile. "Maybe. But is *yours?*"

"Yes, it is. And stop being so drokkin' smug, will you? You haven't seen him in action yet."

I almost said, "And you haven't seen *me* in action," but then I realised that would probably come across as even more smug. Instead, I said, "Open the door and start recording the camera feed. At the very least, if he kills me, then you can show the footage to sub-warden Copus and the others, give them some idea of what they'll be facing."

She said, "All right. If he kills you, you have the consolation that you'll be immortalised in a special how-not-to-do-it training film." Vine tapped at the datapad again, and immediately raised her rifle.

The door in front of me slid open, and a rush of warm air washed over us, carrying with it faint traces of blood, vomit and faeces.

I stepped through, very much aware of the thick smear of blood across the floor that led to a stomachless young soldier lying face up, his mouth and eyes open but unmoving.

Five metres from Armando, I stopped. He hadn't noticed me, or if he had, he was keeping a very tight rein on his reactions. I'm no shrink, but that was a level of control I wouldn't normally attribute to a frenzied killer.

Softly, I said, "Soldier...?"

No reaction.

"Corporal Armando, my name is Rico Dredd. Can you hear me?"

Still nothing.

"Corporal, I'm not your enemy. I'm unarmed. I want you to tell me what happened here, and why. Can you do that?"

He didn't respond, so I took another step, and the grey-skinned man opened his eyes, looked straight at me. But that was it. No twitching of limbs or shifting of his weight. His eyes didn't even follow me as I continued to move.

Keeping my distance, I walked slowly around him. His skin was almost the same shade as mine, and like mine was pockmarked with scars and needle marks where the cold-resistant polymers had been injected between the epidermis and the dermis.

"Corporal... John. I don't know what they did to you, but I'm guessing that it was very similar to what happened to me. Look at my arms, at my face... Can you see, John? We're the same. We're in this together. We can help each other, *protect* each other."

Though barefoot, Armando was a little taller than me. His muscles were as perfectly defined as I'd ever seen, not an ounce of unnecessary body fat. He was also completely hairless.

"I'm not a soldier," I said. "But back on Earth I was a Judge. A good one too. I knew my duty. *Semper Fidelis*. Always faithful."

Clearly, the man was in some sort of trance. Resting to conserve energy, but still on high alert. Soldier's fugue, I'd heard it called.

"John, you're not giving me a lot to work with here. This is a mess, and if we're going to sort it out, I'll need your help."

I'm nothing if not adventurous. Now directly behind him, I took another step closer.

I knew that was a mistake before my foot had even touched the ground.

Armando whirled around, lashing out with his fist. The back-handed blow struck me square in the jaw, hard enough to almost knock me off my feet.

I barely registered the hit when his powerful fist slammed into the side of my head, staggering me, a half-second before his knee caught me in the solar plexus.

But it's not so easy to knock the wind out of someone with an artificial respiratory system: I recovered almost immediately and threw myself to the side, ducking under the third blow. That left his own midriff unguarded, and I didn't waste the opportunity. I hit him hard in the stomach with my fist clenched with the ring-finger knuckle prominent: a very specialised move that some of the perps in Mega-City One referred to as the 'Judges' Incentive.' I've used it to bring down perps—and fellow prisoners—twice my weight.

Armando staggered back, but didn't fall. That was impressive. He launched himself at me again, left fist clenched and his right hand clawed. That didn't look like any kind of move I'd seen before, but I wasn't taking any more chances: I stepped back and to the side at the last moment and managed to grab his left wrist, then turned my movement into a spin, pulling him off balance.

That put me in the position to jab my left heel into the back of his knee and pull harder on his arm at the same time.

Wordlessly, he went down, and for a moment I thought that was it, I'd beaten him.

But he twisted around as he fell, locked his hand onto my wrist and suddenly he was dragging *me* off balance. I tried to pull out of it, but he continued to twist, until somehow I was on the ground, on my back. He had his right hand on my throat and his left fist pulled back.

That was when Vine lashed out towards the back of Armando's head with the butt of her rifle.

But the blow never connected. The grey man saw or sensed it coming—maybe there was a shadow, or he felt the breeze or something—and let go of me long enough to push himself up and back. The butt of the rifle slammed into Armando's back between his shoulder blades, and he reached over his head with his right hand and grabbed it, jerked it free of Vine's grip.

He kicked back at her, catching her square in the stomach: had she not been wearing body armour, that kick alone would have killed her.

He didn't even look to see how effective it had been. Instead, he immediately dropped back into position, again grabbing for my throat with his left hand as he spun the rifle around in his right. By the time his fingers locked around my neck again, he had the rifle aimed at my face with his finger on the trigger.

I had an instant where I told myself "The safety's still on!" but I couldn't take that chance. I grabbed the barrel with my left hand and pushed it aside just as he fired. The gun boomed and the muzzle-flash scorched my cheek, and later I found fragments of the foam-steel floor embedded in my skin.

Still holding onto the barrel, I shoved the rifle back towards him, trying to twist it out of his grip, and at the same time he was squeezing my throat with his free hand. If I'd been a normal man, I might have already passed out from pain or lack of oxygen, but I'm no longer a normal man. My polymer-laced skin and modified respiratory system make my throat a lot more resilient than most people's.

I slammed my right fist into his stomach over and over, as Armando fired four more times—each shot another deafening boom—and it was clear that strength-wise we were very closely matched.

I knew a little about military training, what they put the recruits through. It was intense; the system turned men and women into fighting machines, honed almost to perfection. Almost.

But I'd had fifteen years in the toughest academy on Earth. And for each of those fifteen years I'd excelled. Top of the class. Sure, Armando probably had ten more years' experience than I did, but I'd bet my time in the Mega-City One Academy of Law and my one year on the streets against anything he had.

I went for his eyes.

Now, that's a move that a rookie might make when he's desperate. You go for your enemy's eyes, you're not playing around anymore. That's as serious as it gets. Most people are squeamish about something as harmless as eye drops; even the *thought* that an opponent might attempt to tear out their eyes is enough to send them into an absolute frenzy.

So a seasoned fighter learns not to do that. Eyes are off limits. Unless, of course, you know what you're doing. Could be that there's a time when you *want* your opponent to go into a frenzy.

That's what I did. It was a calculated risk, but it paid off.

I pressed the fingers of my right hand into a point and jabbed straight at his left eye.

Armando flinched to the side, shifting his weight and loosening his grip on my neck. That gave me the leverage I needed. I dropped my hand a little mid-strike, and instead hit him just below his jaw, driving my fingers into the carotid sinus and cracking the heel of my hand against his left clavicle, snapping it. Two points of pain with one blow.

He threw himself backwards away from me, but I was still holding onto the barrel of his rifle. I twisted my arm away, pulling him further off balance and loosening his grip on the gun, giving myself enough room to pull my right leg up and kick out.

The sole of my boot mashed satisfyingly into Armando's face, and he toppled backwards. Have to hand it to whoever trained him, they did a pretty good job: he almost recovered before I was on my feet. Almost.

I stamped down on his broken clavicle to further disorient him, then as he was silently screaming, a quick, hard kick to his left temple put him out. It felt like kicking a breezeblock, but it worked.

I pulled the rifle from his grip, spun it around and quickly checked the breech. It was clear. I held it aimed at Armando, finger off the trigger but nearby, ready.

"Drop it!" Vine shouted from behind me. "I said, drop the weapon, Dredd!"

"You *kidding* me?" I'm not ashamed to admit that the weight of the gun was both comforting and empowering, but I shook off the feeling—this wasn't the right time. "Vine, you should cuff this drokker while you have the chance."

For the second time that day, I felt the muzzle of a handgun poke into the small of my back, and Vine said, "Last warning. Drop the gun."

I opened my hand and let the rifle fall to the floor, then stepped back from it. "Cuff him. He's actually unconscious now, not just in standby mode or whatever he was before."

She passed me a set of cuffs. "You do it."

I rolled Armando onto his side and cuffed his wrists behind his back. "Give me another set. *Two* more sets, if you've got them."

"He's not superhuman, Dredd. Those cuffs are a titanium-based polymer. They're unbreakable."

"It's your funeral. Along with all your former colleagues." As I stood up, I added, "You didn't have to pull your gun on me, Vine."

"You're a prisoner. Said so yourself. I can't let you have a gun."

I straightened up, and gave her my best tight-lipped smile. Like there was any other kind of smile I could give. "This creep killed thirty-four highly-trained and heavily-armed marines, and I took him down on my own and with my bare hands. You really think I need a gun to be dangerous?"

Twenty-Three

VINE USED HER datapad to patch the base's comms system to open a short-range radio link with the prison bus, and we waited for Copus and the others to arrive. Vine told them exactly where to find us: she didn't want to leave Armando alone, and certainly didn't trust me on my own.

I sat on the floor with my back to the wall, watching the grey-skinned corporal. "So what *is* this? You're experimenting on soldiers here?"

Vine was looking at her datapad as she lowered herself down close to me. "Dredd... You should have died out there in the Bronze, but you're made of strong stuff. I've just pulled your records. I know who you were before your sentencing." She tapped at the screen. "You were already exceptional, and *now* look at you. I knew about the modification process when I was assigned to this base, but this is the first time I've seen the results in person..." She hesitated for a few seconds, and it was clear to me that she was debating whether to carry on or just end this conversation right here and now. "No, that's not true. Out in the Bronze, shortly after we found you... We recovered a body. He'd been modified just like you."

My artificial skin crawled at that. "Guildford," I said. "Donny Guildford. He was a friend."

"I'm sorry to hear that. He'd been shot in the head."

"I know." At night, sometimes, I could still hear the echo of that gunshot. I mentally shook myself. This wasn't the time. "So your people examined Guildford's body. Reverse-engineered the process. And now you've done the same to Corporal Armando. To his skin, at least."

"Correct. He..." Again, she faltered. "He clearly didn't take to it as well as you have. We haven't done any work on his lungs or other organs yet, just his skin and eyes. We chose Corporal Armando because physically he was the strongest of all the candidates. Most of the time he's more or less normal, but I know he has nightmares. I think we broken him." She turned to look at me. "How did you come out of the process intact, Dredd?"

"I don't know the details," I told her. "And I don't really *want* to know. They wiped my memory of the procedure. Not entirely—I still get flashes from time to time—but enough that I can't actually recall it. It keeps slipping away, like a dream I can *almost* remember. Lieutenant, are you telling me that your people subjected Corporal Armando to the process *without* suppressing his memories?"

She didn't answer. Instead, she said, "He wasn't a volunteer, Dredd. Seventeen months ago he was stationed on JupSat and got into a brawl with an officer. We don't know the exact circumstances of the disagreement—a lot of the information has been redacted—but the officer didn't survive. Armando was court-martialled and sentenced to forty years. He was offered a reduction in sentence if he participated in this programme."

I leaned my head back against the wall, pretty sure I knew where this was going. "You just said he *wasn't* a volunteer."

"Captain Harrow decided that he was the best fit of all the candidates by some distance."

I swear, if I'd still been a Judge, I'd have arrested her there and then. As it was, I felt sick. Whatever people have said about me, they know I'm not a sadist. I don't get off on people being hurt against their will.

Harrow and her engineers had subjected Armando to unimaginable agony. Was it any wonder that his mind had snapped?

Vine said, "I'm not cleared to know everything they did to him. But something inside him snapped this morning. He shared quarters with Second Lieutenants Baily-White and Underwood, and Doctor Riahi, his handler. And today, before first shift, Armando just went berserk. I saw the CCTV footage: it's dark, hard to see much more than just a triangle of light coming in through the open door. They're in their bunks, Riahi's on her side, facing Armando. She says something to him, and grabs his sidearm and starts shooting. Two in the head and one in the chest for Riahi, same for the others. And then he came for the rest of us."

"So what was it that Riahi told him?"

A shrug. "Unknown. The audio quality is poor, and she was speaking softly so as not to waken the others. She and

Armando were friends; they would often spend hours at night talking, especially when he was finding it hard to sleep."

"You were outside when it happened?"

"Yeah. With Master Sergeant Wegryn and Second Lieutenant Matheson, checking the perimeter sensors." She tilted her head back, looking upwards. "Near as I can tell, the damage to the hull was caused by a sack of blastbombs—shrapnel-less grenades. They were trying to trap Armando in that section. It's the longest run of corridor with an exterior wall. Clearly, they mistimed it. But it was the explosion that drew our attention."

"No radio alert?"

She raised an eyebrow. "Covert ops, Dredd. Emphasis on 'covert.' Radio signals would be something of a giveaway. We do have an emergency link to... let's just say it's another base. I guess Captain Harrow must have figured that she was more likely to get a faster response from the prison than from Colonel D'Angelo."

"Who's that?"

"In charge of this entire operation. He and his elite guard are off-base right now: he has a lot of other projects to oversee."

"So what now?"

Vine shrugged. "Good question. I guess I'm the acting CO until the Colonel makes contact—we have no way to contact *him*—but that could be weeks, even months. I can't stay here with only the corporal for company."

SUB-WARDEN COPUS STOOD in the doorway and looked from me to First Lieutenant Vine to the still-unconscious Corporal Armando, and then back to me. "What the hell, Dredd?"

As Kurya tended to Vine's and Armando's injuries, I explained the situation to Copus, then said, "Either we station some people out here until Colonel D'Angelo makes contact, or we bring them back with us."

McConnach said, "Sir, that could work out all right. Word will already have spread throughout the prison about the out-of-control freighter. We just need to brief Vine and keep Armando sedated, tell everyone that they're survivors of the crash."

Again, Copus looked towards Armando. "And his skin-colour? How do we explain that?"

"Asteroid miner," I said. "We say that they used the same process that we do here. Except that it's voluntary."

McConnach nodded. "Yeah, that's good. And that explains how he survived the crash intact. Extra-tough skin. Vine survived because he shielded her. Makes him a hero. People are less inclined to question heroes."

I didn't agree with that, but this wasn't the time for that argument.

Copus absently chewed on his lower lip for a few seconds, then said, "Drokk it. We have no choice. Standard maritime laws still apply out here—you have to offer help to anyone in distress. But if that psycho gets loose and freaks out, I'm going to put a round between his ears, don't care how much the military want to hide him."

"That's the right call," I said.

Copus turned away. "I don't need your approval or consent, Dredd. You, Wightman and Kurya stay put."

McConnach and Sloane stood guard while Copus and Takenaga coordinated with Vine on the process of checking the base room by room, level by level, locking every door as the rooms were cleared. They had to account for every corpse, every weapon. They left the bodies where they found them— there'd be an investigation at some stage—but they logged and tagged them.

Wightman and I were tasked with carrying Armando back up to the entrance, then everyone took part in a lengthy discussion on how to transport the unconscious Corporal Armando from the base to the bus. With his hands cuffed there was no way we could put him into an environment suit—and it's already hard enough putting a suit on someone unconscious: for a start, it takes forever just to get their fingers into the gloves—so in the end we just put a helmet on him, used strips of environment suit puncture-tape to seal the edges around his neck, rested an oxygen tank on his chest, and carried him out on a stretcher.

Getting him through the bus's airlock was even more tricky, because it can really only take one person at time. Puncture-tape came in handy again: we used it to secure him upright to the inner wall of the airlock—I say "we," but it was mostly me. It wasn't easy with so little room in which to work. When I was sure he wasn't going to topple forward, I left him there, closed the outer door, then watched as the inner door opened and McConnach and Sloane peeled the tape free and carried him inside.

Then Kurya, Wightman and I were each frisked and scanned twice before we were allowed back onto the bus.

I took a last look at the base as we rolled away, but Vine had shut off the corridor light and now all that I could see was a rocky plateau.

The journey back was a little slower, but more direct: no one cared any more about hiding our path.

Along the way, Copus and Vine conversed with a brow-creasing intensity, their voices too low for me to overhear. Takenaga slept, while McConnach and Kurya kept watch on Armando, who was stretched out across the back seat, still unconscious.

Wightman sat in the seat in front of me, with his back to the side window so that he could keep an eye on everyone else. "Thirty-*four?*" he asked.

I nodded.

"Damn. Why the hell didn't Vine just put the drokker down?"

"She won't say."

"Maybe he's bullet-proof?"

"Could be, but I doubt it."

Wightman started patting his pockets. "You hungry?"

I realised that I was. "Haven't eaten since breakfast."

"It's on me." He hauled himself out of his seat and made his way to the storage lockers, then came back with four medium-sized tubes of food-paste. "What do you feel like, Rico? We've got... Vegetable Stew, Mock Chicken Dinner, All-Feast, or Supplementary."

"Like it makes one damn bit of difference." I held out my hand and he slapped the Vegetable Stew and Supplementary tubes into it.

I missed food more than anything else. Real, proper actual food that you could taste and chew. When they modify your body to survive on Titan, they don't just reinforce your skin and replace your lungs: part of the process involves sealing up your mouth and nose. They cut a hole in your throat and fit a voicebox, and it's through that hole that you eat and drink.

Upside: you no longer have to brush your teeth.

Downside: everything else. You can't taste much any more. You have to re-learn how to talk. You spend the first couple of months genuinely worried that you might drown in your own saliva. You can't even properly kiss someone. Can't whistle, either, though that's less of a big deal.

By now I was used to feeding myself through the voicebox, but I was still a little self-conscious about it. I didn't like anyone watching at me as I did it.

Wightman had no such restrictions. He popped out the voicebox and held it in his left hand while he squirted the entire contents of the Mock Chicken Dinner through the hole in one go. Then he sat back and pretended to dab at the corners of his mouth with a handkerchief. "Ah... bland, unsatisfying and soul-destroying, just how I like it. My lack of compliments to the chef."

I consumed half of the Supplementary tube—a brown paste supposedly laced with all the minerals and vitamins a person might need in one day—and tried not to think about a large bowl of macaroni and cheese.

There's a story that gets passed on from one mod to another about the very first guy to get the treatment, back on Enceladus. Apparently he starved to death because he just couldn't keep the food down. Could be true. There were times when I thought I really couldn't face another meal squeezed from a damn tube, but I knew that the only sane approach was to get it over with and try to think of something else.

For any prisoner, in the early days of the sentence, a good distraction is to try to calculate the number of days you have left. But pretty soon you've worked it out exactly, and confirmed it by doing it again a few times, and after that you just subtract another day each morning.

In my spare moments, or when things were particularly tough, I would often think of my patrol routes in Mega-City One, try to recall every side-street, every store, every block. It wasn't easy, and on a couple of occasions I got stuck on a name and that was maddening—I once had to ask sub-warden Giambalvo to look up a map of the city and tell me the name of the block between Sal Schoeppner Apartments and Kenji Mizoguchi Block, because I was sure I'd end up with an aneurysm trying to remember it. I chose Giambalvo because I knew she'd worked in the same sector. She told me to take a hike, but the next day she stopped me in the corridor and said, "You drokker, Dredd. You had me awake all night wondering about that. I had to get up and check it out. Windward Ranch Habitats."

I was just squeezing out the last of the Vegetable Stew paste when Copus shouted for everyone's attention.

"This is the story we're... You *listening*, Kurya? This is the story we're going to tell when we get back to the mine. Do not discuss the real situation even amongst yourselves, understood? Four days ago the freighter *Carol Masters* was en route to Mimas when a power-coupling blew in the engine core. The crew had no choice but to detach the core and use the thrusters to steer towards Titan. They were able to slow a little so that they didn't completely break up in the atmosphere, but they hit hard. It came down four kilometres south of Brunel's Ridge. All hands lost with the exception of Petty Officer Salome Vine and engineer John Armando. In this version of the truth, Armando is a former asteroid miner who voluntarily underwent the same skin-reinforcing procedure as Wightman and Dredd and the other mods. He suffered a serious concussion in the crash and has been reacting with extreme hostility, hence the need for the cuffs. Any questions?"

Takenaga asked, "Why concoct a story at all? We place them both in crew quarters. If we dock at the south entrance, we can go straight through to Admin without encountering any other prisoners."

"Because the chances are they're going to be with us for four months, until the next Earth ship comes."

Vine said, "That's unless my superiors decide to check on Huygens Base, in which case they'll get no answer and come looking. We operated with almost complete autonomy, so there are no visits scheduled, and surprise inspections don't happen this far out."

"Yeah, but what did you actually *do* there?" Wightman asked.

"That's classified."

Copus added, "And it's none of your damn business anyway, Wightman. Are we all clear on the story?"

I looked around at the others. They seemed to be satisfied, but I wasn't. I said, "What was the freighter carrying to Mimas?"

He hesitated long enough for me to know that they hadn't thought that far ahead. "Doesn't matter."

I said, "Tectonic surveillance equipment that's too delicate to launch on its own, and has to be set up and calibrated by hand. The expert in question was Professor... Paxton. Ilia Paxton. Female, forty years old, two kids. She didn't want to be there, but she was the only one qualified."

Copus raised his eyes. "You're overpainting this picture, Rico. No one is going to ask."

"Four months," I reminded him. "Boss, when a new guard

arrives at the prison, we all know everything about them by the end of their first *week*."

McConnach said, "He's right about that. What type of ship was the freighter? How many crew? Captain's name? Where was it coming from? You said it didn't completely break up in the atmosphere, so what parts of it did? Was the hull breached and *that's* how everyone died? How come Vine and Armando came out completely intact? Maybe there was a couple of others who survived the impact, but they died before we got to them. We can build on that, too, if we say that there was a crevasse or something in the way and we had to go around it, but if we hadn't, then we would have got there sooner and maybe we could have saved one of the others. Then..." She trailed off as she realised everyone was staring at her. "Sorry."

I said, "Don't be. Most of us trained to be Judges. We were taught how to spot the holes in fake alibis. And so were at least half of the other prisoners. Consistency and solidity is the key to credibility."

Zera Kurya said, "You are all wrong. We tell the other prisoners and guards that it was a crashed covert military vessel. We give them no further answers because we *know* no further answers."

I didn't want to admit it in front of the others, but she was right. Keep the story as close to the truth as possible.

One by one we drifted off to sleep. The last thing I remember was Sloane singing "The Ballad of Skrimpy Doodle" to himself as he drove. He was getting the words wrong, but I didn't correct him. He looked happy and there wasn't a lot of that to be found on Titan.

Twenty-Four

THE BUS SCREECHED and hissed and clunked to a stop and I was awake before the final judder of its brakes.

Sloane was saying, "Mister Copus...? Oh, drokk... someone wake up Copus." He turned back and yelled, "*Now*, drokk it!"

The sub-warden had been stretched out across two seats. He rolled to his feet and started to haul himself towards the front. "What? What is it?"

First Lieutenant Vine was already standing next to Sloane, looking out through the windscreen. "It's a ship. An Omicron-Twelve. About two hundred metres dead ahead."

Sloane said, "It just set down. Flew straight overhead, hovered for a bit, then set down."

"Check the radio," Vine said, checking the datapad fixed to her wrist. "Scan bands two, four and five if you don't get an immediate signal."

I was in the process of getting out of my seat when Giambalvo said, "Stay put, Dredd. All of you."

Copus asked Vine, "Anything?"

She nodded. "Just come in... It's Colonel D'Angelo. They picked up my call from the base to this bus. We're to hold position until further notice."

Sloane turned around to face Copus, "Nothing on the air, sir. Can't even get a link to the mine."

Vine said, "They'll be jamming everything. We might as well get comfortable. Could be a while before they decide it's safe."

Kurya, Wightman and I settled back. We were prisoners; we were used to being trapped in a small space with nothing to do. And Vine seemed calm enough too. It was the guards who would crack first.

It was almost an hour before Vine's datapad beeped again. She showed the message to Copus and he nodded slowly before turning around to the rest of us.

"Need a volunteer. Dredd, that's you."

I pulled myself to my feet. "I swear, when I get home, first thing I'm going to do is send a dictionary to every guard on this damn moon."

"They know we have Corporal Armando, and they want him back."

"So why am *I* the volunteer? Why not him?"

Copus said, "Walk towards their ship. You'll be met halfway by a member of the colonel's team."

"And...?"

"And that's all we know." He nodded towards the airlock. "Get moving."

I stepped into the airlock and waited for the air to be pumped out, then the outer door opened and I stepped out into the Bronze.

Humans are adaptable and can get used to anything. Occasionally I forget that I'm no longer the man I once was, and then something happens to remind me. As I emerged from the shadow of the Big Bus there was a part of me that expected to be hit by a warm breeze, and when that didn't happen I remembered that I no longer really felt the cold or the heat.

It's the little things that can crush a prisoner's spirit. Common experiences that we all take for granted until they're no longer there. Here's another one: using your teeth to tear open a candy-bar wrapper. Okay, so there's not much candy on Titan, but that's not the point: my teeth were now locked away behind sealed lips.

I glanced back at the bus to see Copus glaring at me with his usual Why-isn't-it-done-yet? expression, then returned my attention to the task at hand: walk until I meet some other person. Not the most arduous of projects.

I'd gone about fifty paces when I saw the ship. It was smaller than the bus. Even smaller than a H-Wagon back home. It looked like someone had taken a large block of metal and hollowed out the inside, stuck the biggest engines they could find on the back, a big window on the front, and an assortment of small wings at odd angles. I didn't know a lot about spacecraft, but this thing looked about as easy to fly as the average kitchen.

A hatch opened in the side and a man wearing full body armour climbed out. He looked in my direction for a second, then reached back into the craft and pulled out a large gun. My eyesight isn't the best, but even from here I recognised a fully-automatic assault rifle.

He slung the rifle onto his left shoulder, then started to stride towards me.

The closer we came, the more of his armour I could see. Close-fitting, like the armour Vine was wearing, but darker. No insignia or rank-markings. A few scratches on the shoulder-plates and chest-plate. Utility belt, with a handgun hanging from it.

His helmet was full face, of course, with an almost opaque visor. Given how poor the sunlight is on Titan, I figured he had to have light-enhancing tech inside the helmet.

We were maybe ten metres apart when the wind picked up suddenly, a brief but powerful gust. I was used to that, but this guy wasn't: he swayed a little, almost stumbled. I liked that. It humanised him.

I called out, "You'd want to watch out for that. We get a lot of weather here on Titan."

He stopped two metres in front of me, but didn't reply.

"So who are you?" I asked, looking at my own reflection in his visor.

"Identify yourself."

"Rico Eustace Dredd. Prisoner. Former Mega-City One Judge. You?"

"Sears."

"That's it?" I asked. "No other name? No rank or title?"

"Identify all persons on your transport. Names, duties, ranks."

I recognised this approach. It's one of the methods we learned during Basic Interrogation back at the Academy of Law. Abrupt, impersonal, to-the-point. It makes the suspect feel like they have no control over the situation. It often works, too, but that depends on the suspect. In some cases it triggers their defences and they clam up even tighter.

I found myself reacting that way. Part of me was thinking, *Don't tell this drokker anything!* but then I caught myself. I wasn't a suspect. I hadn't done anything wrong. Well, not in the current context.

So I told him who was on board the bus, and he just stood there. He didn't nod or react in any other way.

When I was done, he asked, "Have you or any members of your party established contact of any kind with your own HQ since you departed on this mission?"

"Not to my knowledge."

"Return to your transport. Inform your CO that you are ordered to reverse your course and return to Huygens Base."

I decided that it was my turn to be the enigmatic one. I stood still and didn't respond.

He repeated himself, a little more aggressively. "Return to your transport. Inform your CO that you are ordered to reverse your course and return to Huygens Base."

I asked, "Is that an order? Because as far as I can see, you have no rank. And even if you had, that makes not one damn iota of difference to me, because I'm not in the military. You have no authority over me."

Keeping his arms by his side, Sears shrugged his left shoulder and his assault rifle slid down his arm and into his hand. Clearly a heavily practised manoeuvre, but still impressive. And probably very unsettling if you're already nervous around people in authority.

I said, "Cheap trick. But I was a Judge—that doesn't scare me."

He regarded me silently for another couple of seconds. "You have your orders." Then he turned and started walking back towards the small craft.

I called out after him, "What if we don't comply?"

He just kept walking, so I headed back towards the bus.

Before I reached it, Sears' ship had lifted off and passed back overhead.

Back inside, I told Copus what had happened, then he, Takenaga and Vine went to a quiet corner to discuss the situation.

Me, if I'd been in command, I wouldn't have wasted that time. I'd have gone back to Huygens. Not because I felt threatened by Sears, but because I still wanted to know what they'd been doing in that place, aside from getting halfway to turning Corporal Armando into a mod.

Twice during their huddled discussion, Copus turned to me and asked, "You're *sure* he said nothing else?"

"I'm sure."

Eventually, they reached a decision. "We're going back to Huygens Base," Copus said. "Mister Sloane, start us up and turn us around."

As the engines rumbled back to life, Wightman groaned. "Aw hell. Just realised. Mister Copus, me and Rico are gonna have to purge our filters soon."

Copus grunted his annoyance. "How long can you put it off?"

"Couple of hours," I said.

"Our ETA is three hours twenty," Sloane said.

"Should be okay. If not, we can do it here in the bus."

I could see Sloane failing to suppress a shudder at that. He'd clearly been a witness to mods purging their sinus filters.

Copus said, "Hold off as long as possible."

* * *

SLOANE'S ESTIMATE OF the journey time turned out to be on the money: three hours and twenty-one minutes later, the big bus rumbled to a stop a hundred metres from the Huygens Base plateau.

Sitting in the seat behind me, Wightman muttered, "We are never getting home, are we? The marines are gonna execute us or something." His voice was thick, clogged, his breathing starting to sound sticky. I knew mine would be too, if I spoke.

A little under eight hours earlier we'd had the fun and games of carrying a cuffed, unconscious man from Huygens Base onto the bus, and now we were faced with doing the same thing again in reverse, and our supply of puncture-tape was running low. Copus, Vine and McConnach were deep in discussion as to how we were going to manage it when a man's voice from the back of the bus said, "I can walk."

I looked towards Armando. He was still lying across the back seat, facing away from us with his hands triple-cuffed behind his back.

Vine slowly approached him. "Corporal... are you lucid?"

"Is that you, Lieutenant?"

"It's me. Corporal, do you know where you are?"

He twisted around a little. "Prison transport. From what I can see of it, it looks like two old Bekka Trundlers welded together."

Sloane quietly said, "He's not wrong there."

Copus eased himself past Vine and stopped two seats away from Armando. "Corporal, my name is Martin Copus, sub-warden at the prison. You and Vine are the only two survivors of Huygens Base."

A pause, then Armando said, "I know."

Copus glanced back at us. "You know?"

"I know what happened. I remember what went down. But I wasn't in control..."

Vine asked, "Corporal, what did Doctor Riahi tell you that caused you to *lose* control?"

"I... I don't recall that. Lieutenant, permission to speak freely?"

Vine said, "Go ahead."

"I'm starving and I pretty urgently need to use the head, sir."

"Understood. Corporal, we were stopped en route to the prison by Colonel D'Angelo, who has ordered us to return to Huygens. Which is where we are now. We'll get you inside, but we're not taking off the cuffs. Not after what happened this morning."

Armando squirmed around until he was lying on his back, then swung his feet onto the floor, wedged them under the seat in front, and used them to lever himself up into a sitting position. He took a moment to look at all of us, one by one.

When his eyes locked with mine, he just nodded—acknowledgement to the one man who had beaten him—then he moved on.

Lieutenant Vine said, "All right. Let's go. Mister Copus?"

The sub-warden did his usual instruction-barking and they donned their environment suits, then we filed off the bus, with Armando second-last—wearing just a helmet sealed with re-used strips of puncture-tape—and Vine following.

Two armour-wearing marines stood guard outside the blast hole in the wall of the fake plateau.

Copus said, "We don't know the situation. All of you keep

your hands to yourselves, say nothing unless you have to. Lieutenant, lead the way."

I was about to fall in line with the others when Copus put his hand on my arm. When I glanced back at him, he was shaking his head.

He waited until the others were several metres away before nodding and gesturing for me to walk ahead of him.

"I know what you're thinking, boss," I said. "This whole situation stinks like the Resyk drains on a hot summer's day."

"Meaning?"

"If you're running a top-secret military project and something goes horribly wrong and then some civilians come in to rescue the survivors, well, it seems to me that you might get to thinking that those civilians are not part of the solution at all. They've become part of the problem."

"Yeah," he said. "That's what I figured *you* were thinking. Not me. You're a perp, Dredd, so you think like a perp and you assume everyone else does too. I agree that this is a highly-charged situation, but the one thing it does *not* need is you trying to be a hero if something goes wrong. When we get inside, you'll keep your mouth shut unless I say otherwise. Understood?"

"I won't say anything." Not because I felt intimidated by him. Hell, I *liked* Copus. He reminded me of myself in a lot of ways. No stomm, get the job done, we're not here to be friends. If more people were like us, the human race wouldn't be so screwed up.

Take your average start-up small company, for example. It might have, say, ten employees: one boss and nine workers. They all understand each other's clearly-defined roles, they know what they have to do, so they get the job done. Sure, they have some fun along the way, but each one of them knows that ultimately the work takes priority. But then the company is successful and expands. Ten years later, it's got a hundred employees. One big boss overseeing three or four department chiefs, each department divided into sub-sections, each sub-section with five or six people who have no idea what anyone else in the company does, but they're damn sure that everyone else is getting paid more than they are. And now the company's just another cluster of grumbling employees who hate their jobs and do the bare minimum of work to avoid getting fired.

That's why someone like Copus is a good leader. Chief Judge Fargo was the same. If you're doing your job, you don't have time to worry about how much your contemporaries are getting paid, and it's not important anyway.

Some of the guards were heel-dragging daydreamers. Kalai Takenaga was a bit like that. She was pleasant enough, but just didn't seem to care much about the job. When we were out on the surface scanning for iridium deposits, we always knew that she would call a halt to it and end the shift as soon as the quota was reached or the time was up. She would literally be watching the clock *and* the weight of the yield. She didn't care whether we talked or sang or told jokes, as long as the work got done, and she rarely interacted with us unless it was to correct someone who said "could of" or misused "whom."

But the other guards would often push us harder. For some of them it was a matter of personal pride that each shift finished with a higher yield than the last.

Sure, it was practically slave labour and we prisoners hated every minute of it, but that's not the point. In that example, it's not about us. It's about the guards.

Back at the Academy, Judge-Tutor Semple used to tell us, "The average person can make better music by playing the radio than by playing the piano, but it's not nearly as satisfying and it achieves nothing new. There's no pride in that."

Still, it bugged me that Copus had singled me out. I'd never given him any reason not to trust me.

Okay, it could be argued that I'd killed four wardens that time we were trapped out in the Bronze; but that had been to save my own life, and Copus didn't really know the full story.

Some of the prisoners were constantly in trouble, always fighting against the system, but that was a master-class in futility. The best way to avoid drowning is to swim *with* the flow, not against it.

So I let it go. No point in being offended because offence is like worry: it gets you nowhere and it's just one more thing to carry around with you.

Ahead, Vine and Armando passed between the two marines and in through the ragged hole, followed by McConnach, Wightman and the others.

Then it was my turn. As I set foot on the base's foamed-steel floor, a thought occurred to me and I turned around to mention it to sub-warden Copus, but the expression on his face told me to keep it to myself for now.

Twenty-Five

ONCE WE WERE all inside the sealed-off corridor and the air had been restored, one of the marines opened an inner door and said, "Follow me. Single file."

It was the same route I'd taken earlier with Vine.

The marine walked ahead of us, and the other behind us. There was almost no way to tell them apart, not counting different notches and scratches on their armour. No insignia, no numbers, no different blocks of colour.

Wightman must have been thinking along the same lines, because as we passed a third marine standing guard outside a door, he asked, "So, your visors have a HUD that tells you who's who, right?"

He didn't respond to that, but fell into step alongside the one trailing us.

We were channelled into a large, empty room off the main

corridor where a fourth marine was waiting. Again, he was wearing armour identical to the others', but I said, "A pleasure to see you again, Sears."

No reaction, but I was sure that under his helmet he'd be angry. I wasn't about to admit that I recognised a particular scratch on his left boot.

Sears said, "Remove your environment suits and leave them in this room, along with any and all weapons or electronic equipment on your person."

"I'm sub-warden Martin Copus. I want to speak to Colonel D'Angelo."

"Just do as you're instructed, sub-warden."

Wightman and I waited as the others stripped off their suits, then we were all very efficiently and thoroughly searched and frisked. That's something you get used to very quickly as a prisoner: we were frisked every time we returned from the mines or from outside. It soon gets so that if they forget about the frisking, you feel left out.

The marines spent a few moments with me and Wightman, examining our cybernetic enhancements, then they ordered us out into the corridor—I noticed that Sears locked the door as he left—and again marched us through the base.

Our path took us past the infirmary, through a narrow mess-hall, and into an empty hangar that clearly doubled as the base's gymnasium: basketball hoops had been attached to opposite walls and court-lines had been crudely spray-painted on the floor.

Sears said, "Stand in the centre of the room. You will not speak."

Sloane asked, "Why not?"

The soldier closest to him slammed him in the stomach with the butt of his rifle.

Copus jumped forward and was instantly the target of three further weapons.

Then the door opened again, and another marine entered, accompanied by a slender, slightly awkward-looking young man in a somewhat creased dress uniform: he'd clearly been wearing it under an environment suit. Watching his bearing, I concluded that this man had never seen combat.

The young man nodded to Sears, who said. "This is Colonel Peter D'Angelo."

Colonel D'Angelo said, "You will all be silent unless directed otherwise." He slowly turned to look at Copus. "Is that clear, or is a further demonstration required?"

The sub-warden nodded. "It's clear. But, look, what the drokk *is* this?"

A handgun boomed twice and everyone flinched. Copus staggered backwards, clutching his left shoulder. "Son of a..." He collapsed into a sitting position.

One of the soldiers stepped forward and pressed the muzzle of his gun right into the centre of Copus's forehead. "You heard the colonel—not one more drokkin' *word!*"

The colonel said, "Stand down, Lancaster." The soldier stepped back, leaving a scorch-mark on Copus's face where the still-hot muzzle had burned it.

The colonel said, "One of you tend to his wound."

Zera Kurya crouched down next to Copus and tore open his shirt. "Clean shot, clipped the muscle. No major damage as far as I can see." She glanced around. "Steripatch?"

One of the marines pulled a pack of steripatches from a

pouch on her belt and tossed it to Kurya. She peeled off the backing from a patch, and slapped it over the wound.

Colonel D'Angelo gestured to Vine. "Come forward, First Lieutenant Vine and Corporal Armando."

Vine and Armando stepped up to him.

To Armando, he said, "You are a disappointment, soldier. A failure." The colonel's eyes narrowed as he turned to Vine. "You broke protocol, Lieutenant."

She didn't respond to that. I don't blame her; they'd just shot Copus for speaking up.

"This is a covert operation and your primary goal is to keep it that way. You invited civilians onto the base. You are hereby stripped of your rank and will be court-martialled."

D'Angelo moved away from Vine and peered at the rest of us. "Huygens Base is a highly classified facility; you were never supposed to know of its existence. This facility was established at the same time as your prison, along with a direct link connecting the base to your emergency system. That link was supposed to be used only in extreme circumstances. But Captain Harrow used that link to initiate contact with Governor Dodge eight years ago. I believe that Dodge was under the impression that said contact was sanctioned and within the purview of Harrow's mission. Harrow's personal logs show that she and Dodge had an arrangement to supply this base with fresh fruit and vegetables in return for the use of certain unspecified equipment." D'Angelo walked up to Copus and looked down at him. "What equipment?"

Copus shrugged. "This is the first I've heard about it."

"You're lying. Do so again, and the next shot will do permanent damage."

Copus used his uninjured arm to wipe a bead of sweat from his forehead. "Harrow agreed to recalibrate the base's satellite to scan the moon for iridium deposits. Our own scanners can penetrate eighty metres at most, depending on the bedrock. The satellite is much more powerful. The data she returned meant we were able to almost double our yield."

The colonel took all this in without a word. His body language was hard to read, but it seemed to me that he wasn't discovering anything he didn't already know.

He returned to Vine. "You understand what you have done, Lieutenant? The breach of security you have committed? Permission to speak."

"Sir, I—" She abruptly cut herself off, inhaled deeply through her nostrils, and stared unblinking at the slender Colonel. "Salome Pamelina Vine. Marine Corps, First Lieutenant. Serial number M-triple-zero-two-four-seven-four-zero-one."

D'Angelo frowned at her. "You will respect the chain of command, Vine. This is a critical situation and your forthcoming court-martial will not be derailed or delayed by any attempts to claim ignorance or duress. You will answer any and all questions to the fullest of your ability and the best of your knowledge. Subsequent discovery of failure on your part to disclose any related pertinent evidence will be considered an act of sedition or sabotage."

I looked across the room towards Wightman, who looked back and gave me a slight shrug. Everyone else was watching D'Angelo and Vine.

I broke the silence. "I have a question."

Colonel D'Angelo started to turn towards me, but stopped, as though he'd concluded that I wasn't worth the effort. "If that prisoner speaks again, I'll consider it to be a deliberate attempt to hinder this investigation."

No one responded to that, so D'Angelo said, "You are all confined to this room until further notice."

He left, followed by all of the marines except Armando and Vine. The hiss of the closing door was followed by the unmistakeable sound of the lock engaging.

McConnach began, "So... what the *drokk* is that all—"

Armando softly but sharply said, "Room's bugged. No cameras in here, but they could be listening."

Takenaga approached Copus, and as she helped him to his feet softly asked, "Ideas?"

Standing in the centre of the room, Vine looked at all of us in turn. "The corporal is right. The colonel's people will be listening. But it doesn't matter because he's going to execute us all anyway, just as soon as he's sure you haven't spoken to anyone else."

Wightman asked, "Why? What does he think we've *done*?"

Corporal Armando said, "You know about me. That's all. You know I exist." He looked down at his cuffed hands. "I'm proof of the project's failure."

Vine nodded. "The purpose of Huygens Base is to build a better soldier. It has to be done out here, far from the reach of anyone on Earth. Covert factors from Mega-City One, Mega-City Two and Texas-City working together... it's more than enough to have the Sov-Blocks and every other city worried." She turned to me. "A lot of the work was inspired by you, Dredd."

I said, "I'm far from the first prisoner to have his body modified."

"That's not what I'm talking about. A long time ago Morton Judd put into action his plans to build better Judges. You and your brother were the success that inspired Colonel D'Angelo to do the same with the marines. There's a facility on Oberon that's growing clone embryos from heavily-tweaked DNA. I've seen what they have so far..." She barely suppressed a shudder. "The results are not promising. They're a long way from success. That's why D'Angelo has turned to body-modification instead. Again, inspired by you."

"How so?"

"Captain Harrow's reports mentioned discovering you out in the Bronze, almost dead. She wrote that if you and... Guildford, was it? ...If you'd swapped places, you would almost certainly have survived long enough to make it back to the prison on foot."

Wightman said, "Wait, stop! For Grud's sake, the more she tells us, the more likely it is that the Colonel will want to execute us!"

"That's inevitable," Armando said. "I know this is worth nothing, but I'm sorry. It was *my* malfunction that sparked this. Everyone in this room will die and D'Angelo will craft a credible reason. He has almost limitless resources and he'll do anything to prevent his superiors from learning the truth."

McConnach asked, "How long do we have?"

Vine said, "As soon as he's certain that we didn't make contact with the prison, that's it. He'll give the order."

I knew that it was time to make some sort of move, but exactly what I *could* do, I wasn't sure. So I said, "That could be bad... if he suspects that one of us *did* talk to someone at the prison, then he might just decide to wipe them out too."

As I spoke I turned in a slow circle, examining the room. No windows, and the only way in was the doors through which we'd entered.

"Except of course that until a couple of minutes ago, all we knew was that this was a base, not what it was for. That's on *you*, Vine." I looked at Takenaga, put one finger to my lips and beckoned her forward. "And you too, Armando. If you hadn't lost control... But why don't you do that again? Go berserk and break us out of here?"

Takenaga stopped in front of me wearing a puzzled expression. I gestured that I wanted the pen in her pocket, and she reluctantly handed it over.

I crouched down and snapped the pen in two, still speaking: "But you can't, can you? Something triggered that, some part of the experiment. *That's* what he's covering up. Not that you're a failure, because clearly you're *not*. You're rational and in control." I popped out the pen's ink capsule and used the edge of the lid to prise the stopper from the capsule. "But still. You took down over thirty of your fellow soldiers without getting so much as a scratch and there's no way *all* of them were caught unaware." I put the pen's nib flat on the floor under my heel, then slowly rocked back until I heard a tiny *crack*.

Inside was a circuit board half the size of a fingernail clipping that held the tiniest lithium battery in common use, not much bigger than a grain of salt. "Some of them had to have heard the gunfire, right?"

Not a lot of people knew that everything they wrote with their handy, disposable ball-point pen was logged in the pen's memory circuits, and there was a reason for that: if they did, they'd stop using those pens. There've been a number of cases where the evidence provided by such pens has proven vital. Not *many* cases, but even one perp caught is worth it. So the people don't know that their pens are logging their words, and they'll never find out, because Judges are rarely required to reveal the source of their evidence.

By now, everyone was crowded around me, but I tried not to let that distract me. This was tricky enough as it was, let alone having to do it while keeping up a running diatribe to distract whoever might be listening.

"Still, I'm betting that Colonel D'Angelo isn't too pleased that his prototype super-soldier was beaten by a former Judge who hasn't been on the streets in years." I pulled the battery away from the board, then motioned for everyone but Armando to step back.

"He's not going to take that lying down." As I said that, I gestured for Armando to sit down next to me.

He looked puzzled, but curious, and did as I suggested. I made a circular motion with my index finger to indicate that he should roll onto his side, and when he did, I lay down almost flat on my stomach with my face close to the handcuffs on his wrists.

The pen's ink capsule contained about eight drops. Just about enough.

I'd never done this before, and certainly hadn't ever expected to do it in full view of sub-warden Copus, but we weren't left with a lot of choice. "Maybe he should have just recruited *Judges*, right? Let the Academy of Law train his troops for him and then pick the best. If he'd come to me after I graduated, I would have said yes."

Each set of cuffs had an electronic lock that responded to a coded—and uncrackable—signal from its corresponding key. But every electronic device needs a source of power, and in the cuffs that was a battery attached to the internal lock, the whole thing shielded in the cuffs' tough titanium-polymer shell. But batteries run down and have to be replaced or recharged; the polymer shell couldn't be permanently sealed.

Holding Armando's arms steady with one hand, I dripped some ink from Takenaga's pen onto the underside of the cuffs, at the seam, all around the tightly-fitting battery cover.

I silently counted the seconds while some of the ink filtered its way down into the cuffs, then at the six-second mark I dropped the pen's tiny lithium battery onto the ink.

The ink is marketed as safe—absolutely non-toxic, non-corrosive—and that's true. But it *is* highly conductive. The ink seeped into the cuffs' battery compartment, short-circuiting and discharging the battery. That shuts down the cuffs completely; a safety measure in case the prisoners attempt to break them open.

But the cuffs' circuitry is smart enough to know that the battery will have to be recharged at some point, and it can't be recharged if the prisoner is still *wearing* the cuffs: you don't let the prisoners have access to the charger. So to make sure that happens, if the circuitry detects only the tiniest trickle of power, it'll register that as an *almost*-discharged battery and use that last burst of power to open the lock.

Corporal Armando's cuffs went *click*, and fell open.

I stepped back, and everyone else in the room was staring at me.

Have to tell you, having my mouth sealed up was the only thing that kept me from grinning like an idiot.

Twenty-Six

I TOLD THE others, "No need to be silent. We should talk to each other. If D'Angelo's people *are* listening in, let them hear five different conversations. That'll keep them busy."

The others began to speak, awkwardly at first, but with growing confidence—and growing volume.

Leaning close and speaking so low that even someone standing a metre away wouldn't have heard, I asked Vine, "If we can get past the doors, how do we get out of the base?"

I'd realised something on the way in from the bus. We were entering the base via the blast-hole in the wall; but clearly there had to be other entrances. D'Angelo hadn't wanted us to use one because then we'd know where they were.

But Vine and Armando already knew.

She told me, "We're twenty metres underground now. All the useable exits are on the top level."

"And getting to them means going through the colonel's people... okay." I had to think about this. Our assets were meagre, to say the least. Of the guards, only Copus and Takenaga were—in my opinion—in fighting shape, and Copus was currently incapacitated, courtesy the bullet in his shoulder. Sloane moved at the speed of a tortoise trudging through tar, and McConnach was long past her prime. Of my fellow prisoners, only Zera Kurya would be of much use. Kellan Wightman had lost his edge. He would never have admitted it, and certainly worked hard to maintain the illusion that he was still a hard-as-depleted-uranium-nails Judge, but I could see the truth. Titan had broken him, as it had so many others.

Sloane tapped me on the shoulder and pointed towards Copus, who was now sitting against a side wall with the torn-off sleeve of his jacket wrapped around the wound in his arm.

I squatted next to him and he leaned forward a little so that he could whisper in my ear. "That was some trick with the cuffs, Rico. How long have you been sitting on that one?"

"Since long before my arrest."

"Heh. Well, I *know* you have a way out of this, don't you? Do what it takes to get us out. Don't let me down."

"I have some ideas, but mostly they begin with me being on the other side of those doors." I signalled to Vine, and when she was close enough, I asked, "How many marines does the colonel have in his guard? Judging by the size of his ship, it's not more than ten."

"Eleven. And it's safe guess they're all here—he never travels without all of them."

Copus asked, "But who's pulling *his* strings?"

"Unknown."

"Okay... If we can somehow take him down, what sort of retaliation can we expect?"

Again, Vine shrugged. "The project is black ops, so only a handful of people back home will know about it."

I said, "Then we need to take the colonel alive, because *he'll* know who his bosses are."

Everyone stopped talking almost at once, and I realised that they were all looking at the door.

The marine called Sears was entering through the doorway, followed by two of his colleagues. Sears stopped two steps in, and his men took up positions on either side of him. "Colonel D'Angelo has reached a decision. There has been a tragic accident and your transport never returned. Governor Dodge will be informed of the truth to encourage his silence. You..." He stopped, staring at Armando, then glanced at the soldier beside him. "Ordered you to search and scan them for *keys*, Malaki."

"Yes, sir. We did. Clean sweep."

"Then how the hell is Armando out of his cuffs? Put fresh ones on him and bring him. He's the sole survivor of Huygens Base."

The colonel wasn't the only one who had reached a decision.

I had never been the most popular of prisoners, but this was going to relegate me to the bottom of everyone's party list.

But, hey, sometimes you have to grow a pair and make the hard choices.

That's what being a Judge is all about. The hard choices. A perp attacks a citizen, hits him with a fire-axe, for example. So you come on the scene. What do you do? Chase down the perp and leave the wounded cit to bleed out, or tend to the cit in the hope that you *might* get a chance to track down the perp before he kills again? You can't do both. Pick one. And pick *fast*, because that cit is dying and the perp is fleeing.

Every day at the academy we were posed questions like that. Every day from the age of five.

There are few easy or obvious answers to those moral dilemmas. They're rarely clear-cut. A Judge learns to quickly and instinctively weigh up all the options, to make the choice that will lead to the best possible outcome. We don't always get it right—we're only human—but doing nothing is *also* a choice. How do you want to spend the rest of your life? "Damn it, if only I'd done *something*!" or "Damn it, I wish I'd done that *other* thing!"

So you act, because inaction is death, if not of the body, then of the soul.

I chose to act. I weighed up the options and the possibilities and the risks, and even as Sears was saying the words "Governor Dodge will be informed of the truth," I was starting to move.

Four steps to the left, keeping watch on the marines. I couldn't see their eyes behind those opaque faceplates, but I could read their body language: soldiers are trained to point their guns at the most obvious and immediate threat. Even when they're officially not targeting someone, their guns will have a bias in that direction.

All three of them had their weapons angled towards Armando. Understandable, because as far as they were concerned, Armando was the most dangerous person in the room. They clearly weren't taking into account that the only reason he was in the room was because someone had captured him. A wise soldier should conclude that maybe the captor was a bigger threat than the captive.

My step put me directly behind Kellan Wightman. His impressive height and build almost completely hid me from the marines' view, and his mass was vital for my plan.

I grabbed the back of his collar with my left hand, and his waistband with my right, and pushed hard.

I'm not as strong as some prisoners, but I'm no shrimp. I pushed Wightman hard enough and fast enough that he didn't even have time to react as he stumbled forward towards the marines.

They took half a second to realise what was happening: a large prisoner was rushing at them.

Another half-second to swing their guns in his direction.

But that was all I needed.

I pushed Wightman and dropped, ducked down to the side.

The marines opened fire and their automatic weapons ripped twin tracks of five-millimetre rounds across his body.

I hit the ground and lunged forward, crashing into the legs of the marine on Sears' right.

The marine went down, his gun still spraying the room—but I couldn't let myself think about that. We both crashed to the floor and I reached up and snatched the handgun from Sears' belt. Their armour was bullet-proof, I knew that, but at this range even a handgun could get through, if it hit the right spot: the elbow and knee joints... and directly under the helmet.

Two shots into the underside of the marine's jaw and the inside of his visor was red.

But Sears was no slacker. He swung his automatic at me and would certainly have blown me away if Corporal Vine hadn't slammed into the third marine—Malaki—knocking him against Sears. I swear I felt one of Sears' rounds skim across my back.

Vine ripped Malaki's gun from his hands, but Sears was recovering, swearing as he again tried to aim.

That was when Zera Kurya lunged at him and headbutted him square in the faceplate—that *had* to hurt—hard enough to knock him back out into the corridor.

I still had Sears' pistol: two point-blank shots to Malaki's right knee and he was down, screaming.

Then he slid *into* the room and I turned to see Corporal Armando dragging him in by the foot. "Get Sears!" Armando barked.

Kurya threw herself after him, using my back as a springboard, and again crashed into Sears, slamming him against the far wall.

I'd never seen Zera Kurya in action. I'd heard about her hand-to-hand skills, of course, but to actually watch her fighting was a unique experience.

Sears had fifteen, maybe twenty, kilogrammes on her, was wearing full body armour and was armed. She had her fists.

Her first punch cracked his helmet's visor and knocked his head back. The second punch was aimed at his throat, and snapped his head forward again.

A knee to the midriff, then she grabbed his right arm and hoisted him over her shoulder, slamming him face-first into the ground.

She pulled the rifle from his grip, jammed the muzzle under the backplate of Sears' armour and emptied the clip.

By the time she straightened up, blood was seeping from every joint in his armour.

Next to me, Vine was staring in shock. I could see she knew we'd done the right thing, but Sears and the others had been her colleagues, of a sort, and she'd already lost thirty-four others that day.

"They're going to kill us for this," she said to Armando. "At the very least."

I said, "They won't. They'll never find out."

On Copus's instructions, Sloane and McConnach started to remove the marines' armour and take their weapons. That was when I realised that Malaki was dead too.

I'd only shot him in the knee. Armando had broken his neck, barehanded.

But still, the others were looking at me as though *I* were the monster, rather than the man who'd just saved them.

Vine had Malaki's assault rifle aimed at my face. "Hand over the gun, Dredd."

"Not a chance. I just *saved* all of your—"

Armando snatched the gun from my hand before I even noticed him starting to move.

Takenaga said, "Jovus, Rico... Wightman."

I said, "What? It had to be done. They would have killed *all* of us."

"You used him as a decoy."

I nodded. "I know. And if I hadn't, we'd *all* be dead. Wightman was going to die anyway." I didn't see the problem. "You know why he was here, don't you? He was an arsonist. Put the lives of millions of cits at risk in Mega-City Two. Four of them died. And he was absolutely unrepentant. *You* know that, Takenaga—you ran his counselling sessions!"

Sloane said, "He was your *friend*."

I turned to him. "Doesn't change anything. Wightman was scum among scum and you know that. *Everyone* knows that.

He knew it. The only reason he wasn't executed when they caught him was because they need strong drokkers like him in this place. Now, thanks to him, we've got a chance that we didn't have before." I looked down at Wightman's mangled body. "There was no way we were all going to get out of this alive. So well done, Kellan. You became a hero at the last minute, even if you didn't know you were going to do it."

I stepped back, away from the still-spreading pool of Kellan Wightman's blood, and looked around at the others. "Are we going to spend the rest of the day debating the moral issues here, or are we going to deal with the actual threat?"

Copus glanced around the room. "Three down. So that's eight left, plus D'Angelo. Pity their armour is custom-made. Okay... Takenaga and Sloane, you'll stay here, guard Kurya and Dredd. Lock the room behind us."

I put my hand out to stop him. "No. You don't have the skills or the experience for this. We need to move fast and you're wounded. It should be me, Takenaga, Kurya, Armando and Vine. Sloane and McConnach are too slow and too soft."

McConnach said, "Mister Copus, we can't give guns to *prisoners!* Seriously, that's insane! Look what this drokker just did to his best friend!"

Copus stared at me through narrowed but unblinking eyes for a moment. "They're not *getting* guns. But Rico Dredd has got a will to live that dwarfs any of ours—that's what's going to get him out of this. And we don't have time to argue. You do this *right*, Dredd. Do we have an understanding?"

"You can count on me, boss. You *know* that. I—"

"Shut up. We're not friends." He turned to Takenaga, and jabbed an index finger at me. "This drokker gives you *any* reason to doubt him—any reason at all—shoot him in the head. *You're* in command here, Kalai. Not him."

Takenaga nodded. "Acknowledged."

Vine handed a communicator to Copus and tossed one of the marines' rifles to Takenaga. "The walls dampen the gunfire but they'll be expected to check in soon. We need to move."

Twenty-Seven

VINE AND ARMANDO led the way, rapidly swapping positions as they made their way along the steel-walled corridor, checking each room as they passed.

Takenaga followed, her bottom lip firmly clamped between her teeth and sweat on her forehead. I didn't know much about her background before she left Hondo City, but I'd always assumed she'd been a Judge. Right now, I wasn't so sure about that. She did *not* look comfortable. She was holding the assault rifle like it was poisonous.

Kurya and I held back. We'd each had similar training to the marines, but this was their territory, not ours, and we were unarmed. I intended to rectify that at the earliest possible opportunity, even though—as we'd already learned—a standard assault weapon wasn't effective against the marines' armour at much more than a metre.

Ahead, Armando silently signalled the all-clear, and he and Vine moved on.

Kurya gestured for me to go ahead.

I said, "No, you next."

She shook her head. "You still have Wightman's blood on you. Literally. I do not trust you."

"I'm unarmed," I said as I moved on.

"A weapon is not required for strangulation."

"Paranoid," I muttered. Then, over my shoulder, I added, "I had no choice, Zera. They were about to kill *all* of us. You'd have done the same thing."

"I would not. You betrayed a fellow prisoner, Rico. If we survive this and return to the prison, you will have a target on your forehead like you have never known. You'll be dead in a day."

"I don't care," I said. "I made the only logical choice."

"You could have picked one of the *guards!*" I'd never heard Kurya so close to losing her temper.

Takenaga turned back and glared at us, mouthing the words, "Shut up!"

We resumed following them.

Kurya was right. I could have chosen a guard. Sloane was the obvious choice, except that while he wasn't the only one who knew how to drive the bus—I could have driven it myself—no one else knew the way back to the prison.

The next obvious choice was Copus, but the position was all wrong: he'd been sitting with his back to the wall. No way to get behind him.

And Takenaga and McConnach were out for reasons of bulk, or lack thereof. It's hard to hide behind someone smaller than you.

So, yes, Kellan Wightman had died and that was sad on some levels; I'm sure that in most cases he would have had my back. But let's not forget that he was an arsonist, and guilty of manslaughter. Not to mention a racist: he despised the Fornies—the Californian Secessionists—with a fervour usually reserved for the sort of preacher you see on Sunday morning TV broadcasting from a mega-church.

He was not a nice guy, that's what I'm saying.

And it was also true that when, or *if*, we got back to the prison, word would get out about what I'd done, and my life would be a living hell. Every prisoner in the place was going to be out for my blood.

Except, of course, that I was now the only person who knew where Wightman had stashed his barrels of booze. Alcohol can be a great bargaining chip if used wisely.

Vine was crouched next to an open doorway, with Takenaga right behind her and Armando pressed flat against the opposite wall, his gun raised. Vine beckoned me closer, then whispered, "Corridor leads to the port stairwell... They're waiting for us."

"You're certain?"

"Heard the crackle of a radio."

"Armando should hang back. I'm guessing that he's the only reason they haven't rushed us. Without him, the colonel's entire project is a failure."

Then a man's voice, far too close for comfort, said, "You got that right, Dredd."

Vine's eyes widened, as I'm sure mine did too.

The voice was coming from the other side of the doorway, no more than a few centimetres away. If the wall hadn't been there, we'd have been leaning against each other.

Armando called out, "Who are you?"

"Lancaster. I've assumed command. I'm guessing that Sears, Malaki and Pohle are out of commission."

I said, "If you mean 'dead,' then yes."

"Sears was dumb to forget that the prisoners are former Judges," Lancaster said.

Vine said, "We have a situation here that can only end with all of your people dead, or all of ours. There's no middle ground."

"It would seem so. Vine, this facility has already been compromised. If we have to, we'll pull the plug on everything. We'll write off Armando. Colonel D'Angelo's not happy about that idea, but he understands. We've already lost so much. The sunk-cost fallacy can't continue indefinitely. Sooner or later, you've got to admit defeat. He's approaching that point now."

I said, "You don't have to do this, Lancaster."

"In the marines we're trained to follow orders without asking questions."

"In the Department of Justice we were trained to *always* ask questions."

"Is that so? Look where that's gotten you."

Armando said, "So I surrender to you, and you kill everyone here, or we continue to hold out and you kill us all anyway."

"Oh, it's—" Lancaster stopped, and we all heard footsteps approaching. "He's here."

We held our breath for a few seconds, then heard Colonel D'Angelo say, "Enough. I don't *want* to do this, but..." Something clicked on the other side, and the door silently and smoothly slid closed.

Most of the door was thick synthiglass, certainly bulletproof. The colonel now stood behind it, looking in at us.

"Door's locked from this side. Former First Lieutenant Vine knows this base. She'll confirm that there is no other way for you to reach us."

We all stood up, and he peered at us one by one, finishing with Armando. "You killed thirty-four people this morning, corporal. Thirty-four of your own colleagues."

Armando took a step closer to the door. "You're the one who turned me into a weapon."

"Perhaps. But I'm not the one who pulled the trigger. *You* did that."

I said, "So we have a stalemate."

Colonel D'Angelo smiled. "Not really, Dredd. It's not stalemate when one player holds all the cards."

"Cards? I was talking about chess. What the hell sort of game *you* playing?" I asked. I was standing beside and a little behind Takenaga, and she really was focussed on the colonel. "Whatever. Here's my move." Looking back now, it was shockingly easy to pull the gun from Takenaga's grip and press its muzzle against the back of Armando's neck.

He jumped, as did everyone else except for the colonel.

"You let us go or your experiment here is over forever."

"And when he's dead, so are you."

"Right," I said. "Now, that's what I mean by a stalemate. Neither of us can make a move."

"Unless we change the rules."

I nodded. "Now you're getting it."

"No, you're the one who's not getting it." D'Angelo stepped to the side a little to get a better view of the corporal. "You don't know *why* you went into a frenzy this morning, do you, Armando? You don't know what it was that set you off."

Colonel D'Angelo took a long, deep breath and let it out slowly, and it seemed to me that he was coming to a decision about something.

And then he said, "Doctor Riahi didn't only modify your skin, soldier. She reprogrammed the primitive centres of your brain with something she called the Berserker Protocol. You automatically respond to two key phrases. One to activate the protocol, the other to dismiss it. Only Riahi and I knew those phrases."

"That's what happened? *She* triggered the frenzy?"

D'Angelo said, "She did. The CCTV footage of the attack is of low quality, so there's no way to be certain, but I believe that Riahi wasn't awake at the time. She was talking in her sleep."

Armando swayed, and looked as though he was about to collapse. "No. No, that's not true."

"It *is*," the colonel said. "You're not a man anymore, Armando, you're a weapon. You said it yourself. You're a weapon, and you were triggered by accident." He shrugged. "A misfire. Another failure of the design team. Or another lesson learned, if you prefer. But I do still want to bring you in. It'll be difficult without Riahi's expertise, but we will attempt to adjust your programming so that it won't happen again. At least, not so easily."

Vine called out, "If you can do that, then you can probably *remove* the programming too."

D'Angelo nodded. "That's possible, but not what we want. Corporal Armando, we didn't spend billions of credits just to end up with a man who *used* to be an unstoppable killer. You understand that, don't you? Now, you will kill First Lieutenant Vine and your new friends here. And then we can clean up the last traces of this mess."

"I won't—"

D'Angelo said, "Unfettered Hematophagy."

I realised what the colonel was doing even before he had finished speaking the trigger-phrase.

My gun was still pressed against the back of Corporal John Armando's head. I pulled the trigger.

I was still too late.

Twenty-Eight

ARMANDO DODGED THE bullet. At point-blank range. It sounds impossible, I know, but trust me: I was there.

I had the muzzle of my gun pressed against the back of his neck, at the base of his skull, and as I squeezed the trigger he moved to the left, spinning at the same time, flicking his left arm up.

By the time the round exited the barrel, Armando had both moved out of its path and knocked my arm with his left elbow.

As the bullet ricocheted off the wall next to the door, Armando jabbed the heel of his right hand into my sternum, and pulled the gun from my grip with his left hand. And I thought *I'd* been slick, when I'd grabbed the gun from Takenaga.

I crashed back into the wall behind me, but I wasn't winded or wounded—I wasn't out of the fight yet.

In the second or so it took me to recover, Armando had

already disarmed Vine and was slamming my gun into Takenaga's stomach.

Armando tossed both guns aside, grabbed hold of Kurya's arm and was pulling her around, putting her between himself and me. Clearly, in this berserker state, he either didn't remember what had happened with Wightman or he didn't care. A sharp, hard punch to Kurya's face disoriented her, allowing him to manipulate her almost as though she were a plastic mannequin.

I had beaten him before, yes, but that had only been a few hours earlier. I was still aching from that fight, and I wasn't sure that I could do it again.

I could have made a grab for one of the guns, and I might have even reached it, but the angles, the positions... If I opened fire I'd hit Kurya for sure, possibly also Takenaga and Vine. I didn't want that.

Vine slammed her fist into Armando's right side with enough force to put a normal person out for good, but he barely registered it. Instead, he continued swinging Kurya around, shoving her against Vine.

I took a quick glance through the glass door: Colonel D'Angelo was staring back, watching the scene with a cold detachment. It seemed to me that he was studying Armando the same way an entomologist might study a pair of clashing insects.

But this wasn't the time for me to start studying *him*. I needed a plan.

I couldn't risk shooting Kurya, Vine or Takenaga; they were all accomplished fighters, and while they were no match for Armando, they *were* slowing him down.

He would kill them, I was certain, but right now, they were still getting in his way.

Often, the wise warrior knows he has to choose a path that his opponent won't expect. Armando—or whatever part of his brain was in control—knew I'd beaten him before, and expected me to try again. So I'd do something else.

Instead of diving for a gun, I rushed at him, reached past Kurya and slammed my fist into Armando's already-broken clavicle.

He didn't scream, but there was no mistaking the pain registering on his face.

He shoved Kurya aside and advanced on me, half staggering, clutching his shoulder. I knew I had one more shot: a quick side-kick aimed at his stomach. He instinctively dropped his hand to block the kick... That was when I added a last-second flick to my ankle that took some power out of the kick but shifted its aim.

I heard the broken halves of his clavicle crunch under my boot.

Then I ran.

Not because I was scared—I could probably take Armando in a one-on-one fight, especially now—but because the risk to the others was too high. I wanted him to abandon them completely and chase me. After all, I was clearly the bigger threat.

Some of them don't see it that way: they argue that I fled the scene. That's obviously stomm. I had the upper hand. I wasn't running from Armando, I was *leading* him. But I don't care what anyone else chooses to believe. Their opinions are considerably less important than the truth.

And my plan worked, too. I ran in the opposite direction of the gymnasium, and within seconds I could hear Armando scrabbling after me.

I have to admit, at this stage I was seriously regretting cracking his handcuffs.

The biggest disadvantage I had was that I didn't know the base, or certainly not as well as Armando did. This had been his home for seventeen months. He would have been able to move around it blindfolded and not bump into anything.

Ahead, the corridor curved to the right, and against one wall was a long red-and-pink smear—the still-drying blood and brain matter of one of the corporal's dead colleagues. After about four metres the smear dropped down to the floor and led to a thick pool of almost-congealed blood: I could feel it stick to my boots and was all too aware that I was leaving a very easy trail for Armando to follow.

But there was no sign of the body. My guess was that the colonel's men had been cleaning up.

I skidded to a stop at a junction and turned right. A trail of blood-dots on the ground disappeared under a closed door. I couldn't tell whether that meant that a body had been carried into the room or out of it; I was hoping it would turn out to be the latter.

I could still hear him behind me—any second now he'd reach the junction—but I tried the door anyway: locked. I moved on, all too aware that every door I tried would almost certainly be the same.

But a Judge doesn't quit just because the odds are against him. He keeps going. He *changes* the odds. He improvises a weapon, or he uses the enemy's strength against him. Or he changes the playing field. That's what I was about to do.

Armando had killed thirty-four people on this base. Colonel D'Angelo's people had done a rudimentary job of clearing up, but they hadn't had a lot of time. Certainly not enough time to dispose of thirty-four bodies. The smears and blood-drops on the floor told me that they'd just moved the bodies out of the way.

The military mind is efficient and methodical, so I knew that they'd have quickly developed a routine. Find the bodies, identify them, check them against the base's manifest, then move them somewhere. Can't have them stinking up the rest of the base. And you don't want them decaying, either, before a proper investigation can take place. You put the bodies into the morgue, if you have one. And if you don't, you still need to keep them cold.

The surface temperature on Titan rarely goes above minus one-eighty.

I thundered up a metal staircase, taking the steps three at a time. At the top I grabbed the rail and hauled on it hard, used it to quickly swing myself around, heading back along the upper level for the next staircase. Again, three at a time—but by now I could hear Armando on the stairs below.

Another thin line of blood-drops told me that I was still going in the right direction, but I was too slow. Or Armando was too fast, depending on how you look at it. I needed something to slow him down.

There was no way this base would have a morgue large enough to hold all those bodies. Colonel D'Angelo would have ordered his team to carry the stiffs outside to preserve them. And the only way out of a mostly-underground base is through airlocks on the upper levels.

D'Angelo had sealed himself and his team off from the berserk Corporal Armando, but he'd clearly not sealed the entire base.

Even if he *had* locked all the outer doors, the base had started life as a ship... Spaceships' airlocks have manual overrides in case of a ship-wide power-failure.

A third flight of stairs, and as I approached the top, Armando was five metres behind me and moving at twice my speed.

I dropped, planted my hands on the top step and kicked back with both feet.

I got lucky, I admit that. My left heel smashed into Armando's face and he stumbled backwards, his grace stripped away by his sheer fury.

He fell, but I didn't have the luxury of watching him tumble. I scrambled to my feet and kept going.

And there, to my left, I saw it: the inner door of an airlock large enough to take a family car. Piled up in front of it was the base's former crew. About two-thirds of them were in body bags, but clearly they'd exhausted the supply; around a dozen were crudely wrapped in blankets bound with electricians' tape.

At the left side of the door was a large, clearly-signposted recess, and in that recess was a solid, red-painted lever.

I made a dive for the lever and grabbed it just as Corporal Armando's hands locked around my right ankle.

I slammed the lever down, and the airlock's inner door instantly dropped down into its cavity in the floor as Armando dragged me away.

Earlier, Vine had told me that he wasn't superhuman. Now, I wasn't so sure. His powerful fingers felt like they were going to crush my ankle.

But that feeling didn't last long. In fact, I barely had time to register it before Armando—still holding on with his left hand—ploughed his right fist hard into my stomach.

The impact jerked my hand free of the lever and I crashed to the floor, but Armando still hadn't let go. He single-handedly heaved me up and swung me by my leg, bringing my face down to his rapidly-moving foot. There was nothing I could do to avoid it.

His boot hit my forehead with enough force that for a moment I thought my neck was going to snap.

Growing desperate, I flailed around with my left foot and by chance more than anything else I managed to hit him in the side of his neck with my heel. That staggered him for a second, long enough for me to get my right hand behind his left knee. I pulled, and he buckled.

I squirmed free, scrabbling my way across the floor towards the airlock. Ten metres to the second lever, the one that would open the outer door.

And Armando crashed into me again, his shoulder slamming into the small of my back. We tumbled to the floor, skidded a little further into the airlock, but now he was grabbing, punching, kicking. He slashed at my face with clawed fingers and ripped away one of the prosthetic pieces of my cybernetic breathing apparatus. The piece had been bonded to my skin and it tore off a chunk, but, worse, I could feel the ends of tubes scraping the inside of my lungs.

There was no way I could beat him. I knew that now. Armando was too strong, too fast. And you can't reason with an enemy who's in the thrall of a berserker rage.

Then another blow slammed into my throat and I felt my voicebox pop out, heard it clatter wetly across the floor.

And I saw a possible way out.

If you can't outfight your enemy, and you can't outrun them, and you've got nothing else to hand... Purge your sinus filters right into their face.

It's a simple process, something that Wightman and I and the other mods did every day. You remove your voicebox, hit the switch on the cybernetic implant under your right ear, and whoosh. Or 'splash,' if you prefer.

Our sinus implants don't produce a *lot* of artificial snot, but it's pretty nasty stuff. Sticky, stringy, laced with dust and dirt and sand and specks of blood.

I triggered mine and it gushed out, hit Corporal John Armando square in the face.

He flinched, squirmed away to try and clean it.

And I jumped up and grabbed the outer door's manual lever.

If we'd been in space, the air would have been blown out of the base, but on the surface of Titan the air pressure is actually greater than that on Earth—and in the base—so instead, Titan's atmosphere rushed *in*.

I'd planned for that, of course. It wasn't the air pressure that I'd needed. It was the cold.

I had to cover up the hole in my throat while I raced after my voicebox, but that only took a few seconds.

And in those few seconds, Corporal Armando collapsed shuddering to the floor and passed out. His polymer-laced skin shielded him from the cold, but his lungs were still human: ice forming inside your lungs is not a nice feeling.

I closed the airlock door again, gave Armando a few hard kicks just to be sure he wasn't faking, then allowed myself a minute to sit down and rest. I mean, it had been a long day. And it wasn't over.

Twenty-Nine

"I'LL MAKE A deal with you, Colonel," I said into the communicator. I'd found it in a vest pocket on one of the corpses, along with four other communicators, a hand-held computer that I was sure would come in useful back at the prison, a deck of playing cards, fourteen packs of gum—again, great currency among the prisoners—and three hundred and eighty-three credits in cash. Which is, of course, the best currency of all.

No guns, knives or any other weapons, unfortunately.

There was probably a lot more to find on the rest of the bodies, but I didn't have time.

Colonel D'Angelo said, "I don't think you're in a position to negotiate, Dredd."

"Actually, I am." I was walking back through the base. Not running: I was still hopeful of spotting something that might be worth smuggling back.

After I'd resealed the airlock doors—having had a brief look outside to see where I was in relation to the artificial plateau— finding the communicators had been my first priority.

The marines had guns and armour and a small but powerful ship, and I was sure that one of their last acts would be to destroy the base. Or maybe just power up its engines and fly it away. Land it elsewhere on Titan, or any one of Saturn's other moons.

"Corporal Armando is still alive, you'll be pleased to hear. He might not be the super-soldier you were trying to create, given I beat him twice, but then I was an exceptional Judge."

"And what is this deal that you believe is worth my time listening to?"

I descended the second flight of stairs. "You take Armando and leave us alone. Simple as that. We're not going to tell anyone what happened here, because you're going to allow us to raid the base's stores. I know you've got better food than we do. That food will buy our silence."

There was no response, just static, and I was about to repeat myself when D'Angelo finally asked, "You expect me to believe that?"

"Have you ever been to prison, Colonel? We know—we *all* know—that there's no way off this rock before our sentence is done. We hate that, but we accept it. Now we have smaller ambitions, and one of them is nicer food. It's the little luxuries that keep us going."

"Where is Corporal Armando, Dredd?"

By now, I'd reached the curved corridor with the blood-smear on the wall, which allayed my slight worry that I'd gotten lost. "You'll never find him before he suffocates. But you let us all go back to our transport, and I'll tell you exactly where he is."

The corridor straightened out, and I saw Vine, Takenaga and Kurya on the floor. There was no way to tell from here whether they were alive, but I was sure they must be. There had barely been fifteen seconds between when I started running and when I heard Armando following me: surely not enough time to kill three people barehanded.

I slowed as I approached Vine, and if I'd still been in possession of my original lungs, I'm sure I'd have been holding my breath.

Her fingers were twitching. She was alive.

Takenaga, too, was clearly still with us. She was moaning softly.

Kurya was further way, beyond the synthiglass door.

I neared the door, where I could see the Colonel's shadow. I stopped walking and softly asked, "You still there?"

"I'm here. I'm considering your offer." A few silent seconds drifted past. "Dredd, you have no way of knowing that I won't just kill you once I have Armando back."

"I know that." I stepped out in front of the door, and D'Angelo jumped back: he'd not been expecting me. "How old are you, Colonel?"

He lowered the communicator and frowned at me. "Why is that relevant?"

"You seem young for an officer of your rank. And you've never been in combat. I can tell by the way you move. So what is it? You were fast-tracked to this position because you're some kind of military genius? Something like that?"

He gave me a slight smile. "It's exactly like that. I'm twenty-two. Recruited out of elementary school. Apparently I have the ideal combination of a very high IQ, vivid imagination and no moral compass. I am what you would call a high-functioning sociopath."

I stepped closer to the door. "Yeah. Me too. So where are we now, D'Angelo? Where do we stand on our deal?"

"You'd be a fool to trust me, Dredd. And I know you're not a fool. Nor am I. What's your angle?"

"No angle. I know we won't come out of this alive unless you permit that. I was a Judge, we understand these things. Sometimes all you can hope for is a chance to walk away." I glanced down at Zera Kurya. I still couldn't tell whether she was alive or dead. "But I can sweeten the deal a little. You'll like this, trust me."

He shook his head. "There's nothing you can offer me that—"

"I beat your super-soldier. Twice. He's stronger and faster and considerably more experienced than I am, and I beat him." I put my index finger on one of the scratches on my face, then pressed it against the glass, leaving a bloody fingerprint. "Here's my offer. My DNA. I'm a first-generation clone of Eustace Fargo, the first Chief Judge of Mega-City One. You want to find the ultimate super-soldier, an unbeatable living weapon?" I smiled. "Colonel, you're *looking* at him."

THE HANDOVER WAS awkward. Tense as a twelve-string guitar about to get married on a tightrope.

All of the Colonel's people, all of mine, at the same time.

We met at the halfway point between the big bus and the blast-hole in the side of the fake plateau. And we all kept our promises. No weapons, no tricks.

Sloane and McConnach helped carry Kurya into the bus—she still hadn't regained consciousness, but at least she was alive—then we loaded up eleven crates of supplies hastily plundered from the base's stores. Once that was done, one by one the others climbed on board, including First Lieutenant Vine, until it was only me and Copus standing in front of Colonel D'Angelo and his marines. The colonel's faceplate was transparent, so I knew it was him. I still had no idea what Lancaster or any of the others looked like.

"So where is he?" Lancaster asked.

"Not yet," I said. "We *all* have to be on the bus."

The colonel nodded. "I remember. But, Dredd, we've got your DNA now. Why do we still need Armando?"

Sub-warden Copus asked, "How *much* did you spend creating him?"

D'Angelo smiled. "Too much to write off. I'll keep my word, Dredd. You just be sure you keep yours. If word of this place gets out, we'll wipe your prison off the face of Titan. You'll be atomised long before anyone on Earth knows what's happened."

"We'd gain nothing from ratting on you. It's not like we have any leverage."

Behind me, Copus climbed onto the bus and passed through the airlock cycle, then it was my turn. I climbed up and then turned back to give the marines a final nod.

"Top level," I said. "Inside the big airlock. I put the corporal in one of the body bags. You're going to need everyone to dig him out."

Lancaster laughed, then turned away, gesturing to his team to run ahead.

But the Colonel hesitated. "I could get you *out*, Dredd. I know people who have Chief Judge Goodman's ear. You agree to serve the remainder of your sentence working for me and you'll have a much better quality of life."

"Let's just get this deal out of the way first," I said. I gave him a wave, then closed the outer airlock door.

Before the inner door was even open, I shouted to Sloane, "We need to go—now!"

Sloane said, "What?" but he was already firing up the engine.

Copus shoved the door open the rest of the way, and grabbed hold of my collar. "What the hell have you *done*, Rico?"

I forced myself to keep calm. "He tried to kill us. I don't make deals with people who've tried to kill me."

There was no guarantee that it would work; I knew that. But the chances were strong. I might not be as academically gifted as Colonel Peter D'Angelo, but *he* had never worked the streets of Mega-City One.

A lack of conscience was no match for knowing how to fight dirty.

About four minutes into the journey, I pulled my communicator out of my pocket, set it down and jacked up the volume for everyone to hear.

A muffled voice said, "He was lying! Why would he hide Armando in a body bag?"

Another voice: "So we wouldn't see him so easily. That's what hiding something *means*, spugwit!"

Rustling sounds, then a third voice, clearer: "Sergeant Lancaster—something under there! That one is moving!"

I could picture the scene: Lancaster and the others checking through the body bags they'd piled up earlier. It would take them a few minutes to free Armando from underneath his former colleagues. Probably a lot less time than it had taken me to pile their bodies on top of him.

Lancaster: "Get him out of there. You two, keep your weapons ready. And a set of cuffs."

More grunting and thumping as bodies were pulled from the heap, then the first voice again, much clearer now: "Cut him out, Evans."

A knife slicing through thick plastic. I turned to the others in the bus. "Don't worry. I tied him up."

Then Lancaster again: "What...? Oh, right. Dredd put a helmet on him so he could breathe under there. Smart. Okay. Get him on his feet. But leave the tape on his mouth and his hands tied."

Colonel D'Angelo, sounding several metres away. "He's alive. So Dredd wasn't lying."

"No, sir," Lancaster said. "What's our next move?"

"Take Evans and get back to the ship. Destroy the prison transport before it can make contact."

Copus muttered, "Stomm!" then turned to Sloane. "Full speed! We can't outrun it but—"

I laughed. "No need, boss." I picked up the communicator and hit the *Transmit* stud. "Hey, Colonel, you back-stabbing drokker!"

A second's silence, then Lancaster's voice, very clear. "There's a communicator in the helmet—they've been listening!"

"We have," I said. "And now it's *your* turn to listen. All of you. Including Corporal John Armando." I took a deep breath, savouring the moment. "Unfettered Hematophagy."

Their screams were loud, but didn't last very long.

After some debate, Copus ordered Sloane to turn around, taking us back to the base once more.

By the time we got in, Armando had reverted to the same comatose state he'd been in when I first saw him, and, well, I won't say it was *easy* to subdue him again, but between us we managed it.

HUYGENS BASE IS still there, to the best of my knowledge. One day someone will find it, and maybe they'll wonder where it came from and why there are so many corpses on board. They might even wonder why there's a small, unmarked military-grade ship in the hangar.

If anyone *does* ever start asking questions, none of us who survived that rescue mission will talk, I know that for sure.

Corporal John Armando and First Lieutenant Salome Vine were picked up several months later by the next ship from Earth. We will probably never know what happened to them after that.

Kellan Wightman's death was listed as an accident. Unavoidable.

At least the 'unavoidable' part of that is true. I knew him. He might not have wanted to die that way, but I like to think that he would have understood.

I didn't want to do it, but it was the choice that led to the best outcome. I'm not happy with that, but I can live with it.

Just like I can live with the endless winds that howl across Titan, rattling the windows and shaking the buildings, the newbie prisoners screaming and crying and praying and pleading, the mine's machinery that never stops rumbling and grinding. I've become acclimatised. None of that keeps me awake any more.

I can sleep at night.

PART THREE

FOR I HAVE SINNED

"WE DWELL IN darkness. Our physical lives are but a brief flare, nothing more. A flicker. We were devoid of physical form for an eternity before, and will be devoid of a physical form for an eternity after. In the grand scale of the lifespan of Grud's glorious cosmos, we might as well not have lived at all."

Pastor Elvene Mandt Carbonara had been the Senior Arch-Primate of the Eighth Church of Grud the Unforgiving, a religious sect quite popular in southern Euro-Cit. She was about forty, I think. Tall with sallow skin, a wide frame but a narrow head, a noticeably asymmetrical hairline and an unsettling under-bite. Not easy on the eye.

But then neither am I, I know that. I wasn't criticising her looks, just commenting.

She'd go through months-long phases where she spoke solely in quotes from her church's religious tracts and the rest of us were never sure whether she believed any of it, or she was just messing with us, or if it was a smokescreen for something else. That last one is most likely: she was scared, and talked non-stop to mask her fear.

She'd been on Titan for over a year, but this was my first time working directly alongside her. I'd seen her many times, of course, but like most of the prisoners, I kept my distance whenever possible. One of those rules of prison life: steer clear of the ones who talk to themselves, or flinch at the invisible fairies buzzing around them, or claim to have invented a way to turn dirt into coffee... because crazy is contagious.

So the Pastor generated an imperceptible force field around herself by constantly talking about the afterlife, and that kept her reasonably safe from the psychopaths.

But it didn't keep away those who were looking for some form of guidance. The 'lost souls' who seem to be destined to stand behind more eloquent people while angrily shouting, "Yeah!" and waving their fists in the air.

We were out in the Bronze, one-forty-something kilometres west of the prison complex, and the Pastor's latest diatribe had begun within minutes of sub-warden Kalai Takenaga telling her, "Carbonara, you're with Dredd. He'll show you the ropes. Dredd, go easy on her."

As we'd walked away from the bus, Carbonara stared down at her feet and muttered something with each step. I'd made the mistake of asking her what she was doing.

"Blessing the footsteps. She who blesseth the steps of her feet shall forever walk upright and steady in the house of Grud. Colonials, chapter twelve, verse six. Have *you* been saved, Rico Dredd?"

I declined to answer, and that was when she hit me with the piece about dwelling in darkness.

I didn't want to get drawn into any kind of argument or debate. I said, "See all these loose rocks? See those two wheelbarrows? You take one of the barrows, I don't care which. If you see any rocks with a silver streak through them, or silver speckles"—I reached down and scooped up a fist-sized rock—"Like this? See? You find rocks like this, anything from the size of your thumb upwards, you put them into your barrow."

She nodded, but it was more of a bow, her environment suit bending slightly at the hips rather than the neck. "Collect the ones with the silver. Got it. And then?"

"And then you keep going until your barrow is *almost* too heavy to push, and then you push it back towards the truck. The crew there will empty it for you, and then you come back here with the empty barrow and repeat the process until you run out of rocks or the sub-warden tells us it's time to quit. When we've picked this area clean, we come back with diggers and sieves. Got to get every molecule of iridium."

Pastor Carbonara looked down at her gloved hands. "These hands were designed for clasping in prayer, not picking up rocks. These are *blessed* hands, holy instruments of the all-strong Grud who shall—"

"I don't care *how* magic you think your hands are. You ordered the murders of eighty-two former members of your cult, so now you get to pick up rocks. Believe me, this is one of the easiest jobs on this whole damn moon, so my advice is you shut up and get to work."

She raised her head and glared at me through her tinted visor. "There is a special booth in Hell's foetid diner reserved for the likes of you, Rico Dredd. The sins of the wicked are a deposit in the bank of hell, and their reward is a hefty dividend of unbearable torment every day, forever. So it is written in the letter from Saint Brenda to the Pomeranians."

"Just go pick up the damn rocks!"

Sub-warden Takenaga called over to me, "Trouble, Dredd?"

"Not yet," I called back. "Any chance I can trade partners?"

"Take a guess."

Within half an hour of working alongside Pastor Carbonara, I could have happily killed her. After another half-hour, I would have been just as happy for her to kill me.

I had known others who talked as much: Cadet Wagner had been a chatterbox, as had Elemeno Pea, the first prisoner I got to know on Titan. But the Pastor was something else entirely. For four solid hours she methodically sorted through the rocks and scree and did a damn good job of it, but she did not once stop talking about her church, about Grud, about sinners.

We'd been assigned a thirty-metre-square area to clear, so I couldn't move far enough away to be completely out of earshot, but I noticed that the inmates working around us seemed to be keeping to the far sides of *their* patches.

I'd no choice but to try to tune out her rhetoric and let it wash over me.

You don't argue with a crazy Grud-botherer because they train for that. You can't fast-track to the end of their sermon by pretending to agree with them because they have an inexhaustible supply of fresh diatribes lined up and ready to go. And you certainly don't ask a religious nut, "What do you mean, exactly?" because they will *tell* you.

In the Academy of Law back in Mega-City One we were

taught how to remain calm under pressure. A vital skill for a Judge, and handy for inmates, it turns out. I was able to ignore Pastor Elvene Mandt Carbonara, to mentally turn her volume down from eleven to about one or two and just ride it out.

But not every prisoner had that skill. Many of them had never been Judges, or they were out of practice.

Over time, some of them began to listen to what she had to say.

She was a charismatic, imaginative, intelligent, very *persuasive* spiritual crackpot sentenced to life on a half-frozen moon with a little over two hundred of the toughest, most dangerous people who ever walked the Earth.

Any fool should have been able to see that this was not a match made in Heaven.

TITAN

2089 A.D.

Thirty

AFTER KELLAN WIGHTMAN died, there was a small-scale power-vacuum in the prison's hierarchy. Every group of people quickly develops a recognisable, and reasonably stable social structure. People are naturally—often unconsciously—channelled towards certain tasks. You might think that I'd always end up at the head of the table because of my skills and training and natural leadership abilities, but no; I tended to drift towards the edges. The lone wolf, if you like. The one who can do all those dirty jobs that everyone understands need to be done, but don't want to do themselves.

Wightman had been retraining as a Tek-Judge before they caught him. He'd been good at making things, and shortly after he arrived on Titan, he started applying his technical skills towards that Philosopher's Stone of prison alchemy: turning vegetable matter into alcohol.

He'd been successful, too. Not only at making the stuff, but at the harder task of keeping it hidden from the guards.

So when Wightman died in 2084—under tragic but understandable circumstances—there was no one left with anywhere near his skill with fermentation.

Before Wightman's stashes ran dry, six or seven different teams had begun work on duplicating his processes. *They who control the contraband control the prison*, it's said. Some of them already had some experience, or enough to get started. Not that it's hard to turn sugar into alcohol: the hard part is doing it safely, in sufficient quantities to be worth the trouble, without being detected.

It took almost eight months before the first truly successful non-Wightman batch of hooch was delivered. Melissa Parenteau, former Texas-City paramedic, had perfected her process and come up with a cheeky little onion-based brandy that was actually not bad at all.

I couldn't taste it much myself, what with my mouth being sewn up and having to imbibe it by pouring it in through the hole in my throat, but it had a pleasant afterglow and was less similar to engine-degreaser than the other teams' attempts.

Parenteau became the unofficial champion of the competition, her alcoholic concoctions highly prized... Until Benedict Ritter decided that he wanted a piece of the action. Ritter was ex-military, a very tough contender who'd been an inmate for over ten years. He was looking to set himself up as a supplier and figured that Parenteau would be easy to oust. She'd only been a paramedic, after all, and he'd been in the Marines, one of the first wave to land on Apostasy. Toughest of the tough.

So Ritter tried to muscle in on Parenteau, and she threw half a litre of eighty-per-cent-proof alcohol in his face and set it alight. Allegedly, anyway; certainly, something burned away the lower half of Ritter's face, and he never went anywhere near Parenteau again.

Everyone left Parenteau alone after that. For the next few years, she was the prison's chief supplier of booze. She mastered fermentation and distillation, and there was even a story going around that the wardens knew what she was doing but let it slide because her stuff was better than anything they could smuggle in on the supply ships.

But in 2088, Melissa Parenteau died, the victim of an attack by Vivean Kassir.

It was a stupid death, really, and an avoidable one. Kassir was Southern Brennan's second-in-command. Even though Brennan was so big that most of us were sure he had mutie genes in there somewhere, Kassir was his muscle. She followed his orders, relayed his messages and beat the stomm out of anyone who bothered him—or anyone she thought might be *going* to bother him one day. Anyone trying to get to Brennan had to go through Kassir. They were joined at the hip. Frequently, if all the rumours are to be believed.

Parenteau died because Brennan decided he wanted in on the game. This wasn't a bad thing in itself, because Brennan's people controlled C and E blocks and had his own distillers, but Parenteau's product was much better.

But instead of talking to Kassir to thrash out the details, Parenteau had tried to negotiate *directly* with Southern Brennan.

I don't know exactly how that meeting went down, but my guess is that Kassir didn't like being bypassed and decided to express her dissatisfaction using the medium of rock-hammer and saw-blade.

Parenteau had been the only one who knew where all of her fermenting drums were hidden. Most of them were found over the following months—one of them was even found by the wardens, as we concluded one morning when almost all of the guards were nursing severe hangovers—but some of them remained elusive, partly because we didn't really know how many she'd had.

Almost a year after Parenteau's death, a 208-litre oil-drum was discovered in the prison's gardens, buried right at the end of the corn field, at pretty much the furthest possible location from the prison's main building. It was so close to the edge of the dome that some of the taller prisoners weren't able to stand upright at that point.

And the two-inmate crew that found it were friends of mine: Ryan Hubble and Genoa Amin.

I was working in the next field, tilling the dry soil while my own crew—Dustin "The Wind" Enigenburg and Rho Kenworth—took turns throwing in handfuls of the dry chemical fertiliser that pretty much kept all of us alive on Titan.

Kenworth saw Genoa Amin approaching and nudged me. "Rico."

I glanced in the direction she was looking, but not before checking to see if any of the guards or other inmates were watching. Two guards at the airlock leading to the main part of the prison. Two more over at the north end of the dome looking up: outside, overhead, two prisoners were clambering up the dome checking the sealant between the transparent plasteen panels and the girders. No one else paying us much attention.

Genoa was walking steadily towards us, hands in front of her, pressing her right thumb into her left palm as though she was nursing a small wound. Any guard who was watching would think that was exactly what she was doing. It's easy to fake certain kinds of minor ailment. They won't get you taken off a shift, but they might earn you a five-minute break, or an excuse to talk to another prisoner.

"Any of ye got a steripatch?" Genoa called, her strong Glaswegian accent absolutely unmistakeable.

I passed my spade to Dustin and began to walk towards her. "I've got one. Is it bad?"

She stopped in front of me, and I pretended to examine her wound. As softly as I could manage with my artificial voicebox, I asked, "What is it?"

"We found an oil-drum. A big one. Rico, I think it was one of Parenteau's."

I could feel a slight smile creeping across my lips. "Full?"

"I think so. Gave it a tap and it *sounds* full. We started digging it clear, but it's too heavy to lift. Hubble wants to roll it out, but I figure they'll definitely notice that."

"You're right." I peeled the backing off a steri-patch. "Cover it up again. Leave a marker so we know exactly where it is. Our best approach is to take the booze out a few litres at a time."

"That's what I was thinking, too." She smiled back at me and I instantly felt queasy. Not because I didn't like her—because I *did*.

She was barely up to my shoulder. A tiny, fierce, black-haired Scot with a sprinkling of freckles across her nose and a cheeky, twinkling grin that was guaranteed to lift your heart... but I knew what I looked like. Sewn-up mouth, grey mottled skin, half my face taken up with cybernetic implants.

Genoa didn't seem to care that I was a mod. She liked me anyway. Or she pretended she did, and that was kind of the problem. I wasn't sure.

So I refrained from giving her hand an extra little squeeze as I pressed the steri-patch into place over the imaginary wound. "It's in a corn field, so my guess is it's probably distilled corn mash. Moonshine." I glanced towards the far end of the dome, a hundred metres away, where I could just about see Ryan Hubble's head moving around.

Hubble was not the brightest. Genoa had once told him, "Hen... it's pretty clear that yer elevator disnae go all the way to the top floor where the lights are on but no one is home."

I said, "I hope that drokker's not trying to open it. Parenteau used to booby-trap her larger drums, especially if it was a batch she was particularly proud of. She—"

That was as far as I got, because at that moment Ryan Hubble attempted to open the drum. Or maybe he just kicked it, or they'd damaged the seal digging it clear.

Whatever the cause, for a brief moment I saw Hubble illuminated by something at his feet. And then he was gone, instantly swallowed by an orange ball of flame.

The explosion rippled through the gardens considerably faster than the sprinkler system could react—almost faster than *I* could react.

I saw the flare, then the fireball, and then I grabbed hold of Genoa's arm and pulled her towards me, stepped to the side and spun, pushing her down to the ground ahead of me. I threw myself on top of her a half-second before the flames gushed over us.

If this had happened on Earth, none of us would have made

it, but the initial blast shattered the plasteen dome and Titan's oxygen-poor atmosphere rushed in, suffocating the flames almost as fast as they spread. The result was an arc of fire racing through the gardens as the transparent panels overhead blistered and shattered, spraying the area with semi-molten shards.

The fireball rolled over us with enough heat to scorch even my polymer-toughened skin. I heard the airlock between the gardens and the rest of the prison slam shut: an emergency protocol. I heard the rush of the flames as they engulfed our crops, the howl of the winds chasing the fire. Screams abruptly cut off.

A few metres ahead of me, Dustin Enigenburg desperately thrashed about in the loose dirt as he tried to smother the flames burning through his overalls.

Even as the dome's heat-warped steel girders started to crash down, I was up and running, dragging Genoa by the hand, all too aware that she was simultaneously suffocating and freezing.

Ahead of us, Rho Kenworth was hauling the smouldering Enigenburg to his feet. She turned back for a second and our eyes met: we both knew he was not going to make it. He had only barely turned away from the blast before it hit. His beard and hair were gone and the left side of his face was a scorched mass of blisters filled with pus and blood that was already freezing solid.

The logical action would have been for me and Kenworth to leave our non-mod colleagues behind and save our own lives... but the real danger to *us* had already passed. The cold didn't affect us, and we could breathe in Titan's atmosphere. We could have strolled back to the main prison block without any worries other than negotiating the fallen girders and cooling lumps of melted plasteen.

But, like me, Kenworth had been a Judge, and no matter how far we might have fallen, there was one trait we'd learned at the Academy of Law that had stayed with us: you don't abandon the weak, you protect them.

I half-dragged Genoa up to Kenworth, and we swapped. I hoisted Dustin Enigenburg onto my shoulder, Kenworth scooped up Genoa in her arms, then we ran towards the airlock leading into the prison.

Something exploded off to our left, but this wasn't the time to check.

Ahead, a seventy-year-old inmate I knew only as Jexter was lying face-up, eyes open, his hands clutching at his throat.

If we'd stopped to help him, Genoa and Enigenburg would have died too. We stepped over Jexter's thrashing, twitching body and kept going.

Another explosion from the left, this one much, much larger. A lump of shrapnel the size of a dinner-plate shot past my head so fast I almost didn't even see it—but I heard it strike a support pillar.

Later, I found it still embedded there: a razor-edged chunk of a semisolid-oxygen cylinder, buried so deep into the pillar that I wasn't able to pull it out. Matter of fact, it's still there now.

Genoa and Enigenburg almost didn't make it. Have to say, they *wouldn't* have made it if sub-warden Copus hadn't stepped out through the airlock and thrown something over-arm towards us.

Thanks to the moon's low gravity and his good aim, it landed three metres in front of me. I scooped it up without slowing, tossed it back to Kenworth. "Oxygen mask! Put it on her!"

Twenty metres closer, a second oxygen mask landed nearby, and again I threw it to Kenworth: "I can't do it from this angle *and* keep running!"

So Rho became the hero, I guess, and I'm happy with that. She was carrying Genoa Amin, who by now was barely conscious and close to freezing solid, and she still managed to put the mask on Dustin while he was passed out, swinging back and forth over my shoulder.

It was the longest run I'd ever made, even though it didn't take much more than fifty seconds.

Rho Kenworth, Dustin Enigenburg, Genoa Amin and I were the only survivors. Seventeen inmates and four guards lost their lives, thanks to Melissa Parenteau's highly explosive moonshine erupting next to a ten-kilogram sack of high-grade fertiliser.

But that wasn't the worst of it. Not by a long way.

After Doc Mollo and his crew checked me over—a few scorches and scratches, nothing that wouldn't heal—I was dismissed from the med-centre.

I returned to the airlock looking out at where the gardens used to be and saw Copus still staring out through the cracked plasteen window.

He must have seen my reflection as I approached. Without turning around, he softly said, "Dredd..."

I moved next to him, and we both looked out at the devastation where there had once been fields and crops and trees. The soil was a mess of shattered plasteen fragments, black-charred plant matter and newly-formed ice.

"It's gone," Copus said. "Even the tubers couldn't have

survived that. Without the gardens, we are screwed. Next transport is five months away."

I said, "I know. But if we start rationing—"

"The storehouse was hit too." He pointed off to the right, where the remains of a concrete building still smouldered. "The crates were airtight and should have been able to withstand the damage, but..." He shrugged. "That's what you get when you keep your emergency O2 tanks in the same place as your food. All because Governor Dodge was too cheap to build a separate storehouse." He glanced at me. "You mention that I said that, and—"

"I won't. What about the air-recyclers?"

"They're working as long as the generator keeps spinning. They'll sustain us."

That was something of a relief. Without the gardens to convert our carbon dioxide, the recyclers were now our primary source of oxygen.

We stood side-by-side in silence for a moment. Captor and captive, prisoner and guard. We were not friends, but we understood each other.

I said, "We should be okay for water. If there are any leaks, the water will have frozen, so we can just go out and bring it back in. Food's the priority. We need to start rebuilding the dome. Or at least find space to plant *some* kind of garden. Immediately."

Copus nodded. "That's what I'm thinking. The old gymnasium at the end of F-Block is airtight. We can set up lamps; we'll be using a lot more power than if we had a glass dome, but it's somewhere to start. Giambalvo has recommended we plant watermelons, squashes, peas and legumes. They start consuming CO_2 the moment they sprout, a little over a week after planting."

"That'll help keep everyone busy... Mister Copus, how long do we have?"

He shrugged. "Based on what we've salvaged from the storehouse, we figure that if we ration half a food block per person every four days, we can last almost three months."

"A half-block every four days isn't nearly enough."

Copus nodded. "We know. Plus-side, the inmates will be too weak with hunger to riot."

I said, "Down-side, you'll be too weak to stop them." But even as I said that, another thought was running alongside it. "Your calculations are taking into account rationing for *everyone*, right? Not just the inmates?"

His teeth clenched in mild anger—though surely he must have seen the question coming—Copus said, "Yes. Everyone." Then his shoulders sagged, and just for a second I thought that I was seeing the man inside the uniform. He looked old, and weak, and on the edge of defeat. "I need *ideas*, Rico. And I need them now. Otherwise, that ship will arrive in five months to a dead colony."

Thirty-One

ANY HOPES THE warden might have had about keeping the situation under the radar disintegrated within hours.

It was obvious to even the dumbest of inmates that the majority of our food came from the gardens and the storehouse. With both of them destroyed, we'd be tightening our belts pretty soon. Or we *would* be, if they'd let us have belts.

Governor Dodge ordered the kitchen double-locked and triple-guarded. And while every inmate not currently out in the Bronze was sent out into the ruins of the garden to salvage anything that might be edible, the rest of the guards overturned the cells. Every scrap of tucked-away food was confiscated.

Out in the gardens, I was one of the inmates chosen to coordinate the scavenging: I'd worked extensively in the gardens, I didn't need an environment suit, and I'd witnessed the destruction. I had some idea of where to look and what might be out there.

Not much, I was sure.

We had tenuous hopes that the deep-root vegetables might have made it, but, no, they were gone. Every tuber, every root was already black and frozen. The few that looked salvageable were brought back in and thawed, but they just disintegrated into inedible mush.

We started at the airlock and worked outwards, clearing debris and salvaging anything that was potentially useful or could be repaired. Hose-pipes, tools, planters, sacks of fertiliser, unbroken sections of transparent plasteen.

As we worked, I saw an inmate struggling to lift a four-metre-long girder and went to help him. We grabbed hold of one end of the girder and heaved it up, lifting it off the crushed body of another inmate.

"Cadmus Holland," I said. "Damn."

The inmate next to me almost snarled. "No great loss. I owed the drokker seventeen creds."

Great, I said to myself, *Sims*. I hadn't seen his face, and in an environment suit almost everyone looks the same anyway. Lorne Sims was another of Southern Brennan's henchmen, a former Mega-City One Judge. He'd arrived on Titan three years before me, sentenced to forty for the murder of a citizen: they'd had an affair, she'd become pregnant, he'd shot her just in case she tried to blackmail him.

Sims, Brennan and Vivean Kassir ran pretty much everything in C and E blocks, from the contraband to the ore-yield gambling, and I'd had a few bad encounters with each of them over the years.

At least Sims was semi-reasonable, where Kassir was a twitchy, quick-tempered idiot and Brennan was a vicious, muscle-bound monster. You could *talk* to Sims, sometimes, when he wasn't having one of his dark days.

Sims said, "I've got this, Dredd. You pull him free."

I hesitated. The girder was heavy enough to crush my skull if Sims decided to let it drop. "How about the other way around?"

"You don't trust me?"

"Not even slightly."

One of the guards called out, "What's the hold-up, Dredd?"

I shouted back, "Got a body here. Holland."

"Then haul him out of there! That's what you're here for, numbnuts! Do I have to draw you a damn picture?"

Sims smirked. "Not gonna drop it on you if we're being watched, am I?"

"Guess not."

I tentatively let go of the girder, and Sims adjusted his footing a little to accommodate the weight.

"Make it quick!"

I crouched down, grabbed hold of Holland's outstretched arm, and dragged him free.

Sims let the girder crash down, then said, "He might have food on him. Check his pockets."

I was already doing so. "Nothing but lint and..." I stopped. There was something in Holland's left front pocket. I shifted my angle so that I could reach inside, then pulled it out. "Stone." I bounced it up and down in my palm. "Nothing special about it." I shrugged. "Guess it was special to Holland. His totem, maybe." Some of the other prisoners had similar items, though how the tradition had evolved was a mystery to me. They found a small object on their first day and kept it with them at all times. It was supposed to represent their hope or their desire for freedom or something. I never got that. I tossed Holland's stone away.

"We should get him inside anyway, I guess." Sims looked around, saw a couple of other inmates pushing a gurney over the uneven ground, and signalled them over.

I took Holland's arms and Sims took his legs, then we lifted him up onto the gurney. As he was being wheeled away, Sims said, "The crashed ship."

"The what?"

"You remember the ship, right? The freighter that crashed out near Brunel's Ridge—you were *there*, Dredd. You and Kurya and Wightman. Five, six years ago."

"Right. The *Carol Masters*, en route to Mimas. We got those two survivors out of it. What about it?"

"It must have had supplies on board. Emergency rations, at the very least."

"It did, but we took them. There's nothing but a shell left there now."

Sims turned away, annoyed.

There had been no freighter, of course. That was the cover story for our trip out to Huygens Base, the covert-ops military station that only a handful of us knew about.

The base had been on my mind ever since Copus told me how bad the food situation was. We had plundered the base when we left, but there could be more supplies there, stuff we hadn't found or hadn't thought worth taking.

When my shift was over, I went to see sub-warden Copus to present my idea.

*   *   *

COPUS HAD HIS own quarters—along with the rest of the guards—on the eastern side of the compound, but he spent most of the time in his office closer to the general population. He even slept there on occasion.

I knocked on the door and he yelled, "What?"

"It's Rico Dredd."

A tiny hesitation, then, "Enter."

I opened the door and stepped through, then stopped. Copus was sitting on the edge of his desk, arms folded, with the warden—Governor Myles Dodge—sitting in the chair opposite. Both of them were scowling in my direction.

Copus snapped, "What is it, Dredd? You find anything worth salvaging?"

"No. Not unless we're going to eat the corpses."

That comment hung in the air for far too long, then Copus said, "What do you want?"

With a glance at the warden, I said, "Huygens Base. Any idea if it's still vacant? We took a lot of supplies back with us, but we didn't spend much time looking. I'm thinking there could be more. None of our people have been back, have we?"

The warden said, "No. But someone else might have been. Whoever was signing the cheques for Colonel D'Angelo sure as stomm knows by now what happened to him."

Copus said, "For all *we* know, the base could be long gone, or taken over by another division."

"What about the emergency link?"

"Already tried it," Dodge said. "First thing I did. No response." He was still staring at me. I was never sure where I stood with him. With every other guard I'd quickly established a mutually-understood hierarchy, but the warden was so reclusive. This was probably only the sixth or seventh time I'd seen him.

"Then we need to check out the place personally," I said.

Copus shook his head. "We can't do that. We'd need a damn good excuse to leave here. We're not going to get away with another crashed ship."

The warden said, "Hell with that. *We* dictate the rules, not the inmates. We can go wherever we damn well choose." Then he sagged a little, deflated by the reality of the situation. "We have a couple of hours before the evening meal. This place is going to break apart the moment they realise that there won't *be* an evening meal." He pursed his lips, and ran his hand over his shaved head as he made his decision. "Dredd's right. We need to check out Huygens. Martin, you'll lead. Take Dredd and whoever else was there last time. We keep knowledge of Huygens Base on a need-to-know basis. If word got out, then whoever was pulling D'Angelo's strings might decide we're *all* too dangerous to be allowed to live."

"I can't go," Copus said. "It's going to be hard enough keeping the lid on this place."

I said, "I'll lead, governor. I want to take Benedict Ritter with me. He wasn't with us last time, but he's ex-military—he knows how to keep his mouth shut. Plus, he'll have some idea of where to look and what we might find."

"Like *stomm* you'll lead, Dredd," Copus said. "You forget you're still a prisoner here?" To the warden, he said, "We'll sort it out, governor."

"Do. And do it fast and discreet, because all the stomm is

about to hit all the fans at the same time and we just lost our umbrella."

COPUS AND I waited inside the hangar, watching as the prison's Big Bus rumbled and hissed to a stop. Phoebe Sloane, the driver, nervously chewed her lip as she climbed down and approached us.

They'd already been informed of what had happened, of course. They'd cut short their shift out in the Bronze and left the mined ore behind, but on the way back they'd seen the devastation. The gardens had been the lifeblood of the prison; there wasn't a single inmate who didn't look forward to garden-shift coming up on rotation. Sometimes, when the lamps were on high and the air-recycler was blowing gently, you could close your eyes for a second and pretend you were standing in a wheat field on Earth. Now moments like that were gone, possibly forever.

Sloane said, "There's emergency rations in the bus. We..." She spread her arms briefly and let them drop down to her sides, at a loss as to what to do next. "We haven't had lunch yet. Didn't know whether..."

"Unload them," Copus said. "Line them up."

The inmates were not in a good mood, most of them looking as shocked as Sloane. One by one they exited the bus and formed a line. Thirty inmates and four guards, almost all of them watching me with an expression that asked, *What the hell is Rico Dredd doing here?*

Copus answered that as soon as they were all out: "You all heard what happened. Some of you will have had food on you when you found out. You've hidden it, because you'd be an idiot *not* to. And the only place you could hide it—where you can also *get* to it again—is on the bus. Dredd here is going to pick some volunteers and they are going to scrub the bus, check every possible hiding-place." He shrugged. "Or you could all just make it easy on everyone by *telling* us where you've hidden your stash. Who wants to go first?"

As expected, no one volunteered.

Copus said, "Strip. Down to your underclothes."

Among the prisoners was Southern Brennan, and even if he'd been of average size, the casual observer would always be able to tell which one he was by the distance everyone else put around him. But then, I guess if he'd been of average size, no one would have been quite so scared of him.

It was still something of a mystery to me that Brennan and I had never actually had a physical altercation. From the moment he'd arrived, he'd made it clear that he was gunning for me, but it had never gone beyond threats. With other inmates, that wasn't the case. Story goes that he once beat Bryna Ausburn to a pulp with his bare fists, used her flailing, unconscious body as a club to attack Rolando Obi, then used Obi as a battering ram to slam his way through the four guards trying to stop him.

They put him in the coal-shed for a month for that, and the first thing he did when he got out was try to strangle the trustee who'd come to mop it out. Another month in the coal-shed.

That suited everyone else, of course. Having Southern Brennan locked away meant a holiday for the rest of us.

The coal-shed was the worst: solitary confinement. I'd done a couple of stints in that two-metre-cubed concrete hell, and I knew stronger men than me who'd emerged broken after only a week. You're stripped and dumped in. The last sound you hear is the lid being bolted down, then no light, no noise, no human contact. Nothing but your naked body and a single one-centimetre hole in the wall through which air, food and water were pumped—the food was a gritty paste and you didn't know when it was going to show up, so you had to sit close to the opening, waiting for the tiny, almost unnoticeable waft of stale air that indicates that the paste is about to ooze through.

After a day or two, you realised that you had to pick a corner to dump in because the only other option was to push your waste back out through the food opening. And while the floor of the coal-shed was smooth, it wasn't exactly level, so you had to make damn sure that the corner you picked was downhill.

Longest I heard anyone had spent in solitary was eleven weeks. That was in the old prison on Enceladus, and the story goes that the prisoner in question had started a brawl on his first day, within minutes of getting off the shuttle, so he was thrown into solitary and somehow forgotten about. They only remembered him when another prisoner was caught turning a broken chair leg into a shiv and he was hauled off to the coal-shed too.

They unbolted the lid and opened it to find that the forgotten prisoner was still alive—the food, air and water were fed in automatically—but he'd lost his sight, three quarters of his body weight, and his mind. He was squatting ankle-deep in his own waste and could no longer speak. Even under heavy sedation he was still constantly trembling, and flinching whenever anything touched his skin.

I don't know whether that story has any truth behind it, but it isn't beyond possible. There's a lot of weird tales about what happened on Enceladus.

Now, I looked at the line-up of inmates who'd returned from the Bronze and realised that Benedict Ritter wasn't among them. Sub-wardens Takenaga and De Luyando were frisking them one by one and searching their clothing and environment suits, which gave me a little time to think.

I had been *sure* Ritter was on this shift, but I wasn't in a position to ask about him.

At least Zera Kurya was there. She was as much a part of my plan as Ritter. I called her out: "Kurya, you're with me."

She scooped up her clothing and stepped forward, reluctantly. I tried not to watch as she dressed again.

Copus said, hesitantly, "One isn't enough, Dredd. I want this done fast."

I knew what he meant, and he understood my dilemma. I needed to pick someone I could trust and who'd be useful when scouring Huygens Base.

Slim pickings. Of all the inmates present, the most effective was clearly Southern Brennan, but there was no way in Grud's groovy hell I was going to get that rock-skulled drokker involved.

Standing on his left was "Velvet" Judy Cassano, seventy years old at least—not a chance. On Brennan's right was a kid from Luxor whose name I could never remember. Twenty years old, apple-cheeked, bright eyes and curly hair. Knifed his supervising Judge eighteen times in the chest when he learned that he had failed his final rookie test. No way I was going to take him, either.

Murderers and psychopaths, corrupt Judges and big-time crooks, club-wielding henchmen and world-class assassins, poisoners and traitors... Every kind of outlaw, and almost all of them standing on the edge of sanity wondering how long the fall would take if they jumped, or, more likely, if they pushed someone else.

From the far end of the line a voice called out, "I'll do it!" and we looked to see Pastor Elvene Mandt Carbonara stepping forward with one arm raised.

I muttered, "Not a chance," under my breath, but loud enough for Copus to hear.

He said, "No. Step back in line, Carbonara. Anyone else?" Much softer, he muttered to me, "Speed this up, Rico. It's already looking suspicious."

Then I realised what I had to do, but I didn't like it.

"Brennan," I said. "I'll take Brennan."

Copus muttered, "Jovus..." but aloud he said, "All right. Get moving. You've got one hour. Rest of you inmates, get inside, get cleaned up. I want your environment suits checked and tanks refilled: you've got a half-hour break, then you're taking over from the crew currently trying to rebuild the dome."

They grumbled away, with their guards following, but as Sloane and Takenaga were about to leave, Copus called them aside and said, "Hold back."

Sloane glanced towards me, Kurya and Brennan and hesitantly asked, "Why...?"

Copus waited until the last of the others was gone, then said, "Dredd will fill you in." He nodded to me. "Don't let me down." He walked away.

Thirty-Two

"So what the hell *is* this?" Kalai Takenaga asked. She was keeping her distance from us, hand resting on the pommel of her sick-stick.

I said, "You know what happened to the gardens and the storehouse. You know we're in trouble. The food supplies we've recovered aren't going to last long enough for the next ship to get here."

Brennan looked from me to Takenaga and back. "So?"

"So Earth is on the wrong side of the sun right now, and even if there *are* any ships closer who've picked up our distress calls, they're not going to have enough food for all of us."

Zera Kurya had already figured out what was happening. Nodding slightly, more to herself than for our benefit, she said, "Huygens Base."

"Right," I said. "We don't know what the situation is out there, and the only way we can find out is to go look."

Sloane said, "There could be more supplies. Food. I know we took a lot with us, but there has to be more. What was the base's complement? Forty?" She frowned. "Military rations for forty people on a remote covert-ops base... There's no way to know how much is left. *Could* be there's a couple of years' worth. If so, we'd be able to survive long enough for a supply ship to reach us." She took a deep breath to steady herself, then said, "Okay. Let's not get crazy. We did a sweep last time. There's probably not much left at all."

"What the hell is Huygens Base?" Brennan asked.

In a way, that was kind of a relief: it meant that our story about the crashed freighter was widely believed. I had never been sure about that until now. Before I could answer, Sloane started to move towards the bus.

I darted ahead of Sloane, got between her and the door. "Hold it. Huygens Base is still supposed to be top secret. After what we did to D'Angelo and the others..." I corrected myself. "After what *I* did, whoever was overseeing the colonel is not going to sit back and allow us to make its existence public."

Sub-warden Takenaga said, "Yeah, but—"

I cut her off. "We can't just drive out there as though we're going down to the local store to pick up bread and munce. No one but us five—and Copus and the governor—can know what we're doing, because if we get to Huygens Base and it's occupied, or we trigger some alarms... that's it, we're done. If they think it's necessary to protect their secrets, they'll kill us. No, they'll *obliterate* us—all of us—without missing a beat."

Now standing next to me, Kurya added, "Even if this task is successful and we return with supplies, we can never tell anyone."

Brennan said, "Covert military base... So the crashed freighter never existed. Okay. I get that." He paused for a second. "Why pick *me*, Dredd?"

"Because you hate me, and everyone knows that." Of course, that was no answer at all. I couldn't tell him the real reason, so that would have to appease him for now. To Sloane, I said, "Get on board, prepare to start it up. The official story is that we're going out to the freighter, so it's got to *look* like that—we need to go in that direction."

The two wardens exchanged a glance, then Takenaga said, "Copus should have talked to us about this first."

I shrugged. "Yeah, he probably should have. But there's not a lot of time. He wants you two back here ASAP because he figures that we've got at most three days before someone steals someone else's stale cornbread and sparks a prison-wide riot. So are you in? Not that you have much of a choice."

Another exchanged glance, a longer one this time, then Takenaga said, "We're in. But you try *anything*, Dredd, and I swear on all that's holy we will make sure you die last."

"And hungry," Sloane added.

"JOURNEY TIME SHOULD be just about six hours," Sloane said as she ran through the dashboard's pre-drive checks. "That's twelve in total, say another twelve while we're *at* the base... Just to be sure, we're gonna need O2 for forty-eight hours. Hell, the air's not in short supply. Call it ninety-six hours. Just in case."

We started to load up the O2 tanks, with Kurya out in the hangar tossing them one at a time to Brennan, and him throwing them in to me through the open airlock doors. It was a little unsettling to see that Kurya and I had to use both hands but Brennan was catching and throwing them single-handed. I stacked the cylinders beside me; when we were done, Brennan and Kurya scoured the hangar for empty storage crates.

"Six hours... That's shorter than last time," I said to Sloane as I slid the cylinders into their slots on the rack.

"This time we know exactly where we're going." She looked up at me, clearly a little nervous, and softly said, "I've always done right by you, Rico. You know that."

I wasn't sure what to do with that. "Uh, yeah, Ms Sloane. You have." Did she think that this was some sort of elaborate ruse or something? That I was going to turn on her and Takenaga and then... what, head out into the Bronze with almost no supplies and wait for death out there rather than in the prison?

But my answer seemed to take the edge off whatever was unsettling her. As Brennan and Takenaga were climbing on board, she called out, "Settle down. We're going to be moving fast, like our butts are on fire and the only water is over the horizon. Foot hitting the floor for at least the first hundred kilometres. It's gonna be uncomfortable, is what I'm saying. You all okay with that?" It seemed to me that she was excited at the prospect of finally being allowed to push the bus up to its top speed.

Brennan said, "We'll manage."

I looked back towards him. He could barely fit into the double-seat he was lowering himself into. He had his environment suit balled up in one hand. It had been handmade specially for him by cutting up two suits and patching them together.

Wightman had once speculated that the only reason Brennan

hadn't been made a mod was because the cybernetic pieces only came in one size: they didn't make artificial lungs big enough for him.

"So what the hell *is* this base, anyway?" Brennan asked. "How come the rest of us have never heard of it?"

Takenaga said, "Put a pin in that until we're out of here." Then she turned to me. "Are you sure this is worth the trouble, Dredd?"

"What's our alternative? Even if the base has been abandoned and cleaned out, there's bound to be *something* that we can use. At the very least, we could use the base's hangar as a supplementary garden. It'll be cleaner than anywhere in our entire complex. And it's got power, so we'd just need to bring the seeds, soil, water and fertiliser out there."

Once we'd reversed out of the hangar's massive airlock, Sloane swung the bus around much faster than I'd anticipated, before shifting it into second gear and stamping down on the accelerator. I was thrown back into my seat and my head snapped back so hard that if my mouth hadn't already been sewn up, I would probably have bitten through my tongue.

The Big Bus surged over the pitted Titan landscape. For the first hour I couldn't say for certain that there was any one point at which all of its wheels were on the ground at the same time.

After about ninety minutes, Sloane eased off the accelerator and locked the controls into automatic before turning around in her seat. "All right... Ground's a lot rougher from here, so we've got to take it easier."

Takenaga pulled herself out of her seat and came forward to sit opposite me, then she looked back towards Brennan. "Why him? He's the only one of us who didn't already know about Huygens."

I said, "He's strong, and he's not stupid. You guards like to pretend that you wield the only power in the prison, but we all know that's not true. There are gangs and there's a hierarchy. Brennan's people are loyal to him—fear-based loyalty is as reliable as any other—so we're going to need him on our side to keep them under control, especially if we *can't* find any food."

Sloane gave Takenaga a smirking glance and said, "Heh. 'We.' I guess you can take the Judge out of the Department, but you can't take the Department out of the Judge." To me, she added, "Dredd, all of this might be your idea but it's not your show. *We're* in charge."

I nodded. "I know that. Wouldn't have it any other way."

"And you're still prisoners," Takenaga said. "No matter what the situation is, back at the penal colony, that still applies. You step out of *line...*" She dramatically thumped her hand down on the back of the seat in front of her.

I guess that was meant to make me jump, to remind me exactly where I stood, but the dull thud was underwhelming, and her whole demeanour sort of crumbled then. She sighed. "Just don't give us a reason to regret any of this."

They had no need to be concerned. The plan was as I had told them, nothing more, nothing less. Get to Huygens Base and, if it was still there and still intact, plunder it for supplies. That's all.

Well, not counting the real reason I'd picked Southern Brennan for the team: things were going to be bad back at the prison, I was sure, and Brennan was by far the most dangerous of the inmates. He could hardly start a riot by proxy.

Thirty-Three

I'D FAILED TO sleep much on the journey south across Titan's unforgiving deserts. Partly because Brennan *had* fallen asleep, and he was snoring so loud I could hear him over the roar of the engines.

But mostly it was because I was hungry.

When you first learn that pretty much all your stored or growing food is gone, the initial feeling is shock, maybe mixed with a little fear for the future. An hour later, the shock has dissipated—you've accepted the situation—but the fear for the future has grown to fill the void, and then some.

There was food on the bus. Emergency rations locked away behind a battered steel panel close to the driver's seat. Semi-solid fudge-like blocks for the others, tubes of paste for me. I could eat the blocks if I had no choice: I'd have to squash them up first, then use my fingers to push the mash in through the hole in my throat. Very messy, but better than starvation.

I realised I was staring at the battered steel panel again, and looked away... only to see that Takenaga was staring at it too.

There was enough food in that panel to keep the five of us going for a week. Ten days if we stretched it out.

Thirteen days if we killed Southern Brennan before he got hold of any.

An unwelcome thought jumped to the front of the line: *We could survive for a month if we killed and ate Brennan.*

I shook my head briskly, a feeble attempt to scare away the unsettling image. It didn't work. *He's almost solid muscle. Protein. Brennan weighs at least one-twenty-five kilograms, and a kilogram of meat yields about two thousand calories. That's two hundred and fifty thousand calories he's carrying around. Say we restrict each prisoner to five hundred calories per day. That's five hundred portions.*

Over two hundred prisoners and guards... Brennan could feed all *of us for two days.*

I abruptly stood up, hoping that the sudden movement would snap me away from that train of thought.

Across the aisle, Takenaga flinched, her hand once again moving towards her sick-stick. "What? What is it?"

"Nothing," I said. "Foot-cramp."

I walked the length of the bus and back a couple of times, but my gaze kept returning to that silver panel. And I could see that the others were in the same situation.

It had been about six hours since I'd eaten. Not long at all, really.

But the notion that within a couple of weeks I'd be starving to death was hard to shake. The mild hunger pangs I felt now were nothing compared with what lay ahead.

We'll each have one food-block now. No, don't be greedy. We'll have one between all of us. Except me. I'll have a single squirt from one of the tubes. Just about a mouthful, that's all. Keep us going for another few hours. We won't be so hungry when we get to the base and we'll be able to think straight.

And we're probably going to find literally tonnes *of food at the base, anyway. We could eat all of our emergency rations now and that would be a drop in the ocean compared to the amount of stuff we'll be bringing back to the prison.*

This all makes sense, in a way, because the prison was secretly supplying the base with food for years, so now we're just reaping the benefits of that. It's karma. You get out of life what you put into it. We sowed, now we get to reap.

The base might even have its own *gardens. Fresh food, how great would that be?*

Again, I stopped myself. I'd had fresh food that morning.

Behind me, Southern Brennan snorted himself awake, then sat up. "Grud*damn*, I'm hungry."

Sloane said, "Quit that. We have to ration it. The supplies we have on board belong to the whole prison, not just us."

Clearly, she had been thinking along the same lines as I had. As we all had.

Brennan said, "We should take an inventory, just so we know. What if the bus breaks down and we get stranded? We're gonna need to know how long we'll survive."

"Cut that out, Brennan, right now!" Takenaga said. "We all ate this morning. We can eat again *tomorrow* morning."

I dropped down into a seat, and glanced towards Zera Kurya. She was staring straight ahead, but not at the enticing silver panel—she was looking out through the windshield.

"You okay?" I asked her.

Without looking at me, she said, "I skipped breakfast."

"What?" I shuffled closer to her. "*Why?*"

"Heavy period. Always makes me feel queasy in the mornings." Her eyes flicked towards me for a moment. "I'm regretting it now."

I sat back. *We're on a mission. Can't carry out a mission on an empty stomach. We wouldn't be able to think straight. We'd miss something.*

For the good of everyone, we ought to eat.

I began, "Takenaga..."

Without turning around to face me, she said, "That's *sub-warden* Takenaga. And the answer is no."

"I'm just—"

"No. We have an obligation to everyone else back at the colony."

Brennan smirked. "Right. The colony. You ever notice that, Dredd? The guards refer to the place as a colony. See, we're *colonists*, not prisoners."

I hadn't noticed that, but he was right. And I wasn't about to admit that to him. "Sure, I know that. They've always done it. Makes them feel better about their crappy jobs."

"That's enough," Takenaga said.

Brennan laughed, and I couldn't help thinking that if I killed him, it'd probably be best to do it quick. A bullet through the head. Maybe tear out his throat. Anything slower might spoil the meat.

And Brennan wasn't the only one I wanted to see gone. I could have named two dozen prisoners whose absence would only improve the place. *Each prisoner we kill, butcher and eat is one less mouth to feed*, I thought.

Horrifying as that was, I couldn't help but follow it up with the mental image of a rescue ship reaching the prison some months in the future, and its crew disembarking to find that the prison population had been reduced to five or six massively overweight inmates using the backs of their hands to wipe the gravy away from their mouths, before belching and tossing fresh human femurs onto an already teetering pile of bones.

Drokk that. I don't care how hungry I get, I am not resorting to cannibalism.

I WAS STRETCHED out across two seats, lying on my side and trying not to think about how my stomach's gurgles weren't just audible, they were *echoing*, when Sloane called out, "Dredd? We're close."

I sat up. "*How* close?"

"You want time or distance?"

"Both."

"Three kilometres, ten minutes at our current speed."

I made my way towards the front of the bus as Sloane eased off the throttle and gently applied the brakes. She said, "This is almost exactly where we stopped last time."

Takenaga said, "Phoebe, that was *five years* ago. How can you remember that?"

"You're good at your job, I'm good at mine." Sloane turned to me. "How do you want to play this? Same as before?"

"Yeah. We climb over the ridge, get a view of the base from above. Once we know for sure that it's abandoned—or if it's not, but they don't seem overly eager to massacre us—we'll call you in." I glanced back at Kurya and Brennan. "You two up for some climbing?"

We went through the usual undignified process of passing through the bus's airlock one by one, which wasn't easy for Brennan because his shoulders were so wide he could barely fit through even *without* an environment suit, and as we trudged towards the hill, I was not looking forward to the fun and games we'd have loading the bus up with crates of food if we couldn't find a way to get the bus into the base's hangar... Open the bus's outer airlock door, load it up with crates, close the outer door, cycle the airlock's air, open the inner door, someone inside lifts the crates out of the airlock and stows them away. Then close the inner door, extract the air again because you don't want to waste too much oxygen. Repeat until bus is full or there are no more crates.

If the engineers who'd put the bus together had been smart enough to foresee this sort of problem, they might have adapted the air-pumps to be able to extract the air from the whole bus; then we could open up the long-since-welded-shut rear doors and load up the crates that way. We'd get the whole job done in a tenth of the time.

Maybe we could even do that now, I thought. *If we can find the right sort of equipment in the base, we could make those adaptations ourselves. I've never welded anything, but it can't be that hard to learn. I can certainly rig up an air pump.*

As these thoughts rattled around, a deeper, more primitive part of my consciousness understood exactly what the rest of my brain was doing: distracting me from the hunger, and from thinking about the possibility that there might not *be* crates to load onto the bus.

For all we knew, Huygens Base might not be there at all. It had originally been a ship, so whoever inherited the place from the late, unlamented Colonel Peter D'Angelo could have just fired up the engines and flown away.

We were about halfway up the hill—steep enough that we had to use our hands to climb—when Southern Brennan said, "It's Schroedinger's Pantry. Until we get there and can ascertain the truth, the base both does and *does not* have supplies."

Kurya laughed a little at that, which—I freely admit— angered me. Brennan's comment was more clever than funny, and it wasn't even that clever. She was *my* friend, not his. She knew how much Brennan and I despised each other. Petty, I know, but hunger can have a strange effect on a person. Brennan was becoming more talkative, Kurya was getting giddy, and I was growing jealous for no good reason.

It had now been almost ten hours since breakfast. I'd had the usual: bowl of oatmeal, a grey-skinned apple from the gardens—run through the blender—and half a tube of Supplementary, the cardboard-flavoured paste with all the vitamins and minerals a prisoner might need for the day.

I could have had a second apple, but I hadn't been in the mood. Or I could have had toast, though I rarely bothered with bread-based products because I couldn't chew. The one time I did try to eat a bread roll by breaking it up into small pieces and pushing them in through my throat-hole, well, it didn't work out. Regurgitating food is an unpleasant sensation at the best of times; it's worse when the only exit point is the hole in your throat and not your mouth. And out on the surface of Titan, in the sub-zero air and low gravity, an arc of instantly-frozen vomit can reach quite a distance before it hits the ground and shatters into a million pieces.

A little ahead of me, Brennan said, "If the base *is* there, and every part of it is fully functioning, I say we take control. Fly it off this damn moon. You must have contacts out there, Kurya. People who can help us."

"We're not doing that," I said. "We steal a military vessel, they'd shoot us down without thinking. Besides, there's nowhere to *go*. The bases on Mimas and Dione and Tethys are controlled by the military, and they're constantly on alert. Even if we could make it as far as Jupiter without being detected, the patrols to and from the Ganymede Installation would rip us to shreds." I stopped climbing for a moment. "Trust me, I've had five years to think about this from every angle. Our only hope would be to head out into deep space, but the ship doesn't have an FTL drive, so best-case scenario is that we get picked up by a friendly interstellar transport before we run out of food or air. The odds against that happening are billions to one against, and that's if they're *looking* for us."

Brennan had stopped too, and was looking back at me. "You getting tired, Dredd?"

"No."

"Hunger getting to you?"

"Don't push it, Brennan. I don't care how big you are—I'd have no problems bringing you down. You know that."

He smirked. "Sure. Yeah."

Kurya had continued climbing, and now called back, "You are both fools. Conserve your energy."

She was right, and both Brennan and I knew it. We moved on, now almost side-by-side.

His gloves were tight on his massive hands, his muscles almost bulging through the fabric of his environment suit. *One burst seam...*

We were out of sight of the bus, and Kurya was about eight metres ahead of us, concentrating on her climbing.

Do it now, I told myself. *Tear one of the seams on his back. He won't be able to reach around to patch it. He'll suffocate in seconds. I'll keep climbing, and by the time Kurya notices, it'll be too late.*

Sadly missed, a tragic end, just when we were becoming friends. I wish I could tell you what happened, but we were all exhausted, starving, putting every last erg into the climb. At one point I looked back to see how he was doing but I thought he was just taking a break. If only I had realised...

This was a very entertaining notion, but not even close to realistic. The climb wasn't that bad, the hill not really that high. Kurya had already reached the top.

"What do you see?" I called.

"It's there."

Behind me, Brennan muttered, "Thank you, Grud!"

As I stopped next to Kurya, I pointed towards the near side of the base. From this distance the whole thing looked like a natural plateau, but we knew that was a disguise. "The hole in the hull was down there... There was light coming out last time, but I remember we shut it off before we left. Your eyes are better than mine, Zera—what can you see?"

"Just shadows. I *think* the rupture is still here. That suggests no one else has been here since us." She glanced at me, then back to Brennan. "Next step?"

I said, "Let's get down there."

Thirty-Four

THE CORRIDORS OF Huygens Base echoed with our footsteps. The thin coating of dust on the floor was unmarked, undisturbed. No signs of life except the air-recyclers and lights that activated automatically as we passed their proximity sensors.

I nudged Kurya's arm and pointed ahead. "Bullet-hole in the wall. I remember that one."

There were going to be a lot more bullet-holes, I knew that. Colonel D'Angelo's pet mind-controlled super-soldier, Armando, had killed D'Angelo and every one of his people in a berserk frenzy that resulted in absolute carnage.

When we last left the base, we'd taken Armando away, but left the bodies behind.

It didn't take long to reach them. The bodies were on the base's uppermost deck, close to a large airlock. All told, including the base's original complement, there were over fifty.

A vast heap of uniforms and body armour containing picked-clean skeletons with broken bones and fractured skulls.

Brennan stayed back, shocked. "Jovus in a jumper, I..."

"You've seen bodies before, Brennan." I nudged a skull with my boot. It rolled to the side.

"I know it's been five years, but this is a sealed environment. Why are they just *bones* already?"

Kurya answered: "This base was a laboratory. Has to be clean. Automated systems detect decaying matter and sterilise the area. I was expecting this: we left this ship covered in blood, but that's gone now."

Brennan nodded slowly as he stared down at the bodies.

I saw this and said, "I know what you're thinking, but don't bother. Copus searched them for weapons before we left." I looked closer at the skeleton in front of me. "Didn't search them for ration-packs, though..."

The three of us hesitated for a moment, then almost as one we each dropped into a crouch and began patting and frisking.

Kurya was the first to find something edible: a candy bar, still in its wrapper. Sealed and intact, protected from the base's automatic sterilisation.

As it was, Kurya broke the bar into three reasonably equal pieces and tossed a piece each to me and Brennan. I like to think I'd have done the same, but I know that's not true. If I'd been armed at that moment, I would probably have shot her for it.

The candy was a Scrumpty Bar: artificial beanuts wrapped around a mockaramel centre and covered in choklit. So overwhelmingly sweet it makes your eyes squint. Two for a credit at any Mega-City One discount store. The sort of candy you stock up on for Halloween because you're damned if you're going to buy the expensive brand-name stuff for the neighbourhood kids.

I swear, it was the most delicious thing I'd ever eaten, despite it being stale and me having to squash it between my dust-caked hands until it had almost melted before I could feed it through my throat-hole.

Brennan consumed his piece in one go, but Kurya savoured hers. Took tiny bites of the choklit coating, a nibble here and there on the beanuts.

After a couple of minutes she looked up to see that Brennan and I were both staring at her, watching every move.

"You're gonna have to stop that," Brennan said. "Seriously. I'm *this* close to taking it away from you."

I said, "We keep searching. Could be more... And we do the same, agreed? Split it three ways?"

"Sure, yeah," Brennan said, still watching Kurya.

She nodded and licked her fingers, then said, "If we're this hungry *now*..."

"Don't," I told her. "Don't think about it."

That third of a candy bar had not taken the edge off my hunger. It had sharpened it, if anything. It had reminded my body that I hadn't eaten since breakfast.

Now, the pangs were almost crippling, almost too much to ignore as I patted and felt my way through the uniform of a long-dead marine who now existed only as set of dog-tags on a bundle of dry bones.

This was nothing, I knew. If we didn't find a food-packed store-room we'd missed last time, then in a few weeks we'd be looking back on this as the best day ever.

* * *

WE GOT LUCKY. Not as lucky as I'd hoped, but luckier than we deserved, I think. At the back of the base's kitchen was a dry-goods pantry stocked with crates of cereal packets, canned fruit and vegetables, five kilograms of mockpork jerky, more spices than we could ever need... and everyone's least favourite, military ration packs. Exactly one hundred of them, in fact. Each with a Best Before Date of a hundred years in the future. Devoid of taste, but will keep you alive. Just add water. Or, in extreme cases, desperation.

Brennan, Kurya and I piled everything up in the mess-hall as we waited for Takenaga and Sloane to arrive.

Surprisingly, it was Kurya who first brought up the subject of an alternative plan. "There is enough food here for us to survive until the supply ship arrives."

Brennan said, "Enough for three, definitely. Maybe not quite enough for *five* people." Without looking at us, he added, "Who would know? Only Copus and the warden, right?"

I asked, "You're serious?"

"Speculating. Each one of us has killed before. This time, it would be for survival."

"This food will keep everyone back at the prison alive for another couple of weeks."

"You pretending to care about other people now, Dredd? Has the monster grown a heart?" He pointed in what I'm guessing he thought was the direction of the prison. "They're criminals, just like us. The only reason most of us haven't been executed is because we're needed to mine the iridium. Once it becomes cheaper to send robots, we're done anyway. You telling me that those jerks back at the prison have more of a right to life than us?"

"The guards do," I said. "Regardless of what anyone thinks of me, I'm no murderer. Yes, I've killed when it was necessary, and I killed in the line of duty, but that doesn't make me a killer. That makes me a *survivor*."

Then Zera Kurya said, "Tell that to Kellan Wightman."

I turned away from her. That had been a low shot; mean. Not like Kurya at all. I figured maybe it was the hunger, and maybe fear of what the coming months would bring.

Brennan said, "Truth hurts, huh, Dredd? Yeah, she told me. For years we thought that Wightman was killed by a power-surge as you were trying to rescue the crew from the downed freighter. Now we know. You used him as a human shield."

I kept my mouth shut as I turned back. It was clear he wasn't finished and I wanted to see where he was going with this.

"Is that why you picked *me* for this duty? There's not many prisoners left who are big enough for you to hide behind." He took a step back and spat on the floor. "That's you, Dredd. That's your precious bloodline. Corrupt or insane, every one of you. Your *brother* is the one who put me away, did you know that? Judge Joseph Dredd, pride of Sector Thirteen. Even with all that crap on your face, I can see him in you. That same arrogance. But in you, it's worse. He looks at everyone as though they're a potential lawbreaker. You look at people as though they're *insects*."

I almost smiled. "Joe brought you in? Is that what you're telling me? You got taken down by my little brother? Damn it, Brennan, you really *are* dumb. You don't advertise your weaknesses, any idiot knows that. So that's why you've had your sights on *me* all this time." I stepped closer to him. "Joe beat you, and I was always better than him. *Always.* So if you're no match for him, you're not worth my sweat. Or did you forget that I scored the highest marks *ever* in the toughest academy on Earth?"

"We're not on Earth now, Dredd."

He was a metre in front of me. Within reach. A jab to the throat would knock him backwards, or bring him to his knees. Throat, eyes, genitals. Three hits and he's down. I could kill him before he laid a single finger on me and I wouldn't even bruise a knuckle.

Because sooner or later it was going to come down to that. One of us would conclude that the other was more useful dead than alive.

For a big guy, Brennan moved fast; faster than I'd anticipated. I almost didn't see it coming: a single punch—more of a jab, really—straight out, square in the jaw.

In most cases I *would* have seen it coming, because to hit me hard enough to hurt, the average person would have to pull their arm back, pivot at the hip. I'd have time to avoid it or block it, or even retaliate first.

But Brennan was *so* strong that even a jab sent me staggering backwards. The back of my legs collided with a table that, like all the others, was bolted to the floor, and I would have fallen onto it if I hadn't put my hands out behind me.

It wasn't luck that my right hand landed on the edge of a large, toughened-plastic tray. I was a Judge: I've been trained to always evaluate every location. Exits, possible weapons, pitfalls, traps, etc. It all happens automatically, the moment I enter a room.

So while I might not have been conscious of that tray's location, it had certainly been logged in my subconscious.

I grabbed hold of the tray and swung it up, grabbed the other side with my left hand. Out of pure Academy-honed reflex I had the tray in front of me like a shield just before Brennan's second—and much more powerful—punch.

His fist slammed into the tough plastic tray hard enough to knock it out of my grip, but it gave me the time I needed to duck and roll away.

I continued the roll into a half-spinning kick, jamming the heel of my right boot into Brennan's stomach. It felt like kicking a sack of wet sand, and it was only slightly more effective.

My spin brought me to the floor face-down, landing with my hands flat in front of me—as I'd planned. I instantly pushed myself up and to the side, just as Brennan brought his boot crashing down where my head had been.

I darted under another table and rolled to my feet, but I was barely upright when Brennan came lunging at me. It was a frantic, almost desperate scramble over the fixed tables and benches, but the gracelessness of the move would make no difference if he hit me: he was almost twice my weight, and all of it muscle.

So I dropped down again, his outstretched arms missed me by centimetres, and I squirmed back under the table, emerging close to Kurya.

Enraged as he was, I wasn't a match for Southern Brennan. On any other day, sure, but not like this. But with Kurya backing me up, I knew I had a chance.

As I again jumped to my feet, I began, "You get his—"

She stepped away, barely looking at either of us. "Not my quarrel."

I didn't have time to respond to that: Brennan was already leaping at me again. He wasn't concerned about crashing forehead-first into a table or smashing his knees on a bench; he wanted to hurt me, and it didn't matter whether he got hurt in the process.

I couldn't keep ducking under the tables forever: I had to *do* something.

So this time I stood my ground. He was angry, and anger makes people careless. His arms, outstretched and grabbing, would take that much longer to protect his midriff and groin.

A well-placed kick or punch would take the fight out of him.

All that passed through my head in an instant, along with the conclusion that he was actually coming at me too fast for my crude plan to work, and that I was at the wrong angle anyway. I jumped aside.

But I'd been hungry for most of the day, and I was exhausted. I'd already been caught in a fireball and had to dodge flaming chunks of plasteen roofing while carrying two people to safety. I wasn't able to move fast enough.

Brennan's left hand caught my upper left arm and locked on. As he crashed into another table—hard enough to loosen the bolts securing it to the floor—he dragged me with him. His powerful fingers dug into my arm; he squeezed so tight I swear I could almost feel the veins and arteries bursting.

He skidded across the top of the table and crashed down on the other side, still dragging me behind him.

The side of my head smacked against the edge of a bench as we went down, and it was only later that I realised how lucky I'd been: a couple of centimetres to the right and I'd have hit the corner, earning a fractured skull at the very least.

Half-dazed, I grabbed one of the table's legs with my free arm and tried to pull myself away, but Brennan squirmed around and locked *his* free arm around my neck.

That was when sub-warden Takenaga shot him in the arm.

Thirty-five

Thirty-Five

IT WAS A stun-shot. I was disappointed about that at first, but later realised she'd made the right call. If she'd killed him, that would be one less person to help search the base and load whatever we found onto the bus.

As Takenaga and Sloane entered the mess hall—with the discharge hum of Takenaga's side-arm still fading—they seemed almost calm about the fight, as though they'd been expecting it. Perhaps they had.

Takenaga told Kurya to check on Brennan, keeping her gun trained on him.

Sloane unzipped her environment suit halfway down and tied the top half around her waist as she looked around. "So. This place is smaller than I remembered."

Kurya was crouched over Brennan. She looked up. "He's alive."

As I pulled myself to my feet, I began, "He attacked—"

Takenaga circled the table containing the crates and boxes of food. "I don't care. Next time it happens, I'll shoot both of you. And it won't be a stun-shot. This is everything?"

I nodded. My left arm felt like the bone had been crushed to powder.

"And how much did you three eat?"

"Not much," I said. "Check the garbage in the kitchen, you'll see the packages."

Takenaga scowled. "You should have had more control. Now you don't eat again until tomorrow evening. Maybe the morning after. You've searched everywhere?"

Kurya said, "Just the common areas. We haven't had time to go through every room."

Sloane was poking through the crates, lifting out cans and frowning at them. "Then that's our next step. We take *anything* even remotely edible. Sauces, spices, toothpaste. Cosmetics. Anything made of leather or chalk or wax. That includes waxed paper. Pot plants. Any of the grunts here keep a pet? Find their food. Even if it's a goldfish, their food is edible."

When you're absolutely starving, a fish-food and leather-belt salad doesn't sound too bad. But Kurya, Brennan and I had eaten about three ration-packs each. We were now full and not in the mood for hunting down supplies of waxed paper and dog food.

Takenaga added, "Gather up any and all medical supplies, too. A lot of pills are made of sugar or starches. As long as we're careful and watch for side-effects and overdoses, we should be okay."

"What about ropes and cloth, if they're made from natural fibres?" I asked.

Sloane shook her head. "Not going to be any good. Humans can't effectively digest cellulose."

Takenaga decided that we should split up into two teams and properly scour the base. When Brennan recovered, he, Kurya and Takenaga would start at the uppermost levels and work their way down.

Sloane and I headed for the lowest.

In a long-dead marine's footlocker she found a small tub of hair gel and stuffed it into the backpack she was carrying.

"Hair gel?" I asked. "That's edible?"

"This brand is mostly wax." She reached into the footlocker again and pulled out a small bulky envelope, then emptied its contents onto the bed. Four small partly-used birthday-cake candles. "Also wax. Nice." She added them to her backpack.

"How the hell do you know all this?"

"My grandpa was a survivalist nut. He raised me. We spent a lot of time in his bunker out in the woods." She smiled. "He was one of those guys who picked their teeth with a six-inch hunting knife. Wrestled a bear every morning before breakfast—which was a bottle of whiskey—then shaved with a chisel. A blunt one. That kind of thing, you know?" She nodded towards the next footlocker. "You can listen and search at the same time, Dredd."

"Right, sure." I popped the lid on the locker. "Empty." I moved on to the next one. It was packed with clothing that had obviously just been dumped back in after the last time it was searched, five years earlier. "Socks. Pants. Boots..."

"Leather?"

"I don't think so."

"Take them out anyway, I'll check when I'm done here.

Yeah, Gramps was a piece of work, all right. A bigot who despised anyone who wasn't a white, straight, male, gun-owning Presbyterian. Ate almost nothing but meat and potatoes because he was convinced that green vegetables made you gay, drank like an alcoholic fish, never went to a doctor in case they might be Jewish or a woman, got into bar fights at least once a week... and somehow still lived to be ninety."

I didn't respond to that. I was staring at something I never thought I'd see outside of a museum. A small wooden box containing what looked like an antique 2mm Kolibri, one of the smallest handguns ever made. Keeping one eye on Sloane, I ran my fingers over the gun and raised them to my face. My sense of smell had never fully returned after the operation, but it was good enough to pick up the familiar tang of gun oil. Whoever had owned the Kolibri had taken care of it.

This can't be the real thing, I said to myself. *They're too rare. Has to be a replica. But if it still works...* The Kolibri held 2.7mm ammunition, not a common calibre. But the wooden box wasn't engraved or otherwise marked; it wasn't a display, for a collector's item. The owner *used* this gun. Whoever had searched this locker last time we were here obviously missed it.

I continued searching, pulling out more socks and underwear, and then right in the corner, tucked away, was a small cloth-wrapped bundle.

Sloane was already straightening up, about to move on past me to the next locker, so I quickly shoved the gun and the bundle—which felt very much like it might contain a dozen or so rounds of the gun's tiny ammunition—into a pair of thick socks.

"What have you got there?" Sloane asked.

"Socks. Look, I'm *taking* these. The guy who owned them is dead and—"

She shrugged. "I don't care. Take *all* the socks, if you want. Don't care if you go through his wallet, either. Just keep searching for things we can eat. Actually, if you *do* find a wallet, and it's leather, keep it."

The next room was clearly an officer's quarters. A bunk resembling an actual bed, two more lockers, a door leading to a small bathroom.

Sloane looked around with an expression of disapproval. "Sparse."

"For you, maybe," I said. "I had a nice apartment in the Meg for a while, but even so, after nine years on this freezing rock and fifteen in the Academy of Law, this looks like *luxury* to me." An idea struck me, but I brushed it away instantly.

That's the way my brain works, sometimes. Ideas come and they're often *good* ideas, but it's not always the right time to act on them. Sometimes you have to dismiss the idea, no matter how perfect it seems, then if it keeps coming *back,* it might be worth some consideration.

Sloane opened the nearest of the upright lockers to reveal a perfectly-pressed and polished dress uniform. She glanced back at me. "You want to be a master sergeant, Dredd?"

"More than anything."

She half-snorted and opened the next locker. It was lined with shelves containing neatly-folded clothes. "Must have overlooked this last time," she said, a note of optimism in her voice. As she poked through the contents, she added, "Check the bathroom."

I stepped around her and pushed the bathroom door open fully. Washbasin, small cabinet, toilet, small pedal bin, towel-rack, shower. There was nothing in the cabinet but a bar of soap and small plastic tumbler that might once have been used to keep a toothbrush upright, but I took them anyway. There was almost a full roll of paper next to the toilet. Not much good at allaying hunger, but I knew some of my fellow inmates would pay dearly for real, actual toilet paper. I stuffed that into my backpack too, and as I was reaching for the towels next to the shower, my dismissed idea came rushing back. I figured it couldn't hurt to try. I leaned back out through the door. "There's a shower here."

"I've seen one before."

"Yeah, but this is a *good* one. Water recycler with purification and heating elements, very high-pressure. Looks like it's almost never been used. There's a lot of fresh towels, too." I held up the bar of soap. "And this. Actual *real* soap, it looks like."

Sloane dropped to her knees and began to rummage through the master sergeant's collection of boots. "And...?"

"I haven't had a real shower since I got to Titan. Neither have you, I'm guessing. I know the guard's quarters aren't much better than the cells."

She stopped rummaging, then slowly looked up at me. "We're on a *schedule* here."

"Got to take a break sometime. Be honest, Ms Sloane, in a couple of months we'll all be killing each other over the last scraps of half a leather shoe that someone's been boiling for a week. If anyone clips a toenail, there'll be a dozen people clustered around asking, 'Are you planning to eat that?' We are toppling over the edge of the abyss here and it's a long, painful way down. I'd like to have at least a few nice memories to keep me company as I fall. Wouldn't you?"

She straightened up, looking past me towards the bathroom. "Jovus..."

"You take a shower, then I'll take one. No one else needs to know. Who am I gonna tell, anyway? And if I did, who'd believe me?"

Sloane shook her head, but she didn't move away, or say anything. That's when I knew I was getting through to her.

"You don't think you can trust me, is that it?"

"Partly, yeah."

"Phoebe... I mean, Ms Sloane... I could have attacked you at any time, you know that. I'm not a violent prisoner. What happened in the mess hall, that was Brennan attacking me. I mean, I'd have to be an idiot to attack him. You know that. Cuff me to the bed frame if you want to be sure."

She glanced up at me. "No, I don't think we need to go *that* far."

"The others are on the other side of the base. They'll never know. Take ten minutes for yourself. I mean, even if we survive this, how long have you got to serve?"

"Almost six years."

"Six years. At one shower a day, that's two thousand barely-warm, hurried showers before you get to go home and properly start your new life. Two thousand more mornings standing on cold, cracked tiles trying to quickly dry yourself with a paper-thin prison-issue towel."

Sloane sighed. "Damn it... All right. You say *nothing*, Rico. Understood?"

"Sure, yeah." I stepped aside, clearing the path to the small bathroom. "Ten minutes, then it's my turn."

"The others will notice we're clean."

"So? For all we know, they're doing the same thing right now. It's only logical. This is a harsh life, even for you guards; we'd be fools not to avail ourselves of every morsel of innocent pleasure that comes our way."

Thirty-Six

I STRETCHED OUT on the Master Sergeant's bed, face-down and propped up on my elbows, and when I was sure that Sloane was busy showering—I could hear her humming over the hiss of the water—I pulled the sock from my pocket and removed the Kolibri and the bundle of ammo.

A quick examination confirmed that the gun was not a real Kolibri. It looked close enough, but this one held a twelve-round magazine in the grip and the barrel appeared to be rifled. The tech required to construct it didn't exist when they stopped making the weapon a hundred and fifty years earlier.

I popped the empty magazine out and sniffed the chamber. Maybe there was the faintest trace of cordite, but it had been at least five years since anyone had even *handled* the gun, let alone fired it. Then I checked the ammunition: twelve rounds that fit the magazine perfectly.

I clipped it back into place, and tucked the gun into the side of my boot. That felt familiar, and brought back a rush of memories of my days on the streets of Mega-City One. The Judge's boot-holster: looks like exactly the wrong place to keep your gun, but with enough training a Judge can draw from it just as quickly as from any other holster, and has the advantage that it forces the Judge to crouch, making them a smaller target. Critics will say, "Yeah, but it's not much good if you're running after a perp!" but a good Judge should have their Lawgiver already drawn *before* the pursuit begins.

Sloane had progressed from humming to singing: "...*He dined with his cat, his horse, his rat and his poodle, used the last of the bread to mop up the noodles, and then served them all his mom's apple strudel, this is the ballad of...*"

It had been a long time since I'd heard anyone singing with such contentment and satisfaction. And that—combined with the heady scent of the soap and the images my mind was conjuring up—began to awaken my long-dormant libido. It was expressing some interest in what I might find if I opened the door, but I'd had plenty of practice ignoring it.

This wasn't about the moment; it was a long-term strategy. I still had eleven years on my sentence, and favours owed by guards are the ultimate currency in a prison.

So while I *could* have walked into that bathroom and very probably seduced Sloane—even with my cold grey skin and mutilated features, I reckon I stood a fairly good chance—it was far better in the long run not to.

Now she knew she could trust me. We shared a secret. Added to her knowledge that coming to Huygens Base was my idea, Sloane was now in a position where she definitely regarded me as an asset to the prison.

I was not like the other prisoners. Everyone knew that anyway, but this reinforced it. And suppose that Takenaga *did* notice that Sloane had showered? She'd ask questions, and that would inevitably lead to Sloane admitting that she'd left me alone while she showered, that she trusted me. That would also encourage Takenaga to believe that I could be trusted.

With that thought, I rolled off the bed and resumed searching through the room. It would be so much better if Sloane emerged from the shower to discover that I'd not been idle.

Perception is everything, after all. If I wanted the guards to see me as being closer to them than to the rest of the prisoners, I had to give them so much evidence they couldn't ignore it.

So I moved on to the next room, another eight-bunk dormitory. I was halfway through the fourth footlocker when I became aware of how much time had passed—certainly more than ten minutes—so I returned to the master sergeant's quarters where the bathroom door was still closed, and I could hear the water still running.

I knocked gently on the door. "C'mon, Ms Sloane. I know it's tempting, but you can't stay in there forever."

The water shut off, and there was a deep sigh. "Okay... Give me a couple more minutes."

I returned to the next dormitory, and was almost done searching it before Sloane returned, still readjusting her environment suit.

She seemed a lot happier than before. Her hair was still wet, but she looked fresh, cheerful, more relaxed. "Sorry... Look,

Rico, there's still some time if you make it real quick. The others—"

"It's fine," I said, doing my best to smile without being too creepy. "It'll be my turn next time, right? Besides, I have to be more careful in a shower, with my cybernetics. Don't want to have to explain a short circuit." I gestured towards the bunk closest to the door. "This room's spoils. Eighteen and a half ration bars, jar of instant synthi-caf, four candy bars, half a bag of walnuts—real ones, I think—and what looks like a tube of crawbies. Ms Takenaga said we should gather up any drugs we find, but I'm sure she meant prescription medicines, not actual illegal narcotics. Should we dump them?"

She hesitated. "No. Crawbies are an opioid, right? We might need them at some point for an anaesthetic." She tossed me an empty backpack. "Not a bad haul, though. Every mouthful is another day a prisoner gets to live."

IT TOOK US almost an entire twenty-four-hour day to sweep the base of all edible products, and the last step was the hangar. Kurya and Brennan had scoured it, but they hadn't been able to get inside the small, unmarked military-grade ship that had been sitting patiently for five years.

Now, all five of us clustered around it, looking up.

Brennan said, "If we could crack the entry codes, we could *fly* back to the prison. Get there in twenty minutes instead of six hours."

"Someone would still have to drive the bus back," I said.

Takenaga circled the ship for the eighth time. "There *must* be some emergency rations on board. That's how the military works: there are rules for everything, and a ship this size would definitely have a survival pack. Might not be *much*, but it's worth a look."

"Except that we can't get *in*," Sloane said. "We've been gone too long already. We should get back."

Takenaga said, "All right. Yeah, we'll do that." After a last look up at Colonel D'Angelo's ship, she walked away.

Southern Brennan lingered, silently staring at the ship. Even when Takenaga ordered him to follow the rest of us, he backed away rather than turn his back on the ship.

When he reached the door, he said, "Leave me."

We all stopped and turned around to look at him.

He was still staring at the Colonel D'Angelo's ship. "Leave me. Maybe I'll find a way to get inside it. Probably won't. Either way, you're better off. You know that." He glanced back at me. "Tell them, Dredd."

I said, "Brennan, you'll starve long before you get that ship open."

"Maybe the hunger will sharpen my wits." He grinned. "Desperation begets invention, right?"

Takenaga said, "We're not leaving you, Brennan. How would that look? We leave a prisoner alone on a military base that probably still has weapons stored away somewhere and definitely has an escape craft? Yeah, the warden would love that."

He turned to her. "Then do me a favour. Shoot me in the drokkin' head and leave me to rot. I've seen what starvation can do to people. I am *not* going out that way."

Sloane and Takenaga exchanged a glance, then Sloane said, "If they wanted you to have a quick death, they wouldn't have sent you to Titan. You haven't *earned* that privilege."

He snorted. "Right. What do I have to *do* to earn it? Attack you so that you've got no choice but to kill me?"

"You can help us load the supplies back onto the bus, that'd be a start. Do that, and I promise you that we won't let you starve."

Whatever he was thinking then, I don't know, but after a second he straightened up, turned away from the craft and strode out.

He didn't look at me as he passed me. I knew then that whatever happened, he would never really be able to look me in the eye again, because we knew. We *all* knew. In that moment, when he'd asked the guards to leave him behind, Brennan had torn open the veil that had always shielded his true self from the rest of the world. And that's a tear that can never be mended.

IN OUR EXHAUSTING, day-long search-and-plunder of Huygens Base we recovered enough supplies, we calculated, to feed every guard and inmate for almost another month, as long as each of them only consumed the bare minimum to stay alive.

It still wasn't going to be enough.

The journey back was toughest on Sloane: the rest of us could sleep, but even though she had the bus on autodrive, she had to remain at least partially alert.

I woke up at one stage, maybe four hours into the journey, and quietly asked Sloane how she was doing. She said she was okay, but she did seem to appreciate being asked.

As I returned to my seat, I saw Southern Brennan watching

me. He beckoned me closer, then said, "Playing the long game, Dredd, huh? Curry favour with the guards. Get them on your side. I get that." Maybe it was because I really knew him now, but his voice seemed softer than before, his manner less antagonistic.

"How long have you got?" he asked.

"Eleven more years."

He nodded slowly. "Eleven. They're not going to break you. I see that now. You'll do your time, and they'll let you go." He leaned to the left, looking past me towards Takenaga and Sloane. "I'm never getting off this rock. The things I've *done*... There's no place for me back home. You and me and Kurya... We're all here because we tried to live by our own rules, not theirs, and that doesn't work. It's like trying to change the course of a glacier by pissin' on it." He glanced down my feet, then raised his head slowly, smoothly, as though he was a mechanical scanner taking in everything. "I could crush your skull between my fists. I could kill the guards. All of them. I could kill every drokker in the prison, but what would I gain from that?"

"Not much."

"That ship back there... That was *it* for me."

I understood what he meant. In life, whatever your ambition, you look at all the obstacles and possibilities and you deal with them or discard them appropriately. One by one, you learn which aspects or elements to ignore and which to embrace in order to get you closer to your goal.

But sometimes you reach a point where you can't avoid the fact that you're *not* going to win, regardless of what you do. It's not a matter of defeat or surrender, but of acceptance. Of understanding that you can't always get what you want.

Brennan had had his moment of clarity. He knew now that "the system" was bigger and stronger than he was. Fighting it was futile.

I shrugged, because I didn't know what else to do, and sat down. Brennan was right about me, though. I *was* playing the long game. Not fighting against the system, but riding it. Steering it.

I knew that some of the other inmates despised me for generally being respectful to our jailers, but it made sense. Sure, I could have fought them every step of the way, but what good would it have done me? It's not like inmates can earn 'Belligerence Points' that they can later trade in for an upgrade in accommodations. I understood that there was no way off Titan other than to get to the end of my sentence and be released. What sort of an idiot would I have to be to jeopardise that?

Well, I guess, the sort of idiot who generally populates prisons. I've seen inmates attack guards solely on the suspicion that another prisoner was given real margarine for his toast, or because someone took possession of the basketball by "deliberately being clever." Sub-warden Martin Copus once almost had his eyes gouged out by a prisoner who thought that all blue-eyed people were in league with Satan. The prisoner in question had blue eyes himself, but was incapable of grasping the contradiction. More than once, inmates have set fire to their own cells as a protest for being forced to live in a cell: clearly, some people just don't understand the concept of prison.

So, yes, I was playing the long game. And the rules were simple: treat the guards with respect, because they're the ones who are interviewed by the parole board to find out whether we're fit to return to society.

Plus the guards are *people*. Citizens. Law-enforcement officers of a sort, true, but still people. Despite my incarceration, I still believed in justice. Still do to this day. In fact, I'd go so far as to say that the quest for justice is my driving force. It's what keeps me going.

Did I break the law? Yes, no doubt about it. Was it fair that I was incarcerated because of it? That's not so simple to answer. If you're on the edge of a lake and you see a child out in the water in the process of drowning, but there's a *No Swimming* sign, what do you do? Let the kid drown because you don't want to break the rule? No, you swim out and save the kid. Of course you do.

Same with me. I'd been able to see how far Mega-City One was falling, and I'd tried to save it. I'd had to break some laws to do that, but what else was I supposed to do? Stand by and watch my city crumble and then shrug and say, "Well, I *could* have saved everyone but, you know, rules are rules"? Drokk that. And drokk anyone who says I'm wrong.

Judges exist to guide the people, not rule them. Same with the prison guards. It's a city in microcosm, with the guards as Judges and the inmates as the citizens. It's the citizens' duty to obey the rules as long as those rules are fair and safe. Anything else is just a hissy fit.

I drifted off to sleep again, but I wasn't out long before I was disturbed by the rocking of my seat. I opened my eyes to see Takenaga making her way to the front, pulling herself along by grabbing onto the seat-backs.

She asked Sloane, "What is it?"

"We're forty minutes out, give or take. Can't raise them on the radio."

"Is that—?"

"They know we're out here. They should certainly be listening."

Takenaga looked around slowly, pursing her lips. "That's not a good sign. How long before we're in visual range?"

"Twenty-eight minutes we should be able to see the comms tower. Three minutes after that, the top of the... well, no, not any more. I was going to say that we'd see the top of the dome over the gardens, but that's gone now."

I sat up, climbed out of my seat. "Take us in slow. Keep listening, keep your eyes open."

Takenaga said, "You don't give orders, Dredd. Sit back down."

"Were *you* ever a Judge? No. I was. I've trained for situations like this." I nodded ahead. "Something's happened, something bad. Check the radio, Ms Sloane. Scan the channels and *keep* scanning until you get a signal."

Sloane said, "No need to be paranoid about it. Until we know for certain what's happening, we have to assume that all is well."

"The evidence is already telling us that all is *not* well," I said. "If comms are down, that means something is jamming the signals, right? At the very least you should be able to communicate directly with the other guards' radios."

Cautiously, Takenaga said, "This is just speculation, but suppose we triggered an alarm at the base and the same people behind Colonel D'Angelo's operation decided to pay the prison a visit?"

Sloane rolled her eyes. "That *is* just speculation, and it doesn't help anyone."

"All right," I said. "Then... get as close as you can without anyone at the prison being able to see us. I'll go out there, scout the area, report back."

"Not alone," Takenaga said. "I'll go with you."

"You'd slow me down. I don't need an environment suit out there: I can run, hide, whatever. Plus, I've logged more time outside the prison than everyone on this bus combined."

Both Sloane and Takenaga were looking at me now, so I gave them my best lips-sewn-together smile. "Trust me."

Thirty-Seven

WE TOOK A wide arc around the prison so we could approach it from the west, where the Potamia Mesa allowed us to get a little over half a kilometre away without being seen.

As I prepared to pass through the bus's airlock, Takenaga said, "As soon as you know for certain what's happening, you come back, agreed?"

I nodded. "Sure."

"You have one hour, Rico. And you're *not* getting a gun," Sloane added.

I actually felt a little insulted by the implication that I'd be dumb enough to ask, but I held it in. Sloane and I had shared a moment back at Huygens and I didn't want to shatter that so soon. So I smiled as though it had been a joke and said, "I know better than to ask."

I kept close to the wall of the mesa as I skirted around it.

If something serious had happened at the prison—something other than a comms failure, which was just about the only safe explanation I could think of—then it might not be a bad thing for me. Rush in, save the day, Governor Dodge is so grateful he commutes the rest of my sentence.

I knew that wasn't going to happen, but, well, daydreams are free and mostly harmless, so I decided that Dodge would not only free me, he'd give me a medal and a million credits.

Then I reached the side of the mesa and ahead of me was nothing but open ground and the prison itself. I'd never really seen it from this angle. Or rather, I'd seen it—many times—but I'd never really *looked*. It was innocuous. To the casual observer I'm sure it looks no different from any other mining plant: a fenced compound containing living quarters, admin blocks, two foundries, assorted outhouses, hangars and workshops of varying sizes.

Unfortunately for me, there was no wall on this side, just the fence, even though everyone *calls* it The Wall. A fence is easier to climb, but you can't see through a wall. If an inmate should escape, it's important for the guards to be able to see which way the inmate is going, so that they can pick them up later. It's not like there's anywhere on Titan to escape *to*. Aside from Huygens Base, that is, but then almost no one knew about that.

My first friend on Titan was Elemeno Pea, and he once asked sub-warden Siebert, "Hypothetically, if a non-mod prisoner ran for the fence, scaled it, and kept going, how long would you wait until you went after him? If he has a twelve-hour O2 tank, would you wait, say, eleven hours and thirty minutes, so that he has no choice but to return with you? If it was a really old prisoner, would you even bother going after him at all? I guess you'd want the equipment back so you'd have to go find any escaper eventually, right? Track down his GPS implant and, bam, stun-shot to the back of the head. Or, no, wait, maybe you fire a warning shot first and then he stops, and then you make him *walk* back because that'll be tough going and it'll be a lesson he won't forget."

Siebert's response had been to tell Pea to shut the drokk up and get back to work.

There was no sign of life from the prison: no activity, no vehicles, no patrols. Nothing but the usual wisps of smoke from the foundry chimneys, which didn't tell me much since the furnaces would take days to burn themselves out.

If nothing was happening, that meant no one was watching. I could safely emerge from the shadow of the mesa and walk towards the prison.

Still, I felt extremely exposed and vulnerable as I stepped out and began to walk, expecting a shot with every step.

After I'd covered a hundred metres and still wasn't dead, I broke into a run. My artificial lungs struggled to keep up as they pulled water vapour from the air and stripped the hydrogen atoms from it, and I was sure I was pushing them beyond their limits, but this was important. If I ruptured one of the lungs, I could always get another one—or they could put my original lungs back, that would be nice. Over the years, I've had many dreams about waking up to find that the surgery has been reversed and I look human again.

I like those dreams... but they're always followed by the crushing disappointment of reality.

Ahead of me, the four-metre-high fence stretched out on each side without a break. It wasn't electrified, so it was theoretically climbable, but the engineer who'd designed it had been a sneaky drokker: the fence was deliberately loosely strung between posts, making it swing and dip and sway as you climbed. Worse, it was topped with coils of razor-wire and, believe me, that stuff is *not* something you want to mess with. Guildford used to call it 'The Pubes of the Giant Robot Devil.'

Titan's gravity is very low, only about a seventh of Earth's, so an olympic-standard athlete would have a good chance of clearing four metres, but it was too risky for me to try. I veered left, heading towards the south gates.

As I ran, I formulated a plan for getting past the gates. They were just as high as the fence, but lacked the razor wire, and were taut enough to make climbing relatively simple. And if that didn't look like a viable option, there was always the possibility of going *under* the gate. I'm sure that when the gates were built, their lower edge swept the ground with only a couple of millimetres' clearance, but decades of ore-carrying trucks had gouged deep ruts in the ground. It would be a tight squeeze, but I was pretty sure it was possible.

But it turned out that no such plans were necessary, because the gates were open. Definitely not an indicator that all was well.

And just inside the compound, lying on his side in the shadow of one of the admin buildings, was a prisoner I recognised as Jamison Yardley, a notorious counterfeiter who'd finally been caught attempting to grow cloned human eyeballs to fool retinal scanners.

It was hard to tell through his environment suit's visor whether he was unconscious or dead, so I decided to assume the former.

The outer door of the tiny airlock to the admin building was open: I hauled Yardley to his feet and pushed him inside, squeezed in behind him and ran the air-cycle. When the inner door swung open, I carried him through to the office and lowered him on an uncluttered patch of floor.

I removed his helmet and checked his pulse. Strong and steady. There was a scuff-mark on the back of the helmet close to the seal, and a corresponding bump on the back of Yardley's neck. Hit from behind, probably didn't see it coming.

I tapped his face a couple of times. "Yardley? Yardley, it's Dredd. You awake?"

No response, so there was nothing I could do for him right now, and nothing he could do for me. I put his helmet back on, loosely, and straightened up.

I had only been inside this building—the loading bay—once, and that had been several years earlier. The outgoing iridium ingots were logged through here once a year when the supply ship came. There was a large antique mechanical scales next to a state-of-the-art electronic mass-evaluator—which even for a prison mine shows a lack of trust—and half a dozen paper ledgers. For the same reason, I guess. You can't remotely hack a sheet of paper.

Out of curiosity, and knowing that I'd probably never get another chance, I opened one of the ledgers at the last page. *2085 Total Yield: Iridium 10,008.62 tonnes. Iron 461.3 tonnes. Nickel 295.8 tonnes. Gold 324.5 kilogrammes.* A lot more like that. Interesting information to a geologist, I guess, but useless to me.

A door at the rear of the office led to the loading bay itself, a large warehouse with a sliding roof. The door was unlocked, and there in front of me was enough iridium to buy a continent. Two dozen pallets stacked high with crudely-formed ingots, the fruit of half a year's labour by me and my fellow inmates.

But I wasn't interested in that. I ignored incalculable riches as I ran through the loading bay to the exit on the opposite side, leading to the guards' quarters. There, I was sure, I'd find some answers.

THE DOOR BETWEEN the loading bay and the guards' quarters wasn't locked, but it was bolted from the other side, which was worse. Locks, I can pick; opening a slide-bolt from the wrong side requires a giant magnet or telekinesis or a hefty bribe.

I pressed my face close to the small square window set into the door and tried to see in, but the quarters were in almost complete darkness, certainly a lot darker than the storehouse.

It was only as my forehead touched the glass that I realised my mistake: I was now blocking the square shaft of light spilling into the darkened room. Anyone inside could hardly fail to notice that.

I was about to move away when I saw something move. A brief glint of light on metal.

And then I was staring down the barrel of a guard's gun, not more than five centimetres away from my face.

A muffled voice said, "Back up, Dredd. Slowly. I want to see empty hands."

I took four steps backwards and raised my hands, palms out. "I'm unarmed." That wasn't true, of course. I still had the 2mm Kolibri replica tucked into my right boot. I figured it'd remain hidden as long as there was only one person on the other side of the door. Two or more and I might be in trouble, but one person wouldn't be able to frisk me properly and hold a gun on me at the same time.

There was a *shunkk* as the bolt slid back, then the door was pulled open.

Sub-warden Giambalvo's voice said, "Walk in, Dredd. Eight steps. Slowly. Keep your hands raised. Try anything and I'll lighten my gun. Understood?"

"Got it."

"Just you?"

"Just me."

I stepped through the doorway. The door was closed and re-bolted behind me as I took my eighth step, and after a few seconds my eyes adjusted to the darkness. I slowly turned around to see Giambalvo standing with her back to the door, holding the gun on me with both hands. The tip of the barrel was trembling. Never a good sign.

"What the hell happened to you?" she asked.

"I was about to ask the same thing."

"You and the others took off in the bus—I'm guessing you went out to Huygens Base—but now you come back without the others. You tell me they're okay, or I swear to *Grud* I'll—"

"They're all fine," I said. "I give you my word." I looked around properly for the first time. We were in the common area of the guards' quarters. Doors on either side led to dormitories, and behind me was a passage to the kitchen. "Are we alone here?"

Her eyes narrowed even further, and her grip on the gun tightened. "Why?"

I chose to take that to mean, "Yes," and said, "Because the

fewer of us who know about Huygens, the better." I dragged a chair over and dropped into it. "Sloane couldn't make radio contact as we approached, so I came out alone to see what's happened."

She sagged then, a combination of relief and exhaustion. "Thank Grud... Are they willing to help us?"

I hesitated. "They...? No. The base has been abandoned ever since the incident with Colonel D'Angelo and his people." I looked around the darkened room again. "So... We were gone less than two days. What did we miss?"

"IT WAS YOUR fault, Rico," Giambalvo said as she spread an old paper map of the prison across a desk in her office. "Word started to spread that you and Southern Brennan escaped. You took Takenaga and Sloane hostage. The inmates started talking, saying that if you two had broken out together, then the situation was worse than we were telling them."

"You're blaming *us* for other people's rumours?"

She pointed at the map. "Right here. C-Block. There was a gathering. They were angry, getting hungry, most of them exhausted from a six-hour shift trying to clear up the gardens and salvage pieces of the dome's superstructure. They heard that you were gone and word started to spread that you'd taken all the remaining rations with you."

I swore. "Where the hell did they get *that* idea?"

She glared at me. "Very few of the inmates here were arrested for an abundance of intelligence, Dredd. There was food, then you were gone and there was no food. Mob mentality filled in the gaps and created the conclusion they needed to riot. And that drokkin' psycho Pastor Carbonara didn't help matters one damn bit." She nodded towards the desk's monitor, which was showing a list of dates and times. "I pulled the security recordings earlier. Check it out. Third from the bottom. Quadrant two, camera four."

I poked at the workstation's keyboard and after a second or two the screen flickered to show a high-angle view of the cross-junction in C-Block. Among the inmates milling around, I could see Pastor Carbonara shouting for attention.

"Give it a few seconds for the sound to kick in," Giambalvo said. "There's always a lag. Don't know why—we've never been able to iron that out."

I said, "It's not a lag. It's a feature. It's—" Carbonara's voice erupted from the monitor, and I hit the pause button. "There's an option in the security software that allows you to view the images in silence for a few seconds just in case you need to check on the camera feed without alerting everyone around you."

"How do you know *that*?"

"I was a Judge. We study security systems." I tapped at the keyboard, calling up the software's options page. "There: 'DBS 25.' That's twenty-five seconds Delay Before Sound. I'd recommend setting the value to five. Any less than that and you're taking a risk if you ever *do* need to surreptitiously check the cameras." I closed the options page, and stared at the still image of the inmates in C-Block. "So what am I going to hear?"

"Watch for yourself."

I hit *play* and the image unfroze. It played in silence again. Most of the inmates weren't paying any attention to Carbonara, but her usual entourage was behind her. One of them found a plastic crate, dropped it upside-down on the ground in front of Carbonara. She stepped on it and resumed shouting just as the sound kicked back in.

"The Almighty Grud has delivered unto us the challenge of the empty larder, and to you, my children, I say that we are duty-bound to meet this challenge head-on. We should *rejoice* in this misfortune, *celebrate* these difficult times to come. We should wallow in the happy knowledge that Grud has deigned us worthy of suffering this hardship. It is *only* through adversity that we will be cleansed and purified and thoroughly shaken down and thus judged fit to enter into Grud's sacred chambers of holy blessed worthiness. Can I get an Amen?"

A woman in the crowd nearby replied, "No, yeh can't. Go peddle yer sanctified stomm somewhere else, Carbonara."

I smiled at that: Genoa Amin, my favourite of all the inmates.

One of the pastor's acolytes—Sven "Fawn" Svendsen, a former tutor at the Megaheim Law Academy—politely asked Genoa to move along, and made the mistake of putting his hand on her arm.

Svendsen wouldn't be using *that* hand again for a long time.

The fight broke out almost instantly. I'd seen it happen before, first-hand, both here on Titan and on the streets of Mega-City One. Sometimes all it takes is for one person to clear their throat in the wrong way at the wrong time, and suddenly the air is filled with fists and screams.

The first groin had barely been kicked before four of Carbonara's followers dragged her away from the fighting. The rest of the acolytes—a good sixteen or seventeen, by my estimation—swarmed into the crowd with swinging fists and butting heads.

Though smaller and lighter than most of the inmates, Genoa fought like a dervish. I was aware of her reputation, but I'd never really seen her in action before.

She elbowed Yves Venti in the throat, and as he stumbled backwards, leapt onto him and used his body as a platform to launch herself towards Billy-Joe Bungalow, a knuckle-dragging bruiser with a penchant for strangling his victims with their own relatives' intestines.

Bungalow saw her coming and lashed out at her, a powerful backhand to swat her away. But Genoa latched onto his arm and wrapped herself around it. Unbalanced, Bungalow staggered into Peta Rosenberg just as she was in the process of pummelling Hugo Boylan with his own cybernetic arm.

Rosenberg lashed out at Bungalow and Genoa rolled neatly to the ground, skidded past Boylan—giving him a totally unwarranted kick along the way—then leapt to her feet, vaulted over two prisoners who were either desperately trying to bear-hug each other to death or were taking advantage of the chaos to have a sneaky cuddle, and tucked herself into a ball just before crashing into the back of Deathwish Drogan's knees.

"Wow."

Next to me, Giambalvo said, "I know. I've watched that three times already. Two days ago she almost froze to death—*and* suffocated. She recovers fast."

Violence rippled through C-Block like a tidal wave, an irresistible force that swept up everyone and everything along with it.

I flipped through the screens, camera to camera, watching as the fighting spilled out into B-Block. Everything not bolted to the floor became a weapon or a shield, often both. I swear I saw one prisoner attempt to attack another with a damp sponge.

Watching the riot after the fact, via the remoteness of the security-cam playback, it was almost possible to be blasé about it, as I realised when I saw Sandrine Hornby throw a fire extinguisher at Philip Mehta and mentally awarded her only six points out of ten.

But that changed when I saw Sorenta Teffer snatch sub-warden Henry's sick-stick and zap him with it. As he collapsed, spewing vomit onto the ground, Teffer hit him again and again, over and over until long after the spasms stopped and his twitching body was ejecting nothing but blood from every orifice.

I hit the pause button again, and turned to Giambalvo. "All right. What's the current status?"

"As near as I can tell, at least seven guards and twenty-eight inmates are dead. Most of the cameras have been smashed or covered. Someone got into the comms control room and rigged the units to broadcast white noise on every wavelength. Until we can shut that down, no one's getting a radio signal in or out—the comms system has its own batteries that'll keep it running for a week, so even if we could get close enough to cut the power cable from outside, it wouldn't do any good. Carbonara has her people holed up in D; they've taken possession of all our supplies and they've got two guards as hostages. One is definitely Aldrich, and I think the other is Mister Copus—that's the only place he could be. Last time I saw them, they were running towards Carbonara's people."

I said, "So they're either dead or captured. Captured makes more sense; hostages are always better than corpses in a stand-off. Plus, if Copus was dead, they wouldn't *hide* his body. They'd display it."

"As for Kassir and Sims," Giambalvo continued, "near as I can tell they lost most of their crew. Now it's just the two of them and a few hangers-on. But they got past security and into the generator."

"Aw, hell, no. That gives them control of the backup air-recycler, the AG *and* the power!"

She nodded. "That's the stand-off. And everyone else is in the middle. Freeze or starve. Or suffocate. Or die of thirst. We can't get close enough to any of them to even begin negotiations. Frame, Doc Mollo and a couple of the others barricaded themselves in Governor Dodge's office to protect him, but that backfired."

"Right: now they're *stuck* in there," I said. "So if I've counted correctly... Aside from Takenaga and Sloane out in the bus, you're the only guard we know for certain who's still free."

Giambalvo nodded again, and held up her gun. "And this is our only asset."

"Not any more. Now you have me."

Thirty-Eight

I NEEDED ALLIES, that much was obvious. Giambalvo couldn't be one of them. A situation like that, if you're running around with one of the guards, you *deserve* to get turned into paste.

Most of the security cameras had been smashed or torn from the walls, but archive footage showed me that a little over seven hours ago, Genoa Amin had been hiding out in the med-centre.

"You can't get to her without being seen by Kassir's people," Giambalvo protested. "They've got the entrance to D- and E-Blocks staked out."

"I know a way."

"And what good will it do any of us if you *can* reach her, Dredd?"

"She's a good fighter. I'll need people who can fight to get past Carbonara's acolytes. Since you won't give me a *gun*..."

"Correct."

"I can do this," I assured her, trying to sound confident. "I can take back control of the generator and the supplies."

She raised an eyebrow. "*Without* killing everyone?"

I nodded. "Without killing *everyone*."

"That's not what I meant."

"I know."

THE LONG TUNNEL between the guards' quarters and gen-pop was usually much better lit; I was grateful to whichever nameless convict had decided to smash most of the ceiling lights. Not an easy task, given that they were behind reinforced transparent plasteen.

As it was, the tunnel was dark enough that I could make my way along it by sticking to the side and keeping to the shadows. Someone would have to be actively looking for movement to notice that I was there.

As I reached the junction where the tunnel joined E-Block, I heard something scuff against the ground ahead of me.

I dropped into a crouch. E-Block was in almost complete darkness. It seemed bigger, and much more dangerous, than it did in the light.

I moved closer, my hand slipping towards my right boot. The Kolibri replica was still there, and I instantly regretted not test-firing it earlier, just to be sure that it actually worked. But the gun would have to be my last resort; it could become a starting gun for the inmates to resume rioting.

Far better to stick with the heavy, unbreakable baton Giambalvo had given me. I've seen—and felt—the effect of those batons far too often. They were smaller but weightier than a Judge's daystick. A quick tap in the right place and a guard could shatter an inmate's jaw without even breaking stride.

Another scuffing sound, closer now. Something shifted in the darkness, a grey fuzziness slowly moving from right to left.

I shuffled closer to the corner, and called out in a loud whisper, "It's okay, it's just me!" I figured it was worth a shot.

The distinctive voice of a modified female inmate came drifting back, "Did you *get* it?"

"Just about. See for yourself."

The face of Dominie Malasi appeared around the corner, and I immediately jabbed the end of the baton at the voicebox in her throat.

She stumbled back, gasping, and I caught her arm and pulled her forward before she hit the ground.

"It's Rico Dredd," I whispered. "Sorry about that, Malasi, but I couldn't risk you calling out."

She coughed and rasped a little, still clutching her throat. "Drokker!"

"Yeah, I know. Who are you with?"

"No one." She tried to pull free of my grip. "It's just me and Bailey. We were down in sub-level three when it all kicked off. Heard you stole the last of our food."

"You heard wrong. We went out *looking* for food."

Her good eye narrowed at that. "Where?"

"The crashed freighter; before your time. Who else is around? Do you know where Genoa Amin is? Last I heard, she was in the med-centre."

"Who?" Going from her expression, she genuinely didn't recognise the name.

"Scottish, female, about thirty, pale skin, dark hair."

Malasi shrugged. "That sounds like Lauren McRitchie. Short girl, yeah? I can't think of anyone else it could be." Then her sewn-up lips spread into a wide smile. "Oh. Oh, that's great. Damn it, Dredd, have you been calling her by the wrong name all this time? Hah, she smiles a lot when you're around, does she?" If it had been possible, Malasi would have been laughing by now. "That's fantastic! She's let you think her name is Genoa Amin for years and you think she's smiling because she *likes* you!"

I didn't have time for this. I squeezed harder on her arm. "Just tell me where she is!"

"McRitchie, or Amin?"

My other hand tightened on the baton, and I think that Malasi sensed it.

"All right, I'll tell you! She's still in the med-centre, I think. There's a few of them holed up there."

I loosened my grip on her arm. "Tell no one you saw me, okay? We don't want this turning into more of a bloodbath than it already is."

I began to move on, but stopped when Malasi asked, "Dredd, how are we going to survive this? Before the riot, I heard Copus talking about creating a new garden, but we'll all be dead long before anything edible can grow."

For a moment I didn't know what to say. Judges aren't therapists; it's not our job to hold the frightened citizens' hands and tell them everything is going to be all right. So I said the only thing I could think of: "Every inmate on this rock is here, not because we got caught, but because we lived through the worst that our cities' authorities could throw at us. We're not just prisoners. We're survivors." I forced a smile. "Can you think of *any* other bunch of people more suited to get through this than *us*?"

THE CORRIDOR LEADING to the med-centre was blocked by a barricade of desks, stretchers and filing cabinets, and some genius had smashed the overhead lights but rigged up portable spotlights that shone directly along the corridor.

I stepped out into the full glare and could see almost nothing past the spotlights. But they could sure see me.

Genoa's voice came from somewhere behind the barricade. "Rico Dredd. So yeh came back, did ye? I... Dredd, I'd stop walking right drokkin' *now* if I were you."

I kept walking. "You're *not* me." I was taking the chance that they didn't have guns. Sure, they could have taken the guards' weapons, but overriding a gun's handprint-scanner without it exploding in your face isn't an easy task. I'd only ever known one inmate smart enough to do that: Ren Tramatky, former Euro-Cit Judge and current corpse.

"I mean it, Dredd. One more step!"

"I'm not a threat. Not to you." I wanted to say her name, of course, but the conversation with Malasi had thrown me. "You know that."

"Only thing I know is if yeh keep walking, we'll... Ah, drokk it! Give him a shot across the bows!"

A small crater appeared in the floor more than ten centimetres to my left and the sound of the gunshot echoed through the corridor.

I stopped.

Still squinting against the spotlight, I said, "Okay, you've got my attention. How'd you do it?"

"What do yeh *want*, Dredd?"

"I'm going to take back control. Of everything. And to do that I need you with me."

There was a moment of silence that stretched out too long, until Genoa whispered, "Is he drokkin' *serious?*"

I called back, "Yes, I am. Are you with me?"

"Do yeh not know what's *happening* here, Rico? Lot of folks dead already. Now there's eight or nine or ten factions, each one waiting for something to trigger them. Won't be long before the hunger gets into some drokker's brain and a lot more people die."

I shuffled about as I shielded my eyes, risking another couple of steps in the process. "I *do* get that. I'm not an idiot. But this situation won't resolve itself."

Her voice heavy with exasperation, Genoa said, "Yes, it *will*. The more people who die, the more food there is to go around for the rest of us. This *is* the resolution."

I didn't want to admit it, but that was hard to argue with. I was stumped for a second. But only a second. "What if whoever has the remaining supplies decides to torch them rather than let anyone else win? We're not exactly dealing with the most empathic and compassionate people, here."

There was more whispering, then Genoa said, "All right, yeh have a point there. Come on. Drop the stick. Hands where—"

"I know the drill. Everyone always wants to see my hands." I let the baton fall to the ground and stepped forward.

When I walked around the barricade and my eyes readjusted to the darkness, I discovered how they'd managed to get one of the guards' guns to work. They didn't need to bypass the gun's handprint-scanner because sub-warden Morton De Luyando was part of their group. De Luyando and I hadn't crossed paths many times. That made him an unknown quantity.

Past De Luyando was Genoa, armed with what looked like a metal chair leg, with one end sharpened to a point and medical tape wrapped around the other to make a grip.

And behind Genoa, through the glass doors of the med-centre, I could see another seven or eight inmates. I didn't know all of them, but a glance at their nervous expressions was enough: these people were not fighters. They'd been incarcerated for non-violent crimes. In a fight, they'd be a liability.

"What are you doing here?" I asked Genoa. "Thought you'd be smart enough to side with someone who has at least a *chance* of winning."

De Luyando said, "This isn't about winning through violence, inmate. It's about attrition. The other factions expend their energies and ammunition fighting each other, then they need medical supplies to patch themselves up."

"Which you'll trade for food."

Genoa nodded. "Spot on, hen. So yeh want me to help negotiate with the others? I can't see it working. Carbonara's got almost all the food, and she's mad as a bag of spaniels. Sims and Kassir have control of the air and the heat. The other factions are spread out ready to ambush anyone who looks like a soft target."

"That's one of the reasons I need you," I told her. "You have a reputation. Same as me. They're gonna think twice before they mess with us." I glanced at De Luyando. "Guess you're staying here. Keep these people safe."

I again looked through the glass doors and that was when I realised *why* those other inmates were part of this clique. Genoa had chosen them deliberately. Most I didn't know, but I recognised Lyanne-Bette Tyrone, a Mega-City Two surgeon serving twenty years for reclassifying comatose patients as deceased and then harvesting their organs. And next to her was Blake "Diamond-Dust" Chancellor, also of MC2, who killed at least forty random citizens by dropping a variety of poisons into their synthi-caf cups on the morning zoom. A qualified surgeon and an accomplished poisoner: both more than capable of dispensing the right medicines.

De Luyando said, "You bring her back *safe*, Dredd. Intact. Or I'll make sure you draw K-shaft for every duty for the rest of your life. You hear me?"

There was no point in a counter-threat. "Sure. I hear you."

Genoa asked, "Who first?"

"Kassir and Sims."

"They *hate* you, yeh know. My guess is yer sittin' at the top of their must-kill list."

"I've been at the top of a *lot* of people's kill lists. But I'm still here."

Thirty-Nine

THE PENAL COLONY'S chief power-source was the generator room. Located at the northern end of the complex, it was only accessible—without going outside—through one long, easily-defended corridor. Halfway along, Vivean Kassir and Lorne Sims had posted one of their people, Hector Boyarsky, as a sentry behind a barricade of battered steel doors and wide-bore plastic ducting. I was familiar with the stuff from digging out the lower tunnels: it wasn't heavy, but it was almost strong enough to stop even an armour-piercing round.

"No one gets in," Hector said. I didn't know him well, and nor did Genoa, but it was clear he didn't want to be there. It wasn't warm in the corridor, but he was drenched in sweat, and his hands were trembling.

"We don't *want* to get in," I told him. "We just want to talk to Sims."

Genoa said, "Or Kassir," and I inwardly winced, but didn't contradict her.

Kassir was too volatile, too close to Brennan in temperament. Any discussion with her was almost destined to end in threats of violence, if not *actual* violence. Hell, one time she walked over to a guy and punched him so hard in the stomach that he was pissing blood for a week. She said he deserved it, because she'd had a dream in which she'd thrown a birthday cake to him and he'd failed to catch it.

Story goes that she'd committed so many acts of violence and insubordination when she first got to Titan that the guards just kept piling on the months to the point where within the first year she'd almost doubled her sentence.

To Hector, I said, "Just let me speak to either of them."

He dry-swallowed and shook his head. "Can't do that."

I began to speak, but he flinched as though I'd raised my arm to strike him—I hadn't moved at all.

"You want this to end, Hector? I can end it. But I need their help."

He glanced along the corridor, towards a second barricade close to the generator room's doors. "I... No, I can't."

Genoa said, "Ah, drokk this. He's not armed, Dredd. What's he gonna do? Tell yer ma?"

She stepped around me and made to push past Hector. He put his arm out and she bumped into it and stopped walking.

She slowly turned her head to face him.

I've seen a *lot* of things, but I've never seen a man so absolutely terrified. He knew that he had no choice. If he didn't try to stop us, Kassir would make sure he paid.

Genoa said, "Who scares you most, Boyarsky? Me or them?"

He muttered, "Oh sweet grud..." Then, louder, said, "Them. I'm sorry, McRitchie. I respect you, I do, but they... They'll kill me."

She leaned closer. "*I'll* kill you."

Hector gently shook his head. "Not the way *they* would. I'd *rather* it was you."

I'd had enough. I swung my baton, whacked him on the side of the head. He crumpled neatly and almost silently.

From behind the second barricade, Vivean Kassir's voice said, "We know what you want, Dredd. We're not buying."

"I just want this to end," I shouted back. "We got some supplies. Enough to last an extra month, maybe. In fact, maybe even longer given that so many of our fellow inmates are no longer in the respiration club."

Kassir stepped out from behind the barricade. She was also carrying a guard's baton. "Got them from where?"

"The crashed freighter. You remember that?"

"Stomm. If that freighter had been carrying supplies, we'd have heard about it a long time ago."

"Emergency rations. Plus, there was stuff we missed last time. Didn't seem important then to recover five kilograms of mockpork jerky. Everyone *hates* that stuff. In a few weeks it's going to be ambrosia. And not just that. There's canned fruit and vegetables, dry cereals, ration packs. It's not going to be a feast, but it'll help keep us all alive until the ships get here."

"*If* they get here. The mining company might just decide it's easier to hold off until we're dead."

Genoa said, "The guards aren't criminals. If the company abandons *them*, that's a crime in sixteen different city-states. They won't take that chance."

Kassir walked closer. She was as tall as me, with roughly the same build. She stopped a metre in front of me and said, "State your terms."

"We need to take down Carbonara's people; they've got all the supplies."

"This much I know."

Genoa said, "Ye control the power throughout most of the complex... So cut the heatin' to B- and C-Blocks. Thirty minutes, forty max, they'll be *begging* yeh to turn it back on."

Kassir shook her head. "We already thought of that. Can't be done. We can't isolate a couple of blocks like that."

I nodded. I'd guessed that must be the case, or they'd have done it already. But I had a backup option. "The generator... I've seen it. It's big."

"So?"

"It's big enough to stay warm for a few hours after you shut it down. You cluster around it, that'd keep you going long after everyone else has passed out from the cold."

Kassir looked from me to Genoa and back. "Jovus... are you drokkin' *insane?* The surface temperature out there is about negative one-eighty! If we shut down the generator and can't get it started again, everyone would be dead in less than a *day*."

Genoa stepped away from me. "She's right, Dredd. That's just nuts."

"You want this to end before you starve; so do I. And freezing is a better death than starvation."

From the doorway to the generator room, Lorne Sims called out, "The cold won't affect *him*. He's a mod." Sims was wearing an environment suit, everything but the gloves and helmet. The gloves were tucked into his belt, and it was a safe guess that the helmet was close to hand.

Kassir glanced back at Sims. "What are you saying?"

"I'm saying Dredd's a snake, but he's not an idiot. And he's no coward." He beckoned me closer. "Let's talk."

As I moved towards him, Kassir put her hand on my shoulder to stop me. It wasn't immediately obvious from her grip whether she was threatening me or just grabbing my attention. "You killed him, didn't you?"

"What?"

"Brennan. That's why you're here and he's not."

That confirmed my long-held suspicion that Kassir was in love with Brennan. She was almost twice his age, but it's said that love doesn't recognise temporal barriers. From the way I'd seen Brennan treat her, it was a pretty safe bet Kassir's feelings weren't reciprocated and never would be. Sometimes, love is like trying to catch your own shadow in a jar.

Brennan probably didn't even realise why Kassir was so loyal to him.

I was on the edge of telling her what had happened to him, how he'd finally snapped and shown his true self. But I decided to save that for another time. Always good to have something in the bank. "He's not dead. He's safe. For now." I let her stew on that while I asked Sims, "Who does Carbonara have backing her up?"

He began to rattle off a list of names, and Genoa raised her hands to stop him: "Pull the brakes on that, there. Who does she have who's a *threat*?"

Sims said, "It's not a matter of *who*, it's how *many*. We figure at least sixty. Maybe as many as eighty."

Genoa and I exchanged a glance, and I'm sure we were thinking the same thing: we'd been expecting to have to deal with maybe ten of the pastor's acolytes, fifteen at most, and even that would be a lot more than she usually had.

Genoa said, "She's got the supplies. Food buys a lot of faith."

I heard voices from the doorway behind Sims, and asked him, "Who do *you* have in there?"

His eyes narrowed at that. "What the drokk difference does *that* make?"

"Basic strategy, spugwit. If you don't know who your allies are, how are you supposed to be able to recognise your enemies?"

"Yeah. Always the same with you, Dredd. You want everyone to believe you're a step ahead of them. You're not the only one who can strategise."

Genoa said, "I don't think that's a real word."

Sims ignored her. To Kassir, he said, "They want to shut down the generator, everyone else freezes, then we all go and take the supplies from Carbonara. Good plan. We'll take it." A grin stretched out across his face. "And we don't need these drokkers alive to *use* it."

I had been expecting that. If they'd known me better, they'd have understood that I don't respond well to threats, and I certainly don't go anywhere without a backup plan.

Just as Kassir shifted her stance and raised her baton, preparing to strike out at Genoa, I raised my own arm and shot Sims in the face.

I'd taken a risk with the Kolibri replica, but I'd been almost certain it would pay off. Whoever had owned the gun before me had kept it clean; that was a good indication that it still worked.

I liked it a lot. Sure, it didn't have the power, accuracy, range or versatility of a Lawgiver, but a gun small enough to conceal in your hand? A very, *very* useful tool. It might well be my new favourite weapon.

My shot was actually a little off. Maybe I was out of practice, but more likely it was because the Kolibri's barrel-length is just too short to permit perfectly accurate aim. I hit Sims square in the forehead. I'd been aiming for his left eye. That still bugs me a little, but it's not healthy to dwell on stuff like that. The outcome was the same anyway: Sims toppled over backwards, dead, and Kassir flinched.

That flinch was enough for Genoa. She was a head shorter than Kassir and maybe twenty kilos lighter, but she was faster and even more vicious.

Even though my instincts were yelling at me to just finish Kassir, I overrode them and I stepped back to watch the fight.

Genoa's first move was her trademark elbow to the stomach. If she'd been fighting a male, that would have been immediately followed by a punch to the groin. Instead, and because Kassir was still armed with a baton, Genoa formed her fingers into a point and jabbed up at Kassir's right armpit. There's a handy nerve-cluster there, and if you strike it with enough force, the target's arm will spasm and she'll drop her weapon.

Genoa caught the baton before it hit the ground, but as she was adjusting her grip on it, Kassir slammed a foot into her kidneys with enough force to almost knock Genoa sideways.

Next came a blur of swings, blocks, strikes and dodges from both of them and I had to resist the urge to offer suggestions.

Vivean Kassir was tough, but no match for Genoa Amin. The

fight's decisive move was a powerful swing of the baton that was almost stopped by Kassir's front teeth.

Almost.

Kassir staggered backwards, spitting out blood and fragments of broken teeth through split lips. She tried to swear at Genoa, but it was hard to understand what she was saying.

Genoa wrapped it up with a spinning, contorted leap: her right foot crashed into Kassir's already-weakened jaw, then it was followed by a baton-strike to the temple.

As Kassir crumpled to the ground, Genoa straightened herself up, flexed her arms a little, then crouched to use Kassir's shirt to wipe the blood off the baton. As she did so, she casually asked me, "So, Rico, I've been wonderin'. When, exactly, were ye planning to tell me that yeh were carryin' a drokkin' *gun?*"

Forty

It took us four minutes to get Sims out of his environment suit, and another two to get Genoa into it. It wasn't a great fit, but then the suits really only came in one size, not counting Southern Brennan's bespoke outfit.

The door to the generator room opened smoothly and silently on well-greased hinges, and we dragged Sims and Kassir inside.

I always thought it'd be the best place to hide in the event of a disaster. Solid construction, only one entrance, lot of shadowy nooks. It's a mess of gantries and staircases and dangling chains and large machines that hum and vibrate so strongly they're bolted to the ground to stop them from juddering their way across the room.

Inside, eight inmates stood in a line, facing us, each one tightly clutching a makeshift club or spear. My guess is that they would have rushed us before now, if not for the shot that had killed Sims. Most of them looked nervous.

"We're going to end this," I told them. "You get in the way, you'll be hurt. Everyone understand that?"

The man on the far right, Donal Pangione—a permanently calm thirty-something with a long, matted beard and only thee remaining digits on each hand—nodded and let his spear drop. "Sure. Yeah."

He was the one I wanted, a former engineer, and no doubt hand-picked by Sims and Kassir. Possibly they'd even bookmarked him years ago just in case. If so, that was smart: plan your survival team in advance because it's a lot more tricky when there's fire or bullets involved. It was something I realised I should have done.

I pointed to the generator, towering over everything else in the room. "You can shut that down and bring it back online again?"

Pangione said, "I can. Worked on subatomic compression star-drives before—"

"That's good enough." I turned to Genoa. "You think you can handle them?"

"Yeah. But I don't want them ambushing me." She paused, then added, "Give me the gun."

"No."

"I'll give it yeh back when we're done, Rico! I can look after myself, but I can't watch these people and watch the door without a deterrent to prevent some drokker cavin' my head in with a wrench."

"All right." I passed the weapon to her as we strode towards the generator, and the others backed away, watching us. Softly, I told Genoa, "The mag's got eleven rounds left, then that's it. Effective range is a lot closer than you'd like, it doesn't pack much of a punch and I don't think it's very accurate, either. But it's still a gun, so maybe that'll be enough to keep them away."

She started to tuck the gun into a pouch on her environment suit's belt, but I stopped her. "You should hold it first, with the gloves on. Get a feel for it. And be careful because there's no trigger-guard."

She practised pulling the gun from her pouch a couple of times. I'd seen faster turtles.

"What the hell kind of a criminal were you, anyway, Genoa?"

"The *nice* kind. I've never fired a gun. Never even held one before."

"I heard you were in for murder."

She raised an eyebrow. "Yeh think I need a *gun* to commit murder? Hah." She turned the weapon over in her hands. "Where's the satisfaction with something like this? With a knife yeh get to be close enough to feel the drokker's last breath. A metre of piano-wire and yeh can feel them struggling. Even with an ordinary carpenter's hammer there's that lovely *crack* as it hits, y'know? The feeling as the shock ripples up yer arm. *This* thing..." She sneered. "A gun is a *coward's* weapon, Dredd. This is for killers who are too scared to get their hands dirty. Amateurs."

I didn't really know what to say to that. I guess there had always been a part of me so enamoured of her that it wouldn't let me really believe that she *deserved* to be on Titan. She was short and cute—"pixie-like," someone once described her— and most of the time was friendly and bubbly and smiling.

But you don't end up on Titan because of an administrative error. A seat on the shuttle is hard-earned.

I began, "Jovis... Look, Genoa—"

"That's *not* my name, yeh drokkin' idiot!" She stepped back, clearly exasperated.

I glanced around at the others: they were watching. I knew what was coming and I didn't want anyone to witness it.

But Genoa—or Lauren—didn't have the same penchant for discretion. "Damn it, Rico. I know yeh've kept me on a pedestal these past few years, but yeh have to grow up *sometime*! This"—she pointed to me, then herself, then back to me again—"this is nothing. There's nothing between us. There's no romance waitin' in the wings for the right moment. For cryin' out loud, man, can yeh not see the pattern?"

"What are you talking about?"

"Yeh did the same thing with that Sov Judge! Kurya. Same thing. Always including her, checking in with her"—Genoa made air-quotes—"*taking care* of her. She doesn't need yeh, she doesn't *want* yeh. I mean, when was the last time there was an actual conversation between ye that *she* initiated?" She sighed long and loud. "Get over yourself, Rico. Yer a Judge who went bad. That doesn't make yeh special. This is the *planet* of the Judges who went bad."

She turned away, then abruptly turned back. "And my name is Lauren McRitchie. Genoa Amin was a *joke*. Some folks here started callin' me that when I got here, because of my accent. D'yeh know wha' I mean?"

I can't pretend that didn't hurt. I'm human, despite appearances.

And she was wrong about me idolising her and Kurya. Sure,

I liked them both, but I wasn't the love-starved puppy that she seemed to think I was.

But this wasn't the time to correct her. We both had jobs to do.

I said, "Sure. I know that. I just *like* the name Genoa. It suits you. Now are you going to be able to handle this? We've only got one shot at it."

"I can do it."

I nodded. "Good." I looked around, spotted Donal Pangione, and said, "You, the engineer. If we shut down the generator right now, how long before we use up all the oxygen in the complex?"

He shrugged. "People consume about six hundred litres of oxygen per day. Assuming that there's about two hundred of us still breathing, that's a hundred and twenty thousand litres. A cubic metre is a thousand litres, so that's one-twenty cubic metres per day consumed by everyone."

Pangione slowly turned around in a complete circle. "Very rough guess... Taking in the sizes of all the prison's buildings, including the enclosed mines and tunnels... Say it's about half a million cubic metres of air. Twenty per cent of the air is oxygen, so that's a hundred thousand cubic metres of O2. Divide that by one-twenty... We're looking at about eight hundred and thirty-three days. Or about two years, three months. Not counting oxygen we already have in tanks, or what might be generated by plant-life before then."

"So they won't all suffocate before they starve."

"Assuming there are no leaks, and no fires. And no running internal combustion engines, or anything else that consumes oxygen."

"Good. Shut it down."

Pangione consider the order for a second. "Uh... no. No, that'd be bad."

"Genoa? I mean, Lauren? Persuade him."

I don't know what Pangione did to shut down the generator—that is, I saw him flipping switches and typing at the attached keyboard, but I didn't understand the actual process—but a minute later there was the sudden absence of a constant background hum I hadn't realised had been there. The overhead lights blinked out, everyone swayed from the sudden loss of the prison's artificial gravity, and from different parts of the complex came a wave of soft *thunks* as security doors locked themselves shut, followed by a fresh wave of shouts and yells and muffled threats.

The only real light in the generator room now came via the overhead skylights, until one of Pangione's colleagues switched on a flashlight.

I gestured for him to give me the flashlight, then asked, "How long before the loss of heat will be noticed?"

"Depends on where everyone is," Pangione said, gingerly nursing the fresh bruises on his arms and shins from Genoa's persuasion. "The admin blocks are better insulated than anywhere else. They'll feel the cold last. Couple of hours, maybe. Everywhere else... it could be a lot sooner. Especially in the mine and the tunnels." He pointed down at the ground. "We got underfloor heating here, just enough to keep the frost at bay. But out there? Cold as my old man's eyes when he's talking about my mom."

Genoa said to me, "You should get moving. Don't want to get there *after* they've frozen to death. It's hard to negotiate with corpses."

As I left, I said, "If they're corpses, I won't *need* to negotiate."

That was a compelling idea, in some ways, but this wasn't about killing everyone. It wasn't even about making sure that the prison's supplies weren't in the hands of a deranged religious maniac. This was about everyone knowing who it was who'd saved the day.

Sometimes you've got to stand up and be the hero.

Forty-One

WITH THE POWER gone I had to navigate using only the light from Saturn—the flashlight would alert anyone watching, so it was for emergencies only—but it was enough for me to see my breath misting in the air. My polymer-laced skin meant that I didn't *feel* any colder, but I could almost sense the heat dissipating all around me.

Pastor Carbonara's followers had barricaded all the doors and windows, and hadn't left a sentry. They didn't seem to be listening out for anyone knocking on the door, either. I checked every possible entrance, but no one was opening up.

I could *hear* them, though. Constant low-level muttering. It was repetitive, almost soothing.

It took me a minute to realise that they were praying.

I wasn't immediately concerned, but there was some urgency. As I said, I didn't want them freezing to death before I could persuade them to open up.

There was another way in. Most people claim to understand that they live in a three-dimensional universe, but they don't really get it until they realise that *any* hole in a building is a door if someone can pass through it.

I had to go back the way I came. Past the generator room, past the med-centre, back to the guards' quarters, where I again found myself staring down the barrel of sub-warden Giambalvo's gun.

This time, the barrel was trembling with more than fear. Giambalvo appeared to be wearing three insulated jackets at the same time, her breath billowing out the narrow gap in the hoods.

"Get into an environment suit," I told her.

"There aren't any. The hell is going *on*, Dredd?"

"Generator's offline," I said, pushing past her towards the guards' lockers. "I need a rope. Twenty metres at least. And a standard tool-belt."

Giambalvo steered me towards an equipment cabinet. "Bottom shelf. What do you need it for?"

There was no time to explain. As I fastened the tool-belt around my waist, I said, "Just hold tight. Seal yourself in somewhere—it's going to get a lot colder in here." I grabbed the coil of rope and slung it around my chest as I ran.

At the door to the loading bay, I paused and told Giambalvo, "Don't bolt this behind me—I might need to come back in this way, and that'll be tricky if you're dead."

I'd intended that to sound a lot more upbeat than it did.

I pulled the door closed behind me and ran out through the loading bay. In the outer office, Jamison Yardley was still unconscious on the office floor, quietly drooling into his environment suit's helmet. The drool was starting to freeze. At least the suit would keep him warm: I properly fastened the helmet and pulled him up into a sitting position, left him propped up against the wall. I was growing tired: if the prison's artificial gravity had still been active, I might not have had the strength to lift him.

I passed through the airlock, then I was back out in the Bronze. It felt almost comfortable, almost a relief to be outside again.

Inside the prison, two hundred inmates and guards were slowly starving, or hiding, or fighting. Grud knew what the next couple of hours were going to be like, let alone the next few months.

But outside I was in control. I knew what I was doing and I didn't have to rely on anyone else.

That's the secret to a happy life: a job that needs to be done, and is just beyond the margins of your capabilities and experience so that it's still a challenge, still rewarding when it's been completed. For most of my time on Titan I'd been picking up rocks or hauling cables or pushing barrows loaded with ore or running a power-hammer. Hard work where the only challenge was brute strength.

One of the advantages of being a mod on Titan is not needing an environment suit. They're clumsy, awkward things. You're constantly checking everything around you for anything on which the suit might snag, even your own equipment. The helmet forces you to turn at the waist if you want to see what's happening either side of you, and the gloves mean you can't easily pick up or manipulate small objects.

Every external area of the prison and the mine is designed for people wearing suits. So when you don't need one, things are very different.

The buildings are suddenly scalable, for a start. Sure, the handholds and footholds aren't much more than weld-seams and rivets, but when the gravity is only a seventh of Earth's, that's not a problem.

I ran towards the side of the med-centre and jumped, aiming for a thin horizontal rail about halfway up. Years of hauling cables and swinging pickaxes had done a lot to strengthen my grip. I hauled myself hand over hand up the side of the four-storey building. I had to pass a window: I made out one of Doc Mollo's assistants sitting cross-legged on the floor, wrapped in a bundle of insulating blankets. He was reading an old paperback novel as he absently poked his index finger inside his left ear while holding a scalpel with the same hand. The potential for disaster was so great that I almost stopped to watch.

The roof of the med-centre was one of the highest points around—only the Admin building and the framework over the pit were taller—and I could see clear across the compound, but I hadn't climbed up just for sightseeing purposes. On the far side I swung myself over the edge and dropped down to the roof of the long tunnel that led to the cell-blocks.

It was windy up there and the tunnel-roof rattled constantly, which would easily mask my own footsteps as I ran from one end to the other.

The tunnel butted against the D-Block perimeter wall, four metres above me. It would have been a simple task to jump, grab onto the edge and pull myself up, but I decided to climb:

the risk of falling was too great, even under Titan's low gravity.

The roof of D-Block was gently sloped, easy to walk on. It was peppered with circular skylights, transparent plasteen strong enough to weather the worst of the moon's storms.

I crouched close to the nearest skylight to get my bearings. I was in the right place: inside, directly beneath me, was the sealed-off end of the uppermost southern corridor. The floor was three metres below, an easy enough drop if I'd been able to open the skylight; but even if I'd had the tools to open it, Titan's dense, toxic atmosphere would rush in and kill everyone in seconds.

But skylights are not the only openings. Halfway along the roof was a metre-square box, an emergency air vent, designed to help expel smoke or gas or airborne toxins. I'd seen similar vents in city blocks in Mega-City One, where they had strong bars on the outside to prevent any enterprising burglars from climbing through. Here on Titan, all the burglars were already on the inside.

All but one.

Long-term plans for the penal colony included an air-filled dome over the entire complex. When that happened, vents like this would be needed. But right now, it was just sitting there, useless; Titan's atmospheric pressure was greater than Earth.

It was my guess that the fan hadn't yet been wired up. What we had was a square box with two circular openings—one on top, one opening into the room below—and the only thing stopping me from using it as a makeshift airlock was the large motor and fan-blades inside.

The openings were simple irises, somewhat rusted and four centimetres thick, edged with a contact-sealing polymer gel.

I knelt down next to it, sprayed the plates' hinges with an all-purpose lubricant, then pulled a large, flat-bladed screwdriver from the belt and started prising open the top iris. My biggest worry was how much time it was going to take me to disconnect and unbolt the fan-blades and the motor: the longer I took, the greater the risk of someone inside hearing me.

I was able to force the blade of the screwdriver between two of the plates, but the iris didn't seem to want to open no matter how much I forced it. It had probably *never* been opened. I had a mental image of some engineers installing the vent: one of them suggests testing it out, and the other asks, "What for? They're never gonna need it. It's just here because, y'know, regulations."

I grabbed the screwdriver handle with both hands, braced my feet against the side of the vent, and pulled with every last iota of energy.

Something cracked, sending me tumbling back onto the roof.

For a second, I was sure that the screwdriver's blade had snapped, but when I got to my feet and checked, the iris was open. Even better: someone had been cutting corners. The motor and fan-blades weren't there. They'd never been installed. I mentally thanked the long-gone engineers for being even lazier than I'd imagined.

Now freed, the iris mechanism was opening and closing smoothly and silently. The plates were linked: push one plate and the whole iris opened. The polymer gel sealant was still intact, and it seemed to me that it was holding.

At the bottom of the box was another iris of the same size, this one cleaner and less rusted—a good sign. The inner walls of the box had fittings to hold the fan's motor in place: I tied my rope to the two that looked strongest.

I climbed in, keeping my feet in opposite corners outside the circumference of the iris. Now for the tricky part. I crouched down and closed the upper iris above me, then, flashlight awkwardly clenched under my jaw—it's not like I could hold it in my mouth—I started work on the lower iris.

It took a lot less effort than its counterpart. There was a sort of hiss as it popped open—the atmosphere in the vent and the block equalising—and suddenly I was looking straight down into the heart of D-Block.

It made sense that the block's architects would put the emergency vent directly above the centre of the building for maximum efficiency. Unfortunately, the centre of the building was the wide atrium connecting the block's corridors.

The floor was a good eighteen metres below me. No guarantee I could survive that drop even in Titan's lower gravity. Which was why I'd brought the rope.

At this stage I figured I probably should have tied the rope around my waist *before* I opened the inner iris, but in my defence I was exhausted. And hungry.

The block was pretty dark inside, but, far below, I could just about see the inmates. For a second, I thought they were all dead, but then one of them turned over onto her other side, and a male inmate got up, stretching and yawning, and wandered into a cell. I heard the faint but unmistakeable sound of a urine stream splashing into water.

By crouching down a little more, I could see the gantries surrounding the atrium. They were sealed from the atrium by strong wire mesh; I could have used the tools on my belt to snip my way through, but that would take far too long.

My only option was to go straight down.

And then I saw her. Pastor Elvene Mandt Carbonara. The lolling inmates dissipated as she walked slowly and steadily across the atrium, at the head of a substantial wedge of followers, maybe thirty in total. Carbonara was speaking— preaching, I guessed—but I couldn't make out her words. Behind the throng, four more of her followers clustered tightly around one of the guards. I didn't need to see his face to know that it was Copus. His hands were bound. Two of the followers were holding shivs against his throat, another was carrying his weapons, and the fourth was walking backwards behind them, glaring warily around.

It made sense. The guards' guns have handprint-sensors, like a Judge's Lawgiver, and it's very tricky to get past them. So instead of killing the guards and taking worthless guns, you keep the guards alive and force them to use their guns as and when you need them.

I tied the rope around my chest, twice, and did my best in the cramped confines of the vent to check that it was securely fastened. If any of the knots slipped, I was dead. A fall of eighteen metres in one-seventh of Earth's gravity probably wouldn't kill me, but Carbonara's followers would certainly finish the job.

I waited until Carbonara's entourage had passed, then with a tight grip on the rope I took a deep breath and lowered myself over the edge. I had to keep the majority of the rope coiled loosely on my chest, because I hadn't measured it first: it was easily long enough to reach the ground, but I didn't know how much longer it was than that: when you're entering hostile territory stealthily descending a rope is fine unless the rope reaches the ground long before you do and gives you away.

I descended hand over hand, a few centimetres at a time, each second expecting a shout of alarm from below.

Halfway down I happened to glance to one of the gantries and saw a blanket-wrapped middle-aged female prisoner wordlessly staring back at me. She gave me a slight smile and a shrug, then wandered into one of the open cells.

I was two metres above the floor when a whispered voice from the side said, "Dredd?"

I spun about to see Dustin "The Wind" Enigenburg staring up at me. He was lying on his side on the floor outside one of the cells, with a thin blanket draped over him and half of his face covered with a thick bandage.

He propped himself up on one elbow and looked around: no one else seemed to have noticed me. Then he pushed himself to his feet, scooped up his blanket and entered the cell, gesturing for me to follow him.

I dropped the rest of the way and darted over to him, all too aware that I'd left a rope dangling from the ceiling.

Inside the dark cell, Dustin dropped onto the bed, wrapped himself up in his blanket again and whispered, "The hell are you *doin'* here, dude?" His breath misted as he spoke, and he was clearly shivering.

"What do you think I'm doing here?" I asked. "Got to sort out this mess. Why is everyone sleeping out on the floor?"

"The Pastor's people have control of the supplies. We're gettin' fed in the morning. Quarter of a ration block each, she said. But only her most loyal followers will get it." He shrugged. "The Almighty Grud can be petty, I guess. He apparently doesn't approve of pillows or mattresses because they promote comfort, and the only true comfort is in the arms of Grud. All false comforts are to be shunned."

"Don't tell me you've been taken in by all that stomm?"

"Hunger feeds belief, Rico." Dustin looked at me with his uncovered good eye. "What option do we have? There ain't enough food for all the people, and we can't increase the amount of *food*, so..."

I finished the sentence for him. "So we decrease the number of *people*."

"Right."

"Not my way of doing things. We need to take back control. How many people does she have?"

"Pretty much *everyone*. She's got the food, and Copus's and Aldrich's guns. And she's got *Grud* on her side. She predicted the power would go down. How do you explain *that*?"

"She *guessed* it would go down. That's not the same thing, and it's definitely not an indication that she's got a direct line to the Almighty. The power's down because *I* shut it down."

"Jovus... Why would you do *that*?"

"Because I'm hoping that even the most fervent fanatic will realise that they'd rather live than freeze to death. They have the food, but I control the power, the heat and the light." I nodded towards the door. "I need to know where all of her people are stationed. How many at each point, who they are if you know, and any weapons they're carrying. Be *casual*, got that? You're just stretching your legs. So check them out but don't *look* like you're checking them out. Yawn a couple of times. Shuffle. Smile sleepily if anyone looks your way. Do a circuit and come back to me."

Dustin took all this in, then said, "No."

I gave him a good glare, but I must be losing my touch.

"No way, Rico. I'm sticking with what I have. Carbonara's crazy, but she's winning. Winners live, losers die. It's that simple."

"Was it that simple when I carried you out of the gardens while the whole damn place exploded around us?"

He shrugged under his blanket. "I didn't know that was you. Thanks for that. I owe you, but I'll pay you back some *other* way. Dude, you can't beat the odds this time. There are too many of them."

"They're going to freeze to death. I'm not."

Dustin pulled his blanket tighter around him. "They've got guns."

"I was a *Judge*. Top of my—"

"Top of your year in the Academy of Law. We know. *Everyone* knows. We were Judges too, most of us. Open your drokkin' *eyes*, Rico. They've won already. All you've got to do is join them, and then you're on the winning side too."

Forty-Two

IT WAS TEMPTING, I can't deny that. I could approach Carbonara and say, hey, include me in your group and I'll get the power restored.

But I couldn't do that. Carbonara ruled by force and by withholding vital resources. Fighting against that sort of regime was the reason I was on Titan in the first place.

It wasn't like they could outwait me. I could go without food for days, if I had to. But in an hour, maybe less, the last of the residual heat would be gone and any inmate who wasn't a mod would freeze, and then all the food was mine for the taking.

I looked down at Dustin Enigenburg huddled in his blanket. I didn't want him to die. I didn't want *any* of them to die. But the truth was there just *wasn't* enough food for everyone, so some of us were going to die no matter what decision I made.

Which meant that the only logical course of action was that

I had to choose who lived and who died. After all, I had the power. Over everyone. Not just the other inmates.

I held all the cards.

I told Dustin, "Stay put. And forget that stomm about sleeping on the floor. Keep as warm as you can, because it's going to get a *lot* colder before this is done."

I stepped out of the cell and into the atrium. It was quiet, with only the occasional rasping breath or soft cough to let me know that the bundles scattered across the floor contained human beings. But not for much longer, the way things were going.

I strode towards the centre of the atrium, aware that the generator room was probably still very warm, and if I died in the next few minutes, there was a strong chance that Genoa might not order the power to be reactivated in time to save everyone else. Would that make *me* the killer, or *her?*

A voice from my right: "Who the drokkin' *hell*...?"

I turned to see Fawn Svendsen staring at me. He was standing in front of the closed doors to the block's small gymnasium, wearing an environment suit without the helmet and carrying a sharpened metal pole fashioned from a table leg.

Svendsen backed away a little as I started towards him. "Dredd, is that *you?*" His breath was clouding so heavily in the air that I almost couldn't see his face through it. "How did you get in? We got every door and window..." He stopped, looking past me. His head tilted backwards as his gaze followed the rope up to the vent in the ceiling. "Drokk me sideways!"

I pulled the metal pole from his feeble grip—he was unable to hold it in his right hand, thanks to his earlier encounter with Genoa—then flipped it around and held the sharpened end up to his throat.

"Do it," he said, his voice a hoarse whisper. "Do it. Power's gone and even if it does come back, we're gonna starve long before the ships get here. Do it, Rico."

I didn't. But I did crack him on the side of the head with the edge of the pole. He crumpled to the floor and a trickle of steam rose from the blood that briefly seeped from the wound before it began to freeze.

I had to move fast.

Carbonara and her entourage had to be in the gymnasium: it was the only room with enough space for all of them. And clearly Svendsen had been assigned to guard the doors.

I dragged Svendsen aside, then thumped on the door with my fist and called, "We need *help* out here! They're tryna get in!"

I stepped back into the shadow and the doors burst open, disgorging two dozen of Carbonara's acolytes in a mass, a freezing and frenzied swarm. They seemed to all be armed with shivs, or that old favourite of the inmates of crumbling prisons, the half-brick in a pillowcase.

I quickly stepped inside, closed the doors after me, and jammed Fawn Svendsen's table leg between the door handles, effectively locking it.

On the other side of the small gymnasium, Pastor Carbonara stood in the middle of a cluster of her most loyal followers, with the hostages Copus and Aldrich trussed up on the floor nearby. Aldrich was clearly unconscious, but Copus was watching everything. Behind them, the entire back wall, about a fifth of the room, was taken up with crates of food and emergency rations.

Carbonara stared at me in surprise through the visor of her environment suit. "What...? *Rico Dredd?*"

"It's over," I said.

One of her followers was carrying a guard's gun, and he made a move towards Copus.

"Don't," I warned. "It's over. I control the power. Kill me and in a few minutes most of your people will start losing digits to frostbite. But that won't matter, because half an hour after *that,* they'll be frozen solid." To Carbonara, I said, "Concede or die. You have no other options."

Behind me, someone started banging on the doors, but I figured my makeshift bar would hold long enough.

Carbonara said, "*Join* me, Neophyte Dredd. Brother Rico. We will unite our houses under Grud's gracious and forgiving eye and our partnership will... Our partner-*ship* will be the only vessel capable of sailing the rough seas of the coming months. Buoyed aloft by Grud's will and compassion, He will be the wind that blows the sails and lends us the strength we need to reach the calm harbour of—"

"You really *are* just making this stomm up as you go along, aren't you?"

The banging on the door hadn't stopped, and I had to step further into the room for Carbonara and her people to hear me. "Take down the barricades and release your hostages. I won't tell you again."

"No."

"I can wait. Can you?"

"With Grud's help, we can wait an eternity."

I looked around at her followers. "You're the only one wearing an environment suit, Pastor. My guess is that your friends here are already losing the sensation in their hands. Finding it hard to hold onto their weapons. Certainly, they lack the strength to fight me one-to-one. All at once they *might* have a chance, but they'd want to get started right now. Every second they delay is another percentage point off their likelihood of success."

No one moved any closer to me. I knew then that I'd already won. The banging on the doors was starting to weaken.

"Let's say they've got a fifty per cent chance of taking me down. Forty-nine. Forty-eight. And they have to do it without killing me because I'm the only one who can get the heat turned back on. Forty-four. Forty-three—"

The man closest to Copus tossed his shiv to the ground and stepped away.

That broke the seal: the rest of them did the same, leaving Pastor Carbonara on her own in the centre of the room.

She was muttering something under her breath, and I had to step closer to hear.

"Please don't take this away from me."

I turned to one of her former followers, a man I knew only as Waterman. "Open the doors. Get all your people to work on breaking down the barricades. The sooner they do that, the sooner we can have the heat restored."

As Waterman moved towards the doors, I grabbed one of the shivs from the floor and started to cut through Copus's bonds. He was still glaring at the Pastor. I'd known him a long time, watched him deal with a lot of different situations, but I'd never seen *that* look in his eyes before.

Behind us, Waterman had opened the doors, and I turned to see Carbonara's half-frozen acolytes staring back in at me. The fight had gone out of them. Waterman simply said, "It's over," and the crowd dissipated. They no longer cared about the crates of food they'd worked so hard to acquire and protect. Now, their brains were filled with cold and little else.

"The barricades," I reminded Waterman.

"Yeah. Yeah, sure thing, Dredd."

As I started work on the ropes around Aldrich's wrists, Copus stretched slowly, then painfully pushed himself to his feet. "You did good." His voice was weak, but steady. "You've got to get the power back on, Dredd."

"I know. I—"

"*Now*. Leave him—I'll look after him, and protect the supplies." He leaned down and snatched up his gun. "Just go."

I nodded and headed for the door. I knew what was coming next. I guess even Pastor Carbonara did, too.

Before I'd even left the room, the gunshot echoed throughout the prison.

THE DOORWAY BETWEEN D-Block and C-Block had been barricaded by two guards' desks, five prisoners' bunks and Grud knew how many large pieces of gym equipment. Dustin and Waterman were among the inmates staring up at it.

Waterman told me, "We can't... It's sealed. Everything's just jammed in too tight, and now it's iced over."

It didn't take a structural engineer to see that he was right. Even if the inmates weren't suffering from hypothermia and starvation, it would have been a difficult task. They'd sealed themselves up nice and tight, knowing that they had all the supplies.

"Just... Just bring it down. It can't be *that* hard," I said.

Waterman raised his right hand: the palm was drenched with

blood, the skin torn away in strips. There was a corresponding bloodstain on one of the steel bunk-frames. "It's going to take too long to pull it down." He glanced back the way we'd come. "Can't you get back out through the roof?"

The answer was no. As I'd passed through the atrium, I'd noticed that the rope, like almost everything else now, was slick with frozen condensation. And if the rope was iced, so was the vent. Low gravity or not, I wasn't sure I had the *strength* to pull myself up.

"What about the window?" I asked. There was only one window on the ground floor, in the guards' office.

Shivering, Dustin, said, "You d-drokkin' c-crazy? Break the w-window and we all suffocate!"

"So it's the doorway or nothing," I said. I grabbed hold of the nearest bunk-frame and started to pull. Nothing. No movement at all. "Get ropes, get blankets," I snarled. "Wrap them around something! If everyone pulls at the same time..."

I looked back at the other inmates and realised that plan wasn't viable. Only a few of them were still on their feet. The others were huddled together in clusters, sharing what little body heat they could spare. More than a few lay on their own, barely moving.

They no longer had the strength to pull down their own barricade.

We were trapped.

Forty-Three

Salvation comes at a price, as Pastor Carbonara might have said.

For us, it came maybe ten minutes later.

I'd returned to the gymnasium, and ignored Copus as I wordlessly popped open one of the crates and found a tube of banana-flavoured food-paste. Unlike everyone else, I wouldn't freeze to death, and I wasn't going to starve myself just to keep them company.

"That's not yours, inmate!" Copus said. "Drop it!"

"Get drokked," I told him. "I've earned this." I leaned back against the crate and looked down at Carbonara's frozen corpse as I opened the tube. "So you just executed an unarmed prisoner who was already on her knees."

"She took a run at me," Copus said.

"She had a weapon," I suggested. "Hidden in her hand.

Her surrender was a ploy to gain your trust before she turned on you. Luckily, you spotted what she was doing at the last possible instant." I popped out my voicebox and squeezed half the tube of food-paste into my throat.

"Right. A weapon." He turned the gun over in his hands a few times, then returned it to his holster. "I *had* to do it, Rico. Otherwise..."

I replaced the voicebox and said, "Otherwise she'd eventually start again. Twist the facts and claim that *she* was the one who saved everyone. In a place like this, there's always people willing to follow someone with confidence and a promise of a better life. They're like the starving: eventually, they'll eat *dirt,* because that's the only way they can feel full."

Copus started to nod, then stopped himself. "Hell no. Screw *that*. Philosophy is how people who can't *do* things trick themselves into thinking they have something to offer. You get those barricades down?"

"No. No one has the strength... You could shoot out the window in the guard's room."

"And we'd all die sooner." He slumped back against the stack of crates. "Drokk."

I looked out through the gymnasium doors, then back to the body of the Pastor. Maybe she'd been the lucky one after all.

I glanced at Copus, and it seemed to me that he was thinking the same thing.

We waited to die.

Of course, we *didn't* die. Not all of us.

I felt suddenly weak, far too heavy, and at the same time Copus slumped to the floor. Then the overhead lights flickered on.

Genoa had restored the power.

*   *   *

IN ALL, SINCE the morning of the explosion out in the gardens, eleven guards and forty-eight inmates died. Over a hundred had to be treated for minor injuries ranging from frostbite to blunt force trauma.

Eight days after it all began, I was summoned to Governor Dodge's office, where he waited with sub-warden Copus. Both on the one side of the desk, the governor sitting and Copus standing at his shoulder. That was rarely a sign of good news.

I thought the Governor looked a little better than he had a few days earlier, when Kurya, Copus and I had freed him and the others. They'd locked themselves in Dodge's office without nearly enough food and water, having seriously underestimated how long the siege—as Dodge kept calling it—would last.

When I'd failed to return to the bus, Kurya and Brennan had persuaded Sloane and Takenaga to let them investigate. As soon as they'd entered the prison, they heard the generator was offline, so that had been their first stop.

Apparently, Genoa had shot Brennan twice with the Kolibri replica, but the low-powered shots had barely slowed him down. He'd taken the gun and tossed it deep into the heart of the room. We never found it again—my guess it that it hit one of the magnetised parts of the generator and is still stuck there today.

But anyway.

Back in the office, the Governor was looking at me with distaste. He didn't like that a prisoner had saved the day.

Dodge began, "If not for Southern Brennan..."

I raised my hands. "Whoa... What? All *that* drokker did was force Genoa—I mean, Lauren McRitchie—to reactivate the generator. *I'm* the one who broke the siege with Pastor Carbonara and her people. Single-handedly. Didn't Giambalvo make that clear to you?"

"She did," Copus said. "And we're not denying your part, Dredd. But you're the one who had the power shut down in the first place. You know how many inmates died of starvation in those few days? Zero. But we figure at least seven of them died from the cold."

"If I hadn't done it, more would have died in the long term. You know that."

Governor Dodge suddenly looked deflated. "Gruddamn it... Taking into account the number of dead, the supplies your team found at Huygens, and the emergency supplies inbound from the station on Mimas, we have a chance. It'll be tough as hell, but if we start the new gardens now, we might make it." He chewed on his lower lip for a second, then glanced at Copus and nodded.

The sub-warden turned to me. "We're putting you in charge of overseeing and maintaining the new gardens, Rico. This is a privileged position. You'll have eighteen inmates working under you, following your orders. It shows a level of trust that, if broken—if we ever have even the *slightest* reason to believe it is broken—will result in the most severe punishments."

"Do not let us down, Dredd," the governor said.

I smiled, as well as I could with sewn-up lips. "Of course not. Thank you, Governor."

He returned his attention to his desk and dismissed me with a brisk flick of his fingers.

Back out in the corridors, I passed Sven "Fawn" Svendsen attempting to mop the floor with only one functioning hand.

He sported a thick bandage on the side of his head, and winced a little when he nodded at me. "Rico."

"Sven." I pointed to the floor. "Missed a bit."

"I was saving that bit for later." He rested on his mop for a second. "About what happened... Appreciate you not killing me. And sorry about almost killing *you*."

He hadn't even come close to killing me, but I let that slide. "Forget it," I said. "Tensions were high. We were all on edge."

"Sure, yeah," he called after me. "Hey, life's a lot better when we're not carrying grudges, right?"

I didn't respond to that, but I did give him a friendly wave. He was right. What happened, happened, and no amount of whining could make it un-happen.

The past is our foundation, sure, but it shouldn't also be our cemetery.

As Elemeno Pea once told me, "You gotta let sleeping bygones bury the hatchet."

That said...

Sometimes you *have* to go back. Not for yourself, but for those you've left behind. If someone does you wrong, and then you move on to something better, well, the only fair thing to do is to go back to that person who wronged you and show them the light.

It was 2089. I was almost halfway through my sentence.

I knew then that I was going to make it.

EPILOGUE
TEN YEARS LATER

TITAN
2096 A.D.

FABIENNE BROWN FOUND it hard not to stare at the scarred, beaten man on the other side of the steel table. "Are you *permitted* to discuss those things, Rico?" the reporter asked. "The military base, the food riot... I mean, look what they did to you, just to keep you quiet after the *storm*..."

"That was a long time ago," Rico said. "Huygens Base is no longer a secret. Things have happened. And *this*..." He sat back and gestured to his face, throat and chest. "Yeah, it's hell, but they're not going to turn me back while I'm still a prisoner. You can get a lot more work done out there in the Bronze when you're not encumbered by an environment suit."

For hours, he'd been telling her his story, but she still wasn't sure what to make of him. She'd known who he was before she came to Titan, of course: Rico Eustace Dredd, a former

Judge. Brother to Joseph Dredd, who, many said, was tipped to one day sit on the Council of Five.

But Rico had only lasted a year on the streets. Fabienne had wanted to know why. Genetically, he was identical to Joe, and they'd received the same training. So why had one turned out bad, and the other good?

He was the reason she had wanted to come to Titan, and this trip was the result of years of cajoling and deal-making and compromises between her publishers and the Mega-City One Department of Justice.

Now, watching him sitting impassively in the steel chair, cuffs on his wrists and ankles, all she could see was an idealist who'd taken the wrong path.

Or maybe he was steered *down the wrong path*, she told herself.

Aloud, she said, "I'm wondering how much of your story is true, Rico. There are so many inconsistencies. And I've no way to verify most of what you've told me; the full details of your pre-arrest activities haven't yet been made public."

"What reason would I have to lie?"

"To paint yourself as the hero of your own tale, of course. Why else?"

"It's all true," he told her. He shuffled closer, and added, "But you do understand that guards will check your recordings before they permit you to leave, don't you?" He smiled. "My guess is that at least three quarters of what I've told you will be redacted. And of the rest... a lot of names and details will be changed. So what *is* the truth? You're only getting one side of the story. To know the whole truth you'd need to have been there. And even *then*..."

"Our grasp of the truth is tainted by our own biases," Fabienne said.

Rico Dredd nodded. "Right. Pick any event... Say, that time me and Joe got trapped out in the Cursed Earth. I can tell you what *I* perceive to be the truth, but you ask *Joe* what happened, you'll get a different spin on the story."

"You've spent more of your life without your brother than with him, Rico, but you talk about him a *lot*. Do you think Joe was envious of you? You frequently scored higher marks than him in the Academy."

Rico shrugged. "Maybe. He was always a closed book, even to me. Hard to say whether he was jealous or just plain inferior. But he was wrong, I'll tell you that. They're all wrong."

Fabienne asked, "Wrong to incarcerate you? Or wrong in their approach to the law?"

Rico leaned forward, resting his arms on the table. "Now, let me get this clear... Redactions or otherwise, I don't want to be misquoted. The Law said that what I was doing was illegal, so they *were* right to punish me. It's the *Law* that was wrong. Does that make sense?"

"They were right and wrong at the same time."

Rico sighed. "You need sound-bites for your readers, Miss Brown. Pull-quotes, headlines. I get that. But you're oversimplifying things. Good men following bad rules are still good men. Just like bad men who follow good rules are still bad men. Joe Dredd is a stickler for the rules. I've said that before, and I'm sure others will be saying it long after I'm gone."

"You and your brother... You're clones."

"Hardly a secret," Rico said.

"How old were you when you found out?"

A dismissive shrug. "We've always known we were different. I can't remember *not* knowing."

"All right. Then how old were you when you understood what it really *meant*? I'm guessing twelve, thirteen...?"

Rico stared back at her. "I know where you're going with this. You're wrong."

"Am I? Or is all of this—everything you've done, everything you've *become*—just your way of proving to the world that you are *real*? That you're not just a clone? You're a person in your own right. You rebelled against the system that brought you to life, and raised you, and trained you. You don't like the idea of being just a part of the machine, a manufactured cog. Interchangeable with your brother. You want everyone to see you as human."

Rico didn't respond.

"Do you want to know what *I* think?"

His eyes narrowed a little. "Sure."

"I think that's the sort of attitude that *makes* you human." Fabienne reached across the desk and nudged the voice recorder a little further away from the inmate. "You've been on Titan a long time, Rico."

"I know. You have a question to go with that point?"

"It must get lonely out here."

Rico sat back, and smiled as much as his sealed mouth would allow. "So you're a convict-groupie. That's why you pushed so hard for this gig."

"Is that so bad?"

"You don't care that I look like this?" he asked.

Fabienne Brown stood up, her chair scraping back across the floor. "Not one bit. I've checked the rules. It's an offence for a visitor to fraternise with a prisoner. That's one of those rules that don't exist for any good reason. Just like you were saying, Rico." She moved around to his side of the table, and stared down at him.

"Do it, then," he said. "But don't expect me to kiss you, because I can't."

"Who said anything about *kissing?*"

The floor of the interview room was hard and cold. It was awkward, thanks to Rico's cuffs, and it was over in minutes.

Afterwards, she lay beside him for a while, resting her head on his chest. "That was beautiful, Rico. Really special."

"Yeah," he said. "Sure was. No one's touched me like that since they made me into a mod. Thanks."

"When you get out, you'll look me up, right?"

"Sure thing," he lied. "First thing I'll do as soon as I hit the Big Meg."

MEGA-CITY ONE
2099 A.D.

"No, Rico..." Joe said. "Don't make me kill you."

Rico almost laughed at that. He'd spent more than half his life working in the Bronze on Titan. He'd endured hardships that would have killed a lesser man a long time ago. And what had Joe done? Lived here in his cushy, warm apartment in his sheltered city. Plenty to eat, never had to drink his own recycled piss. Never had to undergo surgery that turned him into a monster.

On the day of his release, the new warden had called Rico to his office. "You're getting out. First prisoner ever to get early release that didn't involve a pine box or an urn. Be *grateful* for that. Be thankful that you're leaving this rock and going back to Earth. I want you to bear that in mind, Dredd. Are you with me on that? Do we have an understanding?"

Here it comes, Rico had said to himself. There was going to be bad news. There was something he'd grown to suspect over the years, but had never wanted to find out for sure.

The new warden said, "Your surgery... my predecessors lied to you. It *can't* be reversed. I'm sorry. Maybe in time, ten years, twenty, they might be able to fix you up a little, make you look more normal. But what Copus and Dodge told you about a freezer containing the inmates' removed body parts..." He shook his head. "Again, I'm sorry. There's no freezer. There was only ever the incinerator."

On any other day, Rico knew, he'd probably have throttled the warden. But not when he was so close to release. He'd said nothing, just accepted his fate.

"Maybe back on Earth, they can do something for you. They've got face-change machines, they can grow limbs back..."

"Sure, yeah," Rico had told him.

And now here he was, in Mega-City One, reunited with Little Joe for the first time in almost twenty years, and his brother was pleading with him.

It hadn't been hard to track down Judge Joe Dredd. Just like it hadn't been hard to break into his apartment and seal the place up airtight. Run a cheap vacuum pump to draw out most of the air. Leaving just enough so they could talk. Let Little Joe see what it feels like to eat vacuum for a change.

The hardest part had been the waiting. Even after all that time since his arrest, these last few hours had been almost unbearable.

And now Joe was on his knees, only a few minutes of air left in his helmet's respirator. And he still believed that he could beat Rico.

He's got it the wrong way around, Rico thought. *He can't possibly think that he's actually* better *than me, can he? Is he really* that *deluded? Or... is he stalling?* "Because you know I'm faster, huh?"

He saw Joe's hand begin to slide towards his Lawgiver. But he was still hesitating. *Weak. He's weak. He's always been weak, unwilling to do what's necessary.* "You're yellow, Joe!"

Still, Joe wouldn't draw his gun.

"*Draw*, damn you!" Rico placed his own hand on the gun strapped to his chest, the gun he'd pulled from the dying hands of Evan Quasarano, who'd grown up into a smug, mid-level mobster with a gang of his own. Quasarano had tried to laugh Rico out of his office, told him that he was a washed-up ex-con trying to relive his glory days.

"You sent me to *Titan*, brother Joe—you turned me into a *freak!* Now you're gonna pay for it!"

Joe didn't move. "A Judge that goes wrong has got to be punished! Don't make me kill you!"

"*Draw, I said!*" Rico screamed.

Calmly, Joe said, "Okay, Rico. If that's the way you want it."

Joe grabbed his gun. Rico drew.

There was a moment, the thinnest slice of a second, when Rico knew that he had won. He'd proven to Joe that his way was right, that a rigid, unbending approach to the Law was ultimately flawed...

...That twenty years on the streets of Mega-City One were no match for twenty years in the penal colony on Titan...

...That Joe would always, *always* be second-best. The lesser brother. The flawed clone.

And then Joe's shot hit him in the chest, before Rico's gun was even out of its holster. The shock took the strength out of Rico's legs, and he collapsed to his knees.

Impossible. He...

Rico realised he was toppling to the side, that he would crash to the floor, but Little Joe was there, running towards him, sliding in, catching him before he hit the ground.

His arms growing weak—colder than they had been even in that methane lake on Titan—Rico reached up and grabbed his brother. "You... You... can't be faster than R-Rico...!"

Joe looked down at him, his face barely visible through the helmet's visor and respirator. "Twenty years on Titan slowed you down a split second... But you were the best, Rico... *The best*."

Joe lowered him to the floor, pressed his gloved hands against the entry wound in Rico's chest.

With the last of his strength, Rico pushed Joe's hands away. "Don't. I'm dying, Little Joe. I get to go first. But I *was* right, wasn't I?"

"Shallow breaths," Joe said. "I'll get help. Just hold on."

Rico watched, unable to move, as his brother restored the apartment's environment, then radioed Control for backup.

Rico said, "The Meg, the Justice Department... You're all teetering on the edge. One good push and it'll topple. The whole society will come crashing down because... because you damn Judges are too much in love with your own power. You *know* I'm right."

He was fading fast, and he knew it. There was no way out of this one. Each breath was an agonising rasp that struggled through his artificial lungs. "Admit it, Joe... I want to hear you say it. Admit that I'm right."

As the air and heat flooded back into the apartment, Joe crouched down next to him. "No. You're wrong. We serve the

Law, the Law serves the people. That's how it has to be. It's not perfect, but it's..."

"Hah! Even *now*, you can't back down..." Rico reached up with his left hand, palm open. But his strength was gone and what was meant to be a slap was almost a caress. As his hand slipped back down, he said, "You never... never did learn how to comfort someone, did you? Say goodbye to the old crew for me. Gibson and the others... Whoever's left. You tell *them* I was right, Joe."

"I'll tell them you *said* you were right." Joe hesitated for a moment. "Rico..."

"Yeah...?"

"That reporter, the one who took your story on Titan..."

"Oh yeah, her. What about her?"

"You have a daughter. Her name is Vienna."

Rico Dredd laughed for the last time. "Yeah? That's good. I like that. Take care of her for me, Little Joe. You raise her *right*... understand? Tell my girl all about me."

"I'll tell her what she needs to hear, that's all I can promise you."

"Huh... Not good enough..." Rico's plastic-coated eyes flickered shut. "Things were... the other way around... I'd tell her everything. I'd do it *better* than you, Joe."

"I know you would, Rico. I know."

The apartment door burst open and in seconds Rico and Joe were surrounded by med-Judges. They pushed Joe aside and crouched over his brother.

But they were too late to save him. Twenty years too late.

THE END

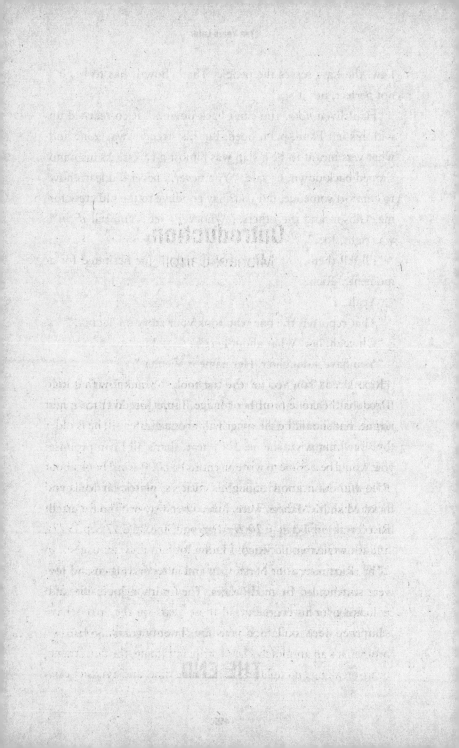

Outroduction
Michael Carroll

HOPEFULLY BY NOW you've read the book so you know that Rico Dredd is the clone brother of Judge Joseph Dredd (Rico might argue that should be the other way around: after all, he is older by a few minutes).

It would be a crime to write an entire 100,000-word book about Rico without acknowledging his creators, writer Pat Mills and artist Mike McMahon. Their Judge Dredd story "The Return of Rico" was published in *2000 AD* prog #30 (dated 17 Sep 1977), and it's a tale that packs a heck of a lot into only six pages... In 2099, Rico returns to Mega-City One after serving his twenty-year sentence on Titan. He blames Joe for his incarceration and is looking for revenge. But all those years on the streets have sharpened Joe's skills. Joe wins the shoot-out, killing his own brother. It's an absolutely classic strip: intriguing, thrilling, tragic, heart-breaking and uplifting at the same time, and a master-class in efficient story-telling. (Mills retells this story eighteen years later in "Flashback 2099: The Return of Rico" in *2000 AD* progs #950 to #952, this time with Paul Johnson on art duties.)

For such an important character his presence in Dredd stories is surprisingly scant. He pops up from time to time—usually in a flashback sequence, or in an alternate reality—but you could count Rico's actual appearances on the fingers of about two and a half hands.

When I was developing the first volume of this series, *The Third Law*, I knew how Rico's story had to end, of course, but I wanted to focus on the journey rather than the destination. And I knew that I wanted it to stand out from the other stories in which Rico appeared, and to do that I chose to tell the tale from Rico's point of view. Now, once or twice Rico has been depicted as actually evil—smug, cackling, grinning, rubbing-hands-together, "I'll show them *all!*" evil, from the same school as Dick Dastardly and Snidely Whiplash—but that never sat right with me. A credible villain isn't the one whose midnight hilltop ranting soliloquies about perceived injustices and intended revenge are always illuminated by well-timed flashes of lightning. It's the one who makes the reader think, "Actually, I kinda see where they're coming from here."

And since I'd decided that Rico would be the one telling us his tale, he might be a tad biased, with a tendency to paint himself as the good guy. After all, every character is the hero of their own story, right?

So he embellishes his past, tweaks the tone here and there... He shines a light on the elements that support his viewpoint and nudges the rest under the carpet. He's a master manipulator, or he *believes* that he is. He has rewritten his own history, inflating his strengths and crowing about his victories while justifying his crimes and redesignating his flaws as positive attributes. He presents himself simultaneously as both hero and victim; the lone champion standing firm against the unstoppable machine, when in reality he is as much a part of that machine as anyone else.

I leave it up to you, the reader, to decide whether he's attempting to fool his audience, or he's just fooling himself.

For me, it's that aspect of Rico's character where he and Joe differ: they're actually much more alike than either of them might want to consider, but the key difference is that Rico thinks he's special. He has an ego. He wants to be acknowledged and thanked for serving the people. Joe doesn't care about any of that: he just wants to do his job. He doesn't need to be raised aloft or to see his name in lights.

So this is the story of a strong man trying to do the right thing, and suffering the consequences. As he might have put it, standing up for others makes you an easy target. But beneath that, it's also the story of a *weak* man who was given more power than he could handle.

My thanks to Pat Mills and Mike McMahon for creating Rico, and of course to John Wagner and the late Carlos Ezquerra for creating Dredd in the first place, to the other creators who have worked on Rico, the awesome behind-the-scenes staff of *2000 AD*, Abaddon Books and Rebellion, and lastly but not leastly to those readers who enjoyed my first Rico book enough to keep asking for more!

Michael Carroll
Dublin, December 2018

About the Author

Irish Author **Michael Carroll** is a former chairperson of the Irish Science Fiction Association and has previously worked as a postman and a computer programmer/ systems analyst. A reader of *2000 AD* right from the very beginning, Michael is the creator of the acclaimed *Quantum Prophecy*/*Super Human* series of superhero novels for the young adult market.

His comic work includes *Judge Dredd* and *DeMarco, PI* for *2000 AD* and *Judge Dredd Megazine* (Rebellion), *Jennifer Blood* for Dynamite Entertainment and *Razorjack* for Titan Books.

His website is at www.michaelowencarroll.com.

FIND US ONLINE!

www.rebellionpublishing.com

/rebellionpub /rebellionpublishing /rebellionpub

SIGN UP TO OUR NEWSLETTER!

rebellionpublishing.com/sign-up

YOUR REVIEWS MATTER!

Enjoy this book? Got something to say?

Leave a review on Amazon, GoodReads or with your
favourite bookseller and let the world know!

JUDGE DREDD
YEAR ONE

Mega-City One, 2080.

Judge Joe Dredd's first year on the streets as a full-eagle Judge. Bred for justice, trained in law, Dredd's no helpless rookie, but he's not the seasoned veteran we know either. Three tales follow the first adventures of the future city's greatest lawman.

With an introduction by the Mighty Tharg!

CITY FATHERS

The brutal murder of a Justice Department-sanctioned spy uncovers something new and dangerous in the sector's murky black market. Unless Dredd can stop it, chaos will be unleashed.

COLD LIGHT OF DAY

A savage killing spree results in the deaths of two highly-regarded Judges, and many consider Dredd to be responsible: a decision he made five years earlier – while he was still a cadet – has come back to haunt him.

WEAR IRON

"Wear iron, that's the rule." Paul Strader is a stick-up man, and a stone cold professional. But when he gets in over his head, he has to risk everything on the word of a corrupt lawman and break every rule he has.
Every rule but one...

 WWW.ABADDONBOOKS.COM

Follow us on Twitter! www.twitter.com/rebellionpub

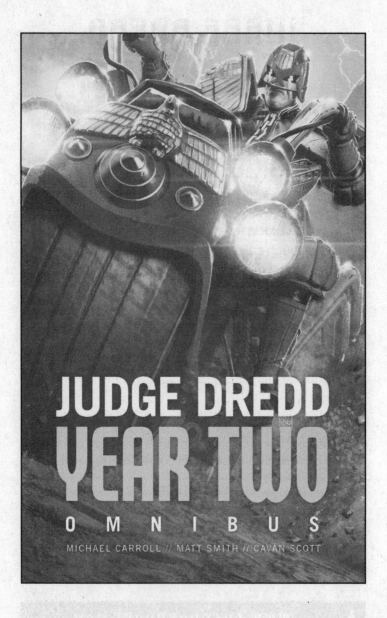

JUDGE DREDD
YEAR TWO
O M N I B U S

MICHAEL CARROLL // MATT SMITH // CAVAN SCOTT

JUDGE DREDD
YEAR TWO

ROOKIE YEAR'S OVER

Mega-City One, 2081.

Judge Joe Dredd's been on the beat for a year. He's made tough calls, tackled hardbitten perps, and seen the consequences of his choices come back to bite him.

But he's not done learning yet. Dredd's second year on the sked will see him back out in the Cursed Earth, where right and wrong are questions that go beyond the easy answers of the Law; he'll tackle an apparent serial killer—or more than one?—targeting journalists; and he'll take his first real beat down, leaving him bent and broken with only his badge and his conviction to protect him...

Including stories by Matt Smith, Michael Carroll and Cavan Scott, *Judge Dredd: Year Two* puts the city's greatest lawman to the test.

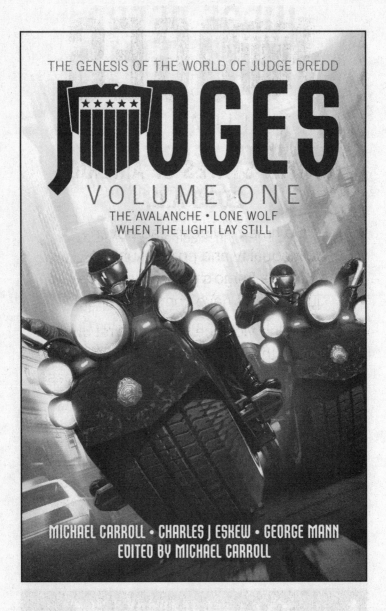

THE GENESIS OF THE WORLD OF JUDGE DREDD

J☆☆☆☆☆DGES

VOLUME ONE

THE AVALANCHE • LONE WOLF
WHEN THE LIGHT LAY STILL

MICHAEL CARROLL • CHARLES J ESKEW • GEORGE MANN
EDITED BY MICHAEL CARROLL

J✪DGES

VOLUME ONE

UNITED STATES OF AMERICA
2033 A.D.

In a time of widespread poverty,
inequality and political unrest,
Eustace Fargo's controversial new
justice laws have come into effect.

Protests and violence meet the first Judges
as they hit the street to enforce the Law; the
cure, it's clear, is far worse than the disease.

Is this a sign of things to come?

**"I did enjoy this book, even though it
made me nervous... I loved the conflict
it caused in me. It's fast-paced and
uncompromising, keeping true to the
essence of the Judges."**

British Fantasy Society

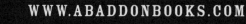

WWW.ABADDONBOOKS.COM

Follow us on Twitter! www.twitter.com/rebellionpub

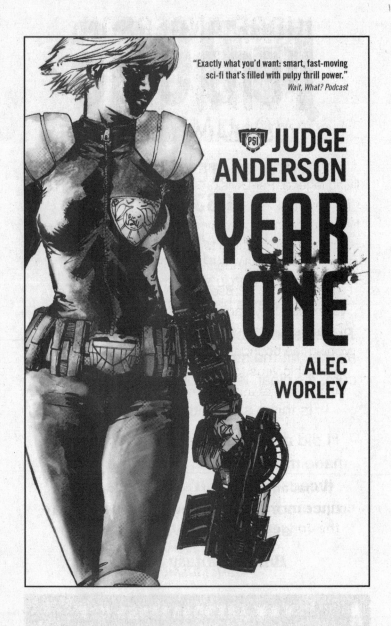

"Exactly what you'd want: smart, fast-moving
sci-fi that's filled with pulpy thrill power."

Wait, What? Podcast

**PSI JUDGE
ANDERSON**

YEAR
ONE

**ALEC
WORLEY**

JUDGE ANDERSON
YEAR ONE
"YOU READY, ROOKIE?"

In years to come, Cassandra Anderson will be a living legend, Psi-Division's most famous Judge. But for now it's 2100, and a young Judge Anderson is fresh out of the Academy, the Eagle still gleaming on her shoulder. It's time to put her training—and her judgement—to the test.

Tackling a love-obsessed telepathic killer at a Valentine's Day parade, plunging into the depths of madness in a huge new psychiatric prison, and probing the boundaries of reality itself as she hunts a psychic virus to its roots, Cass will be forged in the fires of Justice, emerging as something extraordinary.

Includes a bonus short story and introduction by the author.

"What an exhilarating ride! I could easily conjure up the gritty, grimy cacophony, picture the Judges, every smug expression, every inflection of every voice."

Dark Musings

WWW.ABADDONBOOKS.COM

Follow us on Twitter! www.twitter.com/rebellionpub